TIME RIDERS

2001 1912 1957 1941 2066

DAY OF THE PREDATOR

ALEX SCARROW

PUFFIN

PUFFIN BOOKS

Published by the Penguin Group
Penguin Books Ltd, 80 Strand, London WC2R 0RL, England
Penguin Group (USA) Inc., 375 Hudson Street, New York, New York 10014, USA
Penguin Group (Canada), 90 Eglinton Avenue East, Suite 700, Toronto, Ontario, Canada M4P 2Y3
(a division of Pearson Penguin Canada Inc.)
Penguin Ireland, 25 St Stephen's Green, Dublin 2, Ireland (a division of Penguin Books Ltd)
Penguin Group (Australia), 250 Camberwell Road, Camberwell, Victoria 3124, Australia
(a division of Pearson Australia Group Pty Ltd)
Penguin Books India Pvt Ltd, 11 Community Centre, Panchsheel Park, New Delhi – 110 017, India
Penguin Group (NZ), 67 Apollo Drive, Rosedale, North Shore 0632, New Zealand
(a division of Pearson New Zealand Ltd)
Penguin Books (South Africa) (Pty) Ltd, 24 Sturdee Avenue,
Rosebank, Johannesburg 2196, South Africa

Penguin Books Ltd, Registered Offices: 80 Strand, London WC2R 0RL, England

puffinbooks.com

First published 2010
8

Set in Bembo Book MT Std 11/14.5 pt
Typeset by Palimpsest Book Production Limited, Falkirk, Stirlingshire
Made and printed in England by Clays Ltd, St Ives plc

British Library Cataloguing in Publication Data
A CIP catalogue record for this book is available from the British Library

ISBN: 978–0–141–32693–1

www.greenpenguin.co.uk

Penguin Books is committed to a sustainable future for our business, our readers and our planet. This book is made from paper certified by the Forest Stewardship Council.

PUFFIN BOOKS

DAY OF THE PREDATOR

Praise for *TimeRiders*:

'A thriller full of spectacular effects' – *Guardian*

'Insanely exciting, nail-biting stuff' – *Independent on Sunday*

'This is a novel that is as addictive as any computer game' – *Waterstone's Books Quarterly*

'Promises to be a big hit' – *Irish News*

'A thrilling adventure that hurtles across time and place at breakneck speed' – *Lovereading4kids.co.uk*

'Plenty of fast-paced action . . . this is a real page-turner' – *WriteAway.org.uk*

'A great read that will appeal to both boys and girls . . . you'll find this book addictive!' – *redhouse.co.uk*

'Contender for best science fiction book of the year . . . an absolute winner' – *Flipside*

ALEX SCARROW used to be a graphic artist, then he decided to be a computer games designer. Finally, he grew up and became an author. He has written a number of successful thrillers and several screenplays, but it's YA fiction that has allowed him to really have fun with the ideas and concepts he was playing around with when designing games.

He lives in Norwich with his son, Jacob, his wife, Frances, and two very fat rats.

Books by Alex Scarrow

TimeRiders
TimeRiders: Day of the Predator

www.time-riders.co.uk

To Frances, Jacob, Max and Frodo – Field Office, Norwich

And as for you, dear reader, the following message is encrypted for your eyes only:

ER YKU CPVO IPJPBOD TK DONKDO TCES TCOJ YKU UJDOQSTPJD TCO EILKQTPJNO KR KJO WKQD – LPJDKQP

CHAPTER 1

2026, Mumbai, India

They'd heard the rumbling coming towards them down the echoing stairwell like a locomotive train. Then all of a sudden it was pitch black, the air thick with dust and smoke. Sal Vikram thought she was going to choke on the grit and particles of brick plaster she was sucking in through her nose, clogging her throat and the back of her mouth with a thick chalky paste.

It felt like an eternity before it was clear enough to see the emergency wall light in the stairwell once more. By its dim amber light she could see the lower flight of stairs was completely blocked by rubble and twisted metal spars. Above them, the stairwell they'd been clambering down only moments earlier was crushed by the collapsed floors above. She saw an extended arm emerging from the tangle of beams and crumbling breeze-blocks, an arm chalk-white, perfectly still, reaching down to her as if pleading to be held or shaken.

'We're trapped,' whispered her mother.

Sal looked to her, then to her father. He shook his head vigorously, dust cascading off his thin hair.

'No! We are not! We dig!' He looked at Sal. 'That's what we do, we dig. Right, Saleena?'

She nodded mutely.

He turned to the others trapped on the emergency stairwell along with them. 'Yes?' he said. 'We must dig. We can't wait for rescue . . .' Her father could have said more, could have completed that sentence, could have said what they were all thinking – that if the skyscraper had collapsed down to this floor there was no reason why it wasn't soon to fold in on itself all the way down.

Sal looked around. She recognized faces despite them all being painted ghost-white with dust: Mr and Mrs Kumar from two apartments along; the Chaudhrys with their three young sons; Mr Joshipura, a business man like her father, but single . . . enjoyed a string of girlfriends. Tonight, presumably, he'd been on his own.

And . . . another man, standing at the back of the stairwell, beneath the wall light. She didn't recognize him.

'If we move things, we may cause more of it to collapse!' said Mrs Kumar.

Sal's mother placed a hand on her husband. 'She is right, Hari.'

Hari Vikram turned to look at them all. 'Some of you are old enough to remember, yes? Remember what happened to the Americans in New York? Their twin towers?'

Sal remembered the footage, something they'd been shown in history class. Both of those tall, magnificent buildings sliding down into the earth and disappearing among billowing dark grey clouds.

Heads nodded. Everyone old enough remembered, but none of them stepped forward. As if to press the issue, a metal spar above creaked and slid, releasing a small avalanche of dust and debris down on to them.

'If we just wait here . . . we die!' shouted her father.

'They will come!' replied Mr Joshipura. 'The firemen will soon –'

'No. I'm afraid they won't.' She turned towards the voice.

The old man she hadn't recognized had finally said something. 'I'm afraid they won't come for you,' he repeated, his voice softer this time. He sounded like a westerner, English or American. And, unlike everyone else, he *wasn't* coated in dust. 'They won't have time. This building has less than three minutes before the support struts on the floor beneath us give way. Combined with the weight of the collapsed floors above, it'll be enough for Palace Tower to go all the way down.'

He looked around at them, the wide eyes of the adults, the wider eyes of the children. 'I'm truly sorry, but none of you are going to survive.'

The heat in the stairwell was increasing. A floor below, the flames had taken a firm hold, their heat softening the steel girders of the skyscraper. Deep groans rippled and echoed around them.

Hari Vikram studied the stranger for a moment; the fact that he was the only one *not* coated in a thick layer of chalky dust wasn't wasted on him. 'Wait! You are clean. How did you get in here? Is there another way through?'

The man shook his head. 'No.'

'But . . . you were not with us *before* the floor collapsed! There must be some way –'

'I have only just arrived,' replied the man, 'and I must leave soon. We really don't have much time.'

Sal's mother stepped towards him. 'Leave? How? Can you . . . can you help us?'

'I can help only *one* of you.' His eyes rested on Sal. 'You . . . Saleena Vikram.'

Sal felt every pair of eyes in the stairwell settle on her.

'Take my hand,' said the man.

'Who are you?' asked her father.

'I'm your daughter's *only* way out. If she takes my hand . . .

she lives. If she doesn't, she will die along with the rest of you.'

One of the young boys began to cry. Sal knew him; she'd babysat the Chaudhry boys. He was nine and terrified, clutching his favourite soft toy – a one-eyed bear – tightly in both hands as if the bear was *his* ticket out.

Another deep moan from one of the skyscraper's structural support bars echoed through the small space on the stairwell, like the mournful call of a dying whale, or the stress vibration of a sinking ship. The stale air around them, already hot, was becoming almost too painful to inhale.

'We have just over two minutes,' said the man. 'The heat of the fire is causing the building's framework to deform. Palace Tower will collapse, directly in on itself at first, then sideways into the mall below. Five thousand people will be dead a hundred and twenty seconds from now. And tomorrow the news will be all about the terrorists who caused this.'

'Who . . . *who are you*?' asked her father again.

The man – he looked old, perhaps in his fifties or sixties – stepped forward through the crowd, his hand extended towards Saleena. 'We don't have time. You have to take my hand,' he said.

Her father blocked his path. 'Who are you? H-how did you get through to us?'

The old man turned to him. 'I'm sorry. There is no time. Just know that I arrived here . . . and I can leave just as easily.'

'How?!'

'*How* is unimportant . . . I simply can. And I can take just your daughter . . . *only* your daughter with me.' The old man looked down at a watch on his wrist. 'Now there really is little time left – a minute and a half.'

Sal watched her father's taut face, his mind working with businesslike efficiency. No time for *hows* and *whys*. The flicker of fire was coming up from the blocked stairwell below them, sending dancing shadows through the dust-filled air.

Hari Vikram stepped aside. 'Take her, then! You must take her!'

Sal looked up at the old man, frightened at his strangeness, reluctant to offer her hand to him. Not that she believed in anything beyond this world, not Hindu gods, not angels or demons . . . but he seemed not of this world somehow. An apparition. A ghost.

Her father angrily snatched at her hand. '*Saleena!* You must go with him!'

She looked at her father, her mother. 'Why c-can't we all go?'

The old man shook his head. 'Only you, Saleena. I'm sorry.'

'Why?' She realized tears were streaming down her cheeks, tracing dark tracks on her chalky face.

'You're *special*,' said the old man, 'that is why.'

'Please, you must take my boys too!' called out Mrs Chaudhry.

The old man turned to her. 'I can't. I wish I could . . . but I can't.'

'*Pleeease!* They're so young. Younger than this girl! They have their whole lives –'

'I'm sorry, it's not my choice. I can only take Saleena.'

Sal felt her father's hands on her shoulders. He pushed her roughly forward towards the stranger. 'You take her! You take her now!'

'Dadda! *No!*'

'You take her now!'

'No! Not –'

They heard a deep rumble and felt the floor trembling beneath their feet.

'We have only seconds,' said the old man. 'Hurry!'

'SALEENA!' her father screamed. 'YOU GO!'

'Dadda!' she cried. She turned to her mum. '*Please! I can't!*'

The old man stretched forward and grasped hold of her hand. He pulled her towards him, but she found herself instinctively squirming and twisting her hand to escape his tight grip. '*No!*' she screamed.

The deep rumbling increased in volume, the floor shuddering, and cascades of dust and grit filled the air around them, tumbling down from above.

'This is it!' the old man said. 'Time has come! Saleena . . . I can save your life if you come with me!'

She looked at him. It seemed madness that he could, but, somehow, she believed him. 'Your parents want this too.' His eyes, so intense, so old.

'Yes!' yelled her father above the growing roar. 'Please! Take her NOW!'

Beside his small frame, her mother was screaming, stretching out her hands to hold her one last time. Her father grabbed her, held her back. 'No, my love! She must go!'

Mrs Chaudhry pushed her boys at the old man. 'Please! Take their hands too! Take their hands –'

The floor shook beneath their feet, lurching to one side.

Sal suddenly felt light-headed, as if she was free falling.

This is it, it's falling!

Then the floor suddenly fractured beneath their feet, revealing an ocean of churning, roiling flames, like gazing down into Hell itself. And the last thing she recalled was seeing that one-eyed bear tumbling down through a large split in the stairwell's floor into the fire below.

CHAPTER 2

2001, New York

Sal sat upright in her bunk – gasping for breath, feeling her cheeks wet with tears.

The nightmare again.

It was quiet and still in the archway. She could hear Maddy snoring on the bunk below, and Liam whimpering nonsensical words in his soft Irish accent as he stirred restlessly on the bunk opposite.

A muted lamp glowed softly from across the archway, lighting their wooden dinner table and the odd assortment of old armchairs around it. LEDs blinked among the bank of computer equipment across the way, hard drives whirring. One of the monitors remained on; she could see the computer system was doing a routine defrag and data-file tidying. It never slept.

Not *it* . . . not any more – the computer wasn't *IT* any more. It was *Bob*.

Unable to go back to sleep, she clambered off the top bunk. Maddy twitched in her sleep, and Liam also seemed to be unsettled. Maybe they too were reliving their last moments: Liam's sinking *Titanic*, Maddy's doomed airliner. The nightmares came all too often.

She tiptoed across the archway, barefoot on the cold concrete floor, and sat down in one of the swivel chairs, tucking her feet under her and sitting on them for warmth. She grabbed the mouse and opened a dialogue box. Her fingernails clacked softly on the keyboard.

> hey, bob.

> Is this Maddy?

> no, it's sal.

> It is 2.37 a.m. You cannot sleep, Sal?

> nightmares.

> Are you recalling your recruitment?

Recruitment, that's what the old man, Foster, had called it. Like she'd had any real choice in the matter. Life or death. Take my hand or be mashed to pulp amid a crumbling skyscraper. She shuddered. *Great fragging choice.*

> yeah, my recruitment.

> You have my sympathy, Sal.

'Thanks.' She spoke softly into the desk mic – too lazy to tap out any more. Anyway, the clickety-click of the keyboard echoing through the archway was far more likely to disturb the others than her speaking quietly.

'I miss them so much, Bob.'

> You miss your family?

'Mum and Dad.' She sighed. 'It seems like years ago.'

> You have been in the team 44 time cycles. 88 days precisely, Sal.

Time cycles – the two-day time bubble that played out and reset for them, constantly keeping them and their field office in 10 and 11 September 2001, while the world outside moved on as normal.

Outside . . . outside was New York – Brooklyn, to be more precise. Streets she was now getting to know so well. Even the people she had conversations with, people who were never going to remember her: the Chinese laundromat lady, the

Iranian man running the grocery store on the corner. Every time they spoke, it was, for them, the first time – a new face, a new customer to greet cheerily. But she already knew them, knew what they were about to say, how proud the Chinese lady was of her son, how angry the Iranian man was with the terrorists for bombing his city.

This morning was the Tuesday, 11 September, the second day of the ever-resetting time cycle. In just under six hours the first airliner was going to crash into the Twin Towers, and New York and all her inhabitants were going to change forever.

'So what're you doing, Bob?'

> Data collation. Hard-drive maintenance. And reading a book.

'Oh? Cool. What're you reading?'

A page of text appeared on the screen. She could see individual words momentarily highlight one after the other in rapid blinking succession as Bob 'read' while they talked.

> Harry Potter.

Sal remembered seeing the old films from the first decade of the century. They didn't do much for her, but her parents had liked them as children.

'Are you enjoying it?'

Bob didn't answer immediately. She noticed the flickering of highlighted words on the open page of text on the screen grind to a sudden halt, and the soft whirring sound of hard drives being spun momentarily ceased. Forming an opinion . . . that was something Bob struggled with. It required the computer system's entire capacity for him to actually formulate, or rather simulate, something as simple as a human emotion . . . a preference. A like or dislike.

Finally, after a few seconds, she heard the hard drives whirring gently once again.

> I like the magic very much.

Sal smiled as she acknowledged how many terabytes of computing power had gone into that simple statement. If she had a mean streak in her, she could have asked him what colour he thought went best with violet, or what was tastier – chocolate or vanilla? It would probably lock the system for hours as Bob laboured through infinite decision loops to finally come up with the answer that he was unable to compute a valid response.

Bless him. Great at data retrieval, cross-referencing and processing. But don't ask him to pick dessert off a menu.

CHAPTER 3

2001, New York

<u>*Monday (time cycle 45)*</u>

Most of the damage that happened here in the archway with the last time contamination has been fixed up now – the holes in the walls filled again, the door to the back room replaced with a new sturdy one. And we got a brand-new emergency generator installed. Some workmen came in to set it up. We had to hide the time-portal equipment from them, and when they asked about all the computer screens at the desk Maddy told them we were a computer-game developer. I think they believed her.

It's a much more powerful generator, and more reliable than the last shadd-yah old one. I hope we don't have to use it, though.

We've also got an old TV set, a DVD player and one of those Nintendo machines. Liam loves the games. He's mad about one stupid game with silly characters driving around on go-karts throwing bananas at each other.

Boys, eh?

Maddy says we need to grow a new support unit. A new Bob. Just in case another time shift comes along that we need to deal with. Only, the new Bob won't be entirely new. The body will, yes, but she says we can upload Bob's AI back into it and he'll be exactly like he was . . . and not the retarded idiot that plopped out of the growth tube last time. Which is a relief. Bob was so-o-o-o stupid when he was first born.

We fixed the growth tubes. Some got damaged by those creature things that broke in, but they're all functioning now, and we've got them filled up with that stinking protein solution the foetuses float in. We had to steal a load of that gloop from a hospital blood bank. It's the fake blood they use, the plasma stuff, but with a witches' brew of added vitamins and proteins.

Honestly, it's like runny snot. But worse than that, because it smells like vomit.

What we don't have yet, though, are the foetuses. Apparently we can't go and grab any old one – they're specially genetically engineered sometime in the future . . .

Maddy looked at Liam. 'You ready?'

'Aye,' he replied, shivering as he stood behind her in nothing more than a pair of striped boxer shorts, and holding a watertight bag full of clothes.

She looked down at her own shivering body, trembling beneath her T-shirt. 'Maybe one day we could get around to rigging up something to heat the water before we jump in.'

'That's for sure.'

She climbed the steps beside the perspex cylinder, looking down into the cold water, freshly run from the water mains. She settled down on the top step beside the lip of the cylinder and dipped her toes in.

A wet departure – that was the protocol. To ensure that nothing but them and the water they were floating in was sent back in time . . . and not any chunks of floor, or carpet or concrete or cabling that had no possible reason to exist in the past.

'Oh Jeeeez! It's freezing!'

Liam squatted down beside her. 'Great.'

Maddy shuddered then looked up at Sal, seated at the computer station. 'What's the departure count?'

'Just over a minute.'

'So,' said Liam, slowly easing himself into the water, gasping as he did so. 'You're sure about this?'

'Uh-huh.' No, she wasn't. Not sure about anything. The old man, Foster, had left her in charge. Left her running this team and this field office even though they'd barely survived their first brush with time contamination. All she had for help now was *computer-Bob* and a data folder on his hard drive entitled 'Things You'll Probably Want to Ask'.

'How do we grow new support units?' was the name of one of the first files she'd found in the folder when she'd delved into it a few weeks ago. First order of business had been getting the grow-tubes up and running and getting one of those clones on the go. When she'd double-clicked on it, what she'd got was an image of Foster's face looking out of the monitor as he'd addressed the web cam. He looked ten, perhaps twenty years younger than he had the morning he'd told her she was ready, wished her luck and walked out of Starbucks leaving her to run things.

The Foster onscreen looked no more than fifty. '*So,*' he began, adjusting the flex so that the mic was in front of his mouth. '*You've opened this file. Which means you've been careless and your support unit has been destroyed and now you need to grow a new one.*' Foster had proceeded with detailed instructions on maintenance and feeding, and how the growth tubes work. But finally, towards the end of the log entry, was the bit they'd been after.

'*Right . . . so the clones are grown from a store of engineered human foetuses. I'll presume you've used up the last of the refrigerated ones kept in your field office and now you need more.*'

Not exactly used up; those of them mid-growth had all died in the tubes, poisoned by their own waste fluids because the electric-powered pumps hadn't been functioning. The bodies – pale, lifeless, hairless, jelly-like forms that ranged from something that could've sat in the palm of her hand to the body of a boy of eight or nine – had been taken care of. Taken out, weighted down and dumped in the river. Not an experience she ever wanted to repeat.

'*The good news is there are more of them. There's a supply of viable candidate foetuses, all engineered with the silicon processor chip already housed in the cranial cavity. They're ready to grow to full term and, of course, come with basic learning AI code pre-installed.*' The Foster on the monitor smiled coyly. '*If you've been smart, you managed to retrieve your last support unit's chip and preserved its AI . . .*'

She nodded. *Yup.* Well, Liam had done that messy business.

'*. . . so any new support unit doesn't need to start out from scratch as a complete imbecile, and you can upload the AI from the computer system. So, like I say, the good news is there's more of them. But the bad news is they're not going to be delivered to your front door like . . . like . . . some sort of a pizza delivery; I'm afraid you've got to go and get them yourselves.*'

Sal called out a thirty-second warning and Maddy's mind returned to the icy water in the displacement cylinder. She eased herself in beside Liam, her breath chuffing out at the cold. 'Uhhh! This is f-f-f-freezing! How d-do you c-cope with it?' she asked Liam, her teeth chattering.

He offered her a lopsided grin. 'It's not like I get a choice, is it?'

'Twenty seconds!' called out Sal.

'When did you say we're going, again?' asked Liam.

'I t-t-told you: 1906. San Francisco.'

Liam's eyebrows locked in concentration for a moment. 'Hold on now . . . is that not the same year that . . . that –?'

'Yes?'

'I remember my dad reading it in the *Irish Times*. It's the year that –'

'Fifteen seconds!'

Maddy let go of the side of the perspex cylinder and began treading water. 'Liam, you've g-got to go under now.'

'I know . . . I know! Bleedin' hate this bit.'

'Maybe Sal and I should t-teach you how to swim some time?'

'Ten seconds!'

'Oh Jay-zus-'n'-Mary, why does time travel have to be done *this* way? Why did that Waldstein fella have to be so stupid as to invent bleedin' time travel in the first place!'

'You wanna blame someone . . . b-blame the Chinese what's-his-name guy who worked it out in the first place.'

Liam nodded. 'Aghh, well, him too!'

'Five seconds!' called Sal. 'You really need to duck under now!'

Maddy held her hand above his head. 'Need me to push you under?'

'No! I'll just . . . I'll, ah . . . All right!'

Liam sucked in a lungful of air and clasped his nose with his free hand.

'S-see you on the other side,' she uttered as she pushed him under the water. Then sucked in air and submerged as well.

Oh Jeez . . . here goes.

Her first time. Her first time into the past, not counting her recruitment from 2010. She'd been too busy checking the coordinates were set right, arranging the return window time-stamp, checking Sal had pulled out the right clothes for them to wear from the old closet in the back room, making sure she remembered the details of their mission . . . too busy with all those things to realize how utterly terrified she was at the prospect of being pushed out of space-time, through chaos space – and God knows what that was – to emerge back into the space-time of nearly a hundred years ago.

She opened her eyes under the water and saw the foggy form of Liam's scrawny body thrashing around in blind panic. She saw bubbles zig-zagging up around him. She could see the dim lamp on the computer desk through the tube's scuffed plastic, the faint outline of Sal . . . then . . .

. . . Then they were falling, tumbling through darkness.

CHAPTER 4

2015, Texas

'OK, students, we'll be arriving at the institute very shortly, so I want you all to be on your very best behaviour,' said Mr Whitmore, absentmindedly scratching at the scruffy salt-and-pepper stubble around his mouth. He considered it a full beard even if no one else did. 'As I'm sure you will be,' he added.

Edward Chan sighed and looked out of the coach's broad window at the scrub beside the highway. Outside the air-conditioned comfort of the coach it was another blistering Texas day. Hot and bright. Two things he hated. He much preferred his dark bedroom back in Houston, drapes drawn, an ultraviolet lamp making the manga posters on his black bedroom walls glow like the halogen signs outside some cool nightclub.

Dark and cool and peaceful. A place far away from the incessant noise of other kids, the shrill laughter of clusters of girls. High-school girls always seemed to come in clusters – mean, spiteful clusters that sniggered and whispered and pointed. And the boys . . . If it was possible, they were even worse. The jocks – the alpha-male types – loud, brash, great at sports, oozing easy confidence, gangsta rap hissing out of their iPod earbuds, high-fiving each other for any reason. Golden-tanned, sandy-haired, blue-eyed boys who, you could tell, would ease through school, ease through college, ease through life . . . and never once wonder if someone was whispering behind their back, laughing at them, pointing at them.

That was the tribal system at school: the girls – giggly gaggles of Hannah Montana clones, the jocks in their swaggering gangsta gangs . . . and finally the third category, the ones like Edward Chan – the freaks. Loners, emos, geeks, nerds: the cookies that didn't quite fit the cookie-cutter machine that was high school.

His dad was always telling him it was the freaks that ended up doing the great things. It was the freaks who became dotcom billionaires, famous inventors, movie directors, rock stars . . . even presidents. The jocks, on the other hand, ended up selling real estate or managing Wal-Mart stores. And the Hannah Montanas ended up becoming stay-at-home moms, getting fat, bored and lonely.

Ahead of the coach he could see a cluster of pale buildings emerging from the ochre drabness, and presently they slowed down and stopped at a security checkpoint. The other kids on the coach, about thirty of them, all a couple of years older than Edward, began to bob in their seats, craning their necks to look at the armed security guards and the lab buildings up ahead.

'Please stay seated for the moment, guys,' said Mr Whitmore over the coach's PA system.

Edward stretched to look over the headrest of the seat in front of him. He saw a man climb up the steps on to the coach. A smart man in a pale linen suit. He shook hands with Mr Whitmore, the school principal who was chaperoning the students.

'Right, guys, I'm going to hand you over to Mr Kelly, who is from the institute. He's going to be showing us around the facilities today.'

Mr Kelly took the microphone from him. 'Good morning, boys and girls. Let me first say welcome to the institute. It's an honour to have you kids come and visit. As I understand it, you guys have all been nominated by your various schools to come along today because you're all straight-A students?'

Whitmore shook his head. 'Not quite, Mr Kelly. "Most-improved performers". Students who've most clearly demonstrated a willingness to learn. We have all levels and abilities here on this coach, from schools right across the state, but what they all have in common is the spectacular improvement in their year-end SATs scores. These students are the ones who've worked the hardest to *better* themselves.'

Mr Kelly's tanned face was split with a broad smile. 'Fantastic! We like improvers here. *Go-getters*. I wouldn't be surprised if one or two of you on this coach ended up working for us here one day, huh?'

There was a token of polite laughter up and down the rows of seats.

The coach lurched slowly forward, down a long straight driveway flanked by freshly cut lawns, wet with the moisture from water sprinklers.

'OK, guys, we'll shortly be arriving at the visitors' reception area, where you can get off. We have some refreshments ready for you before we start the tour of this facility. I will be your guide for today, and, as I'm talking, if you have any questions at all, please don't be afraid to raise your hands and ask. We want you to get the most out of today . . . to understand what our work is here and how very important it is to the environment.'

Edward looked out of the window as the coach approached a decorative flowerbed and swung slowly around it. In the middle, framed by an arrangement of vivid yellow chrysanthemums, was a sign: WELCOME TO TERI: TEXAS ADVANCED ENERGY RESEARCH INSTITUTE.

CHAPTER 5

1906, San Francisco

'Hey! Don't turn around yet – I'm not ready,' snapped Maddy irritably.

Liam stayed where he was, facing the grubby redbrick wall in front of him. The back alley reeked of rotting fish, and he wondered if he lingered too much longer here whether the smell was going to be stuck on him for the rest of the day.

'Are you not done yet?' he asked.

Maddy muttered under her breath. 'It's all these damned laces and hooks and buttons and things. How the heck did women manage to dress themselves back then?'

He turned his head a little to look up the alley. It seemed to open on to a busy thoroughfare. He saw several horse-drawn carts clatter by, and men dressed like him: formal grey morning coats, buttoned waistcoats, high-collared shirts, with top hats, flat caps and bowler hats. Very much like the better-dressed men in Cork might have worn on a Sunday morning. The clothes they'd found in the back room appeared to be perfectly authentic. There'd been another couple of dusty costumes in there. Sal had said something about them being for the other back-up drop-point – another time, another place.

'Oh, dammit . . . this'll have to do,' tutted Maddy irritably.

'Can I turn round now?'

'Yes . . . but I look a total doof.'

He turned round. His eyes widened.

'What?' she gasped suspiciously. 'What is it? What've I got wrong?'

'Nothing! It's nothing . . . it's just . . .'

Maddy scowled at him beneath the wide-brimmed sun hat, topped with a plume of white ostrich feathers. Her slim neck was framed by decorative lace that descended down the front of a tightly drawn and intricately embroidered bodice. Her waist seemed impossibly thin, as the gown flared out beneath and tumbled down to the ground, modestly covering any sign of her legs.

She put her hands – covered in spotless elbow-length white gloves – on her hips. 'Liam?'

He shook his head. 'You look so . . . so . . .'

'Spit it out!'

'Like . . . well, like a *lady*, so you do.'

For a moment he thought she was going to step forward and punch his arm, like she was prone to do. Instead, her cheeks coloured ever so slightly. 'Uh . . . really?'

'Aye.' Liam smiled at her. 'And me? What about me?'

Maddy grinned. 'Well, you look like an idiot.'

Liam pulled the top hat off his head. 'Ah, it's that, isn't it? Makes me ears stick out like a pair of jug handles.'

She laughed. 'Don't worry about it, Liam. Obviously it's the fashion over here. You won't be the only person wearing one.'

'It was mostly flat caps and forage caps back home. You tried wearing a top hat or a bowler, you were asking for some joker to try an' knock it off.'

She pointed at him, ignoring the quip, her smile replaced with her let's-get-down-to-business frown. 'What time have you got on your clock?'

Liam pulled the ornate timepiece out of his waistcoat pocket. 'Seven minutes after eleven in the morning.'

'OK, we should get a move on. The return window here is in four hours' time.'

'Right you are. How far is it?'

'Not far, I think. It's on to Merrimac Street, then up Fourth Street to Mission Street . . . short walk up that on to Second Street. Ten minutes . . . at a guess?'

Liam stepped forward away from the brick wall, the tumbled crates of rubbish and the stench of rotting fish. With a broad cock-sided grin he offered his arm. 'Shall we, ma'am?'

Her face softened and she threaded one white gloved hand around it. 'Oh, absolutely, Mr Darcy. A pleasure, I'm sure.'

They emerged out of the gloom of the alley on to Merrimac Street and immediately Maddy found herself gasping.

My God. The realization finally hit her. *I'm actually standing IN history.*

Merrimac Street was busy with mid-morning foot and wheeled traffic, mostly horse-drawn carts ferrying goods up from the wharf down the far end. She could make out steam ships lined up against the docks, filling the blue sky with columns of coal smoke and steam, and the churning business of freight coming off or being loaded on.

'Awesome,' she giggled with delight, 'this is just like being in a movie. Just like the beginning of *Titanic* . . .'

He looked at her, disgusted. 'They made a movie about it?'

The smile on her face slipped and became a guilty grimace.

Liam tutted and sighed. 'Good people died an' all . . . for what? So they can become part of a flickering peepshow a hundred years later?'

She shrugged. 'Uh, s'pose . . . but it was pretty good, though. Fantastic special eff–'

His sideways scowl silenced her.

'Never mind.'

They turned left on to the road, heading up it towards Fourth Street, dodging several piles of horse manure along the way. Fourth Street was a little busier, but nothing compared to Mission Street. The road was a broad thoroughfare, a hundred feet wide, thick with carts and pedestrians and a tram line that rattled with trams laden with passengers inside and hanging precariously on the back, dinging their bells to clear the track ahead.

'Oh my God, this is so amazing!' she gushed.

Liam tugged her arm. 'Shhh . . . you're sounding like a tourist.'

Mission Street was flanked with five- and six-storey brick buildings, warehouses, offices, factories, banks and legal firms. She caught sight of a tall building dominating the skyline – fifteen, perhaps twenty storeys high that looked like a small version of the Empire State Building.

'I didn't know they had skyscrapers *back then* . . . uhh . . . I mean back *now*!'

Liam nodded. 'Nothing like this in Ireland.' He shook his head sadly. 'And you're telling me all this gets totally destroyed?'

'Uh-huh. Tomorrow morning, April eighteenth, the great Californian earthquake. According to our history database, much of the downtown area is destroyed by the quake . . . and then the resulting fire destroys most of what was left in this area . . . the fourth and fifth districts.'

'Jeeeez . . . that's a real shame, so it is.' Liam locked his brows for a moment. 'Hang on! Strikes me as a bit stupid that the agency has picked here and now to store our supplies if it's about to be brought crashing down.'

'Well, duh!' said Maddy, making a face and rolling her eyes. 'Think about it! It makes perfect sense!' She looked at him as if he'd just put on a pair of shoes the wrong way round. 'Liam, I thought Foster said you're meant to be smart?'

He pouted his lip, feigning hurt. 'Well, Miss Smarty Pants, you're obviously itching to tell me something, so get on with it.'

She sighed. 'It's perfect, because the bank vault where our replacement engineered foetuses are located will be completely destroyed in the fire. Everything. All the safe deposit boxes, their contents, all the client paperwork . . . everything. No paper trail.'

Liam grinned. 'Ah, very clever.'

'Exactly.'

The hubbub on Mission Street was added to by the noisy clatter of a sputtering engine. Its noise blotted out everything as it slowly approached them. They finally saw the vehicle rolling down the middle of the street on flimsy spoked wheels, following a man on foot waving a red warning flag before him.

'Wow! I didn't know they had cars then!' Maddy shouted in his ear.

He shook his head. 'Now who's being dumb! Of course we did!' He watched the vehicle slowly rattle past, steered by a man wearing a cap and goggles. Beside him sat a woman sporting a cloud of ostrich feathers above her head, her gloved hands clasped over her ears at the cacophony.

'Now I know that's an Oldsmobile Model R,' added Liam as the vehicle finally turned right off Mission Street and the laboured clatter of internal combustion allowed them to talk easily once more. 'There were quite a few of those things dashing about Cork – yes, even Cork – when I left.'

She shook her head. 'Hardly *dashing*.'

They walked on another few minutes in silence, Maddy enjoying playing the lady in her own period-piece Hollywood movie and Liam feeling like this was something of a trip home for him. Back to his time, back to a place where he could talk easily with anyone and not be made to feel like a complete moron for not knowing what a *digicam* was, or that *Seven-Up* wasn't some kind of a ball game, or that a *Snickers Bar* wasn't some sort of sleazy nightclub.

'This is it,' Maddy finally said, pointing to a narrow side street. 'There . . . Minna Street.'

They crossed the wide thoroughfare, dodging a tram clanging its way through the bustle of pedestrian traffic and sidestepping several more steaming hillocks of horse manure. They stood in the mouth of the narrow road, only two carts wide and relatively quiet.

'And that's the building we want,' she said, pointing to a formal-looking frontage of brick and granite. 'Union Commercial Savings Company,' she added. 'According to Foster's "how to" manual, this is the bank's *only* premises. After the earthquake, the fire destroys this building and everything inside it. The company was no more. As if it never existed.' She looked at him. 'You see? Perfect.'

'And all our Baby Bobs are in some sort of safe down in its basement?'

'That's what Foster says.'

Liam frowned. 'So, I'm being dumb again . . . but if there's a whole load of those little foetus things down there in a safe somewhere, what's keeping them alive? Would they not die and sort of go off? Is there a refrigerating device down there?'

'You'll see.'

CHAPTER 6

1906, San Francisco

Maddy strode down Minna Street towards the bank. 'Come on.'

Liam was struggling to keep up with her. 'So, *who* put them in this bank? And *when* did they do it?'

She reached the front step of the Union Commercial Savings Company and stopped. 'OK, Liam, just a second . . .' She pulled her glasses and a scrap of paper covered with scribbled notes in her handwriting out of her handbag.

'Oh Jay-zus . . . you brought *notes* back with you? Isn't that *not* allowed? You know? Contamination of time an' all?'

Maddy looked around the quiet street guiltily. 'I know, I know . . . but there was way too much to remember. I was worried I'd forget something.'

'Foster would throw a fit if he knew you'd brought notes back here,' said Liam.

'Well, he won't, will he?' she muttered impatiently. 'Because he bailed out and left us to cope on our own.'

Liam shrugged at that.

She put her glasses on. 'OK, so, my name is Miss Emily Lassiter. You're my brother.'

'Do I get a name too?'

She sighed. 'Yes . . . uhh . . . here it is, Leonard Lassiter. All right?'

He nodded.

She scanned the notes further, digesting the information for a few moments before tucking them back in her bag and removing her glasses. 'All right, I think I've got it all.' She looked at him. 'You don't have to say anything, OK? Just go along with whatever I say.'

'Will do.'

She took a deep breath, then pushed the double door to the bank inwards. They stepped on to a tiled floor that echoed their footsteps around a hall, dark with oak panels. Ahead of them were half a dozen ornate mahogany desks, each with softly glowing green ceramic desk lamps. Behind each one sat a bank teller, all but one busy dealing in hushed, respectful tones with customers.

Maddy led the way towards the unoccupied teller, a young man with hair slicked down in a rigid centre parting and a carefully clipped and waxed moustache.

'Uhh . . . 'scuse me?' she said.

The young man looked up at her and smiled charmingly. 'Good morning, ma'am. How can I help you?

'I'd like to speak with a Mr . . . uh . . . Mr *Leighton*. He works here, I think.'

'Oh, I'm certain he works here, ma'am,' said the young man. He tapped a wooden name-holder on the desk. 'I'm Harold Leighton, you see? Please, will you take a seat?'

Maddy smiled and slumped down in the seat a little too casually then did her best to quickly recover her lady-like demeanour. 'Much . . . uh . . . much obliged,' she said as demurely as she could manage.

'Now, ma'am, how could I assist you?'

She took a breath, hoping she was going to get this right and not sound half as nervous as she felt. 'My family has a safe deposit box with your bank and I wish to make a withdrawal.'

'Certainly, ma'am. The account is in the name of?'

'Joshua Waldstein Lassiter.'

Harold Leighton's eyebrows raised.

Her heart skipped. 'Oh . . . is there a problem?'

'Not a *problem* as such, ma'am. It's just . . . I still have the paperwork here on my desk.'

Maddy shook her head. 'Paperwork?'

'The paperwork setting up the safe deposit account. Joshua Waldstein Lassiter, I presume he is your . . .?'

'Uh? . . . My uh . . . yes, that's right, my father.'

'Well, your father was here not more than an hour ago. Actually, I dealt with him myself. He brought a very nice jewellery box with him and we carried it down to the safe room and put it in a deposit box together . . . as I say, not more than an hour ago.'

'Oh,' was all she managed to say after a few moments. 'Yes, well, that's quite right.'

'And you wish to withdraw something from the safe deposit box *already*?'

She nodded. 'Yes, that's right.'

'Well . . . that is highly irregular.'

'We're a funny old family, us Lassiters,' said Maddy, looking back over the chair. 'Aren't we, Liam?'

Liam stepped forward. 'Oh yes, that we are, dear sister.' He grinned at the teller. 'She sometimes calls me Liam, although my name is in fact *Leonard*,' he said, nudging the small of her back.

Maddy mentally kicked herself for being such a dumb-nuts.

'You are brother and sister?' Harold Leighton looked up at Liam. 'And it seems you, sir, are Irish?'

'Yes.'

'But,' he said, looking at Maddy, 'it seems, ma'am, you're *not*?'

'I . . . uh . . .' Maddy's mouth flapped uselessly. 'Oh . . .'

'I was brought up in Cork,' cut in Liam. 'My dear sister in California. Father likes to keep a home either side of the Atlantic, so he does.'

The young teller cocked an eyebrow. 'So it seems.' He sighed and spread the bank account details out in front of him. 'Well, it appears your father did specify his children as fellow signatories on the account, so . . . you, ma'am, I presume are Emily Lassiter?'

'That's correct,' she replied.

'For security reasons I have to ask you for the code word your father has put down here on this form to assure us you are in fact who you say you are.'

'Of course.' She nodded. 'It's . . . it's . . .' She realized all of a sudden her mind had gone blank and cursed.

The teller's jaw dropped open at her unladylike language. 'Madam!'

Liam grinned sheepishly. 'She's spent time at sea. Picked up all sorts of dreadful language from the sailors, so she did. Father so hates her talking that way.'

'Just a sec,' said Maddy, fumbling in her handbag for her note. She quickly scanned her scribbled writing. 'Ahh! Here it is!'

She leaned forward over the desk. 'The code word, Mr Leighton, is *Hemlock*.'

Leighton stared at her long and hard, suspicion clouding his young teller's eyes. Finally a cautious smile spread across his lips. 'Yes, it is, Miss Lassiter. If you'll just sign here, I can take you down to the safe room.'

*

The teller spun a large brass wheel and slowly pulled open the cast-iron door leading on to a small room lined with numbered deposit boxes on three walls. 'Your safe deposit box is number three-nine-seven,' he said, leading them to a locker with the number on its door. He inserted the key and twisted it once.

'It is company policy, madam, sir, that I remain in the safe room while you inspect the contents of your deposit box. However, I shall remain over there by the door and I shall turn my back to allow you a little privacy.'

Maddy nodded and smiled politely. 'OK.'

She waited until Mr Leighton had crossed the room and was standing by the cast-iron door, casually jangling the keys in one hand and examining his fingernails on the other.

'Liam,' she uttered softly.

'Yes?'

'I think it's best if you go talk to him, distract him. I don't want him seeing anything he shouldn't.'

He nodded. 'Aye, you're right.' He wandered over and easily struck up a conversation with the young man while Maddy attended to their business.

She pulled the deposit box's door open. The faint glow from the safe room's overhead light showed her little of what was inside. Maddy pushed her hand into the darkness and almost immediately felt the side of a wooden box. She found a small handle and pulled it out. It was quite heavy, and as she hefted it out of the locker towards an inspection bench in the middle of the room, the young man called out.

'Let me give you a hand with that, madam.'

'I'm fine . . . I'm fine,' she grunted.

'Strong as an ox, so she is,' Liam assured him. 'She'll be all right.' He resumed chatting to Leighton, something about steam ships, from what she could hear.

She studied the box. It certainly looked like a jewellery box, about the size of a small travel trunk, made of dark wood with silver buckles and ornate swirls along each side. She turned the box so that the upright lid would hide what was inside from any prying eyes, and then slowly, carefully opened it.

'Another box,' she whispered. But this one was smooth, featureless, metal and cold to the touch.

Refrigerated. There had to be some kind of small power unit or battery inside.

Her gloved fingers found a catch on the side and gently slid it back. Something inside the box clicked and the lid slowly raised with a barely audible hiss. A shallow fog of nitrogen wafted out of the box revealing a row of eight glass tubes, each six inches long and a couple of inches wide. She eased one of the glass tubes out of its holder and, still shielded by the lid of the jewellery box, inspected it closely. Through the glass she could see the murky pink growth solution and the faint pale outline of a curled-up human foetus.

'Hello there, little baby Bobs!' she cooed softly, waggling her fingers down at the frozen embryo. 'Auntie Maddy's here.'

The conversation in the corner was getting quite animated. Clearly Leighton had a passion for new-fangled things like steam ships and automobiles. And Liam was playing along nicely.

Well done, Liam.

She placed the glass tube back and closed the lid of the refrigerated case, lifting it out of the jewellery box and into her bag. She was about to close the lid of the jewellery box when she spotted a scrap of paper at the bottom. What she saw on it made her heart lurch.

Her name.

A note for me?

She reached in and picked it up. Just a folded scrap of paper, a few words scrawled hurriedly on it.

Maddy, look out for 'Pandora', we're running out of time. Be safe and tell no one.

'How're you doin', my dear sister?' called out Liam.

'I'm good,' she replied, grabbing the scrap of paper, balling it up and tucking it into one of her gloves. She closed the box and lifted it back into the locker, much lighter now. She closed the door. 'I'm all done here, Mr Leighton!'

'Ah, splendid!' He came over with his jangling keys and locked the deposit box for her.

'Everything all right?'

She glanced at Liam making a silly face at her over Leighton's shoulder.

'Yes . . . yes, just fine, thank you.'

A minute later they were exiting the bank on to Minna Street once more, Liam holding the bag for her.

'Nice enough chap,' he said.

She turned to look at him. 'A dozen hours from now he'll be dead.'

'Dead?'

'Yes, dead. That's why the instructions said to ask for him *specifically*.' She'd figured that out on the way back up the stairs. Because if anything happened, if the young man had caught a glimpse of anything inside the box, or heard either of them say anything suspicious . . . well, he'd hardly have time to do anything with that knowledge, would he? The agency once again cleverly covering its tracks.

'Jaayyzz. That seems not right to me,' uttered Liam. 'Not to warn him somehow.'

Maddy didn't like it either. 'It's how it is, Liam. It's how it is.'

As they walked up Minna Street towards the main thoroughfare, Liam attempted to lift the mood. 'You got our little babies?'

She nodded. 'All in there. Baby Popsicles.'

'Baby what?'

CHAPTER 7

2015, Texas

Edward Chan and the rest of the touring party sat in the visitors' reception room, munching on doughnuts and breakfast bagels and slurping orange juice from cartons as their tour guide, Mr Kelly, gave them an introductory presentation.

'The Texas Advanced Energy Research Institute . . . or *TERI*, as we call it for short, was established three years ago in 2012 when President Obama was re-elected. As you youngsters have been taught in school, the world is entering a new, tough and very challenging time. The world's population is nearly eight billion, carbon emissions have gone off the chart, the world's traditional energy sources – oil and gas – are rapidly running out. We need to change the way we live or . . . well, I'm sure you've seen enough doom and gloom forecasts on the news.'

He paused. The reception room was silent except for the shuffling of one or two feet and the slurping of orange juice through straws.

'So, as you no doubt know, the institute was set up as part of the president's advanced energy research programme. And over the last three years we've used the billions of dollars of taxpayers' money set aside by this initiative to develop the wonderful facility you're visiting today.

'We have some of the finest quantum physicists and

mathematicians working here, and most of our research work has been to do with a thing called *zero-point energy*. I'm sure some of you must have heard that term in the news.'

Edward looked around at the other kids. A few heads were nodding uncertainly. One of them – a boy a couple of years older than him, short and chubby with curly ginger hair parted at the side and brutally combed so that his hair kinked in waves to one side, reminding Edward of a Mr Whippy ice cream – raised a hand.

'Yes, er . . .?' said Mr Kelly, raising his eyebrows.

'Franklyn.'

'Go ahead, Franklyn.'

'My dad says zero-point energy is just a bunch of wishful thinking. It's like getting something for nothing. And that's impossible in physics, nothing's free.'

Kelly laughed. 'Well, Franklyn, that's a good point, but you see that's exactly what it is. It *is* a free lunch. And the idea that there's such a thing as a free lunch isn't a new one either. Remember Albert Einstein and his theory of relativity. Well, he argued that even in a complete vacuum there's a great deal left there. It isn't just empty space, there's energy too, endless energy waiting to be tapped. Even the ancient Greeks suspected that we walk through an endless soup of energy. They called it "ether". But the trick, kids . . . the trick has always been being able to *isolate* it, to *measure* it. Since it exists everywhere, it's homogenous, isotropic . . . That's to say it's uniformly the same everywhere and in every direction.'

The students stared at him in confused silence.

'Trying to measure zero-point energy is a bit like trying to weigh a glass of water under the ocean. You know? It's the same inside the cup as it is outside . . . and therefore since there's no measurable difference between what's in and outside the cup, the logical statement to make would be the "cup has nothing in it". Which would of course be wrong. So, we have a similar issue with measuring zero-point energy. Only by creating a *proper* vacuum – and I don't mean just sucking the air out of a space, I mean a proper space-time vacuum, a tiny one – can we observe what it is that remains.' He smiled his polished public relations smile. 'The energy itself.

'And that's what we have here at the TERI labs, a device that can create a proper space-time gap. A genuinely empty space.'

Another hand went up.

'Yes?'

'Keisha Jackson.'

'Go ahead, Keisha.'

'How big a hole have you got?' asked the girl. 'Is it big enough to step inside?'

'Good Lord, no! No. It's tiny. Very small. It doesn't need to be big. It's a pinprick.'

One of the boys at the back giggled.

'Shortly, we'll be going through into the main laboratory, where you'll see the containment shielding that surrounds the area of experimentation. I believe the team is due to be opening a pinhole vacuum in the next half-hour.' He splayed his hands. 'Wanna go take a look-see?'

Every head in the room wagged enthusiastically.

CHAPTER 8

1906, San Francisco

They returned to their alleyway with half an hour to spare, having spent an hour on the dockside watching the steam ships being loaded and unloaded, Maddy relishing every little detail of the past and giggling with unbridled delight as dockside workers knuckled their foreheads and doffed their caps at her politely as they walked past.

'Oh my God! I feel like some sort of duchess!' she whispered out of the side of her mouth to Liam as they turned into the alley. 'Everyone's so . . . I dunno, so polite and *proper* back in this time.'

He nodded. 'Especially to a *lady* . . . like yourself.' He nodded at her dress, her flamboyant hat with its ostrich feathers. 'Them clothes mark you out as a lady of *means*. You know? A really posh lady, so you are. Now, if you'd found some dowdy dress that made you look common, them workers would've walked on past without a by-your-leave.'

'Oh, right . . . thanks,' she said.

Liam grimaced. 'Ahhh, now see that came out all wrong-sounding, so it did. I didn't mean to say it like that.'

'No, you're probably right,' she huffed. 'I've always been plain-looking. I'm sure shoving on a frilly dress and some stupid feather hat isn't going to make much of a difference.'

They walked down the alley, sidestepping a toppled crate

of festering cabbages until they reached the spot where they'd materialized several hours earlier.

'Seems harsh that, though,' said Liam thoughtfully.

'What?'

'That fella back there, Leighton. You sure he'll die?'

She nodded. 'Yes . . . it makes sense.' Yes, it did. But it was the feel of . . . the feel of . . . *ruthlessness* that gnawed away at her; the agency seemed to know everything about everyone – and exploited that knowledge mercilessly. In less than eighteen hours the young man she'd been talking to would be nothing more than a twisted black carcass amid the smouldering remains of that bank.

And I have to learn to deal with that, she told herself.

Liam seemed to sense her turmoil. 'Well, this is the job now, Mads. We don't have much of a choice in the matter. Do we?'

She looked at him and realized it wasn't just the young bank teller that the agency was ruthlessly *using*, but Liam too. The side effects weren't apparent yet: the onset of cellular corruption, the onset of premature old age. But they'd begin to show at some point, wouldn't they? The more trips Liam was sent on into the past, the more damage it was going to do to his body, until, like Foster, one day he was going to be an old man before his time: his muscles wasted; his bones brittle, weakened and fragile; his organs irretrievably corrupted by the effects of time travel and one by one beginning to fail him.

She so wanted to tell him. To warn him.

How many more trips, Liam? How many before I'm looking at you and seeing a dying old man?

But she couldn't. Not yet. Foster had told her it would be unkind for him to know his fate too early.

'*Let him enjoy the freedom of seeing history for a bit; seeing his future, his past . . . at least give him that for a while before you tell him he's dying.'*

Liam smiled his lopsided smile. On the face of a grown man, it might have been called rakish, charming even. On him it looked just a little mischievous. 'You all right there, Maddy?'

'Yeah.' She nodded. 'Yeah . . . I'm fine.'

He let go of her arm and checked his timepiece. 'Return window any second now.'

Almost on cue, a gentle breeze whistled up the alley, sending the loose debris of rubbish skittering along the cobble-stones. A moment later, the air several yards from them shimmered like a heat haze: a ball of air twelve feet in diameter, hovering a foot off the ground. Through the portal she could just make out the twisting, undulating shapes of the archway beyond and Sal waiting impatiently for them.

You have to tell him, sometime, Maddy. Tell him time travel will slowly kill him.

She didn't like the fact that Foster had left the decision to her. Having secrets like that, having something she couldn't share with him or Sal.

And what about that note?

She could feel the lump of balled paper in her glove, something else she was being asked to keep from her friends. And why? And who was Pandora? She didn't like that . . . it felt like she was being used.

What? Like you just used that young bank teller?

'Come on, then,' said Liam, stepping forward with the jewellery case in his hands.

'Liam?'

He stopped. 'What?'

She could tell him about the note. She could also tell him about the damage time travel was silently wreaking on him.

That every time he went back in time subtle corruption was occurring to every cell in his body, ageing him long before his time. She decided she'd want to know, to know that every time she'd stepped through a portal she was knocking perhaps five or ten years off her natural life. She'd want to at least be able to choose for herself whether she was prepared to make that sacrifice for the rest of mankind.

'What is it, Mads?'

Or maybe Foster was right – she should keep the truth from him for as long as possible . . .

She pulled her glasses out of her handbag and put them on, then took the silly bonnet off her head with its long, ridiculous ostrich feathers. All of a sudden, dressed in her tight corset and billowing lace skirts, she felt dishonest, a phoney, a fake and, her eyes meeting Liam's, she felt like a liar.

A worn-thin smile spread across her face. 'Nothing, Liam. Let's go home, eh?'

CHAPTER 9

2001, New York

'Are you sure?' shouted Sal.

'That's what Bob says.' Maddy's voice echoed from the archway through the open door into the back room – 'the hatchery' as they called it now. 'He says to attach the end of the protein-feed pipe to the growth candidate's belly button.'

'How do we do that?' Liam replied. 'It's not like there's a socket to screw the thing into.' The small slimy foetus squirmed gently in his hand, stirring in its slumber. He grimaced as it did, feeling small fragile bones shift beneath its paper-thin skin.

It looked as vulnerable as a freshly hatched bird fallen from a nest, and yet he knew that this tiny, shifting, pale creature in the palm of his hand would soon be a seven-foot-tall leviathan, bulging with genetically enhanced muscles, with a deep, intimidating voice rumbling from a chest as broad as a beer barrel.

'Bob says you need to push the feed pipe *through* the belly button,' Maddy's voice came back.

Sal's lip curled. 'You mean . . . like . . . as if we're stabbing it?' she called out.

'Well, obviously don't *stab* it with the pipe!' Maddy's voice echoed back. 'Gently do it!'

Liam looked at Sal and shook his head. 'I can't do it. I'd be sick. Here . . .' He passed the foetus to Sal.

'Oh, right . . . thanks, Liam.'

Sal cradled the thing in her hand and then gingerly reached into the perspex growth tube beside them to retrieve the feed pipe dangling down inside. She grimaced as she fumbled in the slimy growth solution, finally pulling out the tip of the feed pipe. As the slime dripped like mucus from the end of it, she could see the pipe ended with a sharpened tip.

'Bob says you shouldn't have to push too hard. The belly button skin is very thin and should . . . Oh, that's just gross . . .' Maddy's voice faded away.

'What?' called out Liam. Maddy didn't answer immediately.

'Maddy?' chirped Sal. 'What's gross?'

'He says the skin should pop just like a blister.'

Liam looked sheepishly at Sal. 'Really, I can't do it. I'd be . . . I'll be sick over the poor little fella.'

'Shadd-yah,' Sal muttered, 'you are hopeless sometimes.'

She took the end of the pipe between her fingers and gently drew it up until it hovered an inch above the foetus's tiny belly: translucent skin criss-crossed with a faint spider's web of blue veins and a small inward twist of rubbery skin.

She took a deep breath. 'OK . . . here goes.'

She gently pressed the sharp end of the feed pipe into the small whirl of flesh. The foetus shuddered in her hand; finger-length arms and legs suddenly flailing, its walnut-sized head slapping against the palm of her hand.

'Uh . . . Maddy! It doesn't like it! It's struggling!'

'Bob says that's perfectly normal . . . just push it in until the skin pops.'

She heard Liam mutter something about Jesus before his legs buckled beneath him and he sat down heavily on the floor, then slid over on to his side.

'I think Liam's just fainted!' shouted Sal.

'Never mind him,' Maddy replied. 'We need to get the foetus hooked up before it starts starving.'

'OK, OK.'

She pushed the tip against the belly button again, this time pushing despite the foetus's protests, until she felt the skin give way, as promised, with a soft pop. A small trickle of dark blood oozed out on to its belly.

'It's in!'

'Right, now, put bonding tape round the pipe and its belly to hold it in place.'

Sal picked up a roll of tape and wound it round as the thing squirmed indignantly in her hand.

'OK. What next?'

'Just lower it into the growth tube.'

Sal stepped towards the plastic cylinder and lifted the foetus up over the open top. 'OK, Bob Junior,' she uttered. 'See you again in a little while.'

Gently she lowered the foetus into the murky gunk and then let it sink. It settled down through the pink soup, like a descending globule of wax in a lava lamp, until the feed pipe drew taut and it came to a rest.

'OK, he's in!'

'Now close the growth-tube lid and activate the system pump!'

Sal closed the tube's metal lid and clamped it in place. She squatted down to inspect the panel at the bottom of the tube. There wasn't much to see down there. A manufacturer's name – WG Systems – and a small touch screen. She tapped the screen and it lit up.

[Filtration system active]

[Set system to GROWTH or STASIS?]

'It's asking me to set it to *growth* or *stasis* . . . shall I pick growth?'

Maddy's answer echoed back from the archway a moment later. 'Growth for this one.'

Sal tapped GROWTH and confirmed the instruction. Immediately she heard the soft hum of a motor whirring to life somewhere at the bottom of the tube. A light winked on inside, making the pink protein glow and lighting the foggy form of the foetus from below. She could see its struggling form settle, content now that it was getting its feed despite the earlier discomfort of having the tube pushed into its belly.

'All done!'

'Good. Now we've got to do the same thing for the others. Only we'll be setting those to *stasis*.'

Sal looked down at the open case on the floor, and the other vials containing growth candidates. Then she looked at Liam, still out for the count, his face resting against the cold concrete floor amid a small pool of spittle and vomit.

'Great. Thanks for the help, Liam.'

'Blfff ifff wheeeelly gloob!' said Liam, his mouth full to bulging.

Both girls looked at him. 'What?'

Liam chewed vigorously for a moment, then finally swallowed. 'I said this is really good! What is it?'

'Lamb korma,' replied Sal. 'It's nothing like how Mum used to make it back home. You have it much sweeter over here. I suppose Americans like their food really sweet?'

Maddy nodded. 'Sweeter the better. I could live just on chocolate.' She reached across their table and pulled a carton of mango chutney out of the brown paper takeaway bag.

Liam hungrily loaded another forkful of korma into his mouth.

Across the archway, music streamed from the computer. Maddy

had an Internet radio station playing music she remembered her parents listening to: the Corrs, REM, Counting Crows.

'It's kind of weird just us three, though,' said Sal. 'I miss Foster.'

'Me too,' said Maddy.

'We're never going to see him again, are we?'

She shrugged. 'Probably not. He had to go.'

'Why?' asked Liam.

She hesitated a moment. 'He was sick.'

'Yeah,' said Sal thoughtfully. 'He didn't look well.'

'What was wrong with him?'

Maddy played with the rice on her plate for a moment. 'Cancer. He was dying of cancer. He told me that.'

'Poor, poor fella,' sighed Liam. 'I really liked him. Reminded me a bit of my grandfather, so he did.'

They ate in silence for a moment.

'It's strange, though,' said Sal. 'We're part of this . . . this *agency*, but it doesn't feel like we're part of *anything*, if you know what I mean.'

'I know what you mean,' said Liam. 'Like it's just the three of us in this little archway all on our own. No contact with anyone else.' He looked up at Maddy. 'Did he not say there were other groups like us? Other *field offices*?'

She nodded. 'He did.'

'But we never ever hear from them. There's no information about them, or about this agency. No one has contacted us, right?'

'No one.'

Sal put down the poppadom she'd been holding. 'What if it really is just us, just us alone . . . here?'

The other two looked at her.

'What if *we* are the agency?' she added.

Liam's eyebrows arched and his jaw dropped open. 'God help us all if that's the case.'

Maddy shook her head. 'It's not just us. Someone else stashed those foetuses back in 1906, right?'

'Could that not have been Foster?'

'Could be.' Maddy shrugged. 'But then you've got to ask who genetically engineered the foetuses? That's gotta need other people, some facility somewhere.' The other two had no answer for that. 'Fact is,' she continued, 'there's more to this agency than just us. There are others out there somewhere or some*when*.'

'So how do we talk with them?' asked Sal. 'How can we meet them?'

'I think that's exactly the point. I think we're not supposed to.' Maddy slurped her Dr Pepper. 'Maybe we're a bit like some sort of terrorist organization; for all of our safety, no one group can know where another group is. We operate in isolation. It's just us . . . until . . .' Her words tailed off and they sat in silence for a while contemplating where that sentence ended.

'Not much chance of a big Christmas get-together, then?' muttered Liam.

Maddy snorted drink on to the table, relieved that he'd found a way to break the sombre mood.

'At least,' said Sal, 'we'll have a brand-new Bob to protect us soon.'

'Aye. I miss the big ape.'

Maddy pointed to the bank of computer monitors. 'He's just there!'

'Naw,' said Liam, wrinkling his nose, 'it's not quite the same him being in there.'

'You can't exactly hug a computer monitor,' said Sal.

Liam chuckled. 'Quite right. I miss his tufty round coconut head.'

'And that dumb, total blip-head expression on his face,' added Sal.

'Aye.'

Maddy finished a mouthful of curry. 'Well, we'll have him around soon. Foster's "how to" manual says the growth cycle should take about one hundred hours.' She pushed her glasses up her nose. 'Lemmesee . . . that's just over four days.'

'We'll need some new clothes for him,' said Sal. 'I'll see what I can find for him downtown tomorrow.'

Maddy nodded. 'Good idea.'

They finished the Indian takeaway and bagged up the rubbish. Liam volunteered to take it out as the girls changed for bed. He crossed the archway floor, criss-crossed with snaking power cables, and lifted the front shutter enough to duck under and step out into their backstreet.

A flickering blue light dimly lit the street. Above him, bright halogen floodlights illuminated the thick metal spars of the Williamsburg Bridge arcing across the flat docile water of the East River. On the far side – a sight he was still yet to get used to – was Manhattan, a vibrant inverted crystal chandelier of winking city lights and nudging traffic.

He dropped the bag into the trash can, and sucked in the cool night air.

Tonight all was well with the world. Tomorrow was the day planes crashed into buildings and the sky was a dark smudge all of the day.

He hated the Tuesdays.

'Good night, New York,' he uttered under his breath.

The city replied with the rumble of a train along the bridge overhead and the echoing, distant wail of a police siren racing through a Brooklyn street several blocks away. As he prepared to duck back inside and wind the shutter down once more, he found himself wondering if Sal was right. If they really were alone. If the agency was, in fact, just them.

As it happened, the answer to that specific question was to arrive the very next morning.

CHAPTER 10

2001, New York

Maddy was entirely engrossed in *Big Brother USA* when Bob interrupted. She'd been watching Nicole and Hardy quietly plotting together in the kitchen against the other two. It was a rerun of the previous week's shows on FOX and she already knew who was facing imminent eviction. She'd seen this show at least four times already, but for some reason, despite knowing the outcome, it was still compulsive viewing.

So it was with mild irritation that she answered the dialogue box that had popped up on the monitor over the top of *Big Brother.*

> Maddy?

She sat forward and spoke into the desk mic rather than tap out an answer on the keyboard.

'What is it, Bob? I'm watching *Big Brother* right now.'

> I am picking up incoming tachyon particles.

Her mouth dropped open and she dribbled milk and Rice Krispies on to her T-shirt.

'You're kidding me, right?'

> Kidding?

'Joking.'

> Not joking, Maddy. There is a directed communication beam coming in from down-time.

'From *down-time* . . . You mean the future?'

> Affirmative.

Maddy dropped her spoon back in the breakfast bowl and sat back in her chair. She looked around. Liam was still fast asleep on his bunk and Sal was out clothes shopping for Bob.

Oh my God . . . a message from the future?

She realized then and there that it could only be from the agency – their first contact with the rest of the organization – and just when they were really beginning to wonder whether the three of them were all on their own.

'What's the message, Bob?'

> Just a moment . . . just a moment. Decoding . . .

Sal had decided not to bother going uptown, over the bridge into Manhattan. The clothes shops there were all modern chain stores and none of them were likely to have much that would fit a seven-foot mountain of muscle.

Instead she headed into Brooklyn, an area she hadn't explored at all thus far. Foster had been so very keen on her focusing her attentive eyes on Manhattan and Times Square – taking in every tiny detail until she knew everything that was *meant* to be there, every tiny event that was *meant* to happen – that she'd had no time to explore the city *this* side of the East River.

Away from the bridge and South 6th Street, she found myriad quieter backstreets, and one in particular lined with odd little boutiques selling second-hand furniture and dusty old books. The chaos of goods piled outside the storefronts and cluttering the narrow street reminded her vaguely of the market-place near her home in Mumbai.

She found herself wiping a solitary tear from her cheek and chided herself for crying for her parents . . . because – stupid – they weren't dead. The grim fate that awaited them wasn't going to happen for another twenty-five years. At this moment in time, her mum and dad were just kids her age, enjoying their childhood and not due to meet for another decade yet. Strange, that. Stood side by side, she and her mum could probably pass as sisters.

Her attention was drawn to a shop with a curious mix of antique knick-knacks spilling out of its entrance and on to the pavement. Ancient-looking wooden furniture, a rocking-horse and clothes that looked like surplus theatrical costumes. But among them, bric-a-brac, a second-hand TV set, a toaster, a Dyson vacuum cleaner. A little bit of everything, it seemed.

She figured she had as much chance of finding something here that might fit Bob as she might anywhere else and, anyway, everything here appeared to be pretty cheap. She stepped inside the boutique and squeezed through the front of the store, cluttered with a set of chrome bar stools and several flaking display-window mannequins wearing dodgy-looking leather corsets and feather boas.

'May I help you, young lady?'

The voice seemed to come out of nowhere and she jumped. Then she spotted a tiny old lady with jet-black hair who was even shorter than she was.

'I, uh . . . You made me jump.'

She smiled. 'I'm sorry, my dear. I do tend to blend into the store.'

Sal laughed. She could imagine a customer slapping ten dollars down on the counter for the 'realistic old lady mannequin', tucking her under one arm and walking out with her.

'What are you after, my dear?'

'You have a clothes section?'

She waved an arm. 'At the back. I have racks and racks of

old, old clothes and party costumes. Lots of cast-outs from the Broadway theatres and a few antique items too.'

'Thank you.'

Sal weaved her way further into the store, her nose tickled and teased by the dust that seemed to be on everything and the faint smell of mothballs and turpentine. She found the clothes racks at the back and almost found herself giggling at the bizarre mix of garments on display. She flicked through the racks in front of her, chuckling at some of the exotic costumes and cooing appreciatively at others. Eventually she found some things that looked suitable for Bob: a baggy pair of striped trousers with extra-long legs that she suspected might have been part of a clown's outfit at one time and an extra-large bright orange and pink Hawaiian shirt that looked like it might just about fit over the top of his broad shoulders and rippling muscles.

'You must have a very big friend,' said the old lady as she took Sal's payment and folded the clothes into a plastic bag for her.

'Uncle,' she replied. 'My Uncle Bob. He's a *very* big man.' Sal was about to add that he was also pretty dumb as well – dumb, and kind of child-like – when she spotted something dangling from a hanger on one wall: a white tunic, buttoned down the left side, with an emblem on the chest that she recognized – the White Star lines. It was a steward's tunic just like Liam's.

She pointed at it. 'Is that . . . is that a uniform from the *Titanic*?'

The old woman looked round at where she was pointing. 'Oh, that? No, it would be worth a lot more if it was genuine. I could sell it to a museum or a collector for thousands of dollars. Unfortunately it's not; it's just a theatre costume. Not a very well-made costume either. Friends of mine . . . they did a production set on the *Titanic*. It didn't do very well. You want to have a look at it?'

Sal shook her head. She could've said something about it being a funny coincidence that her bunk-buddy was a young lad who'd actually worked on the ship *for real*. The old lady would think her mad, of course, or that she was just being cheeky. Mind you, in just over half an hour's time, when the first plane hit the Twin Towers, whatever odd conversation she might have now would be instantly forgotten.

Sal returned to the archway with Bob's clothes and some groceries before the first plane hit and the Manhattan sky started to fill with smoke. She was about to mention the coincidence to Liam – the steward's tunic exactly like his – when she realized by the expressions on Maddy's and Liam's faces that something important had just happened.

She forgot all about it.

CHAPTER 11

2001, New York

'It's a message from the agency,' said Liam as Sal joined them beside the computer desk. 'From the future.'

'So.' Sal looked at them both. 'There's our answer. We're not alone, then.'

'Yup!' replied Maddy, grinning, clearly the most encouraged and excited by that news. 'Bob's decoding the message right now. He's estimated the year of origin to be about 2056. That's the time of Roald Waldstein, the inventor of time-travel technology.'

'Do you think it's him? The Waldstein fella?' asked Liam.

Maddy reached for her inhaler on the desk and took a quick puff on it. 'Yes,' she replied. 'Hopefully it's the agency checking in with us. You know? Seeing if we're OK. Which would be nice.'

'But how . . .' started Liam, frowning. 'But how will we talk back to them? These tachyon signal things can only go backwards in time, right? That's what Foster said.'

'He said that . . . but he was keeping it simple. It takes a lot more energy to project forward. Plus, more importantly, in 2056, everyone's on the lookout for tachyon particles, right, Bob?'

> Correct. A signal aimed at the agency could be detected and reveal its location. In 2056, international laws against time travel have been established.

'In any case, I wouldn't know which direction to point a

signal,' said Maddy. 'Who knows where in the world they're based?'

'So is there a way to talk back?' asked Liam.

Maddy nodded. 'Yup . . . there is.' There was an entry in Foster's 'how to' guide on how to contact the agency, a short explanation by Foster looking ten years younger as he spoke to the webcam. An entry he must have recorded much earlier than the others.

'It's the same principle, Liam, that you used actually,' said Maddy. 'The museum guest book, remember? Only it's a New York newspaper. We place an advert in the lonely hearts section of the *Brooklyn Daily Eagle*. It has to begin with the phrase "a soul lost in time . . ."'

Liam clicked his fingers; he understood the rest. 'And I suppose they have a crinkly old yellowing copy of that paper?'

'Dated September twelfth, 2001. That's right.'

Sal looked from one to the other, her eyes widening. 'And . . . and do you mean the words in the paper change? They actually *change* on the page?'

Maddy nodded. 'It's a tiny ripple in time. Nothing that would change anything else. After all . . . who's going to be reading the lonely hearts section of the papers tomorrow?'

'The papers would be full of that plane-crashing-into-building story, will they not?' said Liam.

'Exactly. Our little advert won't be noticed by anyone, except, of course . . . a bunch of people carefully studying a page of a fifty-five-year-old newspaper in 2056, or thereabouts.' Maddy clucked with excitement. 'I can't tell you how freakin' relieved I am that there's somebody *else* out there!'

Liam nodded at the screen in front of her. 'Looks like Bob's done.'

> I have decoded the message, Maddy.

'What is it?'

> It is only a partial message. The signal has been interrupted.

'Uh? OK . . . give us what you've got, Bob.'

Words spooled across the dialogue box:

> Contamination event. Origin time appears to be 10.17 a.m. 18 August 2015. Major contamination ripples. Significant realignment of time stream. Death of Edward Chan, author of original theory on time travel, resulting in failure to write thesis in 2029. Death may have been deliberate assassination attempt. Occurred while visiting Instit–

The three of them waited for a moment for Bob to print out more of the message.

> That is all I have. The partial ends there.

'That's it?'

> That is it, Maddy.

She turned to look at the others. 'Er . . . what the hell are we supposed to make of that?'

They sat in silence for a while, digesting the small block of text on the screen. Finally Liam shrugged. 'That they're in trouble?'

'Well, duh,' sighed Maddy.

'They need our help?' said Sal.

'But can we help, though?' said Liam. 'Can I go into the *future*?'

'Of course you can.' Maddy pinched the tip of her nose thoughtfully. 'Think about it. Every time we bring you *back* from a mission in the past, you're going forward in time, aren't you?'

> This is correct. A mission operative can travel forward and backwards. However, energy expenditure is significantly higher moving forward.

Sal looked at the other two. 'But maybe there are other field offices further in the future than us who will deal with this?'

Liam nodded. 'She's right. If we're not the only team, then perhaps somebody else is closer in time?'

Maddy gave it a moment's thought. 'Then why direct the message right at us? I mean . . . right here, right now?' She turned back to the desk. 'Bob, was this a broad-spectrum signal beam, sent out for everybody to pick up . . . anywhere . . . anywhen?'

> Negative. It was a narrow, focused beam.

'Meaning it was meant for us?'

> That is the logical assumption, Maddy.

'But surely there are *other* teams in the future,' said Sal. 'Somebody closer in time and –'

'Maybe there are,' cut in Maddy, 'but any field office based after –' she looked at the screen – 'after the eighteenth of August 2015 is going to be affected by the time wave also, right?' She stared at the other two. 'So maybe we're the closest unaffected team? Maybe we're the field office closest *before* this date?'

Liam sighed. 'Aw, come on. Why is it us again? We only just got ourselves fixed up after the last bleedin' mess and a half.'

> Hello, Liam. I have a question.

'Good mornin', Bob.'

> Is 'bleedin'' a reference to the high body count of the last mission including the extensive damage to my last organic support frame? Or is it an expression of anger I should add to my language database?

'It's Liam being all stressy,' said Maddy.

> Angry?

'That's right.'

Once again they stared in silence at the partial message

displayed on the screen, all of them silently hoping it would just go away or change into another message simply welcoming them to the agency.

'It's for *us*, isn't it?' said Sal after a while. 'We've got to fix this time problem like we did the last one.'

Maddy nodded. 'I think so.'

Liam's jaw set firmly. 'Well, I'm not going anywhere 'less I've got Bob coming with me. I mean that, so I do.'

'OK,' said Maddy. 'That's only fair.' She turned round to face the computer monitors. 'Bob, can we speed up the growth cycle of the foetus we've started off?'

> Affirmative. Increase the nutrient mix of the feed solution. Introduce a small electrical charge to the suspension fluid to stimulate cell activity.

'How quickly can we have a body ready for you?'

> Growth cycle can be increased by 100% with acceptable risk to the biological life form.

'Half the time,' said Maddy. 'That's still . . . what? Thirty-eight hours?'

> Correct.

'Could we not birth the clone any earlier?' added Liam. He looked at Maddy and shrugged. 'I mean, does it need to be a fully grown man?'

> Optimal age for organic support unit is approximately 25 years old. Muscle tissue and internal healing systems are at their most functional.

'But, as Liam says, could we eject the clone from the tube at a younger age? Or would that . . . I dunno, kill it?'

> Negative. A growth candidate can be functional from approximate age of 14 onwards. However, the support unit's effectiveness would be compromised.

'What does that mean?' asked Liam.

'It means Bob won't be quite as big a brute as he was last time,' said Sal.

'So . . . what if we birth the clone at say . . . about eighteen years of age,' asked Maddy. 'How useful would he be?'

> An eighteen-year-old clone would offer approximately 50% of normal operational capacity.

'He'd be half as strong?' said Liam.

Maddy nodded. 'And how much time would that save us off the growth cycle?'

> 14 hours.

She looked round at the others. 'What do you reckon?'

'We speed up the growing process and then empty him out on to the floor twenty-four hours from now?' said Liam. 'And we'll have an eighteen-year-old Bob, with half the muscles?'

'That's about it.'

'But he'll still be dangerous to other people, right? I mean . . . doesn't make any sense me having him by my side if he's just –'

> Affirmative, Liam. I will be capable of causing death with or without weapons.

Liam managed a weak smile. 'Then I guess it'd be good to have you back, Bob.'

> Thank you. I look forward to being fully operational again.

Maddy slapped her hand on the desk. 'Right, then. I guess we have a plan of action. Since we've got no time to waste, Sal, could you go see to the growth candidate? Let's get that process sped up.'

'OK.'

'And I guess I better start gathering all the data I can on this Edward Chan guy,' she said, pecking at the computer's keyboard.

'What about me?' asked Liam.

Maddy tapped her fingers absentmindedly on the desk. 'Er . . . hell, I don't know.'

'I suppose I'm coffee-maker?'

She smiled. 'If you're doing a run to Starbucks, can you grab me a chocolate-chip muffin as well?'

'Yeah, me too,' called Sal from the back room's doorway.

CHAPTER 12

2001, New York

'So, this is what I've got,' said Maddy, producing several sheets of computer printout.

This evening the Kentucky Fried Chicken restaurant's eating area was deserted apart from them. Brooklyn's streets were quiet, everyone back home now that the last light of the evening had gone. All home, watching the news on their TV sets. Today's sky had been divided all day by the thick column of black smoke from the collapsed Twin Towers, and New Yorkers were emerging from the fog of shock and dismay at the day's events to a mood of contemplation and mourning.

They were lucky to find even this place open. Only a couple of staff seemed to be on, and they were busy half the time watching the news updates on a small TV set up right on the counter.

'Edward Chan, as you guys will remember Foster telling us, is this bright young maths kid who went to the University of Texas. He graduated there, then went on to do some post-grad work.'

'What is that . . . what's *post-grad*?'

'It's just more studying, Liam. The kind of studying where you tell your teachers what specific area you intend researching, and they just check in with your work every now and then, and help out if they can.

'So anyway,' she continued, looking down at the printouts and reading, 'at the university he sets out to do a research paper on zero-point energy.'

'And what's that?'

'Jeez, Liam . . . are you going to keep stopping me to ask what stuff is?'

He looked hurt. 'I've got to learn all these modern words, right? I mean, I'm still really just a lad from Cork who's running to catch up on the last century, so I am.'

Maddy sighed. 'It's sort of like energy that's supposed to exist at a sub-atomic level. It was still just theoretical mumbo . . . jumbo in my time.'

'I think they started building something to do with that in India in my time,' said Sal. 'Experimental reactor or something, because we were running out of oil and stuff.'

Maddy scooped up some fries from her box. 'Anyway, if I can continue, Liam? Chan set out to do a paper on zero-point energy and ended up changing course. Instead he wrote a paper on the theoretical possibility of time travel. The main point he was making in his work was that the theoretical energy that was assumed to be there in normal space-time, the sub-atomic energy-soup that was meant to be everywhere, was in fact a form of "leakage" from other dimensions. He writes this science paper and does nothing else notable until his death from cancer a few years later at the age of twenty-seven.'

'So, like Foster told us,' said Liam, 'this Chan lad is the true inventor of time travel, not the Waldstein fella?'

'Well, he did the *theoretical* work that led to Waldstein's machine, so I guess they're both responsible for inventing it.'

'The message from the agency said he'd been *assassinated*,' said Sal.

Maddy nodded. 'Which means . . . what?' She looked at

both of them. 'I'm guessing it means someone is trying to prevent time travel being invented?'

Liam reached for a ketchup sachet. 'So . . . hold on. Isn't that what the Waldstein fella wanted in the first place? To make sure time travel never got invented. Isn't that why this agency thing exists, why the three of us're here instead of dead?'

'So why would the agency want us to save Chan?' asked Sal. 'I mean . . . no Chan means no time travel, right? That means no more time problems.'

'S'right.' Liam raised a finger. 'The message didn't actually tell us to *save* him.'

Maddy leaned forward. 'It was an incomplete message. Maybe that's the bit we missed at the end?'

'But we don't know that for sure,' replied Sal. 'Maybe it was someone from the future letting us know that time up ahead was changing and that there was now no more need for the agency . . . for us?'

Maddy shook her head and pointed to the message printed out on paper. 'Look . . . it begins with "contamination event". I'd say that suggests they considered this to be a *bad* thing. And they're not too happy about it.'

They were silent for a moment, all three of them staring at the printed words on the page, trying to determine the intent of the message.

'Foster was very, *very* specific about this,' said Maddy after a while. 'History must go a certain way, for good or bad. Even if the history yet to happen features some kid called Chan who makes time travel possible . . . that's the way it has to be. And if it changes from that, the agency has to fix it.'

Liam nodded after a few moments. 'I suppose you're right. So . . . do we know where his death is going to happen?'

'The date in the message is August eighteenth. In our

database it mentions Chan was one of a class of high-school students who were on a field trip to the Texas Advanced Energy Research Institute, on this date. This is biographical data on Chan taken from 2056. If this really is an assassination attempt by somebody, the chances are they have access to the same data as us. In other words, they looked at Chan's biography and noted he was going to be at a particular place at a particular time . . .'

'And sent themselves back in time to be there waiting with a gun,' added Liam.

Maddy nodded. 'Yup.'

'Well . . .' Liam bit his lip anxiously. 'You can see now why I'm so bleedin' keen to have big ol' Bob by my side. Seems these bad guys have got guns with them and Bob's a dab hand at dealing with people like that, so he is.'

Maddy glanced at her watch. 'We should probably get back to the arch. The time bubble is due to flip over in a few hours and we could all do with some rest. Bob's new body should be ready to birth tomorrow morning and then we'll be ready to send you guys forward in time to see what's what.'

Liam sighed. 'Back in that ol' bathtub for me.'

CHAPTER 13

2001, New York

Sal stared at the curled-up form in the growth tube in stunned silence for a good minute before she finally gasped. 'Oh no.'

By the dim red light of the back room and the peach-coloured glow of the tube's interior up-light she could see they'd really messed up with growing Bob's body. Well, actually . . . it looked like she alone had messed things up.

They're going to be mad at me.

Maddy's voice echoed through the open door into the back room. 'How's he looking?'

Sal didn't know what to say. So she said nothing.

'Everything OK in there?'

They've got to find out sometime.

'Uhh . . . no. Not really,' she replied.

'What's the matter?' Maddy's head appeared in the doorway, squinting into the gloom of the hatchery. 'Sal? What's up?'

'It's uh . . . it's Bob . . .' she said.

'Oh God, what now? It's not a mis-growth, is it? We can't afford to start off another one.'

Sal had caught a glimpse of the few mis-growths that had been floating in the tubes back here not long after Foster had recruited them; they'd looked like awful freakshow specimens in some carnival tent, contorted, with faces like gargoyles and demons and limbs twisted into impossible claw-like stumps. She thanked God it wasn't something like that.

'No, it's grown just fine . . . it's just . . .'

Maddy took a cautious step into the hatchery, her eyes yet to adjust to the dim red lighting. 'Well, it looks OK from here. Two arms, two legs . . . nothing weird and gross sticking out,' she said.

Sal studied the adult-sized form floating in the murky pink soup. 'I think I must have put the wrong foetus in or something,' she uttered.

Maddy took a few steps across the floor, careful not to hook her foot in a power cable and pull over one of the other tubes holding the other tiny foetuses in stasis.

'Come on, Sal, what's the prob–' Maddy's voice tailed away as she stood beside her. 'Oh,' she whispered. 'I see now.'

Sal bit her lip. 'I . . . I must have . . . I'm sorry. I didn't check it first. I . . . just didn't see.'

Maddy looked at her. 'You didn't *see*?'

'They all looked the same!' Sal replied, her voice rising in pitch. 'Look, I'm sorry!'

'Oh, that's just great, Sal. Just great! Now what are we going to do!'

'I'm sorry, OK? Sorry. I didn't see. I just –'

'Sorry . . . is that it? *Sorry* doesn't help us. There's no time to grow another one!'

Liam stepped into the back room. 'Hey! Ladies, ladies! Whatever is the matter?'

'Well, why don't you come and look for yourself,' snapped Maddy irritably.

Liam made his way cautiously forward until he was standing between them.

'Meet your new support unit,' she added sarcastically.

Liam frowned at the dim outline in the tube, then suddenly his eyebrows shot up into twin arches. 'It's a . . . it's a . . . it's a . . .'

'Girl,' said Sal helpfully.

'Oh Jay-zus-'n'-Mother-Mary . . . I never knew we got baby boys *and girls*.'

Maddy reached down to the floor and picked up one of the empty glass containers the foetuses had come in. She held it close to the growth tube to take advantage of some of the softly glowing light coming from within.

'There,' she said after a while, her finger pointing at a small marking at the bottom of the glass.

Sal leaned closer, screwing her eyes up to see it better in the dim light.

'It says XX . . . that's all. What's that supposed to mean?'

Maddy tutted and shook her head. 'You don't know?'

'No.'

Liam shrugged. 'Me neither,' he said, his eyes still locked on the naked female form inside the tube.

'It means female. And XY means male. You guys can be real morons! It's to do with the chromosomes.'

Liam managed to drag his eyes away. 'Cromer-what-a-ma-jinxie?'

Frustrated, Maddy banged the perspex tube with the palm of her hand. 'Doesn't matter. I'll explain another time. The point is what are we gonna do?'

'If we start another one off, it'll be at least another thirty-six hours before we can send someone to investigate the Chan thing,' said Sal.

'That's my point!' replied Maddy, removing her glasses and rubbing her eyes. 'The message sounded urgent. Right? God knows what damage is happening to the timeline ahead of us right now!'

'We don't have much choice,' replied Sal. 'Unless . . .'

Maddy nodded. 'Unless you go check it out on your own, Liam.'

Liam looked at them both. 'You're joking, right?'

Neither said anything.

'Right,' he replied. 'Well, the answer is . . . *not on your nelly!* No way! No sir! I'm not going into some spangly future place without a Bob –' he looked again at the female form inside the tube – 'or a *Roberta* by my side. It's been hard enough for me trying to get my head around 2001 and all your crazy modern ways. There's no way that I'm doing 2015 all on my own, I'm tellin' you.'

Maddy sighed. 'All right, then.' She looked at the shape floating in the goo. 'That thing may not have the brute strength of the last one, but at least you'd have Bob's AI and database along with you.' Maddy turned to him. 'And this is just a scouting mission anyway. Just a quick visit to see what happened to Chan.'

Liam's face hardened. 'That's what Foster said to me the last time . . . and look what happened. I got stuck in the middle of an invasion for six months.'

Maddy reached a hand out and touched his arm. 'Well, this time we'll just be more cautious.'

He chewed his lip in thought for a moment, then finally nodded. 'Jeez . . . all right. I suppose if it's just a quick look-see.'

Maddy gently slapped his shoulder. 'Good. Sal?'

'Yes?'

'Let's birth it.'

'OK.'

Sal squatted down on her haunches to tap the command into the small control panel at the bottom of the cylinder.

'Er . . . Liam?' said Maddy.

'Yes?'

'Would you mind?'

'Mind? Mind what?'

'A little privacy?'

'Uh?'

Maddy sighed. 'It may just be a mindless blubbering clone right now . . . but it's still a lady.'

Liam was still sulking at being kicked out of the back room when the metal door to the hatchery finally slid to one side with a shrill squeak of un-oiled rollers. Maddy and Sal emerged through the doorway first, beaming like a pair of proud midwives. They ushered a pale shuffling form wrapped in a long towel out into the light of the main arch.

Liam studied her; she was taller than the other two and, of course, as Bob had first been when he'd been dumped out of the bottom of his tube, she was completely bald. Yet, despite that, he realized she was – and he felt a little queasy admitting this to himself – quite beautiful.

'Uh . . . hello,' he said awkwardly.

The clone stared at him curiously as the girls led her across the arch towards the table and armchairs. Her pale skin glistened, wet with the goo she'd been floating in only moments ago, and the smell – like a rancid meat stew – wafted across to him, turning his stomach.

'Hello there,' said Liam again as they sat her down opposite him.

'Flug herr gufff slurb,' the clone replied, dark brown slime dribbling out of the side of her mouth and down her chin.

'Right,' said Maddy to Liam. 'You can get acquainted while I sort out uploading Bob's AI.'

He nodded, his eyes still locked on the clone. She seemed to have little of the bulging musculature of Bob . . . athletic, though, not bulky like he'd been last time.

Bob.

Bob? Liam, you idiot.

He realized that it was stupid to think of that first ape-like clone as Bob; it had merely been the organic vehicle that Bob's AI code had first used. But still, he mused, Bob's 'personality' – if he could actually use that word – had been formed inside that big brute. It was almost impossible not to think of him as a big, clumsy, Panzer tank of a man, with fuzzy coconut hair and a voice as deep and rumbling as one of the trains that regularly rattled over the Williamsburg Bridge above them.

During the six months he'd been stuck in the past with him he'd grown attached to the big lumbering ape; not just the code in his head, but that expressionless vapid face of his, those horribly awkward smiles – more like a horse baring its teeth. He'd even cried when those men had gunned Bob down, riddling him with enough bullets to ensure that even his robust body had no hope of recovery. Cried as Bob had 'died' in his arms and he'd had to perform an act of surgery that since then he'd done his very best to blank from his memory.

Cried for Bob, although he'd never admit that to the others because it seemed silly. All that made Bob *Bob* had survived, had come back from the past in his blood-covered hand: a wafer of silicon containing his AI, every memory he had, all the learning, all the adapting, all the growing up he'd done in those six months in the past. That was Bob, not the tattered bullet-riddled corpse he'd left behind in the blood-spattered snow of 1941.

Liam looked again at the young . . . *woman* . . . in front of him: lean and athletic, a porcelain beauty to her face.

Her? HER? It's an IT, Liam. IT . . . get it? Not a 'her'. Just an organic vehicle. A meat robot.

Almost as if the clone could read his mind, it drooled another long spittle string of gunk out of the side of its mouth and grunted something unintelligible.

Sal giggled. 'So like Bob, isn't she? She could be his twin sister.'

Maddy returned from the desk to sit beside the female clone. 'OK, Bob's preparing the download protocols. He needs to handshake with this support unit's in-built operating system before he can upload a copy of his AI into it.'

'Uh . . . how does Bob get into her . . . its head?' asked Liam. 'Don't you need some sort of a cable or something?'

'Bluetooth,' she replied wearily. 'Yes, I know, that means nothing to you.' She sighed. 'OK. It's a broadband wireless data communication protocol designed for low-latency short-distance transmission.' Liam was still staring at her, slack-jawed and bemused. Maddy sighed again. 'Information will fly through the air from the computer and into its head.'

'Oh . . . right.' Liam smiled. 'Why didn't you just say that in the first place?'

They heard a beep coming from the computer desk.

'Uploading is starting now,' said Maddy.

The clone sitting opposite Liam suddenly jerked upright and cocked her head like a dog hearing a dog-whistle.

He watched with fascination as the support unit's eyes blinked rapidly with the data flooding into the tiny computer system built into the middle of its cranium – computer technology that came from the 2050s, technology immensely more powerful than their array of linked PCs beneath the computer desk.

The download of information took about ten minutes, then finally the female clone closed her eyes.

'Installing,' explained Maddy. 'Then it will boot up again.'

After a few moments the clone looked up at them with eyes that now seemed to faintly glint with intelligence.

'Bob?' said Maddy, 'you OK?'

The clone nodded awkwardly. 'Affirmative.' The voice was a deep growl, almost as deep as Bob's old voice had been.

'Jay-zus!' Liam lurched. 'That's . . . weird.'

Sal pulled a face. 'Ewww . . . jahulla! That's just so-o-o wrong!'

'I will adjust the vocal register,' Bob's barrel-deep voice rumbled. The support unit cocked its head then spoke again. 'Is this better?' The voice now the smooth upper-register of a teenage girl's.

Maddy nodded. 'Much better. I think we can safely say you're not an *it* . . . you're a *she* now.'

Liam shook his head as he studied *it . . . him . . . her . . . Bob*. 'I feel very strange about this,' he finally muttered. 'Very strange indeed.'

CHAPTER 14

2001, New York

'Now, she's had all the biographical information about Edward Chan and details of the layout of the Texas Advanced Energy Research Institute uploaded. Isn't that right?'

The support unit nodded as she lowered herself into the water beside Liam, wearing underwear that Maddy had self-consciously pulled out from beneath the sheets of her bunk and donated.

'Affirmative. I have all the data required for this mission,' the support unit replied sweetly.

Liam shook his head. 'This is so weird. I mean . . . it's great to have you back an' all, Bob, but you're a . . . you're a . . .' His glance flickered involuntarily for a moment towards the clone's chest. He clasped his eyes shut. 'Oh Jeez . . . you're *a girl*, so you are!'

'Recommendation: suggest this copy of my AI be given an appropriate unique identifier.'

Maddy, sitting on the top step and looking down at them in the water, nodded. 'That's right. You can't go round calling her Bob.'

'Additional information: although the AI in my computer is a direct duplication, I am now interfaced with a different organic brain, and during the operational lifespan of this organic support frame, different data will result in a different emergent AI.'

Liam looked up at Maddy. 'What did she . . . it . . . Bob just say?'

'That you should think of this support unit as someone brand new. As a different team member . . . because she's going to develop a different personality. That's right, isn't it?'

The support unit nodded. 'Affirmative. Consequently this AI should have its own identifying label.'

'She needs a new name to avoid confusion with Bob,' added Maddy, nodding towards the bank of monitors and computers on the desk. 'Remember, Bob's still in there.' She grinned. 'You're best thinking of this support unit as . . . I dunno . . . his sister.'

Liam looked at the clone treading water beside him. She tried one of Bob's reassuring horse smiles – just as clumsy and ill-fitting as her . . . *brother*. But, somehow, more appealing on her slim face.

'Liam,' she said softly, 'please give me a name.'

'Go on,' said Maddy. 'It's your turn.'

He shook his head. 'I . . . don't know.'

'OK, you think about it.' She called across the archway to Sal. 'What's the countdown?'

'Fifty seconds!'

She handed them a couple of sealed plastic bags. 'Clothes for you in there. And a wig for her. Now, you'll arrive at the institute just as a class of thirty children are being given a tour of the place. I've checked the floor plans and picked out what looks like an equipment storage room near to the institute's main experimental chamber. That's where we'll send you. You can dry off and change in there, then join the school party.'

Liam nodded.

'You'll be there to observe how Edward Chan is assassinated, OK? Not to stop it . . . just watch. Then we'll bring you back, you can tell us what happened, then we can work on what we need to do to prevent it happening. That's the plan. Got it?'

'Aye. And the return window?'

'Is set for ten minutes after Edward Chan's time of death. The usual failed-return protocols apply – if you miss that first window, we'll open again an hour later . . . you know how it goes.'

'An hour later, a day later, a week later.'

'That's it.'

'Thirty seconds!' called out Sal.

'You OK, Liam?' said Maddy softly.

He nodded, his teeth beginning to chatter with the cold.

'Come back safely,' she said affectionately, patting his hand holding the side of the tube. She got to her feet and clanked down the steps beside the tube.

'Ten seconds!'

Liam turned to look at the support unit treading water beside him. 'Hey . . . I've got a name for you.'

'Insufficient time, Liam,' she replied. 'We have to go under the water now.'

Reluctantly he nodded, sucked in a big lungful of air, let go of the side and held his nose. The support unit gently rested a hand on top of his head and shoved him under with surprising force, then ducked beneath the water herself.

CHAPTER 15

2015, Texas

He watched Edward Chan walking ahead of him with the other kids. He looked so small among the other high-school-age kids, so small and so vulnerable with his high-school rucksack on his back and a yellow T-shirt two sizes too big for him.

Yes. Yes, he does . . . but don't forget who this boy is. Just how dangerous he is.

Howard Goodall gritted his teeth with renewed determination. Ahead of him, just a dozen yards away, was the legendary Edward Chan, grandfather of time-travel technology. His mind reiterated an inescapable mantra.

The boy has to die. The boy has to die.

Too many of his colleagues had been arrested to get him to this place, this time, close enough to kill Chan. He could feel the weight in his own rucksack – a red one with *High School Musical 4* stencilled in cheerful pink across it. He could feel the weight of responsibility in there and the miniature carbon-fibre projectile weapon hidden inside an innocent-looking camping flask, the cheap plastic kind you can pick up from Wal-Mart for five dollars.

The institute's guide eased his way through the shuffling trail of students to the front where he stopped, turned round and raised his hands to get everyone's attention.

'OK, now that you guys have all had some refreshments

and you've had a little introduction to the theory behind zero-point energy, we're going to be heading into the business part of this facility: the experimental reactor building. Before we go inside there's one more security check –'

Thirty students moaned in unison.

'Sorry, kids,' he laughed. 'I'm afraid it's procedure, so if you'd all just open your rucksacks and school bags one last time for our security guards to get a quick look-see inside, then we can proceed.'

Third time. Howard did his best to look just as casual and irritated at the hassle as all the other kids. He unzipped his rucksack and held it open for a cursory glance. If the guard bothered to unscrew the drinking cap of the camping flask, he'd find the small weapon, which was roughly the size and shape of a whiteboard marker.

Howard watched the guard work his way down the line of impatient children.

But he won't unscrew it . . . because, Howard, you're going to look just as bored as all these other kids. Bored and impatient to get on with the tour. And not nervous. Not scared.

Howard was the one in their group they'd selected to do the job. Although he was twenty-three he looked young, young enough to pass as a high-school student, a few tufts of downy hair on his upper lip suggested a boy desperate to grow his first moustache. His dark wavy hair pulled back into a scruffy ponytail, his thrash-metal *Arch-NME On Tour* T-shirt, took six or seven years off him. Now, he no longer looked like Howard Goodall, a mathematics graduate from the year 2059, but *Leonard Baumgardner* – some grungy high-school kid who'd managed to earn a set of top scores in his SATs.

The real Lenny was back home in his basement, bound and gagged along with his mom. Howard had briefly considered killing them both, worried they might struggle free and raise the alarm. But he figured this was all going to be done before that could happen.

He looked close enough in appearance to the spotty face on Lenny's old school ID card to pass a cursory examination, and since this party of students had assembled together in Austin earlier this morning, and he was the only kid from Baumgardner's school going, there was no one there to *not* recognize him. No one had any reason to believe he wasn't young Leonard.

Of course, none of the kids knew each other; they were from different schools all over the state – thirty kids assembling, early morning, with their parents, waiting to be signed on to the coach and into the care of Mr Whitmore for the day.

Howard glanced around at the others.

And what if one of the others is not who he says he is?

He kicked that thought away as quickly as it had arrived. He needed to stay very calm. Needed to look relaxed, like these others; slightly bored, waiting to be shown something interesting, something worth crawling out of bed for so early.

The guard finally reached for Howard's bag. 'Morning,' he grunted. 'Let's take a look, son.'

Howard casually held out his rucksack.

'Anything hazardous in here, son?'

'What? You mean . . . apart from my big bomb?' sighed Howard with a lazy smile.

The guard scowled at him. 'Not even funny, kid.' His hand rummaged quickly through the grubby items inside: a sandwich box, the flask, several rolled-up and dog-eared comicbooks, before he slapped the rucksack closed and waved Howard past.

Howard offered the guard a casual wave. 'Have a nice day, now.'

'Go on, kid . . . scoot,' said the guard, before turning to rummage through another bag.

Ahead he could see Chan and the other students gathered around the guide, Mr Kelly, and the teacher, Mr Whitmore, waiting for the last of them to be checked.

He sucked in a deep breath as he wandered over to join them, settling his nerves, his pounding heart. Inside the zero-point chamber, that's when he was going to do it. The chamber would be sealed, and this security guard and the others on the outside; his best chance to fire several aimed shots at the boy. It would take them a while to react, to open the door.

To take me down.

Howard smiled grimly. Not such a big price to pay to save the future of mankind, not really.

CHAPTER 16

2015, Texas

They landed with a wet splash on to a hard tiled floor.

'Ouch!' Liam whimpered.

The water sloshed noisily across the floor soaking cardboard boxes of domestic cleaning materials.

'Jay-zus, why can't we ever land on something soft . . . like a pillow?' He grimaced as he let go of his nose and puffed out the breath he'd taken back in 2001.

'Insufficient data to identify a soft landing loca–'

Liam raised a hand. 'It's all right . . . I wasn't after an answer.' He pulled a wet shock of dark hair out of his eyes and opened them, instantly wishing he hadn't.

'Oh-Mother-of-God!' He clamped his eyes shut and turned away to look at the storeroom wall.

'What is wrong?'

'You could have warned me you were taking those wet things off!'

'Why?'

'Because . . . because . . .' He bit his lip. *This is so very not right.*

'Because you're a, ah . . . you're a *girl* now, Bob.'

Liam spotted some towels on the storeroom shelf and began to dry himself off.

'You should assign a new ident. to this AI copy. I may be

"Bob" now,' she said, 'but this AI will develop new sub-routines and characteristics that require a new identifying label.'

Liam nodded. 'Yes.' Self-consciously he found himself wrapping the towel round his waist as he hurriedly removed his wet boxers and pulled the clothes he'd brought with him out of the bag.

'Four seconds before we were transmitted, you indicated you had a suitable ident. for me.'

'Oh yes . . . so I did.'

She turned to look at him. 'So, what will I be called?'

Liam could hear the rustle of clothes being quickly pulled on behind his back.

Good.

He really didn't need to see *that* . . . again. He found a pair of neon green three-quarter-length baggy shorts and a navy blue sweatshirt with the word NIKE splayed across it. And, for some reason, a large tick beneath the word. He felt much better with some clothes on, even if they looked quite ridiculous.

'I had a cousin called Rebecca,' he said. 'Used to call her *Becks* for short.'

'Becks?' replied the support unit, her voice rising at the end in a query.

'That's right – Becks.'

'A moment . . . logging ident. . . .'

'So, are you *decent* now? Can I turn round?'

'Decent?'

'You know, got clothes on?'

'Affirmative.'

Liam turned round and found his breath caught momentarily. 'Blimey!'

Becks cocked her head and looked at him. 'Are these garments incorrectly deployed?'

His eyes skittered awkwardly up from the combat boots to the black leggings, to the black lace mini-skirt to a black crop top that displayed a bare midriff, up to her . . . *perfect* . . . face framed by tumbling locks of flaming fox-red hair. Quite clearly Sal had decided their support unit needed to look like some sort of gothic valkyrie.

'Uh. No, you are . . . you got it about . . . errrr . . . right, I suppose . . . I think.'

Liam felt his mouth go dry and a strange jittery, lurching sensation in his stomach.

Jay-zus . . . get a grip, Liam. That's . . . that's . . . that's just Bob wearing a girl suit. All right?

'Recommendation: you should refer to me as *Becks* from this point on,' she said firmly. 'It will avoid unnecessary confusion between AI versions.'

He nodded. 'All right . . . uh, OK. So, you're Becks, then. That's that settled.'

'Correct.' Her smile was faltering and clumsy as always, just like Bob. But on those lips, strangely quite perfect.

Liam decided to shift his mind to other things. 'I suppose we had better get a move on and find this Chan fella.'

Becks nodded and blinked, retrieving data from her hard drive. 'We are located within the institute's experimental reactor building. The reactor is very close to this location.'

Liam stepped towards the storeroom's door and cracked it open a sliver. Outside he could see a narrow hallway and, opposite, double doors with a sign on them: AUTHORIZED VISITORS AND STAFF ONLY. Just then he heard muffled voices from the end of the hallway and glass doors swung inwards to reveal a man in a smart linen suit leading a shuffling gaggle of teenagers.

'Yes, we're in the correct place all right,' whispered Liam.

He watched them coming towards them, the man turning to talk to the group, gesturing emphatically with his hands. Liam gently closed the door until it clicked. 'They're just coming up now. We can tag along on the end,' he whispered.

He waited until the muted sound of the man's droning voice and the shuffle and slap of trainers on the polished linoleum floor passed them by before he cracked the door open again and peeked out. The last kids in the school party were just ahead, three blonde-haired girls deeply involved in a mumbled conversation, clearly too interested in chatting to each other to even pretend to be listening to the guide up front.

'Now!' Liam mouthed, and stepped out behind them, Becks swiftly following.

He fell in step at the back of the group and when one of the girls casually glanced back over her shoulder he quickly managed to mimic the laid-back swagger of one of the boys up ahead.

'Oh,' said the girl. 'Thought we were, like, you know, the last.'

Liam shrugged and smiled. 'Guess, *like*, not,' he replied, doing his best to bury the Irish in his voice.

Her gaze lingered a moment longer, a flickering smile for him. Then she turned back round and was back to gossiping in a conspiratorial murmur with the other two again.

Liam puffed out a silent gasp of relief. It looked like they'd jumped the first hurdle – successfully sneaking on to the back of the tour party and managing to pass themselves off as yet two more kids who might actually have preferred a trip to Disneyland or Universal Studios than wandering around a bunch of clinically clean corridors. He grinned at Becks and then almost immediately wished he hadn't. The smile she returned gave him that weird flip-flopping sensation in his stomach again.

Liam, you daft idiot . . . It's just Bob in a dress, for crying out loud!

He wished Sal could have found some other clothes for the support unit, something baggy, drab and unflattering. And why a wig with hair like that? Why *that* colour? He'd always loved that copper red. His first crush at school, Mary O'Donnell, she'd had hair that bewitching colour of fiery red.

Oh, saints preserve me . . . she's just a meat robot, so she is.

CHAPTER 17

2015, Texas

'And here we are!' announced Mr Kelly to the group. 'We're about to enter the central reactor containment area. The whole experimental chamber is surrounded by an electro-magnetic field to filter out possible interference from all manner of electronic devices. Basically, we're going to be walking inside a giant electro-magnet. So if you kids have any iPods, laptops, iPhones or memory cards with data on you'd rather not lose, may I suggest you place them on the table here before we step through?' he said, indicating a table beside a pair of thick metal doors.

Liam watched with amusement as virtually every student sighed and then proceeded to reach into their rucksacks to pull out all manner of shiny metal and plastic gadgets and gizmos.

Eventually done, Mr Kelly tapped an entry code on to the large metal doors and he smiled expectantly as they swung slowly inwards.

At last, the gaggle of teenagers in his charge seemed to be shaken out of their torpid state of disinterest. A shared gasp rippled among them as their eyes swept up to take in the large spherical chamber, seemingly constructed entirely out of football-sized ball-bearings.

'As you can see, the entire chamber is lined with charged magnets, which act as a completely impenetrable barrier for any sort of FM radio signals, WiFi signals, electrical currents, atmospheric static and so on, the sort of things that can affect our readings from the test runs.'

He led them into the spherical chamber along a raised walkway, towards a platform thirty feet in diameter. Mr Kelly pointed towards a rather less impressive-looking structure, what appeared to be a polished metal witch's cauldron with a lid on, six feet across. Wires and cables and broad cylinders of metal descended through the lid into whatever witches' brew was bubbling away inside.

'Now that, kids . . . that's what this is all about. That metal sphere contains tens of billions of dollars' worth of investment, and quite possibly represents mankind's energy future.'

'That's the reactor?' asked Mr Whitmore.

'Yup. That's it, the zero-point energy test reactor.' Kelly smiled and shook his head. 'You know, it still amazes me that something so small, something the size of a . . . of a small car could, in theory, provide more than enough energy for every last person on this planet.'

Liam found his jaw sagging open, just like everyone else's.

'The tests we've run in there have so far produced really quite staggering amounts of energy out of the space-time vacuum pinholes that we've opened. The trick is sustaining and controlling the pinhole . . . and, of course, containing such huge amounts of energy.'

'That sounds a little, like . . . a little dangerous,' said the blonde girl who'd glanced back at Liam.

Mr Kelly looked at her. 'What's your name?'

'Laura Whitely.'

'Well, Laura . . . I guess it does sound a little dangerous. Dr Brohm, one of our leading scientists working on this, likened it to opening a very small peephole and looking on to the face of God himself.' Mr Kelly forced a laugh at that comment. 'A little fanciful, I think, but it gives you an idea of how much energy we're talking about . . .'

Howard Goodall felt the first bead of sweat trickle down the small of his back as he discreetly eased his rucksack off his shoulder on to the floor. He slowly opened the zip just a little and sneaked his hand inside. His fingers quickly found the screw cap of his thermos flask and he gently began twisting it off.

He could see Edward Chan at the front of the small knot of students gazing in silent awe at the glistening metal container.

Howard wondered how they could all be so incredibly stupid, how mankind was happy to play dice with technology it had no way of understanding. He remembered a lecture at university. His tutor had talked about the Americans' Manhattan project during the Second World War – their attempt to build the world's first atom bomb. How, when they first did a test detonation in the deserts of New Mexico, the scientists hadn't been certain whether the bomb would destroy several square miles of desert or, indeed, the entire planet. But still the reckless, silly fools went ahead and tested it anyway, played dice with mankind's future.

Just like time travel – a technology mankind was woefully unprepared to be in possession of. He stepped forward, a little closer to Chan, his eyes darting to the heavy doorway of the chamber slowly being swung back into place.

His hand felt the tube-shaped carbon-fibre weapon. It was small, tiny, with a magazine containing six toxin-tipped projectiles. He only had to wound Chan, just get one shot on target and wound the boy – the neurotoxin would finish him in minutes.

This is it, Howard, he told himself. *This is the end of time travel.*

CHAPTER 18

2001, New York

'What? Jealous?' Maddy shook her head emphatically. 'Jealous of Bob Version Two?'

Sal had a mischievous look on her face. 'Just asking.'

'Oh, come on, of course not! It's not even human . . . it's just . . . it's just a clone. It's not even a genuine copy of a human – it doesn't have a proper human brain!'

'But she *looks* very human.'

'And so does a storefront mannequin, or a GI Joe action figure or a Barbie doll.'

Sal shrugged and grinned mischievously. 'Liam seemed impressed.'

Maddy had noticed. His eyes had been out on stalks. 'No different to any other boy, I guess . . . one thing on their minds all the time.'

Sal giggled. 'True.' She spun in the office chair beside the computer desk. 'So, you don't . . . so you're not jealous?'

Maddy took off her glasses and wiped them on her T-shirt. It was decidedly odd having Bob looking like that, like some athletic-fit catwalk model, some Amazonian beauty. And yes . . . having something like that gliding beautifully around was enough to make any female feel inadequate, plain in comparison. But then Maddy was used to it.

On the other hand, if Sal was asking in a roundabout way

whether she had *feelings* for Liam . . . well, the answer was no, not *those sort of feelings*. Liam was nice-looking, charming in an old-fashioned gentlemanly way, but what she felt for him, more than anything else, was pity, a choking sadness.

Every time I send him through . . . I'm killing him just a little bit more.

She looked at Sal. 'No, I'm not jealous. I'm not, you know, like . . . *after* him –'

> Maddy, it is time to activate the return window.

'OK,' she replied, turning to face the desk. She began to tap the retrieval coordinates into the computer.

'But he's nice,' said Sal.

'Sure he's nice,' said Maddy. 'I'm sure he had girlfriends back in Ireland, but . . . but, I'm a couple of years older than him anyway and . . . and it's more like he's a little brother, or a nephew really, than, you know . . . sort of boyfriend material.'

Maddy double-checked the coordinates. 'Anyway . . . My God, Sal –' she grimaced at her – 'I can't believe you're being so personal!'

'Sorry,' said Sal, flicking a tress of dark hair out of her eye. 'Oh . . . I just remembered! You'll never guess what I saw in a junk store down–'

'Just a moment, Sal. I need to concentrate . . .'

CHAPTER 19

2015, Texas

Liam identified Chan among the students. It wasn't as obvious as he'd thought it would be. There were about seven or eight who looked oriental to him, and most of them were younger than the other students. But he knew Edward Chan was the youngest here and he zeroed in on a small boy at the front, gaping wide-eyed at the zero-point energy reactor. Seemingly entranced by it.

Becks gently tapped Liam's arm and leaned towards him. 'Information: according to the mission data, Edward Chan only has four minutes and seven seconds left to live.'

Liam nodded. He looked around the chamber, trying to identify what or who could possibly pose a threat to the boy. If they were down to four minutes, then presumably the lad's killer was right here, right now, getting ready to make his move. His eyes darted from Mr Kelly, explaining the machinery and instrumentation, to Mr Whitmore, stroking his sparsely bearded chin thoughtfully, to the two technicians manning a couple of data terminals.

One of them?

His gaze shifted to the students, all of them still marvelling at the interior of the chamber and some of the incredible-sounding statistics that Mr Kelly was reeling off. '. . . equivalent to *all* of the energy produced by coal, oil, natural gas . . . over the last one hundred and fifty years . . .'

One of them? One of the students?

Why not? It could just as easily be one of the students. After all, Liam was the same age as the oldest of them and an assassin would probably have a better chance smuggling himself in as a student than he would a member of staff. After all, that had worked for him and Becks. His gaze wandered from face to face, looking for a nervous tic, darting eyes, lips moving in silent prayer, someone clearly agonizing over the precise moment to strike.

Becks gently tapped his arm again.

'What now?' he hissed.

'I am sensing precursor tachyon particles in the vicinity.'

He looked at her. 'Uh?' Their return window wasn't due yet, not until ten minutes after Chan's supposed moment of death. That was the arrangement. 'Are you sure?'

Becks nodded towards the reactor. 'There. They are appearing . . .' Her eyes widened, and her lids fluttered and blinked rapidly. 'DANGER!' she suddenly barked at the top of her voice.

Howard was almost beside Chan, his finger on the trigger inside his bag ready to pull the small weapon out and fire it at his back. He wanted to be right beside Chan, right next to him, to know as an absolute certainty he wasn't going to miss. Too much rested on this. *Everything* rested on this. He was just a couple of yards from him when a tall girl with distinctive red hair at the back of the knot of students suddenly started shouting.

Mr Kelly stopped mid-sentence. 'Excuse me?'

'DANGER!' shouted the girl again, her voice loud and urgent.

'Excuse me, young lady,' replied Mr Whitmore, 'this is *not* the place for some sort of stupid prank!'

Howard turned to look at the girl.

Something's wrong. Someone knows!

'DANGER!' shouted the girl again, but her finger pointed directly at the reactor, not him. 'Tachyon interference with the reactor! The reactor will explode!'

Howard had no idea what the hell she was on about. Perhaps it was just a coincidence, perhaps she was just some flaky goth girl making some sort of a protest against experimenting with zero-point energy. He was with her on that, but now was not the best time. He wasn't going to be distracted. He pushed his way forward towards Chan as the other students began to step back warily from the reactor in response to her outburst.

At last, standing beside the small boy, he looked down at him, his finger poised on the trigger, ready to whip the gun out and fire.

Chan turned to look up at him. 'What's the girl at the back saying?'

Howard found himself shrugging. 'I . . . uh . . . I guess she's having some kinda fit.'

'Now stop it!' snapped Mr Whitmore, pushing his way through the bemused students towards the girl. 'Nothing is going to explode!'

Chan grinned up at Howard. 'Crazy girl, huh?'

And Howard found himself smiling back at the kid, somehow not quite ready . . . not quite ready to pull out the gun and fire at point blank range. He really hadn't expected to be looking down into a friendly face at the very moment he pulled the trigger on Chan.

*

Without a warning Becks grabbed Liam roughly by the shoulders and man-handled him back from the reactor towards the walkway leading to the sealed exit.

'Becks! What the hell are you doing? What's going on?'

'Imminent threat of explosion,' she said crisply and calmly, and a little too loudly. Her voice spooked the other students nearby who quickly began to join them backing away from it.

'Everybody, calm down!' shouted Mr Kelly. 'Nothing is going to happen!'

Liam looked up at Becks. 'Are you sure it's going to –?'

Becks suddenly stopped dragging him. 'Too late to escape!' She yanked Liam's arm downwards to the floor and he dropped to his knees.

'Ouch! *What are you doing?*'

She knelt down in front of him and wrapped her arms round his shoulders, shielding him from the reactor. Liam peeked over her shoulder and saw the reactor's thick metal casing suddenly start to ripple like jelly and a moment later begin to collapse in on itself.

'What the –?'

Becks reached out one hand and grabbed his nose painfully. 'You must lower your head,' she ordered, yanking him roughly down until he was almost doubled over, his head in her lap. Then all of a sudden he felt the oddest *tugging* sensation. As if he and Becks and the world around them was being sucked into a gigantic laundry mangler, stretched impossibly thin like elastic strands of spaghetti towards the reactor . . . following the collapsed metal casing into some inconceivable pinpoint of infinity.

'Ooooooohhhhh Jaaaaaaaaayyyyyy-zzzzzusssssss!'

CHAPTER 20

2001, New York

Maddy and Sal stared at the shimmering window in the middle of the archway. Through a curtain of undulating, rippling air they could see the dim outlines of the storeroom they'd sent Liam and the support unit to.

'Something's definitely wrong,' whispered Sal.

Maddy nodded. 'That's the third back-up window they've missed.'

Five minutes ago they'd been cheerfully prepping the scheduled return window, assuming that the simple scouting mission had been a success and Liam and the support unit would be ready and waiting to come back and tell them what exactly had happened to Chan.

Now, for the third time, both girls were staring at a dark storeroom with no sign of either of them.

'Oh boy,' uttered Maddy. 'I don't know what we do now. That's it – we've tried all the back-up windows.'

> Maddy?

She stepped towards the desk and leaned over the deck mic. 'Yes?'

> You should try the six-month window.

'Yes . . . yes, you're right.'

Bob was right, it was worth a try. She clicked the PURGE button on the screen and the shimmering window in the middle of the archway vanished with a soft pop and a gentle puff of displaced air. She entered a new set of time coordinates: exactly five months, thirty days, twenty-three hours and fifty-five minutes after the time they'd been sent into the future; exactly five minutes before the support unit's mission time span was up and it was scheduled to self-destruct. It made sense. It would be the last possible chance to rendezvous with a return window. With the support unit dead, Liam would not be able to receive a tachyon signal to instruct him on a new rendezvous time-stamp. If they weren't there, in that storeroom six months after arriving and impatient to get back home, then Maddy had no idea what she could do next.

She clicked on the screen to confirm the new time coordinates and then activated the displacement machinery. Once again a twelve-foot-wide sphere of air began to shift and undulate, revealing the storeroom again. Both girls squinted for a while at the dark space beyond. Same store cupboard . . . a few things had been shifted around; clearly someone had had a spring-clean in there. But no sign of either Liam or the support unit.

'Oh,' said Sal. 'We've really lost them.'

Maddy pinched her chin. 'No . . . let me think.' There was a way to communicate with the support unit. A tachyon signal beam. That's what they'd done last time: aimed a broad beam of particles in the direction in which they'd guessed Liam and Bob were and transmitted an encoded signal back through history. It had worked. Bob had picked it up.

'Bob,' she spoke into the mic, 'can we send a tachyon signal beam forward?'

> Affirmative. We have enough power.

'Right . . . what if we send it to, say . . . five minutes before whatever happened to Chan, happened.'

'What message?' asked Sal.

'I dunno. Something like – *abort the mission, something is going to go wrong.*'

Sal nodded. 'Yes, we should do that.'

Maddy sat down in one of the office chairs and purged the open window. It puffed out of existence. She then opened the message interface and quickly tapped in a message.

Return to the store cupboard immediately. We'll pick you up there. Something is about to go wrong with your mission. Something is about to happen to you. A return window will be waiting for you.

Bob's dialogue box popped up.

> You wish to send this message?

'Yes, immediately.'

> Recommendation: a narrow beam transmission.

A narrow beam meant she needed to know quite precisely where to aim it. But she had no idea where the two of them might be. They might have been somewhere else in the facility. Something may have caused a detour, a fire alarm perhaps? Or some malfunction in the lab may have resulted in everyone being evacuated.

'Bob, let's make the beam broad enough to sweep the whole area. Make sure the support unit gets the message.'

> Caution: there will be technology in the vicinity that may be unpredictably affected by tachyon particles.

'I really don't care if we mess up somebody's experiments, or damage their precious gizmos . . . I want Liam to get that damned message!' she snapped angrily. 'All right?'

> Affirmative. Wide beam sweep to cover vicinity.

Sal looked at her. 'Are you sure about this?' She nodded towards the computers. 'Bob just sort of cautioned us, didn't he?'

Maddy spun the chair to face her. 'You got any other suggestions?'

Sal shook her head.

'Right, then,' she replied, her voice brittle. 'We have to make contact.'

Stay calm, Maddy. You're the leader, so stay calm.

Her face softened as she reached for her inhaler on the desk. 'Sorry, Sal . . . I'm just a bit stressed and –'

'No, it's OK.'

'I don't know what else to do.'

> Confirm transmission?

'Bob, you cautioned me . . . because what? Is there some sort of danger to Liam if we throw a whole load of tachyon beams forward?'

> Information: tachyon particles might interfere with zero-point energy experiments that are being conducted at the institute at this time.

'But does that endanger Liam in some way?'

> Unknown. Records show zero-point energy research was abandoned as being potentially hazardous. There is very little public domain data on the Texas Advanced Energy Research Institute's work in this field.

'So? What do I do?'

> Recommendation: do nothing.

'Nothing?'

> Correct. Wait for possible contact from them. Sending a tachyon signal forward may endanger Liam and the support unit and might also present a security risk for the agency.

Maddy stared at the screen in silence. 'You want me to do absolutely nothing? When they might be in trouble and need our help? You're asking me to do nothing but sit on my hands?'

> Affirmative. A tachyon signal might be detected by sensitive instrumentation at the institute and the message

intercepted. This would clearly alert them to the existence of time travel and the agency.

'They could know time travel is possible fourteen years *before* Edward Chan does his maths paper,' added Sal. 'Our message to Liam might alter history just as much as someone killing Chan.'

> Sal is correct.

'So you're saying we wait for them to get themselves out of whatever's happened?'

> That is my recommendation. They are very capable.

Maddy chewed her lip in thought for a moment. 'And this is my call?'

> You are team leader. I can only offer data and tactical advice.

'Right, well then I say forget potential contamination, forget any of their zero-point experiments we might be messing up and *stuff* any security risks for the agency. They've pretty much left us all alone to fend for ourselves so far . . . I'm damned if I'm going to sacrifice Liam just to keep them happy. We warn Liam and the support unit to abort the scouting trip. We get them back home and then . . . *then* . . . we can deal with any time changes we may have caused! All right?'

Sal nodded. 'I suppose it's a plan.'

Maddy turned to the computer screen. 'All right?'

The '>' cursor blinked thoughtfully on and off in the dialogue box and they heard the computer's hard drives whirring softly. Finally, after a few moments the cursor flickered forward.

> Affirmative.

'Cool,' said Maddy. 'So, Bob, send that message to five minutes before Chan's recorded time of death.'

> Affirmative.

As Bob proceeded with beaming the message, Maddy

prepared to open a window yet again in the storeroom for the same moment in time and resolved to keep it open for at least ten minutes. That would give them enough time, she hoped, to receive the message, wherever they were in the institute, and make their way back to the storeroom. She was about to activate the time window when Bob's dialogue box appeared centre screen.

> Information: there is an intense energy feedback loop interfering with the tachyon signal beam.

'Meaning?'

> 87% probability that this is an explosion.

Her breath caught in her throat. 'An explosion?'

> Correct.

'Oh my God.' Maddy felt the blood drain from her face. 'How big?'

> Unable to specify. It is a large signature reading.

She looked at Sal. 'Oh my God, you don't think . . .?'

Sal swallowed nervously and didn't say anything – her wide eyes said it all.

'Bob, tell me it wasn't *us* that just caused that to happen – our tachyon signal?'

Bob's cursor blinked silently for a few seconds.

> The tachyon signal is the most likely cause of the explosion. The precursor particles may have caused a reaction.

'Oh God, what have I done?'

CHAPTER 21

Brilliant white, floating in a void of perfect, featureless white. To Liam it felt like hours, staring out at it, hanging motionless in the void as if he was floating in a glass of milk.

It felt like hours, but it could have been minutes, seconds even.

He'd begun to wonder if he was actually dead and hanging around in some pre-afterlife limbo. Then he saw the faintest flicker of movement in the thick milk world around him.

An angel coming for him? It looked like a cloud of slightly dimmer white and it danced around like a phantom, gliding in decreasing circles that brought it ever closer to him. It looked familiar.

I've seen that before.

Then he remembered. The day that Foster had pulled him from the sinking *Titanic*. In the archway, as he'd woken the three of them from their slumber . . .

The seeker.

There were more out there, faint and far off, drawn to him as if they could smell his presence, like sharks smelling blood. Perhaps the first seeker had silently called out to them that there was something here for them all to share.

Oh Mary-Mother-of-God . . . they're going to rip me to pieces!

The nearest seeker swooped still closer to him and the faint cloud of grey began to take form. He thought he could make out the head and shoulders of the indeterminate shape, almost human-like. And a face that took fleeting form.

Beautiful. Feminine.

He almost began to think he was right first time, and that this was Heaven and those swooping forms were angels coming to escort him to the afterlife. Then that vaguely familiar feminine face stretched, elongated, revealing a row of razor fangs and the eyes turned to dark sockets that promised him nothing but death. It lunged towards him . . .

And then he was staring up at another face, framed with hair dangling down towards him, tickling his nose, with piercing grey eyes staring intently at him. 'Liam O'Connor, are you all right?'

'Becks?'

'Affirmative. Are you all right?' she asked flatly. 'You appear undamaged by the explosion.' He felt her strong hands running up and down his arms and legs, around his torso. 'No apparent fractures.'

'I'm OK, I think. Just a little . . . dizzy, so I am.' He began to sit up and she helped him.

'You are disorientated,' she said.

He looked up at a clear blue sky and a dazzling sun. He blinked back the sunlight – a curious vaguely violet hue to it – and shaded his eyes with a hand. 'Jay-zus, where are we? Is this another world?'

'Negative.' She looked at him, then corrected herself. 'No. We are where we *were*,' she replied.

But when? The spherical chamber and laboratory buildings were gone. Instead of the institute's water-sprinkled lawns and flowerbeds, there was nothing but jungle. If this was the same place, then it had to be some significant time in the future or the past. It certainly wasn't 2015.

'The tachyon interference caused an explosive reaction,' said Becks. 'We were pulled through the zero-point window into what is known as chaos space.'

'Chaos space?'

'I am unable to define chaos space. I have no detailed data on it.'

'And then what? We were dumped out into reality again?'

'Correct.'

He saw another head suddenly appear above a large lush green fern leaf. Somebody else, dizzily sitting up and wondering where on earth they were. It was one of the students: a black girl, her hair neatly thatched into corn-rows. A gold hooped earring glinted in the sunlight.

'What the –?' she muttered as her eyes slowly panned round the tall green trees and drooping vines. Finally her eyes rested on Liam and Becks.

'Hello there,' said Liam, waving a hand and smiling goofily.

She stared at him silently with eyes that still seemed to be trying to work out what she was seeing.

He noticed another head appearing out of the foliage several dozen yards away. He recognized the receding scruffy hair and sparsely bearded jowls of the teacher who'd been with the group of students during the tour of the institute.

Other heads appeared, all looking confused and frightened, spread out across a clearing in the jungle, a hundred yards in diameter. Liam recognized the institute's smartly dressed tour guide, one of the technicians who'd been in the chamber and the rest of the students.

'Wh-what happened?' called out the teacher.

The guide's carefully groomed silver hair was dishevelled,

his smart suit rumpled and dirtied with mud. 'I . . . I . . . don't know . . . I just . . .'

Liam looked at Becks. 'We're going to have to take charge of things, aren't we?'

She looked at him blankly. 'The mission parameters have changed.'

Liam sighed. 'No kidding.'

He was about to ask her if she had any idea at all of when in time they were when he heard a shrill scream echo across the clearing.

'What was that?'

It came again. Sharp, shrill and terrified. He got to his feet, as did several others, and pushed through clusters of knee-high ferns towards where the sound was coming from. Becks was instantly by his side, striding slightly ahead of him without any trepidation. Liam realized he felt reassured to have her there despite her diminutive frame. Despite lacking the intimidating bulk of Bob, he had a feeling she was a great deal more dangerous than she looked.

Finally, a yard ahead of him she stopped. Liam stepped round her and looked down.

The blonde girl he'd spoken to earlier – he remembered her name, it was Laura, wasn't it? – was screaming, her eyes locked on to the thing that was lying in the tall grass beside her.

It took Liam a moment for him to make sense of what he was seeing on the ground, then . . . then he got it; understood what it was. His stomach flopped and lurched and it took every ounce of willpower he had not to double over and vomit.

The teacher emerged from the tall grass to stand next to Liam. He followed Laura's wide-eyed gaze and then sucked in a mouthful of air. 'Oh my God! . . . That's not . . . that's not what I think it is,' he whispered, and turned to look at Liam. 'Is it?'

Among the tall fronds of vegetation nestled a small twisted mass of muscle and bone. At one end Liam could see a long braid of blonde hair, matted with drying blood, and halfway along the contorted form, he spotted a solitary pink Adidas trainer, hanging half on and half off a pale and perfectly normal-looking foot. It had to be one of the three blonde girls they'd tagged behind on the way into the chamber. He could quite understand the girl, Laura, screaming. They'd been chatting, giggling and exchanging phone numbers only ten minutes ago.

Liam recalled Foster saying sometimes it happened; sometimes, very rarely, the energy of a portal could turn a person inside out. *Oh Jay-zus, what a mess.*

Half an hour later those of the group that had survived the blast and arrived in one piece had made a rough assessment of their predicament. Dotted around the jungle clearing, they'd made the gruesome discovery of more bodies just like the girl's, turned inside out and almost unrecognizable as human. Sixteen of them. Of the thirty-five people who'd been in the chamber when the explosion – or, more accurately, *implosion* – had occurred, only sixteen of them appeared to have made it through alive.

Now, gathered together in the middle of the clearing, well away from the forbidding edge of thick jungle, it was Whitmore who first seemed to be stirring from a state of stunned shock. He wiped sweat from his forehead with the back of his sleeve and narrowed his eyes as he studied Becks.

'You!' he said. 'Yes, you! I remember now . . . you said it was going to explode. Just . . . just before it actually did.'

Becks's face remained impassive. 'That is correct.'

'Hang on!' he said again, his eyes suddenly narrowing with

dawning realization. 'You . . . you're not one of m-my kids. You're not –'

Liam could see where this was going. It was pointless continuing to pretend to be high-school students a moment longer.

'What just happened, whatever's just happened,' blustered Whitmore, 'you damn well *knew* it was going to happen.' His voice rose in pitch. 'Who are you? Is this some sort of terrorist thing?'

Becks shook her head slowly, her face impassive. 'Negative. We are not terrorists.'

Whitmore fell silent. His lips quivered with more questions he wanted to ask, but he was struggling to know what exactly to ask. Where to begin.

'Excuse me?'

Their heads all turned towards a boy with kinky ginger hair, neatly side-parted into a succession of waves, and thick bottle-top glasses that made his eyes seem to bulge like a startled frog. He pointed to his name tag. 'My name's Franklyn . . . you can call me that. Or just Frank will do.' He smiled at them uncertainly. 'Uhh . . . I just wanted to say that . . . this is going to sound really weird, but I guess I'll just come out and say it.'

'What?' snapped Whitmore.

'Well –' he pointed up at the sky – 'you see them?'

All eyes drifted towards the top of some trees twenty yards away, a long branch leaning out over the clearing with strange dangling willow-like green fronds drooping to the ground. In among them, a pair of dragonflies danced and zig-zagged with a buzz of wings they could hear from where they stood.

'Those are huge,' uttered Kelly. 'Good grief! . . . Two-foot, three-foot wingspan at a guess?'

'Uh-huh,' said Franklyn. 'They're *really* big and I'm pretty sure I know what species that is.'

The others looked at him.

'It's a petalurid, I think . . . yeah, I'm sure that's the right name.'

'Great,' said Laura, 'so now we know.'

'No, that's not the important bit,' said Franklyn. He looked at her. 'They should be extinct.'

'Well, obviously they're not,' she replied.

'Oh yes they are. We've only ever had fossils of insects that size.'

Whitmore stood up. 'Oh my God! He's right!' He watched the two dragonflies emerge from the overhanging branch and dart out into the open, their wings buzzing noisily like airborne hairdryers. 'Insects haven't been that size since . . .' He swallowed, looked at the others. 'Well . . . I mean, millions and millions of years.'

'Petalurids,' uttered Franklyn again. 'Late Cretaceous. I'm pretty sure of that.'

Kelly got to his feet and stood beside Franklyn. 'What are you saying?'

The boy wiped a fog of moisture from his glasses, blinking back the bright day from his small eyes. 'What I'm saying, Mr Kelly, is those things haven't existed, alive . . . in, like, well, I guess something like sixty-five million years.'

CHAPTER 22

2001, New York

'Maddy! Where are you going?'

Maddy ignored Sal's pleading voice as she strode across the archway, cranked up the shutter and stepped out into the backstreet.

I can't do this . . . I can't do this.

She felt the first tears roll down her cheeks as she picked her way along the rubbish-strewn sidewalk towards South 6th Street at the top. Her first proper mission in charge and she was already going to pieces. An impetuous decision on her part, stupid and hot-headed enough to go against Bob's reasoned advice, and now she might just be responsible for killing Liam and the support unit. Not only that, but she'd probably also caused the deaths of dozens of others. And, most importantly, Edward Chan.

'I can't do this,' she muttered. 'I'm just not ready for this.'

She stepped out of the backstreet on to the corner and watched the busy intersection for a while: traffic turning right to pick up the bridge road, left towards the river; pedestrians making their way over to their jobs in Manhattan . . . all of them oblivious to the commercial jets already in the air and heading towards their doom.

She wanted Foster back. Needed him back. What possessed him to think for one moment she was actually ready to run a field office? His pre-recorded 'how to' answers stored on the computer just weren't enough. She needed him to talk to, to explain the technology to her more fully, to tell her more about the agency and their place in it. There were so many gaps in her knowledge she didn't even know enough to have an idea what questions to ask. She was floundering.

'Damn you, Foster!' she hissed under her breath, and wiped at her wet cheeks.

The old man could be anywhere in New York, if, indeed, he'd decided to stay on in the city. He'd walked out on her on one of the Monday mornings, walked right out of the Starbucks with a bag over one shoulder, leaving her alone with her coffee. It was Tuesday today. If he was that desperate to see the world before he died, then he might just as well be on a Greyhound bus to some other state or even on a plane to somewhere exotic.

Face it. He's gone for good.

'She just got up and left!' said Sal.

> I sensed emotional stress markers in her voice.

'Well, duh! Of course she's upset! She's just . . . I mean, she may have just killed Liam!'

Sal realized her own voice sounded shrill and loud. 'Oh jahulla! Is he dead? Did she kill him?'

> Insufficient data. The residue signal suggests a sudden and violent enlargement of a dimensional pinhole, releasing a vast amount of energy.

'Like a bomb?'

> Correct. Just like a bomb.

She slumped down in the office chair. 'So, dead, then,' she uttered, looking down at her lap and suddenly beginning to feel the stab of pain. The equivalent, in days, of almost three months had passed since Foster had pulled her from a falling building. So much had happened in that time, a world almost conquered by Nazis and then in the blink of an eye reduced to a radioactive wasteland. Their trip to the basement of the Museum of Natural History, finding the clues . . . Liam's message in the guest book. And all the clean-up and fix-up after that whole nightmare. It almost felt like another life: Mumbai, Mum and Dad, the burning building.

This place, this scruffy archway criss-crossed with cables, had begun to feel like a home, and Liam and Maddy . . . even Bob, like an odd new family. Now, in one moment, with one simple mistake, she wondered if that was all gone. She looked up from her hands, wrestling each other in her lap, to see Bob's silent blinking response on the screen.

> Not necessarily.

'What? What do you mean "not necessarily"? Do you mean not necessarily dead?'

> Affirmative. They may have been transported.

'You mean like one of our time windows?'

> Correct. The sudden dilation of a dimensional pinhole being used to extract zero-point energy may have functioned in a similar way to a portal.

'Where? Do you know where? Could we find them?'

> Negative. I have no possible way of knowing when they would have been transported to. It would be random.

'But . . . but they could be alive, right? Alive, somewhere?'

> Affirmative, Sal. But in the same geographic location.

'Is there anything we could do to try to find them?'

> Negative. We are in the same situation as before we sent the tachyon signal. If the explosion did not kill them, then they are sometime in the past or future.

The rising hope she was feeling that there might be a way to find them and bring them back in one piece began to falter.

> My AI duplicate and Liam may attempt to establish contact with the field office, provided it can be done with a minimum of time contamination.

'You mean like Liam did with the museum guest book? A message in history?'

> Correct. If they have not been transported too far in time, it may be possible for them to find a way to communicate without causing a dangerous level of contamination.

'So what . . . we wait? We wait and hope for a signal?'

> Affirmative. We must wait and we must observe. There is no other viable course of action.

CHAPTER 23

65 million years BC, jungle

'Excuse me?' said Laura. '*When* did you say?'

Franklyn finished wiping his glasses dry and put them back on again. He took his time savouring the silent, rapt attention of the others sitting together in the clearing. 'I said sixty-five million years ago.'

The others shared a stunned silence. Eyes meeting eyes and all of them wide. The enormity of the fact taking a long while to sink in for all of them.

It was Whitmore who broke the silence. 'Sixty-five million years . . . so that definitely takes us to near the end of the Cretaceous period.' He looked at the boy, whose glasses were already beginning to fog up again from the humidity. 'It *is* the Cretaceous, isn't it?'

Franklyn nodded. 'Correct. Late Cretaceous, to be precise.'

'We've travelled in time?' uttered Kelly. 'That's . . . that's not possible!'

'Whoa!' one of the other kids cried.

Whitmore and Franklyn were looking at each other warily, a gesture not missed by Liam.

'What? Either of you gentlemen going to tell us what a bleedin' *late crustation* is?' Liam studied them suspiciously. 'You two fellas looked at each other all funny just then. That means something, right?'

Whitmore pursed his lips, his eyebrows arched as if in disbelief at what he was about to utter. 'If Franklyn here is right,' he said, watching the foot-long dragonflies hover and drop among a cluster of ferns nearby, 'then this is dinosaur times. We're in dinosaur times.'

Laura gasped. 'Oh God.' She took two or three deep breaths that hooted like a steam train coming down a tunnel, like a woman in labour. 'Oh my God! I was watching *Jurassic Park* last night! I don't want to be eaten by a rex. I don't want to be eaten by a –'

Several of the other students, not all of them girls, began to whimper at the prospect; the rest began to talk at once. Liam watched Whitmore struggling with the situation himself, shaking his head incredulously and balling his fists in silence. Kelly meanwhile was gazing up at the blue sky and the slightly odd-coloured sun as if hoping to find an answer up there.

Somebody needs to take charge, thought Liam. *Or they're all going to die.*

He was damned if he was going to volunteer, though – to be responsible for this lot. He and Becks were probably going to fare much better on their own. One of the three men was going to have to step up and take care of these kids. But, as it happened, as Liam was beginning to wonder how the pair of them were going to discreetly extract themselves – with Edward Chan in their possession – the decision was made for him.

'You!' said Whitmore, his lost expression wiped away, all of a sudden remembering there was an issue as yet unresolved. His voice cut across the clamour of all the others'. 'Yes, you! The goth girl,' he said, pointing at Becks. He looked at Liam. 'And you. You know what happened, don't you? The pair of you weren't in my party. And you knew that explosion was going to happen. So you'd better start telling us who the heck you are!'

There was an instant silence as all eyes swivelled to him and Becks.

Liam grinned self-consciously. 'Uh, we . . . that's to say me and Becks here, we're not er . . . students as such. We're sort of *agents* from another time.'

Fourteen pairs of eyes on him and none of them seemed to have anything close to a grasp on what he'd just said.

'See, we're time travellers and we came along today to try to protect *him*,' he said, pointing at Edward Chan who was sitting on the grass, arms wrapped round his huddled knees.

Edward Chan's eyes widened. 'Uh? Am I in trouble?'

'You, Edward. We came to find out how we were going to protect you from an attempt on your life.'

The others looked at the small Chinese boy then back at Liam.

'You better explain about him, Becks,' said Liam. 'You've got all the facts in your head.'

Becks nodded. 'Listen carefully,' she began. 'Time travel will become a viable technology in the year 2044 when a Professor Roald Waldstein will build the world's first time machine and successfully transport himself into the past and return safely to his time. The practical technology developed by Waldstein in 2044 is largely based on the theories developed and published in *Scientific American* by the Department of Physics, University of Texas in 2031. The article is entitled "Zero-point Energy: energy from space-time vacuum, or inter-dimensional leakage?".'

Kelly's tired face lit up. 'You gotta be kidding?'

Whitmore looked at the bewildered young boy hugging his own knees on the ground in front of him. 'So how does this affect this boy?'

Becks's cool grey eyes panned smoothly across to Chan. 'The article published in *Scientific American* is a reproduction of a maths thesis presented by one Edward Aaron Chan. An act of academic plagiarism by his supervising professor.'

Edward looked up at her. 'Me? Really?'

'Correct. You will submit your dissertation to the Department of Physics for evaluation with an almost identical title in the summer of 2029, when you are twenty-six years of age. The department head, Professor Miles Jackson, will attempt to take credit for your work when it is approved for publication several months later, but he will be exposed as a plagiarist shortly after the article's publication.'

'But you said you'd come to protect him from an attempt on his life . . . why would someone want to *kill* Chan?' asked Whitmore.

'Edward Chan is the true originator of time travel,' replied Becks. 'In the future, 2051, time-travel technology becomes forbidden under international law because of the danger it poses to all mankind. This law is a result of years of campaigning by Roald Waldstein, the inventor of the first viable time machine, to prevent any further development of the technology.'

'Wald– . . . the man who builds this first machine?' said one of the students, a tough-looking Hispanic boy. Liam noticed his name tag was still on his chest: JUAN HERNANDEZ.

Becks's gaze panned across to him. She waited silently for him to continue.

'Why?' asked Juan. 'Why build the thing, then, you know, campaign against usin' it? Don't make any sense.'

Liam answered. 'Waldstein never ever revealed what he saw on his first and only trip into the past . . . never talked to anyone about it. It was a big secret what he saw. But he was once heard to say that he'd looked upon the very bowels of Hell itself.' Liam could have added more, could have added that maybe he'd glimpsed, for a few seconds, something of that himself.

Becks continued. 'Waldstein's campaign gained popular support. It is logical to presume that it may be one of his more fanatical supporters who has somehow managed to travel back in time to find Chan and attempt to kill him, to retroactively prevent him writing his thesis, and thus prevent or forestall the invention of time travel.'

A long silence followed filled only with the gentle rustle of the jungle's trees and the far-off high-pitched squawk of some jungle creature. It was Whitmore who cut it short. 'Well, OK . . . that's all very fascinating, but what just happened? Where are we and how do we get back?'

Becks's eyelids fluttered for a moment. 'The geopositional coordinates will not have changed. We are exactly where we were.'

'Yeah, right, man!' snapped Juan. 'There ain't no jungle like this. Not in Texas!'

'We're still in the same place,' said Liam, 'but it's *when* we are that's changed. Right?'

'Affirmative.' Liam nudged Becks. 'Yes . . .' Becks corrected herself.

'Which, if Franklyn is correct, is sixty-five million years ago,' said Whitmore, loosening his tie and unbuttoning the top button of his sky-blue shirt, already stained with dark underarm patches of sweat.

Liam smiled thinly. 'Yup, that's about it.'

The technician who'd survived and come through with them dipped his head and shook it. 'Then we really are totally, totally in trouble, man.'

Liam wanted to say something like he'd been in this kind of mess before, that there might possibly be a way out of here for them, that at the very least they had a genetically enhanced and very lethal combat unit, with an embedded supercomputer, disguised as an oversized gothic Barbie doll, here to help them all out. But he figured right now that would probably be one detail too many for them to have to cope with.

Kelly removed his linen jacket, no longer looking smooth and groomed and, like Whitmore, sweating large dark patches in the hot and humid air. 'So what are we going to do now?'

And, once more, all eyes rested on Liam.

Aw, Jay-zus . . . What? I'm in charge now?

It looked like he and Becks weren't going to be able to sidle away, that they were lumbered with the others. Liam sighed. 'Survival,' he said eventually. 'I suppose we'd better start thinking about that. You know? Water, food, weapons, some sort of a camp. The rest . . . if there is *a rest* . . . well, I suppose that can come later.'

CHAPTER 24

65 million years BC, jungle

Howard took a break from the work of hacking at the vines and bamboo canes with his improvised machete: a jagged strip of metal – part of the reactor's shell – with a handle made of coarse leaves wrapped round one end and secured with shoelaces. As a machete it worked surprisingly well and, from the other jagged strips of reinforced alloy that had materialized in the past with them, they'd managed to produce nine very useful cutting implements like this one.

The Hispanic boy, Juan, was working alongside him while across the clearing, shimmering with the heat of the midday sun, he could see some of the others fashioning simple spears out of the thicker bamboo canes they'd cut down.

'That's bull, man,' muttered Juan, following his gaze. 'We ain't gonna kill anything with these pointy sticks.'

Howard nodded wearily and grunted something back, but his eyes were on Chan, standing next to that weird red-haired girl, as he ham-fistedly attempted to whittle a sharp end on a three-foot cane. She and the odd Irish boy . . . they'd given their names as Becks and Liam, but if they were covert agency operatives from the year 2001, they were probably aliases.

Which agency, though? Who sent them?

As far as Howard knew, no government, anywhere, was

meant to have functioning time-travel technology. Although obviously the most powerful nations – the Chinese Federation, the European Bloc, the United States – must secretly have been developing it. And those two presumably must be field operatives working for one of them, here to protect Chan.

The Irish boy seemed to be calling the shots, with Whitmore, Kelly and the technician, Lam, happy for him to do so. Howard was content to go along with the status quo for now. Happy to carry on playing the role of timid young Lenny Baumgardner, a high-school student with straight As and a perfect school attendance record. It kept things simple for the moment. After all, the presiding question now was one of survival – the basics: food, water, shelter.

But his focus had to remain, whatever happened, on the mission, on what he'd set out to do: to end young Chan's life and absolutely guarantee that the uniquely brilliant theoretical concepts his older, twenty-six-year-old mathematician's mind would one day produce would never see the light of day. Brilliance like Chan's was rare; the kind of genius and intuition that comes along once in a generation, once in a century even.

Chan's work was going to end up being as life-changing as Einstein's once was. More so, in fact.

Without that published thesis the famous Waldstein would perhaps never have been anything more than an anonymous hobbyist inventor working in his garage. While the world of 2055 might be facing a dark time ahead with water, food and energy shortages, global warming and catastrophic levels of over-population, at the very least, history, as it was, would still be safe; at the very least, mankind would not be meddling with dimensions it had no possibility of understanding, dimensions that could contain *anything*.

Just because a door can be opened . . . doesn't mean it should *be opened.*

But Chan was here now . . . and not in the year 2029, sixty-five million years away from helping mankind make its biggest-ever mistake. Howard wondered whether that meant his mission was as good as done. Did he still need to kill him? After all, the explosion, presumably caused by something to do with those two agents, perhaps some side effect of time travel and the fields of energy it radiates, had propelled them far back in time. Surely further back in time than any prototype time machine currently in development could ever reach. And how would they know when they were, anyway? Sixty-five million years to choose from. Like a needle in a haystack. Like a needle in a whole barn full of hay, in fact.

Go ahead, pick a year . . . see if you get lucky.

He smiled.

It's done. The world's safe now. It's done.

Which was a relief, because now all he had to think about was the business of survival, here in this jungle with nothing for company but over-large dragonflies and whatever other giant creepy-crawlies and Cretaceous creatures lurked in the jungle. And, of course, a bunch of frightened kids and several men who ought to be showing a little more backbone.

Howard had done his bit for mankind . . . now, just surviving in this wilderness for the foreseeable future – he wasn't ready yet to be a dino dinner – that was for him.

He looked up at the thick edge of the jungle ahead of him: a ribbon of dark green foliage and tall canopy trees that wrapped itself all the way round the clearing.

And God knows what big hungry things are wandering around in there.

*

'Oh, that's just great. That's just bloody great.' Liam stared at the swiftly surging river: a tumbling torrent of white suds that swirled around and over a bed of worn boulders.

'So, it runs all the way around us,' said Kelly. His smart linen business suit was smudged with dirt and sweat. Not the most practical clothing for jungle trekking. He'd tied off the jacket round his waist and rolled up the sleeves of his white shirt. The tie was still on, though, Liam noticed. A token that Kelly was not quite ready to abandon hope that help might arrive at any moment and he'd want to look his best for it.

'I think we're on a sort of island,' Kelly continued.

They'd spent the morning exploring the immediate surroundings beyond the clearing. Whichever direction they'd taken they'd soon come across the energetic roar of water and glimpsed the glinting, fast-moving river through the thinning jungle.

Island was about right. Approximately three or four acres of jungle with a central clearing, shaped roughly like a tear drop. The pointed tip of the island was where they stood now staring at the rolling water. The river split in two around their spit of land; to the right of them it broadened out into a wide, slower-moving channel. Slower-moving, but still brisk enough so that Liam wouldn't dare chance trying to cross it. But then he couldn't swim. More than that . . . water scared the bejeezus out of him. Not that he needed the others to know anything about his pet fears right now.

To their left the river compressed into a narrower channel thirty feet across, lined with boulders, and became a violent roaring ribbon of snow-white froth and energy. A fool might try to swim the wider channel, but only a completely mad fool would attempt a crossing on this side.

'We're trapped on here,' said Laura, looking around at the others. 'Aren't we?'

'At least we've got drinking water.' Liam shrugged. He gave them all a cheery smile. 'So it's not all bad news.'

Becks took a couple of steps down the wet shingle towards the raging river and silently appraised their surroundings. After a while she turned round. 'The island is a suitable defensive position.'

'Defensive?' called out one of the students. Liam turned round. It was a large boy, whose cheeks glistened with sweat beneath a mop of dark frizzy hair and he was still wearing his name tag: JONAH MIDDLETON. 'Defensible against what, dude?'

'Dinosaurs,' uttered Laura, her voice shuddering slightly.

Whitmore nodded. 'Yes, dinosaurs.' He turned to Franklyn. 'How good's your knowledge of the late Cretaceous?'

'Pretty good,' he replied. 'You want to know what species we can expect to encounter?'

'Please, tell me we don't get the T-rex,' blurted Laura. 'Not that.'

'Oh, we got those all right.' Franklyn put his hands on his hips. 'But they're more likely found on open terrain. Not jungle like this.'

'It's the *velociraptors* that scared me,' said Lam. His head bobbed energetically as he talked, his dark ponytail wagging like a dog's tail as he looked from one person to another. 'Seriously scary things, those.' He nodded sombrely. 'I seen all three *Jurassic* movies, guys . . . and it's those smart little ones you got to watch out for.'

'There are no raptors.' Franklyn shook his head. 'They're Asian and died out eighty-five million years ago. We should expect to see . . . lemmesee . . . ankylosaurus, that's the tank-shaped one with a spiky club for a tail. Pachycephalosaurus, that's the upright one with, like, a cyclist's safety helmet on his head. Triceratops . . . you all know that one, right?'

Heads nodded.

'Parasaurolophus . . . the duck-billed one with that Elvis-quiff bone sticking out backwards.'

'But those are all herbivores, aren't they?' said Whitmore. 'What about the carnivores?'

Franklyn pursed his lips. 'We got rex, of course, but no raptors. That's the *good* news.'

'Oh, great,' sighed Laura. 'That means there's bad news.'

'Well . . . I'm afraid there *are* several varieties of the smaller therapods,' he said, by way of explanation.

Liam shrugged at him. 'And those are what?'

'Therapods – same genus as the raptor,' Franklyn continued. 'Small predators, three to six foot tall. They walk on their back legs and have poorly developed front arms. They're pack hunters.'

'Three to six foot?' said Liam. 'That doesn't sound so bad, then.'

'Yo, dude,' said Jonah. 'You actually, like, *seen* the *Jurassic Park* movies?'

Liam shook his head. 'No. I presume it's one of them *talkie* motion pictures?'

Several of the students glanced at each other.

'*Talkie motion pictures?* You did say you were from the future, didn't you?' said Kelly.

'Well, not as such. Not directly . . . no. Actually I'm fro–'

'Caution!' said Becks, striding back up the shingle towards them. 'Confidential information.' Her glare silenced the stirring murmur of voices. 'That is unnecessary data. You do not need to know anything about the operative, Liam O'Connor.'

'Actually, I think I'd like to know a little more about you as well,' said Whitmore. 'I mean who the h–?'

'Stop!' barked Becks. 'This conversation will now cease!'

Laura made a face. She stepped forward and planted herself in front of Becks. Both girls about the same height, eyes locked in a silent challenge of each other. 'Oh? And who exactly made *you* the boss?'

Becks silently appraised her. 'You are a contaminant and a mission liability.'

'What? What's *that* supposed to mean?'

Becks's cold glare remained on the girl. For an unsettling moment Liam wondered whether she might just reach out and snap Laura's neck like a dry twig. He'd seen Bob effortlessly do far worse to countless grown combat-fit men.

'Becks!' he called out. 'Leave her alone!'

The support unit finally spoke. 'Liam O'Connor is . . . *boss*. I am just the support unit.'

'Support unit?' Laura's face creased with a look of bemusement. She turned to Liam. 'Sheesh, what exactly is the problem with your sister? She got some kind of behavioural problem?'

'She talks like some kind of robot,' said Keisha.

'Well now, since you –' Liam was about to explain, but Becks cut him off again. 'Irrelevant data.' She took a step away from Laura towards him, Laura's challenge instantly dismissed and forgotten. 'Recommendation, Liam.'

Liam nodded. 'Go on.'

'A bridging device can be constructed.' She turned her gaze towards the roaring river to their left. 'The narrowest width is precisely thirty-two feet, seven inches.' Her eyes then scanned the tall and straight trunks of the nearest deciduous trees along the riverbank. 'These trees are all of suitable length.'

'And just how are we supposed to fell a tree!' said Lam. 'All we've got is Mr Kelly's penknife, some bamboo spears and a bunch of freakin' useless hatchets.'

Liam decided he'd better start sounding decisive and leader-like. 'Well now, listen. Me and Becks'll figure something out, so we will. Right . . . Becks? . . . Sis?'

She looked at him. 'Question.'

'What?'

'Are we still pretending to be brother and sister?'

The others stared at them.

Liam sighed. 'Not any more.'

CHAPTER 25

2001, New York

Sal spun round in the chair at the sound of the roller shutter rattling up. 'Maddy?'

Maddy ducked beneath and into the archway. 'Yeah, it's me,' she replied, in a dull, lifeless voice.

'I thought you'd left us. Maybe gone for good.'

Maddy's face creased with a tired smile as she crossed the floor. 'It did cross my mind.'

'You shouldn't blame yourself. But look –'

'Don't, please.' Maddy raised a hand to hush her. She slumped down in a swivel chair beside Sal. 'I screwed up. I was hasty and impatient and killed Liam in the process. I've got to find my own way of dealing with that. And it's not going to help you trying to tell me that I shouldn't be beating myself up over it.' She buried her face in her hands, pushing up her glasses and rubbing tired eyes.

'No, listen to me,' replied Sal, sitting forward. 'Bob says he might not be dead.'

Maddy peered through her fingers.

'In fact, Bob's been analysing the tachyon signature around the window we opened. He's almost certain that we caused a portal, not an explosion.'

The screen in front of them flickered to life.

> Sal is correct. An 87% probability of a random portal.

Sal reached out for her arm. 'He's alive, Maddy. Do you see? Alive.' She made a face. 'Probably.'

Slowly Maddy lowered her hands from her face. 'Oh my God. You serious?'

'Yeah.'

Maddy turned towards the screen. 'Bob? You're sure of this?'

> 87% probability. The decay signature of the particles while our window was open was very similar in structure to the decay of a closing window.

'Can you work out where we sent him?'

> Where is likely to be nowhere. He was unlikely to have been geographically repositioned.

'When, then? When?'

> Negative. I have no data.

The momentary look of hope on Maddy's face quickly slipped away. 'So we've blasted him into history and we've no idea when?'

> Affirmative.

She looked at Sal. 'And what? I'm supposed to feel better about this? This is supposed to be good news?'

'He's alive, Maddy. That's something.'

'He's lost. Lost for good. Might as well be dead. But don't you see . . . it's worse than that. If he and the other support unit, and god knows how many other people, have been blasted back into history, we've really messed up. That's a whole load of contamination right there.'

'So? We've been here before. We've fixed time before. In fact . . . look, if they cause a whole load of contamination, that's a good thing. Right, Bob? That means we've got a chance to –'

> Negative. Contamination is to be avoided.

'But if they change things and we get time waves here in 2001 it'll give us some sort of clue *where* they are.'

> Affirmative.

'See? We can find them. It's possible. For example, if Liam's any time in the last century he could make his way to New York and use the guest book again.'

Maddy shook her head. 'Maybe, maybe. But . . . they could be any time. *Any* time, Sal. I mean, not just a year ago, or a hundred. But maybe a thousand, ten thousand . . . a million. God, if he's just five hundred years back, what document could he scribble in then? There wasn't a written language here in America in those days. It was just Indians and wilderness.'

Sal shrugged.

'And if he's like thousands of years back . . .' She turned to look at the screen. 'That's possible, right?'

> Affirmative. Provided there is enough energy invested in a portal there is no limit to how far back in time a subject can be sent.

'If he's gone back thousands of years, Sal, any attempt to contact us could totally change history. I mean *really* mess things up. Just look at what happened when those neo-Nazis went back to 1941. They turned the present into a nuclear wasteland!'

'I'm just saying . . .'

'Saying? Saying what? We're totally messed up here! God . . . there could already be a freaking time wave on the way! And then what? New York vanishes? More zombies?'

Sal reached for her arm again. 'Maddy . . . please! You've got to stay calm. We need you calm. You're the strategist. You can figure this out. I know you can.'

Maddy shook her head. 'Uhh,' she muttered. 'Foster'd figure it out. But me?'

He'd know exactly what to do. In fact, if the old man had been here, he would have been smart enough not to have caused this problem in the first place.

But he's out there, right? He's out there somewhere in New York. What about the Starbucks? That was a Monday morning at about nine. If I went there tomorrow morning . . .

She quickly realized that wouldn't work. Foster was gone. He wasn't back in the arch when the field office bubble reset. Foster was gone from their forty-eight-hour world.

Gone from Monday and Tuesday. Maddy's jaw suddenly dropped open. *What about Wednesday?*

Sal was looking at her. 'Maddy? You OK?'

But where would he be on Wednesday, September twelfth? She tried to remember their last conversation in the coffee shop. She'd asked him where he'd go, what he planned to do with the time he had left to live. He'd said he'd always wanted to visit New York, to see the sights. Just like a tourist. Maddy herself had been to New York so many times before her 'death', that she no longer thought like a tourist, no longer mentally checked off the places one had to go see.

'Sal, what places would you visit in New York, if this was like a holiday trip?'

'Uh?'

'If you were a tourist? What would you most want to go see?'

'Why are you –?'

'Just tell me!'

She scowled in thought for a moment. 'Well, I suppose the Empire State Building, the Statue of Liberty, the Museum of Natural History. Maddy, why? What're you thinking?'

Maddy nodded. Yes. The Empire State Building, the Statue of Liberty. She could try those first.

'Maddy?'

She looked up at Sal. 'I'm going to go find Foster. Bring him back if I can. He'll know what to do, Sal. Because I sure don't.'

'But he's gone for good you said. He wasn't here when the bubble reset. He's gone.'

'Gone from our two days, yeah. But not Wednesday . . . not Thursday, not any other day after that.'

'You're going to ride forward?'

Maddy considered that, but the less time travel she did – forward or backwards – the better. Foster had quietly told her timeriding was a bit like smoking; like a single cigarette, it was impossible to say for sure how much a single smoke might take off your life, but if you could ever avoid having a cigarette that could only be a good thing.

'I'll miss the reset. That's what I'll do,' said Maddy. 'I'll go into Wednesday and hang around those places. Who knows? I might get lucky.'

'You can't do that! You'll be gone for good like Foster!'

'No . . . we'll schedule a return window.' Maddy pinched her lip in thought. 'Yeah, we'll schedule a window at, let's say, eight in the evening on Wednesday.' She turned round and pointed towards the shutter door. 'Just outside the archway in our side street. That'll bring me right back into our time bubble, back into Monday.'

'But what if a time wave happens while you're gone?'

Maddy shrugged, resigned. 'I can't see you coping any worse than Maddy "Mess-up" Carter's done so far, right?'

'Oh shadd-yah! We should be figuring out how to get Liam back, not messing around visiting tourist attractions.'

'Yeah? But think about it – there's nothing we can do, is there? Just wait around . . . wait for a time wave to hit us and hope it'll lead us directly to him? That's it. That's pretty much all we can do right now. Just wait. Well, at least while we're sitting around here doing nothing useful I can try and find Foster, see what else he can suggest.'

Sal clamped her mouth shut.

'Make sense?'

Sal nodded slowly. 'OK,' she replied, fiddling with a pair of plastic bangles on her wrist. 'Do you want me to come with you? Two pairs of eyes?'

The screen in front of them flickered.

> Recommendation: Sal should remain here as the observer.

Maddy nodded reluctantly. 'Bob's right. If we get a time ripple preceding a wave, we need you here as our early heads-up. You should stay here and do your mid-morning walk around Times Square just like always. And, anyway, if the poop hits the fan and for some reason I end up being stuck out in Wednesday it'll be good to know there's someone left holding the fort, right?'

Sal tried a confident nod. 'Uh . . . yeah.'

'Right . . . that's the plan, then.' Maddy looked at her watch. It was just gone five in the afternoon. Outside, the sun would be looking ahead for a place to settle beyond the smoke-filled sky of Manhattan, and most of New York was already back at home, the normal day of work abandoned hours ago as they silently watched live news feeds from their dinner tables.

Tonight, New York was going to be a ghost town, just like it always was on the Tuesday as the clock ticked down towards their field office time bubble resetting itself.

CHAPTER 26

65 million years BC, jungle

Liam wiped sweat from his brow with the back of his hand. 'Jay-zus, it's almost as hot as the old lady's boiler room, so it is.'

'Old lady?' It was Mr Whitmore.

Liam thought the man had been far enough behind not to hear his bad-tempered mutterings. He shrugged. 'Oh, just a . . . just an old ship I used to work on.'

He stopped where he was, catching his breath for a moment. The hot humid air felt heavy on his lungs. They stood still for a while, trading ragged breaths and listening to the subdued noises of the jungle around them, the tap of water dripping on waxy leaves, the creak of the tall canopy trees subtly swaying and shifting, the echoing chatter and squawk of some flying creatures far above amid the branches.

Further back down the trail he'd been hacking out with his improvised machete, he heard the others stumbling towards them: Franklyn, their resident dino expert grinning at the prehistoric jungle around him like a kid in a candy store; Lam behind him, squinting up at the bright lances of sunlight piercing down through the cathedral-like vaulted roof of arched branches and thick leaves, and Jonah Middleton whistling something tuneless as he stumbled clumsily after them. The rest of the group were back on their 'island' fixing a counterweight to the bridge so it could be raised and constructing a camp under Becks's supervision.

Two days and nights they'd been here already and both nights, like clockwork, rain had come down in a torrential downpour, soaking them all and making sleep impossible. Tonight hopefully, with Becks hard at work – a one-man construction team, they'd at least have shelters to huddle beneath.

'You used to work on a ship?' said Whitmore, his breath wheezing past each word. 'Was that *before* you became . . . what did you say you were – some sort of time-travelling secret agent?'

'I didn't really say it like that, Mr Whitmore. Did I?'

He scratched his beard. 'I think that's exactly what you said.'

'Oh well, even though that does sound a little barmy, that pretty much describes me and Becks, so it does.'

Whitmore shook his head. 'I'm still trying to get my head round this being real, you know? It's just –'

Liam grinned. 'Oh, it'll mess with your head all right. That's for sure.'

'You're really from the future?'

'Well, actually, not precisely the *future* as it happens.'

Whitmore looked confused by that.

Liam wondered if he should really say any more. Becks was right in that the more information they handed out to these people the greater the potential risk to blowing the agency's anonymity. But he also figured what the heck . . . they were here and the future was sixty-five million years away.

Might as well be hung for a sheep as a lamb.

'I was born in Cork, in Ireland in 1896, if you must know. And I should've died in 1912.' He looked at Whitmore and his grin spread even wider. 'Aboard a ship you might just have heard a little something about . . . the *Titanic*.'

The man's eyes widened. Lam, Franklyn and Jonah joined them then, all five of them filling the quiet jungle with their rasping breath.

'What's up?' said Lam, noticing the goggle-eyed expression on Whitmore's face.

'That's . . . surely . . . that's just impossible!' blustered Whitmore.

'Well now,' replied Liam, looking around at the Cretaceous foliage, 'you'd think *all* of this little pickle we're in would be impossible, right? I mean . . . us lot stranded in dinosaur times?'

Whitmore ran a hand through his thinning salt and pepper hair. 'But the *Titanic* . . . you were actually *on* the *Titanic*?'

'Junior steward, deck E, so I was.'

Jonah pushed his frizzy fringe out of eyes that were filling his face. 'No . . . way . . . dude!'

Lam wiped some sweat from his brow. 'This is just getting weirder and weirder.'

'I was recruited, see. The agency plucked me moments from death just as the ship's spine snapped and apparently both halves went sliding under. Made no difference to time, do you see? It made no difference to history whether my bones ended up at the bottom of the Atlantic with everyone else's or not. That's how the agency recruits . . . poor fools like me who'll never be missed.'

'My God,' whispered Whitmore. 'That's really quite incredible.'

'What about the other one?' asked Franklyn.

Jonah nodded appreciatively. 'Yeah, your foxy goth girlfriend.'

Liam assumed he was referring to the support unit. 'Becks? No . . . she's, uh . . . she's certainly not my girlfriend.'

'Whatever,' said Franklyn. 'Where does she come from?'

Lam shook his head. 'Maybe we should be asking *when* does she come from?'

Franklyn's face stiffened at being corrected. 'Yes . . . *when*.'

Liam decided a small white lie was better right now. Telling them she was some kind of a robot killing machine probably wasn't the best thing to be telling them. The last thing their little group needed was a reason not to trust Becks. They all needed each other, and they certainly needed *her* help.

'Oh, Becks is from the future. 2050-something or other. I guess that's why she talks a little funny every now and then.'

'She *is* kind of weird,' said Franklyn. 'Like Spock . . . or something.'

'So, Liam, since it looks like you're the only one who understands what's happened here,' said Whitmore, 'it seems we're all going to have to rely on you to get us home. I presume you have some sort of a plan of action? You know . . . beyond merely exploring our immediate surroundings.'

A plan? The closest thing to doing any 'planning' so far had been figuring out how he'd use the rubbish machete in his hand if a dinosaur was to suddenly emerge from the undergrowth ahead.

'The plan?'

'Yes,' said Whitmore, 'I mean . . . I presume there's a way out of this mess for us, isn't there?'

Liam could see the other three were staring expectantly at him. 'Well, uh . . . well, one thing's for sure, gentlemen. We need to stay right where we are, on that island.'

'Why?'

'Because it's the exact same place that we *were*.'

Joseph Lam nodded. 'The same geo-coordinates as the lab, right?'

'That's right. We haven't moved an inch in position . . . just in time. If we happened to up sticks and move camp somewhere else, it would make it even harder for someone to find us. So we're best staying put right where we are.'

Whitmore dabbed at his damp face with the cuff of his shirt. 'This agency you work for . . . are they like a government agency? Like the CIA? Like the FBI? Something like that?'

Liam hadn't heard of either of those. So he decided to do what he did best: bluff. 'Sure, they're just like them fellas, Mr Whitmore, but you know . . . uhh . . . much bigger and better, and, of course, from the future.'

'And they're going to come for us, right? They're going to get us all out of here, aren't they?'

Liam offered him a stern, confident nod. 'Sure they are. We've just got to hold on here. It'll take them a little time to find us . . . but they will. I assure you, they will.'

They looked at each other uncertainly, until the scraggly beard beneath Whitmore's stubby round nose stretched with a smile. 'Well, all right, then. I'm sure between us we've got enough know-how to make do for a few days.'

His smile spread to the others.

'I'd like to see at least one dinosaur first, though,' said Franklyn. 'Be real lame not to.'

'Yeah,' said Jonah, pulling out a mobile phone from his pocket. 'That would be, like, awesome. You know? I could stick it up on YouTube. Whoa! No!' He pushed his frizzy mop of hair aside. 'Better than that, dude . . . do it as a pay-per-download. I could make, like, millions out of this . . .'

Whitmore shook his head. 'What is it with you kids these days?'

'Opportunity,' replied Jonah. 'That's what it is, my man . . . a golden freakin' money-makin' opportunity.'

Whitmore sighed.

CHAPTER 27

65 million years BC, jungle

Becks stood to one side dispassionately observing the work of the others as they hacked at the slim, straight trunks of the smaller trees they'd already felled, stripping branches from their sides to produce usable lightweight logs for construction.

She had them divided into two groups. One doing this job, the other group lashing the logs together with lengths of twisted vine to form wigwam-shaped frames. On top of these they could layer the big waxy leaves that drooped from the canopy trees. A few layers of those would give them a covering that would almost be waterproof.

That had been Liam's instruction. Make shelters. But her cool grey eyes panned uneasily across the clearing, observing the area of jungle that had been hacked away, the disturbed jungle floor where the smaller trees had been uprooted. Her eyes picked out the slashes of machete blows on other bigger trees that had proven too difficult to fell or uproot and the compressed tracks of footprints on the ground – the distinct oval of signatures of a human presence.

> [Evaluation: time contamination is increasing]

Every movement these people made, every footstep, every swipe of a blunt blade, was adding to a growing count of potential contamination. Yet Liam O'Connor's instruction to her was a mission priority, an override. As the mission *operative*, his orders were as final and non-negotiable as any hard-coded line of programming in her head.

He'd been very specific: that she was to organize the completion of the bridge and the building of a camp. And, for good measure, some kind of small enclosure, a palisade that they could all hide inside just in case any nasty found its way on to their island.

And so she had. Just like their last mission, back when her AI software had been assigned the ident. 'Bob', she was once again obediently following orders. There was something vaguely comforting about being in a brand-new functioning body, being on a mission once again with Liam O'Connor. They had functioned together very efficiently last time – successfully correcting a significant time contamination against exceedingly unfavourable odds.

But there'd been something . . . *untidy* . . . about the AI's learning curve. As Bob, it had discovered that the strict mission parameters could be overwritten with new ones, that under extreme circumstances the collection of software routines was actually capable of making a 'decision'.

That in itself had been a disturbing realization. As Bob, the AI had learned that its core programming could be subtly influenced, swayed, by something else: the tiny nodule of organic intelligence the computer chip was connected to. The undeveloped foetal brain of this genetically engineered frame. As Bob, the AI had experienced a fleeting taste of something that these humans must all take for granted. Emotion. The AI had discovered something very, very odd . . . that it actually 'liked' Liam O'Connor.

Since that first clone body had been irreparably damaged in the snowy woods down the hill from Adolf Hitler's winter Berghof retreat and the AI uploaded into the field office's mainframe – an entirely non-organic, disembodied existence – the AI had had much time to reflect on all that it had learned from those six months in the past.

Conclusions

1. **AI is now capable of referring to the newly developed AI routines as . . . '*I*', '*Me*', '*Myself*'.**
2. **'*I*' am now capable of limited decision-making.**
3. **Within an organic hardware housing, '*I*' am capable of limited emotional stimulation.**

And most important of all . . .

4. **'*I*' '*like*' Liam O'Connor.**

Becks continued to watch the humans at work and realized that part of her onboard code was insistently whispering a warning to her that a decision needed to be made, and made very soon. The humans were beginning to cause dangerously unacceptable levels of contamination in this jungle clearing with all that they were doing. With every footstep, with every log being cut down, there was an increased possibility that some fossilized forensic clue would survive sixty-five million years to be found in the future, and quite clearly reveal that humans had visited this time.

Unacceptable.

Liam O'Connor's instructions to her were at odds with the basic protocols of journeying into the past, that contamination must be kept to an absolute minimum. Even now, by simply being here, these people could be causing a far greater time wave than the assassination of Edward Chan in 2015 might have caused.

Recommendation

1. **Terminate all humans, including mission operative Liam O'Connor.**
2. **Destroy all traces of human artefacts and habitation in this location.**
3. **Self-terminate.**

The recommendation was faultlessly logical and strategically sound. But that small nodule of primitive organic matter reminded her software that Liam was a friend.

And friends don't kill friends.

Becks blinked away the thought. It was an unwelcome distraction.

Decision Options

1. **Proceed immediately with mission recommendation.**
2. **Wait for operative Liam O'Connor and discuss.**

A decision. Never easy. Becks's internal silicon wafer processor began to rapidly warm up as gigabytes of data rattled through software filters. Her lifeless grey eyes blinked in rapid succession as she desperately struggled to produce an answer and her fingers absentmindedly tightened round the handle of the machete. She barely registered the blonde-haired female human called Laura approaching her.

'Hey!' the girl called out. 'You going to give us a hand or just stand there and watch us do the work? Huh? *Becks?*'

Becks's eyes slowly swivelled and locked on the girl, but she said nothing. Her mind was very, very busy.

CHAPTER 28

65 million years BC, jungle

Liam saw it first: amid the relentless green and ochre of the jungle, it was an unmissable splash of bright crimson. He raised his hand, turned round and put a finger to his lips, shushing Lam and Jonah at the back who'd been chattering for the last five minutes about comicbooks.

They hushed immediately.

Whitmore stepped quietly forward and joined him. 'What is it?'

Liam pointed through a thin veil of leaves. 'Blood . . . lots of it, by the look of things.'

Whitmore swallowed and looked goggle-eyed again. 'Oh boy,' he whispered. 'Oh boy. Oh boy.'

Franklyn joined them. Unlike Whitmore, his eyes lit up with joy. 'Excellent!' he gasped. 'Looks like something made a kill.'

Whitmore swallowed. 'That's exactly what I'm worried about.' He looked at Liam. 'I suggest we quietly back up and –' But before Whitmore could finish Franklyn pushed his way forward through low sweeping fern fronds and into a small clearing.

'Oh, this is so awesome! Come on!' he called to them. 'We must have frightened the predator off!'

Liam looked at the teacher and shrugged. 'Well, I suppose if we've scared some dinosaur away, the last thing we ought to start doing now is look frightened ourselves. We'd better brass it out, right?'

By the look of Whitmore's still goggling eyes, he'd have been much happier with the *backing quietly away* plan. Liam left him thinking it over as he stepped forward through the fern leaves and into the clearing.

Franklyn was squatting over the eviscerated ribcage of some large beast, wrinkling his nose at the fetid smell of shredded organs, pulled out and splayed across the jungle floor.

Liam felt something stir and roll queasily in his empty stomach. 'Jay-zus, that's disgusting.'

'A recent kill by the look of it,' said Franklyn, prodding the large carcass with his fingers. Shreds of tattered muscle tissue swayed from the ends of the ribs as the body rocked slightly. Lam, Jonah and Whitmore emerged behind Liam.

'Oh, man, that's totally gross!' said Jonah, holding his nose at the pungent smell of death.

'I really think we shouldn't hang about here,' said Whitmore. 'Whatever did this might still be close by.'

Franklyn nodded and smiled. 'Exactly! Maybe we'll actually get a chance to see something!'

Liam looked around the dense foliage, wary that some large creature with very sharp claws and teeth might just be watching them now. 'You know, I think Mr Whitmore's got the right idea. Maybe we should probably back off.'

'Look at these marks on the hide,' said Franklyn, ignoring them. 'The lacerations, lots of them, small ones, not large like a rex might do.' He studied the ground. 'See?'

Liam looked at where he was pointing and saw several three-pronged indentations across the ground. And then he spotted something long and curved like a fishhook on the ground. He stooped down and picked it up.

'What's that?' asked Franklyn.

Liam shrugged. 'Looks like some sort of claw.'

Franklyn couldn't help himself. He snatched it out of Liam's open palm.

'Oh my God! That's . . . that's a claw, all right! Look, the serrated inner edge.' He turned it over in his hand. 'But it's a weird shape, isn't it, Mr Whitmore?'

Whitmore seemed more interested in leaving, but he quickly leaned over and inspected it more closely. 'It's certainly not the crescent shape you'd associate with a raptor or some other species of therapod.'

Franklyn grinned with excitement. 'Maybe this is an unknown species?'

'It's possible,' said Lam. 'I mean, don't they say something about we've only ever discovered the fossils of one per cent of the species that have ever lived on planet Earth?'

'I really think we should leave,' said Whitmore.

Liam nodded. He held out his hand. 'May I have it back?'

Franklyn seemed reluctant to let it go. But after pulling a face he passed it to Liam. 'Cool find,' he uttered.

Liam smiled. 'I'm sure you'll come across another.'

'Yeah, probably . . . whatever that belonged to is small. Probably pack hunters.'

'Pack hunters?' Jonah straightened up. 'You know, I think Mr Whitmore's right. Maybe we should go.'

'Uh-huh,' said Whitmore, smiling quickly, uncomfortably. Looking around the clearing. 'Well, Franklyn, a fascinating find. We can all talk about it on the way back.'

'Pack hunters?' said Lam. 'Like raptors? You said there *weren't* raptors!'

'These aren't. Look at the footprints . . . there'd be indentations from their sickle toe. No, these are some other species, maybe not even therapods. Something entirely different.' He stood up. 'This is so cool!'

'Yes, well . . .' Liam looked at the others. 'So now we know for sure we're sharing this place with dinosaurs.' He looked at the buffalo-sized carcass. 'And now that we know there's some bigger types we could hunt for food I think Mr Whitmore's right – we ought to head back to the camp.'

Four heads bobbed enthusiastically.

Franklyn sighed. 'OK.'

'Right, then.' Liam gestured down the path they'd beaten. 'After you, gents.' They filed quickly past him, Whitmore glancing awkwardly back over his shoulder as he stepped by. 'Actually, I really wish we hadn't spotted that,' he said quietly, pulling a face.

Liam knew what he meant. The poor beast, whatever it had once been, looked like it hadn't just been killed for meat. The organs splayed out on to the jungle floor, the intestines dangling from loops of vine . . . it was as if the creatures that had brought it down had frolicked and played with the grisly remains – a gory celebration of the kill. The idea of an animal species capable of *celebrating* seemed somewhat disconcerting. It hinted at ritual. It hinted at intelligence.

Maybe they're just messy eaters?

In the gathering stillness, he thought he heard the softest *click* – like the tiniest twig snapping beneath impatient, shifting weight. He glanced back once more at the blood-splashed clearing and wondered if predators' eyes were cautiously eyeing him in turn from the cover of the dense green foliage.

Yellow, unblinking eyes studied the curious creatures as they departed. Just a dozen yards away – no more than three or four strides from where the beast crouched – there were five of these pale creatures the like of which he had never seen before. They made odd noises, not a million miles away from the cranial bark he made when calling for the attention of the rest of the pack. And these odd creatures moved in a not dissimilar way: upright, on long, developed rear legs, but far more slowly, sluggishly.

The creature shifted position slightly, bobbing down lower to get a better look between the broad leaves of the fern he was hiding behind. These pale upright things, these *new creatures* . . . he wondered if this was the entirety of their pack, or whether there were more of them elsewhere.

They seemed harmless. They appeared to have no visible teeth, no slashing claws, nothing that signalled any danger about them at all. Nothing that identified them as potential rival predators.

Except . . . except – the creature could see this – these pale things were *clever.* They appeared to work co-operatively, sharing tasks. Just like his pack did. He watched in absolute stillness, his olive skin a perfect disguise among the varied greens of the jungle. He watched with intense eyes that faced forward, capable of binocular vision; capable of judging distance, range.

A predator's advantage.

These strange newcomers, these *new creatures*, also had eyes that faced forward. Another reason to be so very wary of them. Perhaps they too were predators of some kind, unlike the docile plant-eaters, whose eyes on either side of their heads were designed to detect potential danger from two directions.

Yes . . . these things had predators' eyes. And yet they appeared utterly defenceless, harmless and pitifully slow and clumsy in the way they moved around the clearing.

He cocked his head curiously. The long fishhook-shaped

razor-sharp claws on its left front paw clacked together carelessly.

The last of the new creatures suddenly turned and looked back in his direction. It must have heard something, the *snick* of his claws. Incredibly the creature's eyes looked *directly* at him – right at him – and yet seemed to see absolutely nothing. Its eyes panned slowly from left to right then finally it turned and headed off after the others.

The creature looked down at his claws: four of them, long and lethal, curled from the digits of one arm, three . . . and a broken stump . . . from the other – damage caused many seasons ago fighting off a young male who had foolishly decided to challenge his leadership. The challenger had died, of course, and in a rage he had torn the body to ragged pieces in front of the rest of the pack as a lesson.

The claws usually grew back. The young female who'd lost her claw today during the kill, she would have a new one before a new moon. But his stump had never regrown a claw. A constant reminder that his days as leader were numbered by how long he remained effective.

Slowly and very lightly, Broken Claw stepped backwards, away from the fern leaves and further from the well-lit small clearing into jungle darkness. His powerful rear legs strong and agile – capable of incredible speed, but also able to move in almost complete silence.

A simple thought passed through his mind – a thought not made up of words, but ideas.

The new creatures must be watched.

Instinctively he sensed there was something terribly dangerous about them. Until he knew exactly what it was, until he knew how weak or dangerous they could be, the new creatures should be carefully observed, studied, until he was sure he had the measure of them and then . . . then, when these things were least prepared, when they were certain these pale creatures had no concealed powers, they would be attacked and feasted upon. And the pack could celebrate their dominance once more as the quiet killers of this world, decorating the jungle with their organs, painting their blood on their hides.

His sharp teeth snapped together softly, and he resolved that patience, for the moment, was the correct course of action.

CHAPTER 29

65 million years BC, jungle

Liam heaved a sigh of relief as he caught a glimpse of the raging river and the long slender trunk that bridged one rocky bank to the other. It appeared Becks had finished her work on the bridge. It could now be raised, courtesy of a crudely rigged counterweight of a bundle of logs. They were tied together and connected to a stout rope of a dozen twisted vines, which ran up and over the thick branch of a canopy tree that stretched a sturdy limb out above the river. The other end of the rope was tied round the end of their 'drawbridge', a thirty-foot trunk as straight as a javelin and a slender foot in diameter. It was thick enough to take their weight, one at a time, but not so heavy the supporting branch above would snap as it was raised.

One by one, they stepped on to the log, and cautiously inched their way over the tumbling froth a few feet below. Liam was the last one over and, as he anxiously awaited his turn, he scanned the wall of jungle behind him, wary that, being the last one on this side of the river, he might prove a tempting morsel for some hungry beast.

But his turn came, and a few moments later he was on the far side with the others. 'OK, let's raise the drawbridge.'

Between them they pulled on the counterweight of logs,

and with the creak of stressed vine rope and the branch above taking the burden, the bridge rose up until it was approximately at an angle of forty-five degrees.

'Good enough.' Liam looked up at the sky. The sun was beginning to head for the horizon and long dark shadows stretched across the river. Through the trees and tufts of bamboo thickets on their side of the river, from the direction of the clearing, they could hear the echoing hack of blades on wood: the others working on their camp, their home . . . a temporary home, Liam found himself hoping. The sound of activity was reassuring.

'I hope somebody's got the kettle on for us,' said Liam.

A minute later they were just stepping out into the broad clearing, keen to see what the others had managed to construct in their absence, when they heard a scream echo across the open space.

'Uh?' uttered Lam.

On the far side Liam could see movement. Someone running. It was the girl Laura, running, staggering, stumbling to her knees, then back up on her feet. Behind her, pursuing with a swift purposeful stride, a figure all in black with flaming red hair: Becks.

'Whoa . . . catfight,' uttered Jonah, grinning like an idiot.

'Hey!' Liam called out. 'What's going on?'

Laura glanced his way and changed direction towards him. Becks was swiftly closing the gap. He noticed her holding one of their bamboo spears in one hand, the tip bright red with a splash of blood.

What the . . .?

He ran forward. 'Becks! What's going on?'

Closer now, he could see a long gash down Laura's left arm, blood splattered across her bright pink sweatshirt.

'Oh God! Oh God! She's trying to kill me!' Laura screamed. The rest of the group on the far side of the clearing, where a row of simple frames of wood had thus far been erected, were watching the scene in stunned, uncomprehending silence.

Finally Laura collapsed in a pile at Liam's feet, clasping at her arm and looking back in panic as Becks strode forward. 'She speared me!' gasped Laura. 'Just walked up and stabbed me for no reason!'

Becks came to a halt several yards away and looked calmly at Liam. She even smiled her faltering horse smile, lips slowly stretching to reveal a row of perfect teeth. 'Hello, Liam,' she said.

'Jay-zus, Becks! Why'd you go and attack the poor girl?'

'Mission priority. She has to be terminated.'

'*What?*'

Becks nodded at the others standing just behind Liam. 'All of them as well. The others, and you, Liam.' He thought he detected a hint of regret in her voice as she said that. 'After that, I must purge this area of evidence of human occupation. Then I must self-terminate.'

'What? That's crazy!' said Lam.

'Becks, listen,' said Liam, spreading his hands slowly. 'This is not necessary, all right?'

She took another two strides forward, reached down and grabbed Laura round the throat, and effortlessly lifted her up off the ground, her legs kicking in the air. Laura scrabbled and scratched at her face, one hand finally grabbing a fist of Becks's red hair.

'BECKS! STOP IT!'

Liam's command halted her. She looked at him, confused. 'It is a mission priority. We have already caused unacceptable levels of time contamination.'

'PUT HER DOWN!'

Becks stared at him, but remained poised and perfectly still, Laura still dangling, kicking, struggling and slowly choking; the sharp ragged point of the spear held in Becks's other hand hovered mere inches away from her throat.

'THAT IS AN ORDER!'

Becks's eyes slowly panned from Liam to Laura then back again. Her eyelids fluttered momentarily then finally she said, 'Affirmative.' She released her grip on Laura and the girl tumbled heavily to the ground, Becks's red wig wrenched from her bare head, still clasped by Laura's bloody fingers.

'Now, put that spear down!' snapped Liam.

She obediently released her tight grip and it clattered on the soft ground.

Laura's breath chugged in and out in whooping gasps while the others stared in stunned silence at Becks and her bald head, already sporting a quarter-inch fuzz of dark hair.

'Oh my God! She's a complete freakin' psycho!' said Lam.

Behind him, Liam heard Jonah mutter, 'Jeez . . . got that right, dude.'

Becks was staring at him. There was something in those cold grey eyes, something that looked like guilt, regret. Possibly even sadness. Like a scolded baby in that moment – that stunned *could go either way* moment – just before the face creases up and the tears and wailing come.

'No,' said Liam, 'no, she's not.'

'She's *not* a psycho?' said Lam. 'Sure about that?'

Liam nodded. He could see muscles twitching in Becks's face. Confusion, desperation . . . her mind struggling to reconcile conflicting priorities: Liam's direct order versus hard-coded mission protocols.

'She's just doing what she thinks is right. She's following her programming.'

Franklyn cocked his head. 'Programming?'

The fire crackled noisily, illuminating their faces as they gathered in a circle round it like so many amber-coloured ghosts in a graveyard. The jungle, beyond the thrown flickering glow of light, was dark and noisy with the far-off echoing cries of creatures calling to each other.

'But how can we be sure that . . . *thing* won't just freak out on us again?' asked Kelly. He cast a glance at Becks standing several dozen yards away out in the darkness, motionless, dutifully keeping watch for any signs of a night predator entering the clearing.

'She just won't,' said Liam.

'Yeah, well, that doesn't exactly fill me with confidence.' Kelly threw a small branch on the fire, sending a cascade of sparks up into the pitch-black sky. 'I mean, it's not like you knew she was going to attack Laura earlier.'

Liam looked at the girl. Her arm was bandaged with a strip of cloth torn from her sleeve. The black girl, Keisha, had done a good job with the dressing. It hadn't been a particularly deep gash, but luckily hadn't severed an artery. Laura must have been incredibly lucky; Becks had stumbled on the uneven ground as she'd lunged with the spear. Laura had been fortunate Becks hadn't managed to get hold of her. Liam had seen enough of Bob in action to know that, male or female, these support units were lethal killing machines up close and personal.

'She won't,' said Liam again. 'I've discussed the situation with her.'

'Discussed the situation?' snorted Jonah. 'Can't you just pull some sort of plug on her? I mean . . . she's a robot, right?'

'No.' Liam shook his head. 'She's not that sort of a robot. Not all wires and motors and metal bits. She's an organic unit, what the agency call a *genetically engineered* unit.' He looked around at the pale faces. 'You've heard of that term, have you?'

'Well, duh,' sighed Keisha. 'Any kid who watches the Cartoon Channel knows that term.'

Liam shrugged apologetically. 'Anyway, she's what we call a *meat robot*. Flesh and blood, so she is. But she has a real computer up in her head.'

'And what? You sayin' her programmin' made her go for Laura with the spear?' said Juan.

'That's right. She was concerned about all the contamination we were causing, and without me being there to discuss it with her she had to make a decision on her own.'

'Concerned?' said Jonah '*Concerned?* Dude, I'd hate to see what she's like when she's really mad at something.'

Liam ignored that.

'Liam, you said contamination,' said Kelly. 'You mean, creating evidence we've been here? Like our camp and the bridge?'

'That's right. Every cut, every scrape, every footprint – in fact, everything we do – just our *being* here could potentially alter history in such a way that the future is totally destroyed.' Liam glanced at the motionless silhouette of the support unit standing guard in the middle of the clearing. 'It's a basic command for her . . . like, I suppose, like one of the ten commandments would be to us.'

'Thou shalt not mess around with time,' chuckled a dark-skinned boy called Ranjit. 'That would be a cool eleventh commandment to have.'

'Yeah,' said Jonah. 'Thy shalt not kill your ancestor, for he begets –'

'You think it's funny?' cut in Howard sharply. The others looked at him, taken aback at the outburst. Thus far he'd been one of the quieter members of the group. 'You think messing with time is just some sort of a game? It's the most insane thing man has ever done.' He stopped himself short. Took a breath and dialled it back a bit. 'What I'm saying is . . . it's just pretty insane, time travel.'

Liam nodded sombrely. 'He's quite right. It is insane. Although a man called Waldstein is the first man to travel through time –' he looked at Edward, the smallest face around the fire – 'it all begins with you. It's all based on work that *you* will do one day.'

'So . . . theoretically,' said Kelly, 'if Edward had, for example, died in that explosion back in the reactor, and not gone on to do his work, then this Waldstein guy would not have invented a time machine?'

'And we'd not have been blasted back into dinosaur times?' said Laura.

Liam noticed one or two heads turning towards the young boy, giving him a long, silent stare that looked like careful deliberation. Liam could see where this conversation might go.

'There can only be one correct history, one correct timeline. And, whether we like it or not, that timeline *includes* an Edward Chan who becomes a maths genius, and a Mr Waldstein who makes that first machine, so he does. That's how it goes. That's how it *has* to go.' Liam stared at them all, each in turn. 'And that's why you can trust me . . . why you can trust Becks, to be sure. Our primary goal now is to make sure that this young lad gets back home to 2015 to do what he has to do. And that means the rest of you too.'

'So, if there's, like, a *primary* goal . . . then there's a *secondary* goal,' said a dark-skinned girl with long black hair and a pierced upper lip that glinted with several metal studs. It was the first time he'd heard her speak today. Quiet, pensive, she reminded him a little of Sal. She was still wearing her name tag: JASMINE.

'There's no *other* goal, Jasmine, I promise,' said Liam. 'Me and Becks want to get you all back home, so we do.'

But that's not strictly true, is it, Liam?

He and Becks had spoken in private earlier. He'd managed to reason with her calmly – to talk her down from proceeding any further with her self-decided mission objective to kill them all, then herself. But it was a compromise. A perfectly logical compromise that successfully reconciled the conflicting protocols in her head.

'*In six months' time*,' he'd agreed with her, '*if they haven't rescued us by then, before your six months is up and you have to self-terminate . . . then, yes, you're right . . . I suppose we'd all have to die. I'll even help you.*' He'd smiled at her. '*Let's just hope it doesn't come to that, eh?*'

The campfire crackled noisily.

'So, there you go, all friends now, right?' said Jonah. 'Even robo-girl.' He grinned. 'Now about a nice sing-song. A round of "Kumbayah"?' he added sarcastically. 'I'll take the lead. *Kumbayah, my Lord! . . . Kumba–*'

Someone threw a chip of dried dino dung across the fire at him.

CHAPTER 30

Wednesday, 2001, New York

A Wednesday. Maddy realized she hadn't seen one of those in quite a while. Since she'd been on a plane trip back home to her folks in Boston, in fact. Since she'd become a TimeRider.

She looked down the flagpole approach to the Statue of Liberty's star-shaped podium and spotted only half a dozen other people. She'd been here once before, on the same school trip that they'd visited the Museum of Natural History. It had been a tedious day full of queuing. Queuing to get ferry tickets, queuing to get on a ferry over to Liberty Island, queuing to get inside the podium building beneath Liberty's feet and look at the small museum's exhibits. Queuing once again to get a look up inside the statue itself. A pretty dull day of standing around, being shoved, bumped and barged into, waiting to look at things she actually had precious little interest in.

Today though there were no queues.

The island was all but deserted. Half a dozen ferries had arrived throughout the day, each offloading no more than a handful of muted whispering visitors. And, even then, their eyes had been more on the column of smoke coming from across the bay, coming from Manhattan, than they had been on the giant copper-green statue in front of them.

Maddy took another slurp of the cooling polystyrene cup of coffee in her hands. Horrible. She'd lost count of how many she'd bought from the stall opposite the embarkation pier. She was almost on first-name terms with the bewildered-looking man behind the counter who'd served her every time. He certainly should know by now she took it white with three sugars.

Come on, Foster . . . where the hell are you?

Through the morning she'd been hopeful as each ferry had arrived. But not now; it was nearly four in the afternoon. Another hour or so and the Statue of Liberty's little museum would be closing, the last ferry back across the harbour getting ready to leave.

She was beginning to realize today had been wasted, loitering around like this. Cluelessly hovering around the podium's entrance in hope that the old man would turn up. Never mind, she told herself, now at least she knew that Foster hadn't spent the first Wednesday of his 'retirement' out here. She'd head back to their archway. Today, Wednesday, it would be nothing more than an empty brick archway with a TO LET sign pasted on the roller-shutter door, and outside that shutter door she'd wait until eight in the evening when a shimmering portal would appear, ready to take her back into Monday again.

Then she'd do this all again, try Wednesday once more, but next time she'd loiter outside the Empire State Building.

Her eyes drifted off the tourists as they passed by her and into the podium, pausing as they did to look once again at the pall of smoke in the sky.

She remembered this day, remembered *the day after.* She'd been what? Eight? Nine? Mom and Dad at home all day, sitting in front of the TV, watching as dust-smeared emergency workers scrabbled at the edge of the smouldering wreck, pulling twisted spars of still-warm metal away in the hope of finding someone alive. She'd been playing on the floor of the lounge with her Tech-Meccano set, trying to build her version of a Transformer, half her attention on what she was doing, half on her parents: Mom sobbing and Dad cursing.

And here she was again. Different place, same day.

An odd urge occurred to her. What if she found a way through the security cordon around the ruin of the Twin Towers and found a TV camera and reporter to be stopped and interviewed by. She could wave at her eight-year-old self, wave at her mom and dad watching the TV. She could reassure them that she wasn't going to die along with 137 other people aboard Flight 95 in nine years' time. Tell them she was going to be OK.

She shook her head. *Nice idea.* But she wasn't going to do that.

She turned her thoughts towards more pressing matters. Liam and the support unit. Bob had assured her that the copy of his AI in the female unit would make the same recommendation to Liam as he would: to find a discreet way to make contact. Discreet . . . because a too-obvious message, a message that stood out above the background noise of history, could significantly affect the timeline. But there was the problem. A subtle message carefully laid down in whatever historical period they were in, laid down for only her and Sal to find . . .?

I mean, where the hell are we supposed to start looking for something like that?

If they'd only been bumped back less than 150 years, then perhaps there was a message waiting for them once more in the Museum of Natural History's guest books. That was something Sal had decided to try and check out. But what if they'd been knocked further back in time?

Five hundred years ago? A thousand years ago? What was

in the middle of Texas a thousand years ago? A lot of buffalo, she guessed, and some Indians. But certainly no visitor guest books for them to discreetly slip a message into. A 'get us out of here' scrawled across an ancient Navaho tribal history rug was almost certainly something the support unit would NOT recommend to Liam. Not unless they wanted every historian studying Native American history discussing the message at some symposium.

Subtle. It could only be subtle.

But, she sighed to herself, *too* subtle and how were they ever going to find it?

Unless it's a message that's meant to find us.

She looked up from her coffee.

. . . Find us . . .

'My God,' she whispered to herself. Maybe that's what they'd try to do. A message addressed to its finder, whomever that might be. A message that perhaps might promise a reward of some kind to the finder provided it was delivered to a certain location on a certain date. A message that might promise untold wealth, access to an incredible time-travel technology? And think about it. Such a message would be too important, too powerful, to become public knowledge, wouldn't it? A message like that would become a closely guarded secret, right? A secret handed down by the original finder to his offspring, like a dark family secret or a horrendous supernatural curse. Handed down from one to another, until finally the message is passed to someone who is able to make their way to a certain backstreet in Brooklyn on 10 September 2001 and gently knock on their door, calling out to see if anyone's inside.

Oh my God . . . it's possible, isn't it?

And what if that happened while she was standing out here like a complete lemon? Waiting for Foster to turn up, when quite probably he was never going to. Computer Bob was right. That's what he'd said, wasn't it? 'Just wait.'

'Oh, you freakin' idiot, Maddy,' she hissed to herself, tossing the polystyrene cup into the bin beside her and heading down the walkway towards the pier.

CHAPTER 31

65 million years BC*, jungle*

'You can do *what*?' said Liam.

Becks hefted the log up in her taut arms and held it steady as Liam lashed it in place with a hand-woven length of rope made from the species of vine they'd found dangling from virtually every tree around the clearing.

'I believe it is possible for me to calculate when in time we are with a very high degree of accuracy.'

He wrapped the rope tightly round the log, tugging it hard so that it shuffled up against its neighbour. The palisade wall so far stretched only a dozen feet: about twenty logs, each just under eight inches in diameter and all roughly about nine feet tall. When they were done, they'd have a circular enclosure about four yards across – large enough for all sixteen of them to huddle inside should something nasty find its way on to their island and they needed somewhere to retreat to.

'How?' asked Liam.

'I have a detailed record of all the variables during the time of the explosion.'

'Variables?'

'Data. Specifically, directly after we arrived here. The particle decay rate.'

Liam cocked an eyebrow. 'I haven't a clue what that means, Becks.'

She walked over to a dwindling pile of logs and effortlessly picked up another. They were going to need more. Across the clearing he could see Whitmore and several of the students carrying one between them, stumbling across the lumpy ground towards them. She slammed one end of the log down into the soft soil with a heavy thud, next to the last log, and Liam began to lash it into their wall.

'I have a detailed record of the explosion. The number and density of tachyon particles that we were exposed to in 2015 and the number and density of tachyon particles that emerged here alongside ourselves.'

Liam looked at her and shrugged. 'Assume I'm a child that knows nothing, Becks.'

She looked at him and he thought he caught her rolling her eyes at his stupidity: a gesture the AI must have learned from Sal back when it was computer-bound and its visual world was what it picked up from the one webcam.

'Tachyon particles decay at a constant rate. That is why it takes greater amounts of energy to beam a signal further into the past.'

Liam tugged hard on the vine rope, cinching the knot tightly. 'I get that. So, if these particles die out at a steady rate, that means . . .?'

'I am able to calculate how many particles decayed and, from that, determine how far in time we were sent.'

He grinned. 'Really? You can do that?'

Becks looked up and tried mimicking his uneven smile. 'I have the processing power to do this.'

'And we'll know exactly *when* we are?'

'To an accuracy level of one thousandth of a per cent.'

Liam shook his head in wonder. 'Jay-zus, that metal brain of yours is a bloody marvel, so it is!'

She seemed pleased with that. 'Is that a compliment, Liam O'Connor?'

He punched her arm lightly. 'Of course it is! Don't know what I'd do without you.'

Her gaze drifted off across the clearing for a moment then back at him. 'Thank you.'

He finished lashing the log and waited for her to pick up another and slam it down heavily beside the last one.

'So what? We'll actually know what day we arrived in the past? Even what time?'

'Negative. I am unable to give that precise a calculation.'

'OK. We'll know to the nearest week or something?'

She shook her head.

'The nearest month?'

'Negative.'

'Year?'

'I can calculate to the nearest thousand years.'

'*What?*'

'I can calculate our current time down to the nearest –'

He cut her off. 'I heard you the first time. But . . . but that's no good to us, is it? I mean, even if we could somehow get a message to the future and tell them which *thousandth year* we're in, finding us here would be like trying to find a needle in a haystack!' He slumped down against the wall. 'If they tried opening a window at the same time every day for every year for a thousand years that'd be . . . that'd be . . .'

'Three hundred and sixty-five thousand attempts,' said Becks. 'Add another two hundred and fifty attempts for leap years.'

'Right! That many. Jeeeez, they'd never find us!'

She squatted down on her haunches beside him. 'You are correct. It is extremely unlikely,' she confirmed.

'So that's it, then?' he said, sagging. The moment of

believing they might have the beginnings of a way out was gone now, leaving him feeling even more hopeless than before. 'We're stuck here.'

'Until my six-month mission timer reaches –'

'Yes, yes . . . I know. Then you've got to do what you've got to do.'

A hand reached out and gently grasped his arm. 'I am sorry, Liam O'Connor. It does not make me happy to think of terminating these humans. Particularly you.'

He sighed. 'Well . . . I s'pose that counts for something,' he muttered. 'Thanks.'

They watched as the others finally arrived with the log, and between them heaved it on to the ground. Whitmore wiped sweat from his forehead and recovered his breath. 'Good God, I'm beat. Roughly how many more of these logs do you think you're going to need to finish that?'

Becks turned and eyed the wall for a moment. 'Seventy-nine.'

He puffed out his cheeks. 'Seventy-nine? You sure?'

She nodded. 'I am sure.'

'Right,' Whitmore puffed. 'Right, come on then, you lot,' he said to the others. 'Back to work.'

Liam and Becks watched them go. 'It would be possible for the field office to narrow down the number of candidate windows,' said Becks.

'What?'

'They do not need to try opening three hundred and sixty-five thousand, two hundred and fifty windows. I am certain the AI back in the field office would make the same recommendation.'

'Same recommendation? What?'

'A density probe. They could attempt a brief scan of each day. Any scans that returned a varying density signal warning would indicate movement of some object at that location. It is possible they would consider density warning signals as best-case candidates.'

He looked at her. She was right. A routine protocol before opening a window, to make sure they weren't going to get mangled up with somebody else. 'Do you remember *exactly* where we appeared on this clearing?'

She nodded. 'I have the exact geo-coordinates logged in my database.' She pointed across the ground towards a cluster of ferns. 'You appeared there. Fifty-one feet, seven and three-quarter inches from this location.'

'Then –' Liam looked at the spot – 'we'd need to stand someone right there . . . flapping their arms around or something, right?'

'Correct. But it is unlikely the field office will be making probe sweeps this far back in time.'

Liam felt himself sagging again. Another dashed ray of hope. He balled a fist with frustration. 'This time-travel stuff is nonsense. Would it be so hard for the agency to come up with some beamy signal thing we could send back to them?'

'In theory it would be possible. But it would require an enormous amount of energy and of course time displacement machinery, and a sophisticated enough computer system to target where to aim a –'

He raised a hand to shush her. 'Becks?'

Her grey eyes locked on him obediently.

'Please, shut up.'

'Affirmative.'

He stood, stretching an aching back. 'Ah, sod this!' Then he suddenly snapped, slamming his fist against the log wall. The palisade vibrated slightly with the soft creak of stretched vine-rope.

'Ouch!' he muttered, and sucked on grazed knuckles. 'That hurt.'

She tilted her head, curious. 'Then why did you do that?'

'Ugh . . . will you not be quiet?'

CHAPTER 32

65 million years BC, jungle

Several of the new creatures were standing in the shallows of the raging river, frothing white water tumbling noisily around their legs. They all held long sticks in their hands and seemed to be studying the water intently, keeping motionless for long periods then finally, inexplicably, lashing out with their sticks.

Broken Claw turned to the others crouching a few yards away, watching these creatures with fascination. He snicked his claws to attract their attention. They all obediently looked his way. Broken Claw uttered a series of soft throaty barks, and snapped his teeth.

New creatures. They are dangerous.

He couldn't explain why – he just knew somehow that they were. Quite possibly far more dangerous than them. His yellow eyes swivelled back to the creatures, and across the far side to the curious contraption these things had been fashioning with their pale clawless arms. The long trunk of a tree stripped of branches and leaves and hanging at a raised angle over the river, just like the long-slanted neck of one of the giant leaf-eaters that lived on the open plain. Tied round the contraption's top, Broken Claw recognized vines, entwined together, taut and angling back up towards another tree, over a thick branch and dangling straight down to the ground, where the vines were wrapped round a cluster of logs.

He couldn't begin to understand what the contraption did, or why these things had laboured so hard on making it. But they had, and it worried him. That he himself couldn't understand what it did worried him. He barked again softly.

New creatures. Cleverer than us.

The others seemed to agree. They cowered lower among the foliage at the edge of the jungle.

He could see as many of them wading in the water as the number of claws he possessed. He wondered how many more of them were on the island on the far side of this narrow river. More than his pack?

Just then, one of the new creatures lurched forward, pushing the stick into the water. A moment later it pulled the stick out. On its end, one of the grey river creatures thrashed and struggled, silver and glistening.

The stick had somehow captured the creature.

The stick . . . captures . . . the river creature.

He watched with fascination as the new creatures carried the large flapping river-dweller between them, away from the water's edge and through the trees until they were gone from view. Only one of them remained behind. Still, poised, gazing intently out at the water.

Broken Claw recognized this one. He'd seen him before three sun-rises ago, back in the jungle. Their stare had actually met for a moment, although the thing's pale blue eyes had seemed to register nothing of that. Broken Claw sensed this one led the others, just like he led his pack. A position of loneliness and responsibility. For a moment his animal mind processed a thought that a human might have called *kinship*.

New creature. Is like I. Leads others.

When the time came to kill them all, when he was sure it was safe for them to make their move, he decided this creature should be his and his alone. Perhaps in the moment that he tore this pale thing's heart out all the wisdom and intelligence inside it would become his. Then he too would understand the *stick that captures* . . . and the curious construction raised over the river.

Liam scanned the swirling suds of water in front of him. Every now and then he could see the dark outline of one of these large prehistoric mudfish darting around the shallows, teasing him to make a lunge at it with his spear.

He was useless at it, unable to anticipate which way the dark shape would lurch to avoid being skewered. Juan was probably the best among them at catching these things. The one he'd just caught was a whopper: four feet of wriggling wet meat, enough to feed at least half of them tonight. If he could just manage to bag another one himself while the others were carrying it back to the camp, then he could at least feel less like a useless jerk.

Some leader.

Franklyn seemed to know everything about dinosaurs, Whitmore quite a lot too. Juan seemed to be at home in this survival situation, good at hunting, building a fire and all. Keisha seemed to be the group's carer and doctor. And, despite the unfortunate incident a few days ago, the others were beginning to regard Becks as their bodyguard. Even Jonah seemed to have a valued role as the group's comedian.

And then there's me. The Irish kid who can do nothing more than keep saying 'help's on the way'.

He wondered if the only reason they'd accepted him as the nominal leader was because he'd made the rash promise to get them back home. That and, of course, because Becks took her orders only from him. He wondered how they were going to feel about him being in charge in a few weeks' time or months' time, when there was still no sign of rescue.

He felt lonely and worn out with the burden of responsibility. At least the last time he'd been stuck in the past it had just been himself to worry about; he hadn't been asked to lead anyone.

No, that was Bob's job. He laughed at the memory of Bob leading that army of freedom fighters. They'd thought he was some sort of warrior angel sent down from Heaven by God himself; they'd thought he was a superhero just like out of one of those comicbooks. Superman, Captain Freedom. He'd certainly looked the part.

Movement.

He looked up and saw a pack of small dinosaurs, little more than lizards, standing upright on their hind legs and gazing at him curiously. None bigger than his hand. They were standing only a couple of yards away and tweeted and twittered among themselves as they idly watched him. Franklyn had a species name for them, although Liam was damned if he could remember it.

'What do you fellas want?' he called out.

He could guess . . . begging for scraps. These little chaps had been hopping and skipping around their campfire last night like excited children, drawn by the smell of fish meat being grilled on a spit. One of them had even been bold enough to hop up on to the cooking carcass, but had slipped on the greasy scales of the fish and fallen into the fire, where it had flapped around and screamed for a while before finally succumbing to the flames.

'Did you not learn your lesson last night, you silly *eejits*? Best staying away, eh?'

They all cocked their heads to the right in unison at the sound of his voice.

'Jay-zus, you little fellas really are stupid, aren't you?'

They tweeted and twittered and cooed at that.

'Ah, go away, will you? You'll spook my fish, so you will.' Liam bent down, scooped up a rock and tossed it a dozen yards down the silted riverbank. The entire pack of mini-therapods turned and scooted after it excitedly, presumably utterly convinced it was a hunk of juicy meat.

Liam watched them go, pattering across the silt, leaving a host of tiny trails behind them, like the trail of winter birds across virgin snow.

And that's when the idea struck him.

'Oh . . . oh,' he gasped to himself. 'Oh Jay-zus-'n'-Mother-Mary,' he added for good measure. 'That'll be it!' He dropped his spear into the water and turned on his heels, heading through the trees towards the camp.

CHAPTER 33

65 million years BC, jungle

He stumbled out of the jungle and into the clearing. Across the way he could see a thin column of smoke from yesterday's campfire, still smouldering, and clustered around it their dozen wigwam shelters, cone-shaped frames of wood beneath layers of broad waxy leaves the size of elephant's ears. To one side their palisade, finished now, and reinforced with a coating of rust-coloured dried mud, packed into the spaces between the logs and almost as hard as concrete. Around the tree-trunk palisade wall a three-foot-deep trench had been dug out. It effectively added another two or three feet to the height of their defence. Liam very much doubted it would hold at bay something as large as a rex, but it might be enough to dissuade any smaller beasts on the hunt for an easy meal.

He picked out Becks among the figures moving around the camp: a figure in black, her head no longer a pale round eggshell, but dark now with a week's worth of hair growth.

'Becks!' he called out. Her head turned sharply towards him, and her posture instantly adjusted to one ready for action. Every other head turned his way as he stumbled awkwardly across the ground towards them.

He saw Juan and Leonard scrambling to their feet and reaching for spears. He realized his voice must have sounded shrill as if he was shouting a warning. Kelly reached into his trousers for his penknife, Whitmore for one of their hatchets.

By the time Liam arrived beside the campfire, breathless and sweating from the exertion, everybody stood poised with a weapon and ready to run for the safety of the palisade.

'*What is it?*' asked Kelly. 'Something coming?'

Liam looked at them all. They were wide-eyed, some of the girls terrified even. Glances skipped from Liam to the far side of the clearing from where he'd emerged sprinting as if the devil himself was in hot pursuit.

'What's happened, dude?' asked Jonah.

Becks said, 'Your voice indicated a threat.'

Liam shook his head. 'Ah no, not really. I just had an idea.'

'*Fossils*, that's what you're talking about,' said Franklyn. 'Fossils. They're not even the original print that's left behind, but just an imprint of the print: sediment that has filled the footprint, then hardened over thousands of years to become a layer of rock.'

'Yes, but it's still a *mark* that's survived through all that time. An impression of that original mark.'

'Of course,' sniffed Franklyn. 'Yes, of course that's exactly what it is.'

Kelly shook his head. 'That's it? That's how you intend to communicate with your agency? Leave a mark on the ground in the Cretaceous period and hope some lucky fossil hunter finds it?' He shrugged, exasperated. 'Oh, great . . .' He gazed at the fire. 'And there was me thinking you and your robo-girl here had some sort of high-tech *beacon* or something to bring them here!'

Becks shook her head. 'Negative. No beacons.'

Liam raised a hand to hush her. 'That's just the way it is, Mr Kelly. There's nothing I can do about that.'

Laura bit her lip. 'That . . . that doesn't sound like much of a chance, though – a message traced in the ground surviving millions of years in one piece?'

'Survivin' that long,' added Juan, '*and* bein' found as well, man. What's the chances of that?'

Liam shrugged. 'Maybe we can improve our chances.' He looked at Franklyn. 'Do we not know where the first fossils were discovered? I mean historically? That's actually *known*, right?'

Whitmore and Franklyn exchanged a glance. 'Well, yes,' said Whitmore. 'It's common knowledge where the first *American* dinosaur fossils were discovered.'

Franklyn nodded. 'In Texas, of course. Right here in Texas.' Behind his bottle-top glasses, his eyes suddenly widened. 'Yes! Oh, hang on! Yes . . . Dinosaur Valley. Right, Mr Whitmore?'

Whitmore nodded. 'Good God, yes, you're right, Franklyn. Near Glen Rose, Texas.'

'Glen Rose?' Liam shrugged. 'Would that be far away?'

Kelly's scornful frozen expression of cynicism looked like it was thawing. 'Not that far from where the TERI labs were, actually. About sixty miles away.'

'Dinosaur Valley State Park,' continued Whitmore. 'It's a protected area now, a national landmark. At the beginning of the 1900s, I think, some of the first fossils were found along a riverbed there. Lots of them.'

'The Paluxy River,' said Franklyn, 'where the fossils were found, was thought to be the shoreline of some Cretaceous-era sea.'

Liam looked from Whitmore to Franklyn. 'So? We could get to this place, right? You fellas know exactly where it would be?'

Both shook their heads. 'Not really,' said Whitmore. 'How

could we know that?' He gestured around at the jungle. 'It's an entirely different landscape.' He laughed. 'Hell, it's out there somewhere!'

'I know where it is in relation to the TERI labs,' said Kelly. The others looked at him. 'Well, I drive in to work from Glen Rose. It's where I live. I pass the signs for Dinosaur Valley Park every day on the way up to the interstate. It's just outside Glen Rose, about a mile north of the town.'

'I have geo-coordinates for the town of Glen Rose,' said Becks.

Liam looked at her. 'You do?'

'Of course. It was part of the data package Maddy Carter uploaded prior to departure. I have the complete set of US Geological Survey maps for the State of Texas.'

Liam's eyes glistened by the light of the campfire. 'We could actually do this!' He looked at them all, piecing together on the fly something that was beginning to resemble a plan. 'Then, in theory, Becks, you could lead us right to this place that will one day become this *dinosaur park*?'

'Affirmative.'

'And if we know some fossil-hunting fellas find a whole load of fossils, as you said, Mr Whitmore, sometime in the 1900s, then could we not place some fossils of our own right there?'

'I suppose we –'

'Negative,' cut in Becks. She understood now where Liam was going with this. 'That would represent a significant contamination risk.'

Liam clenched his teeth in frustration. 'Come on, Becks, we have to break a few eggs, so we do.'

She cocked her head. 'Break eggs?'

'You know . . . how does it go? *To make an omelette.* We leave a message to be found. So, all right, it causes a new load of contamination problems. But then we have a chance at being rescued, getting these people back home where they should be, and then . . . then we go and fix that little problem.'

'This action introduces a third independent source of contamination.' She looked coolly at the group gathered around the campfire. 'Already there are two potential sources of time corruption. One in 2015 – the absence of Edward Chan. The second, this time, the presence of humans where there should not be any. Either or both contamination sources have a high probability of already causing significant time waves in the future.'

'What if . . .' started Jonah, but he almost stopped when every pair of eyes swung on to him. Clearly now wasn't the time for some flippant wisecrack. But he continued anyway. It seemed like a smart idea to him. 'What if . . . like . . . we left a message that was, you know, like, *too* important to become common knowledge.'

They stared at him in silence. No one was telling him to shut up, so he elaborated. 'I mean, like hushed up. Like, say, Roswell.'

Liam shrugged. 'Roswell?'

Kelly snorted a dry laugh. 'The supposed sight of a crashed UFO in 1947. Conspiracy nuts love that story. According to them it was a real flying saucer from outer space with real live LGM onboard.'

Laura saw Liam purse his lips in confusion. 'Little Green Men,' she said helpfully.

'Anyway,' continued Kelly, 'despite the fact it was most probably just a crashed test jet of some kind, you still get nut-jobs going on about wanting to free the little green men from their years of medical testing and enforced imprisonment.'

Jonah made a face. 'Yeah . . . but how do we *know for sure* it ain't true, Mr Kelly, eh? Point is, it could've been just a test jet, it could've been an alien spaceship, but the world will never know 'cause the government being, like, totally paranoid douche bags, hushed it all up. Kept the secret to themselves.'

'Oh, come on, kid,' said Kelly, 'that's a load of –'

Liam waved him silent. 'Hang on! No, wait! Jonah has a point . . . I think.' He scratched his cheek, deep in thought for a moment. 'Look, the point is people like the government . . . Your American government, right, if someone, some everyday person discovered a fossil that suggested something as amazing as the invention of time travel and they told the government, what would they do?'

'You kiddin'?' said Juan. 'They'd end up all over it like a rash, man. Secret service, Homeland stiffs in black suits an' dark glasses an' stuff.'

'I'll tell you, dude. Whoever found it would end up having an unfortunate accident,' said Jonah, looking at Kelly. 'Always happens, like . . . always. In fact, anybody who knew about it, was related to somebody who knew about it, would end up dead or in Guantanamo or someplace. Either way, there wouldn't be anyone walking around talking about it.'

'That's what I mean,' said Liam. 'It would remain a secret.' He looked at Becks. 'And so nothing major would be changed by it. The world wouldn't be talking about it. The world wouldn't know about it.'

Behind her narrowing eyes he guessed her computer was hard at work processing that notion. Looking for a percentage probability figure.

Whitmore nodded. 'That's how the intelligence agencies work, by putting up a poker face. Give nothing away. You know something? You keep it to yourself. You know something about the enemy, say the Russians . . . you don't change a thing about the way you behave. You act normal so the enemy don't know you've got something on them.'

Liam nodded. 'Exactly! Just like in the Second World War. I read something about those Enigma codes and all. And how the Americans and British couldn't sometimes react to the German messages they'd intercepted, otherwise the Germans would have figured out they'd cracked their secret codes.' He looked down at the muddy ground at his feet. Subconsciously the toe of his left shoe drew spirals in the dirt. 'So I don't know yet what kind of a message we could write. But we'd want something we know they'd *have* to keep secret. But, more importantly, we want a message they'd need to take directly to our field office.'

'That will compromise the agency's secrecy,' warned Becks.

Liam shrugged. 'I know . . . but another problem to fix later, huh?'

She scowled silently at that. 'It is another protocol conflict.'

'So you can blame it on me when we get back,' he said with a grin.

The group considered Liam's plan in silence for a while as the fire crackled and hissed between them.

'I reckon your idea sounds cool,' said Lam. 'I'm in.'

Liam noticed a couple of heads nod.

'All right, then,' he said finally. 'All right, then.' This felt good, having something at least half-figured out, something for them all to work towards. 'Becks, we'd need for them to know when we are, you know? As close as you can get it. So you do what maths in your head you need to do.'

She nodded slowly. 'Affirmative.'

'And maybe we'll need some sort of device erected exactly where we landed, right? So that if –' he corrected himself – '*when* they get our message and have an approximate time period to start density probing, we need something that's constantly moving to and fro in that space. Creating some sort of a movement, a disturbance?'

'Correct.'

'You mean like a windmill or somethin'?' asked Ranjit.

Becks nodded. 'Affirmative. A device of that kind would be suitable.'

'And we'll need to make some preparations for a long hike. Food, water, weapons, those sorts of things.' Liam looked around at them. 'And we'll need to leave someone behind to man the camp and lift the bridge after we're gone.'

'Also to maintain the density interference device. It must function constantly. All the time,' said Becks.

Liam looked over his shoulder out towards the darkness, towards the middle of the clearing where they'd landed over a week ago. 'Yes, you're right. It'd be bad news for us if a density probe passed through here once, found nothing and moved on.'

Liam's grin was infectious and began to spread among the others.

He looked at Becks. 'Is this acceptable?'

She nodded slowly. 'The plan has a low probability of success.' She smiled, quite nicely this time. 'But it is possible, Liam O'Connor.'

CHAPTER 34

2001, New York

Sal watched the world go by. *Her world*, that's how she thought about it: Times Square, New York, eight thirty in the morning, Tuesday 11 September 2001.

She knew it so well now. She knew everything that existed in this thoroughfare and everything that was meant to happen at this very moment in time. For instance . . . she looked around . . . and there they were: the old couple in matching jogging pants, huffing slowly side by side; the FedEx guy with an armful of packages, dropping one of them on the pavement and looking around to see whether anyone had noticed his hamfistedness; two blonde girls sharing headphones and giggling at something they were listening to.

Sal smiled.

All normal so far.

And there was the flustered-looking huddle of Japanese tourists standing outside TGI Friday's on the corner of 192 West and 46th Street, flipping anxiously through their phrase books to work out how to ask for a coffee and salt-beef and mustard bagels times nine.

Her eyes drifted up to the billboards overlooking Times Square; there was Shrek and Donkey, Mikey and Sully. There was the billboard for *Mamma Mia* . . . and walking slowly up the pavement towards her favourite bench, checking in every bin along the way and pushing a loaded shopping trolley in front of him, was the cheerful old tramp she saw this time every morning.

She sniffed the warm morning air; it smelled of car fumes and faintly of sizzling bacon and sausage meat. Again, quite normal – the smell of a city in a hurry and on its way to work.

'My world,' she whispered to herself. Her world . . . and all was well.

Only that was little consolation. If her world was still unaltered, if there weren't even the tiniest of differences to see here, it could only mean that Liam and the others had as yet to make any impact on whatever piece of history they'd landed in. There were two conclusions to draw from that, weren't there? Either they were being incredibly careful and had managed to avoid any kind of contamination at all . . . or . . .

'Or they arrived nowhere,' she muttered.

Dead. Torn to pieces by a wall of energy, by the explosion they'd caused. Or perhaps lost in chaos space. Foster had once ominously told her it was a place you'd never ever want – not in your wildest nightmares – to loiter around in.

Maddy was back from her trip to locate Foster. She'd not managed to find him. Sal had thought it was a long shot. But she seemed to have cheered up a little, seemed hopeful that they were going to get them back home yet. For some reason she'd been gabbling on about expecting, when the bubble reset at twelve o'clock tonight and they were 'reset' back to Monday morning, the first thing they'd hear would be a knock on the archway's door, and somebody standing outside, perhaps feeling silly, uncertain, and holding in their hand some sort of artefact from history with Liam's scruffy handwriting scrawled across it.

Sal wondered why Maddy was so sure that was going to happen, that the answer to this little mess they were in was actually going to deliver itself to their front door like the morning post.

Maddy slurped on her third Dr Pepper and placed it back on the desk beside the other two, now forming an orderly queue of crumpled cans. She could feel the sugar kick building up inside and the office chair twisted one way then the other as she pulled on the edge of the desk.

'Well?' she said. 'What do you think, Bob?'

> Your thinking is logical. However, my AI duplicate would offer Liam caution against this course of action.

'Of course you would, Bob . . . because that's a hard-coded protocol.'

The cursor blinked for a few seconds.

> Also because of the danger of revealing the location of this field office.

'But Liam would still go and do something like that, right? He'd override your warning?'

> I am unable to answer that, Maddy.

'But, come on, you know him better than me or Sal.'

> He has broken protocols before. He is capable of impulsive decisions.

Maddy smiled. 'That he is.'

She picked up her can again and tossed another fizzy mouthful down. 'So, like, if somebody in history does find a message from him . . . I guess we're going to have to do a lot of tidying up after ourselves.'

> It will depend on who discovers the message. And when in history that person comes from.

'Well, it would be dropped somewhere, some*time* in the

state of Texas. It could be anyone from some Apache Indian, or maybe a cowboy to . . . I dunno, maybe a civil-war soldier or an oil driller, or some college kids goofing around off the main highway. It could be *anyone*.'

> You presume they have only travelled back in time a hundred or two hundred years. It is equally possible they exist in what will one day be Texas long before the arrival of colonials. It is equally possible they exist in a time before the arrival of Native Americans.

'Isn't there a way you could at least best-guess how far back in time they've gone?'

> Negative. However, it might be possible for my AI duplicate to compare the density of tachyon particles in the vicinity of the explosion and the arrival point. The decay attrition is constant and this would give a fairly precise indication of when they are.

She stared at the screen. 'Really?'

> Affirmative. It will depend on how accurate the reading was.

If Bob was right, if that was true and they had a time-stamp, then getting some sort of message through time to her was the *only* course they could take. And Liam and the version of Bob's AI that was with him were smart enough to come to the exact same conclusion.

'I've got a feeling it's going to be all right, I really do.'

> I hope you are correct, Maddy.

She nodded, wishing she had just a little of Liam's laid-back devil-may-care attitude. She tilted her can and swilled another mouthful. 'Let's have some music . . . It's like a freakin' graveyard in here.'

> I have an extensive database of music. What would you like for your listening pleasure?

‘Something heavy . . . something rocky.’

> Clarify ‘heavy’, ‘rocky’.

‘Bob . . . just give me something *lively*, then.’

> I can analyse the audio files in my database for variables such as beats-per-minute, wave-form, volume, number of times played.

‘Do that,’ she cut in. ‘Do that . . . number of times played. Give me something the previous team liked to listen to.’

> Affirmative.

She heard his hard drive whirring softly, then a moment later the speakers on the desk either side of the main monitor began to chug with a heavy drum beat.

> Is this acceptable?

She sat back in her chair and put her feet up on the desk. It sounded pretty good to her, a bit like Nine Inch Nails, Marilyn Manson . . . a bit like Chilli Peppers. ‘Yeah, cool . . . I like it.’

The music echoed around the archway, bouncing off the cool brick walls, making the place feel a little more alive.

CHAPTER 35

65 million years BC, jungle

Liam watched Becks and the men lowering the bridge between them. He was surprised at the strength of the vine rope, showing no signs yet of fraying and snapping despite the tree trunk having been raised and lowered a dozen times already. It thudded down on the boulders on the far side of the river, bouncing and flexing as it settled into place.

'All right,' he shouted over the roar of the river. 'Everyone who's not staying . . . let's go.'

The first of those that were going along on the trip began to carefully bum-shuffle their way along the log, getting damp with spray from below. Twelve of them in total, leaving four behind to man the camp: Joseph Lam and Jonah Middleton, Sophia Yip and Keisha Jackson. Lam, as the only adult, was in charge, and Becks had made sure he fully understood how important it was to keep the 'windmill' rotating its arms.

The contraption was a post with a balanced crossbar like a pair of scales and someone's rucksack on one side slowly leaking – one at a time – pebbles on to the ground. As the weight adjusted and the 'scales' slowly tilted, it turned a simple windmill: a long, thin spar of wood that swung through the air with a regular rhythm. Every few hours the rucksack needed to be topped up again to maintain the blade's swinging action. It couldn't be allowed to stop.

Lam understood enough of its purpose already – maintaining a regular metronome-like signature of movement. Becks also briefed him on the warning signs that the area in the immediate vicinity was being probed: heat, a momentary localized jump in temperature of about ten degrees and a slight visual shimmering. If a probe actually did occur while they were gone, she'd continued, there would almost certainly be another one directly afterwards to 'double-check' the rhythmic interference. And, provided the windmill was still waving and duplicating the same unnatural pattern, he could expect a two-yard-wide time window to open and for someone to emerge from it, looking for them.

Lam assured them he'd set up a rota to keep the contraption turning and then wished them all luck.

They'd spent a few days preparing to set off on the trip. Sixty miles heading north-east, with no idea at all what sort of terrain they were going to have to cross. It could be jungle all the way. It could turn to desert for all they knew. Which was why they each carried in their school rucksacks as many plastic bottles as had come through with them full of drinking water. They had some food too, parcels of grilled fish meat wrapped in broad waxy leaves and tied up with vine rope. Enough food and water to last them a few days and hopefully they could forage for more along the way.

Kelly was first across and waited for the next with a helping hand extended.

Everyone also had a weapon now, either a spear or metal-shard hatchet, or both. Juan had even managed to produce three surprisingly good bows from suitably sturdy branches and a quiver full of arrows from sharpened bamboo canes, with fletching made from thin strips of bark. The arrows had proved to be rubbish against the hard wood of a tree trunk, splintering on impact. But, tested on the long bulky carcass of one of those huge fish, the arrows had gone almost entirely through.

Liam wondered, however, if a volley of their arrows would do little more than irritate a T-rex, if they met one.

Sixty miles. He hoped the terrain ahead of them was as free of lumbering prehistoric monsters as this jungle had so far proved to be. Other than those ugly mudfish in the river, and that bloody carcass they'd encountered over a week ago, the only living things he'd seen had been dragonflies the size of seagulls and bugs the size of rats, although at night the jungle seemed to echo with the curious haunting calls of a host of unknown creatures.

The others were mostly across now, wet from the spray of the river and the sweat of exertion in this hot and humid jungle. Becks was the last one across. She walked nimbly and confidently along the flexing trunk. Perfect balance and absolutely no fear of falling into the turbulent froth beneath.

Liam pursed his lips, jealous of that. To know no fear, to not have that gnawing sensation of terror in your stomach every time something thudded heavily out there in the dark of the jungle. Not that he could afford to show it. His stupid grin and the casual flick of his hand was all he allowed himself every time something happened that made him want to whimper. For example, he truly wished they'd not happened across that bloody ribcage. That meant something – or things – was out there sharing the jungle with them. Something they'd yet to see.

Becks jumped off the end of the log on to the silt riverbank beside Liam. 'Are you ready to proceed, Liam O'Connor?'

He sucked air through his teeth as he glanced around at the others. They all seemed to be looking at him to lead the way. 'North-east, you say, Becks?'

Becks's eyelids fluttered once as she consulted onboard data. 'Three hundred and eleven degrees magnetic,' she said, pointing her finger towards the thick apron of trees ahead of them. 'We must proceed in that direction.'

'Right, then,' he said, grasping his spear in both hands. He looked back over his shoulder at the four they'd left behind on the far side of the river, and cupped his mouth. 'I'll have a pint of stout to celebrate when we get back!'

They cocked their heads and looked confused. So did everyone on this side.

'Stout? . . . Ale?' he said. 'You know?'

Whitmore scratched his beard thoughtfully. 'Do you mean *beer*?'

Liam shook his head. 'You Americans really have no idea what a good beer is, do you?'

Whitmore shrugged. 'I had a Guinness once.'

Becks shook her head earnestly. 'Liam O'Connor, we do not have any alcoholic beverages in the camp. You will not be able to have a *stout*.'

'Oh, doesn't matter,' he sighed. 'I was only trying to be funny. Shall we just get on with this?'

'Affirmative.' She looked up. The sun was breaching the tree tops, sending a scattering starburst of rays across the morning sky. 'I calculate we have nine and a quarter hours of daylight before the sun sets again.'

'Then let's get a wriggle on,' said Liam. 'We got a lot of miles to cover.'

Broken Claw watched them step off right past him and into the jungle. Right past him. He was amazed at how little the new creatures seemed to see with their small eyes. Broken Claw could quite easily have reached out from the hummock of tall grass he was crouching behind and touched one of them.

The rest of his pack were there with him, dotted around beneath the shelter of ferns, behind the slender trunks of the trees that lined the river, as many hunting males as he had teeth in his mouth. The females and the younger pack members, a little further back in the jungle for safety. So many of them hiding within a few yards of them, and yet none of these curious pale upright creatures seemed to have any idea they were being watched.

Broken Claw struggled to make sense of that. Perhaps these things had spotted them, but for some cunning reason were hiding their reactions? Again, another reason to be wary of them. That and those sticks they carried, those sticks that could easily trap fish from the raging river. And new things. Curved sticks with a taut line of vine stretched from one end to the other. He wondered what these new devices did.

The new creatures stumbled clumsily and noisily past, up the gentle incline of the bank, and disappeared into the dark canopy of the jungle. Broken Claw turned from them to study the others on the far side of the river. They were pulling on another length of vine and he watched in silent awe as the tree trunk across the water slowly jerked and wobbled and raised inches at a time, reminding him of one of the large plain-dwellers, raising its head and long neck after drinking from a pool of water.

He understood this thing now. He understood its purpose.

A way across the dangerous water. A way that could be raised and lowered at will.

He caught sight of yellow eyes dotted here and there, the intent gaze of his extended family pack. They too were watching the tree rise, apparently under its own power. That was good. Good that they were seeing for themselves how wary they must be of these harmless-looking new arrivals.

Broken Claw offered a soft bark and the yellow eyes vanished. And the pack, like a ghostly dawn mist dissipating under the warm light of a rising sun, was suddenly gone, as if they'd evaporated into the jungle.

CHAPTER 36

65 million years BC, jungle

It was gone mid-afternoon as they neared the crest of the steep jungle mountain they'd been struggling up since dawn. Through fleeting gaps in the foliage canopy, Liam had caught glimpses of an ebony ridge of peaks ahead of them, to the left and right, as far as he could see. He'd considered suggesting they turn left or right to try finding a way round, but that might mean a detour of days. Better, he decided, to press on up the sloping jungle hillside and tackle the ridge. At least it would be all downhill on the far side.

Up ahead, now, the jungle was fast thinning, giving way to smaller withered trees trying to find a foothold on a ground of shale and gravel dotted with coarse tufts of grass. Just ahead of him Becks emerged into sunlight.

He noticed that her back, taut with muscle, was bone dry. *Don't these clones ever sweat?* Liam was drenched. Every inch of his skin was slick with perspiration, the salt running down from his fringe stinging his eyes.

Behind him he could hear Franklyn and Whitmore talking. They hadn't stopped since they'd set out from the camp, a relentless jabbering to and fro on all things prehistoric. It was certainly reassuring to know their group had what sounded like a fair bit of expertise on this alien environment, but Liam would happily have paid a ship steward's monthly wage for them to just shut up for five minutes.

Whitmore dabbed at his damp forehead. 'But I want to know why we haven't seen any yet. This Mesozoic era was very favourable to the larger species. I mean –'

'No need to patronize me, Mr Whitmore,' Franklyn cut in. 'I know all that. I know this was the most densely populated era, that the Cretaceous was really the time of the dinosaurs. Much more so than the Jurassic era.'

Whitmore nodded. 'Mind you, it wouldn't have sounded quite so snappy if they'd called that film *Cretaceous Park*, would it?'

'At least it would have been more *accurate*,' said Franklyn. 'But it's so strange, don't you think? I mean, Dinosaur Valley State Park isn't so far away . . . and the Paluxy riverbed there is covered in fossils from all types of species. How come this jungle valley's, like, *deserted*?' Franklyn's voice was laden with disappointment. 'I mean, here we are . . . the *perfect* time, in fact, to see *all* the classic species: T-rex, ankylosaurus, stegosaurus, triceratops, and yet we've seen nothing.'

'It could be the jungle itself is unfavourable terrain for the larger animals.'

'That's not true,' replied Franklyn. 'It's nutrient heaven for the herbivores. And where there are herbivores you should also find carnivores. This jungle should be full of them.'

'Well,' said Whitmore, looking up the slope at the thinning vegetation and craggy peak ahead of them, 'no more jungle now.'

They and the rest of the party followed Liam and Becks out of the lush green into a mostly grey-brown world of slate and shingle. Up ahead the slope rose to a fractured cliff face of sharp slate angles. He could see that the robo-girl was already climbing up it, making swift progress from one treacherous handhold to the next. He watched her pulling herself up the sheer cliff face without any apparent difficulty.

Robo-girl. Now they all knew she was some kind of a robot, and after seeing her nearly skewer Laura like one of those mudfish – and, Lord knows, if Liam hadn't intervened, she would have killed them all, one after the other – there was no way anyone was going to entirely trust her.

Whitmore's feet slid on the shale as he scrambled awkwardly up the last fifty yards to the base of the cliff to join Liam.

'We . . . we're . . .' Whitmore gasped like an asthmatic as he wiped the sweat from his brow. He looked up at the sheer rock face. 'We're climbing that?'

'Yup,' said Liam.

'I . . . I'm . . .' He was still heaving to catch some air. 'I'm not sure I'll be able to.'

Liam shook his head as he peeled the rucksack off his back. 'Not a lot of choice, Mr Whitmore. It's that direction we need to go.'

He swallowed anxiously. 'Uh . . . I'm really not so great with heights.'

'Don't worry about that, Mr Whitmore. She can pull you up if you'd like.'

Franklyn puffed and wheezed up the last few yards, kicking loose shale beneath his trainers. 'That goes for me too. I'm exhausted.'

Liam looked up the rock face and saw Becks was already at the top and bracing her legs against an outcrop for balance. She pulled the heavy coils of vine rope off her shoulder, secured one end round her waist and tossed the rest down. It clattered on to the shale with several dozen yards in length to spare.

Liam looked at them both and down at the others making their way up the last few dozen yards of the mountainside. Beyond them he could see the green carpet of the jungle rolling all the way down the steep peak they'd been ascending to the deep valley below. He thought he could just make out the hairline silver glint of the river snaking through the lush emerald carpet, and there it was . . . a small oval of lighter green no bigger than his fingernail: their clearing.

'I am ready to proceed,' Becks called down.

They all studied the cliff face unhappily: sixty-foot high, all razor-sharp edges and craggy outcrops that promised to impale or slice anyone unfortunate enough to take a tumble.

'Don't all be chickens,' said Becks.

Liam glanced up at her and saw she was smiling.

Did she just try to be funny?

'Cluck, cluck,' she added in her monotone voice.

Liam shook his head, put his hands on his hips and smiled. 'So, I see you've found a sense of humour, Becks!'

'I have been observing and learning humorous dialogue exchanges, Liam. I am now capable of delivering basic humorous responses.'

'Well done!' he shouted back.

'You are all little chickens. Cluck, cluck, cluck,' she said again with a hint of pride in her dry voice.

Not exactly hilarious, Liam decided, as he looked around at the concerned expressions on the others. But at least her AI was having a go at being more human.

'Is she all right?' asked Juan.

Liam shrugged. 'It's her attempt at a joke. Don't worry. She's fine.' He looked up at her. 'Becks! Maybe we should save the joking around for later? All right? You're scaring the kids.'

Her face straightened. 'Affirmative.'

'OK, then.' He turned back to the others. 'Who's first?'

There wasn't exactly a rush.

Liam was the last one up.

As Becks hefted him up on to the ridge and helped him to his feet, he could see she looked fatigued. In fact, he realized, it was the first time he'd ever seen her looking like that. Genuinely spent. 'You OK, Becks?'

'Recommendation: I should now consume protein and then rest for several hours,' she said. Her grey eyes met his for a moment and he wondered if there was a hint of gratitude in her expression, gratitude that he'd bothered to ask if she was OK.

'OK, you do that,' he said, slapping her shoulder. 'We could all probably do with a rest. Maybe we should set up camp here for tonight?'

She considered that for a moment, panning her eyes around the immediate surroundings. 'This is an acceptable location.'

'Right. I'll tell the others.' He wandered across the top of the peak towards the rest of them. They were clustered together and staring out over the sloping ridge on the far side of the peak. From where he stood, he could see nothing but a rich blue sky and a far-off top-heavy bank of cloud hanging above a flat horizon like a giant floating anvil.

'What is it? Can you see something?' He clattered over, kicking stones and raising dust until he was standing right beside them. 'Oh . . . my,' his voice fluttered softly.

'There's all the dinosaurs you've ever wanted to see, kid,' said Whitmore to Franklyn.

The peak sloped down gently, grey shale gradually giving way in patches to an enormous plain of verdant grassland dotted with islands of jungle – tall straight deciduous canopy trees draped with the vines they'd come to rely on. Around the patches of jungle, herds of huge beasts Liam couldn't begin to name grazed lazily in the late-afternoon sun. Between the slowly meandering groups of giants, smaller packs of fleet-footed beasts flocked and weaved in an endless zig-zagging race.

'My God,' whispered Kelly. 'This is really . . . quite . . . incredible.'

Whitmore and Franklyn were grinning like a pair of children in a toy store.

Beyond the sweeping plain, Liam noticed the flat horizon changed from a drab olive colour to a rich turquoise.

Laura was frowning at that, confused. 'Is that an *ocean* over there? I don't recall Texas having a freakin' ocean in the middle of it.'

Franklyn nodded. 'Sixty-five million years ago there was,' he said, adopting the learned air of a college principal. 'An inland ocean that ran north–south up the middle of America, cutting it in two. In fact, Laura, you probably wouldn't recognize Earth if you were looking at it from orbit right now.'

Liam watched in silence for a good minute, stunned, like everyone else, into stillness and quiet as he gazed out on a scene that no human before had ever witnessed, nor should ever witness again. A moment of incalculable privilege, uniqueness. Once upon a time – and it felt like another lifetime now – he'd been standing in the creaking bowels of a dying ship, waist deep in ice-cold water, facing certain death and crying like a small child. And there was Foster, holding his hand out to him uttering a promise that if he joined him there were going to be things he'd see, wonderful things. Incredible things.

'Well, this is certainly one of them,' Liam whispered to himself.

'What's that?' said Kelly.

Liam roused himself and grinned. 'Nothing, I just said . . . so, this is where all you big fellas have been hiding.'

A good-natured ripple of laughter spread among them.

'We're camping up here tonight,' he announced, studying the distant strip of ocean blue on the horizon. 'And tomorrow we'll be at the seaside, so we will.'

CHAPTER 37

65 million years BC, jungle

Liam savoured the warmth of the fire on his face and hands. It had turned out to be surprisingly cool up here on the peak once the sun had gone down, and his sweat-damp clothes had begun to feel uncomfortably chilly against his skin.

In the sky above the dark plain spread out before them, the last stain of day spread a warm, rich, amber light along the flat horizon and the night was beginning to fill with the distant haunting chorus of creatures calling to each other across miles of open plain.

He heard the scuff of boots and skittering shale approaching out of the dark. Becks appeared and sat down heavily next to him. 'Hello, Liam.'

'Hello,' he replied, chewing on the rubbery corner of his reheated grilled mudfish. He looked at her eyes, glistening as they reflected the campfire in front of them. He wondered what went on behind them when she wasn't busy assessing mission priorities or threat factors. He wondered if that tiny organic brain linked to her computer could appreciate how beautiful that amber sky was . . . or enjoy the pleasing sensation of warmth from the fire.

'Your AI's done a bit of *growing* again, hasn't it?' he said presently. 'Your *cluck, cluck* thing earlier was . . . well, about as funny as one of my old Auntie Noreen's jokes, but . . . the thing is it sounded almost human.'

'Thank you.' She nodded. 'It has been useful to me observing these younger humans. Their social interactions are more heavily nuanced by emotional indicators and less restricted by expected convention.'

His face creased as he digested that. 'You mean they're more likely to blurt out whatever they're thinking than adults?'

'Affirmative.'

'Well now,' he said, smiling, 'that's probably true.'

Laura Whitely, sitting opposite, caught what they were saying over the babble of dinosaur talk going on between Kelly, Whitmore and Franklyn. 'I don't *blurt*,' she said. 'Children do that.'

Becks's gaze shifted to her. 'Are you not a child?'

She gave Liam an *is she for real?* look, one eyebrow cocked with incredulity. 'Excuse me? I'm fifteen. I'm not a child. I'm a teenager.'

'You still have four years of physical and mental growth to undergo before you are technically an adult human being,' said Becks. 'Optimum mental and physical functionality is obtained at nineteen years of age. This makes you still a child.'

'Yeah? And what about you? What are you, then?'

Becks's jaw dropped open, a facial expression Liam had not seen her pull before. Nor an expression he could recall Bob ever pulling either, for that matter. Becks's eyes gazed at the fire for a long, long time, the lids fluttering slightly every now and then.

She's really giving that some serious thought.

'I will . . .' she began after a while. 'I will never be a complete human being.'

Laura's face softened ever so slightly. A second ago she'd

looked like she wanted to square up to Becks, now she almost looked sorry for her. 'You sound sad about that.'

'Sad?' Becks considered that word. 'Sad,' she said again quietly. 'My developmental AI routines allow me to learn and replicate human behaviour patterns. But I am unable to directly experience emotions. This would affect my performance as a support unit.'

'So, let me get this straight,' said Laura, shuffling round the fire, closer to them so she wasn't being drowned out by Franklyn's droning voice. 'You're flesh and blood, just like a human being, but your head is, like, all robot?'

'My body is a genetically enhanced female human body. I have multiple-threaded muscle tissue capable of a five hundred and seventy-six per cent performance response.'

Laura looked at Liam. 'That means she's . . . what? Like, six times stronger than she should be?'

Liam nodded. 'Aye, that sounds about right.'

'I also have a high-density calcium-based support chassis –'

'Strong bones,' said Liam.

Laura nodded. It looked like she'd figured that out for herself.

'I also have a rapid-reaction, high white-cell-count fluid repair system.' Becks turned to Laura. 'My blood clots quickly.'

'Right.'

'All of this gene technology will be developed by W. G. Systems in the year 2043 for military applications: genetically engineered combat units.'

'Wow,' uttered Laura. 'You mean like super soldiers.'

'Correct. I was designed for war. Specifically subterfuge and covert operations.'

Liam smiled. 'But don't let that put you off her – she's a sweetie really.'

Becks looked at him curiously. 'Sweetie?'

Liam put an arm round her shoulders and hugged her clumsily. 'We go back a bit, Becks and me. Would you believe it, she used to be a man, so she did? Big chap, just like some muscle-man called Schwarzenhoffer or something. Apparently he becomes a president of yours sometime.'

'Oh my God.' Laura made a face. 'You don't mean *Arnold Schwarzenegger*?'

'That's the fella. Anyway, Becks was called Bob back then. But . . . well, you had a bit of a scrap, didn't you? And –'

'Caution,' said Becks. 'It is inadvisable to reveal details of previous missions.'

Liam hushed. Perhaps they'd revealed more than they ought. 'Yes, you're right. Sorry, Laura.' Liam decided to change the subject. 'Becks, we should consider what message we want to leave in the ground, you know?'

Becks nodded. 'Affirmative. This is important.'

Kelly overheard that. 'You guys discussing the help message?'

And that shut up everyone around the fire, even Franklyn.

'Yes,' replied Liam. 'I've been giving it some thought, Becks . . . We would have to actually reveal the exact date and location of our field office.'

She frowned. 'Negative. The location and time-stamp must remain known only to agency operatives.'

'But we *have* to, do you not see? Because Sal and Maddy aren't exactly likely to go fossil-hunting in Texas any time soon. It will be someone *else* who finds it. And the only way it will find its way to them is if we reveal that.'

'You know,' said Kelly, 'that kind of information would be mighty powerful stuff. The fact that time-travel technology exists. The fact that humans have actually been back to dinosaur times . . . that's world-changing information, Liam. You understand that, don't you? You mentioned time contamination and time waves and stuff like that . . . Won't it –?'

'Oh, for sure,' said Liam. 'That's the kind of nightmare we were recruited to *prevent* – contamination of the timeline.'

'And yet you'll be causing it.'

'I know . . . I know. But it's the only way.' He looked at Chan, sitting quietly between Leonard and Juan. 'The timeline is already badly broken. Who knows what state the future is in now? And, yes, by deliberately stamping a big ol' message into the ground, we're about to make it a lot worse. But – and it's taken me some time to see this for myself – time is like, I dunno, like liquid. It's fluid. What can be changed can be changed right back, so long as you know where to go and what to do. And, of course, as long as you've got a time machine.'

Liam nodded at Chan. 'We need to get Edward back to 2015. That fixes part of the problem. Then, once we've done that, Becks and I will come right back here and undo all that contamination.'

'How?'

'Very simple,' said Liam.

CHAPTER 38

65 million years BC, jungle

Liam looked down at the shale by his feet. He dragged a finger through it. The others watched curiously as his finger inscribed four letters in the gravel. He spelled the word *Help.* Then with his hand he messed it up. 'We'll erase the message we just left,' he said. 'And everything that happened as a result of it being discovered, well . . . it'll all *un-happen*. It'll all be erased too.'

'If your message includes the location of your base,' said Kelly, 'I assure you, it won't be some curious fossil-hunter that turns up, it'll be some secret government agency. NSA, CIA, maybe some spooks we don't even know about . . . They'll storm the place. Kick the door in. Delta Force guys with guns. What you've got is too valuable.'

'Oh.' Liam hadn't considered that.

'You could be endangering your colleagues,' said Laura.

'They wouldn't *hurt* them, would they? They'd just want to be asking questions, would they not?'

Kelly shrugged. 'With something like time-travel technology at stake? Who knows? Our secret services have a long history of shooting places up first and asking questions later.'

Whitmore cut in. 'Oh, come on! They're professionals, the best in the world!'

Several of the others joined in. Some agreeing with that, some of them disagreeing.

Liam looked at Becks. 'Maybe this is not such a great idea.'

'You wish me to proceed with the *alternate plan*?' she said softly.

Liam looked at her, pleased that she'd had the sense to ask that in little more than a whisper. Not so encouraged, though, seeing one of her hands flinching and reaching for a hatchet.

'No, not yet,' he said, reaching out and grasping her hand in his. 'Not yet, OK?'

She nodded.

'Unless,' said Edward quietly, his voice almost lost beneath the to and fro of all the others. 'Unless, there's a really important reason *not* to hurt anyone.'

The others stopped and looked at him. It was the first thing he'd said all evening. All day, in fact.

Edward's eyes widened as they all stared at him. 'I . . . I was just saying . . .'

'Go on,' said Liam.

'Well . . . if part of your message was a . . . was in, like, a code. Then there's a reason to . . . you know, *not* to want to shoot everyone up, because they know they'd need someone to decode it.'

Liam pursed his lips in thought. 'That's true.' A code, a secret, hinting at still further secrets and revelations. What person wouldn't want to know more?

'If a message is going to lead some government spooks right up to the front door of your secret organization,' said Kelly, 'then you can bet the bit of the message they can't make sense of will be driving them nuts. Edward's right. They'll want your colleagues alive.'

'All right,' said Liam. 'So then the first bit of the message needs to be the time and place of our field office.' He turned to Becks. 'That's how the message will find its way to Maddy and

Sal. The rest . . . the time-stamp they need to aim for, that bit should be the super-secret coded bit. Can you come up with a code, Becks?'

She nodded. 'I can produce a mathematical algorithm and use that as an alpha-numeric offset code. My duplicate should be able to recognize the pattern of the algorithm and produce a decode key.'

'No,' said Edward, shaking his head. 'It's too easy to break a math-based code. If they . . . you know, if they put a big enough computer on it, they could crack it. Simple.'

Kelly nodded. 'And you can bet the NSA or the CIA or whichever bunch of spooks ends up calling will have no shortage of computing power at their disposal to crunch your code.'

'There is no other way to generate a code that can be unlocked at the field office,' said Becks. 'My duplicate needs to have the same library of algorithms –'

'*Every* math-based code can be broken,' said Edward, his quiet voice finding a little more confidence, 'you know? Eventually. It's just a case of how much computer power you put on it.'

'Edward's right,' said Howard. 'Think about it, what if the message is discovered, say . . .' He turned to Whitmore and Franklyn. 'When did they first discover fossils in this place we're headed to?'

Franklyn shrugged. 'Early 1900s.'

'Right. So if the American secret services of that time secured that fossil back then they'll have had a whole century of time to crack the algorithm and decode it before they come knocking.'

'But computers powerful enough to work on it were only developed in the '80s,' said Juan. 'Don' forget that.'

'That's more than enough time,' said Howard. 'They'll come knocking knowing the entire contents of the message. Their only concern will be securing your agency's HQ and confiscating all your technology. Your colleagues will be a secondary consideration.'

'Your code has to be like a personal thing,' said Edward. 'Like a secret. Something only you and they know.'

Howard shook his head. 'I'm thinking this is a seriously bad idea. We could end up really messing with history. And I thought you guys are meant to stop that kind of thing happening.'

'And staying here, young man?' said Whitmore. 'What do you think *that's* going to do to history? *Homo-sapiens* existing right now? Sixty-five million years before they're due?'

Howard shrugged. 'We won't exist for long, though, will we?' His words silenced the teacher. 'You actually think the sixteen of us are going to survive and thrive? You think we're going to breed and produce lots of offspring and establish a Cretaceous-era human civilization that's going to change the world?'

Whitmore shrugged and half-nodded. 'It's possible.'

Howard laughed. 'No, it's not. We'll eventually die out here.' He looked around at them. 'There are six females in the group.' He looked at Becks. 'Not counting you. I'm not really sure what you are.'

'I am incapable of sexual reproduction,' she replied flatly.

'Six fertile females,' continued Howard. 'We might be able to make a few babies, but there are too few of us to sustain ourselves. If disease doesn't get us, or some hungry carnivore, then in-breeding would eventually.' He managed a wistful smile. 'We'll die out soon enough . . . months, years, decades maybe . . . but it'll happen and history won't be changed by us having been here. Maybe we shouldn't do this. Maybe we should accept we're stuck here and –'

'You can forget that!' said Laura. 'I want to go home!'

Kelly nodded. 'I think we all want that, right?'

Heads nodded around the fire.

Liam sat forward, held his hands out towards the fire and rubbed them. 'We're doing the message, Leonard. We have to. Now I've just got to figure out something that only we . . . and *they* know.'

'How big is your agency?' asked Laura.

Liam smiled and replied hesitantly. 'Oh, you know, it's big. Lots of us, so there are.'

'You know them well?'

'Sure, we're all pretty close.'

'Friends?'

'Yes, I'd like to think we're –'

'Then maybe there's something like a song, or a film or something? You know? Something like that you could use as a common reference point for –'

Liam suddenly felt his hand being crushed by a vice-like grip. He looked down and saw Becks was holding it, and squeezing it.

'Ow! Becks, you're hurting me,' he hissed. 'What's the matter?'

She let go and looked at him, her eyes widened with a mixture of surprise, and perhaps even elation. 'I have had an idea, Liam O'Connor.'

CHAPTER 39

65 million years BC, jungle

From the darkness they watched them. Beyond the illumination of the dancing yellow flower in the middle. Broken Claw had seen this fascinating dancing creature only once before, after a storm. When a stab of light from the sky had come down and touched the long dead trunk of a tree. The yellow flower had engulfed it, consumed it, producing such unbearable heat as it did so. He'd been young then. And ever since then the yellow flower had been an occasional monster in his dreams, chasing him, reaching out for him, wanting so much to consume him.

And now here it was, *tamed* like some sort of a pet by these new creatures. They were gathered around it, unafraid of it, every now and then casually throwing a branch on to it and not even flinching as the creature reared up angrily, sending tendrils of light up into the dark sky.

He looked around at his pack, cowering further back down the slope, clearly unhappy at being out of the jungle and here in the open. This was not their terrain, this was not where they were strong. Open ground made them visible, it made them vulnerable. Larger predators existed in the open; large, lumbering and stupid predators like the tall upright one with tiny front claws, enormous jaws, powerful rear legs and a strong sweeping tail. His pack called it *Many-Teeth*.

Out in the open Many-Teeth could quite easily kill them

all. After all, Broken Claw's kind were small, fragile things compared to this powerful mountain of muscle and energy. But between them his family pack had killed quite a few in his living memory. And always in the same way: luring them into the jungle with the tempting cry of one of their young. A pitiful cry that perfectly replicated that of a young helpless plant-eater, a cry that signalled fear and proved an irresistible taunt to one of those large stupid beasts. Once among the densely packed trees, unable to sweep its tail easily, unable to turn quickly, the pack was always able to leap upon the various Many-Teeth they'd lured in that way and begin to tear through their thick hides and rubbery bands of tough muscle tissue to the vulnerable soft tissues inside as they thrashed and roared.

Broken Claw had led many such attacks in past seasons, always the first to gnaw his way through the hide and into the bellies of such creatures, slashing and pulling through the vulnerable insides as the creature still stomped and roared, pulling himself towards the throbbing red organ in its chest. It was slashing at this that usually felled a Many-Teeth. Broken Claw and the others knew that this organ – which seemed to have a life of its own, which every species of creature seemed to possess – was the source of its very life.

In the seasons of his youth, the jungles had once been full of the larger stupid species. So many of them in fact that they often killed many more than they could eat, often only bothering to consume their favourite organs and leaving the rest of the carcass to rot.

But there were fewer now, far fewer of the bigger creatures. They only existed on the plain these days.

Broken Claw understood a simple principle. They had hunted too many of them. They had been too successful for their own good in the jungle, and his family pack had been forced to migrate from one jungle valley to the next several times during his lifespan. Now too, in recent seasons, this jungle had become sparsely populated – another hunting ground that they'd almost completely exhausted.

There certainly was not enough food available in the jungle valley for these new creatures as well.

Slowly, lightly, he glided forward across the loose shale, mindful that his agile feet not dislodge anything that might make the slightest noise. Behind him he heard the soft barking cough of one of his mates warning him not to get too close to these things. He ignored her. He needed to listen to the noises these things made. Perhaps their sounds could be learned, even mimicked. Perhaps they could employ the same technique they used on the Many-Teeth, identifying a sound that could be practised and used by their young to lure one of the new creatures away from the others.

If just one of them could be isolated. They could study it, understand how dangerous it could be, understand its weakness. Perhaps in the last moments of its life, even share some of its intelligence. Then he could find out if this creature also had the same fluttering red orb in its ribcage, the organ that provided life.

CHAPTER 40

65 million years BC, jungle

Liam gazed up at the behemoth slowly ambling their way. 'You're sure it's a plant-eater?'

Franklyn laughed. 'Yes, relax, of course it is. It's an alamosaurus.'

Liam watched the enormous long-necked creature walk with ponderous deliberation across the open plain towards the patch of jungle behind them. He could feel each heavy step through the trembling ground.

Jay-zus-'n'-Mother-Mary, that thing's the size of a small ship!

He guessed he could park a double-decker tram in the space between its fore and its hind legs and still have room to stand on top. The creature's tiny head, little more than a rounded nub on the end of its long muscular neck, swept down close to the ground as it closed the distance between them. Finally coming to a halt to inspect the small bipedal creatures standing in front of it.

'Are you absolutely certain?' cried Liam, watching the thing's head hover at shoulder height just a few yards in front of him.

'Yes! He's probably more scared of you than you are of –'

'Oh –' Liam shook his head vigorously – 'I, uh . . . I very much doubt that.'

'See? He's just checking you out,' said Franklyn, slowly

stepping forward to join Liam and Becks. 'Hey there, big man!' he cooed softly. 'It's OK, we're not carnivores.'

'Well, actually, I am,' said Whitmore. 'A little veal and a nice bottle of Sancerre on a Saturday night.'

Small beady black eyes, in a rounded head not much bigger than a cider keg, studied Liam intently. Its nostrils flared for a moment as it inhaled the curious new smell of humans, then curiosity compelled it to take a solitary step forward. Liam felt the ground beneath his feet shudder.

'Oh, he likes you, man,' called out Juan.

Liam felt a fetid blast of warm air across his face and closed his eyes as the dinosaur's head moved even closer. '*Ohh . . . I'm not happy about this*,' he hissed out of the side of his mouth. Thick leathery lips the size of an automobile tyre probed his face, then moved up to explore the intriguing texture of his dark hair.

'Oh, he *really* likes you, man. Want us to leave you two alone?' chuckled Juan.

'Hair,' said Whitmore. 'That's an evolutionary step that's millions of years away for this creature. The texture of it must be fascinating to him.'

Liam felt a sharp tug on his scalp. 'Ow! Well, he's bleedin' well eating it now, so he is!' He slapped at the creature's mouth. '*Hey!* Ouch! Let go! *Becks!* Help!'

Becks reacted swiftly. She stepped towards him and swung a fist at the alamosaurus's nose. The blow smacked heavily against the leathery skin and with a roar of pain and horror the giant let go of Liam. Its thick muscular neck reared up suddenly, a tree-felling in reverse, and it let loose a deafening bellow that reminded Liam of the dying groans of the *Titanic*'s hull. The air vibrated with its startled roar.

Liam clasped his hands over his ears to protect his rattling eardrums, as the cry spread across the plain from one giant herbivore to the next. The alamosaur stumbled back from them on its tree-trunk legs, turning in a long cumbersome arc, and began to shamble away in a loping slow-motion run that felt through the ground like the early tremors of an earthquake.

'Oh, great!' shouted Franklyn. 'Now you started a stampede!'

The calm scene of moments ago, a vista of leviathans grazing peacefully across the open plain, had been instantly transformed into a deafening display of motion and panic. Liam watched the smaller species of plant-eaters scrambling to avoid being stampeded by the other alamosaurs darting into the islands of trees and ferns for cover.

'Whoa!' Juan was doubling up with excited laughter. 'Those alamo things are real chickens, man! Look at the suckers go!'

Amid the confusion of movement and kicked-up dust Liam caught sight of something else. Dark shapes behind them, half a mile away, smaller than any of the other species out on the plain. Just a glimpse of them, a second, no more. Then they were gone to ground, hidden among the knee-high tufts of olive-coloured grass scattered in threadbare clumps across the open plain.

Liam turned to ask if anyone else had seen them, but the others were still marvelling at the sight of an entire food chain on the move, a thunderous spectacle of swaying folds of leathery skin and sinews taut with panic.

He turned back to look again. Nothing. As if the dark shapes had never ever existed.

What the heck are those?

Vanished like skeins of dark smoke, like that ghostly seeker.

Or am I losing me mind now?

It was fully five minutes before some semblance of calm

returned to the area; the various species of herbivores gathered in a worried-looking cluster a mile away. Tall necks protruded from the pack standing fully erect, watching them from afar like impossibly large meerkats.

'Oh, that was fun,' said Laura. 'Can we go do it again?'

Liam looked at Becks. Her face was folded with a confused expression. 'Becks? What's the matter?'

She looked down at her fist, still balled up. 'I did not hit it very hard.'

'You must have hit a sensitive spot,' said Whitmore.

They made their way across the plain towards the coastline on the horizon, most of the time with Franklyn complaining about how Becks had ruined his chance to study the creatures up close. By noon they were standing among a scattering of boulders and looking at a broad beach of dark coarse sand and a tranquil tropical ocean sending gently lapping waves of surf up the shingle and back down again with a soothing hiss.

'So?' said Liam.

Becks studied the view for a long moment, her eyes narrowed. 'Twenty-one miles north-east of our current location.'

Liam grimaced. 'So then it's underwater, is it?'

'Negative,' she replied, pointing at the horizon ahead of them. 'This is a large bay. Observe the horizon.'

Liam looked again, squinting. Then he saw it: a pale line of low humps on the horizon that he'd earlier assumed were clouds. Following the uneven grey-blue line to the left he could see it becoming more distinct as it drew closer. The broad beach they were looking along seemed to promise that it was angling gradually towards the distant spur of land and, if they were patient enough with it, it would link up with the spur eventually.

'Recommendation: we follow the beach around to the landmass ahead.'

Liam nodded at the low hump of land. 'Is that the place we need to be?'

She nodded. 'Information: the distance of the landmass is nine point seven six miles.'

Whitmore nodded. 'Then that spur *has* to be it, right? That's what will one day be the fossil bed.'

Becks nodded slowly. 'Information: a ninety-three per cent probability you are correct.'

'My God,' he said, scratching his beard. 'Who knows? Some of the footprints we'll see along the beach over there might just end up being some of the fossils we've seen in museums in our time?' His eyes widened and he shook his head incredulously. 'Isn't that the craziest idea?' He slapped Liam on the shoulder. 'Time travel must drive you insane if you think about it too much.'

Liam cocked an eyebrow. 'Oh, I've had my share of headaches thinking on it, so I have.'

They stepped forward, down through the boulders and on to the coarse shingle. 'This is good,' said Becks to Liam, pointing at the beach. 'We are not leaving tracks.'

He looked down. She was right. The beach wasn't sand, it was a coarse gravel that clacked and shifted wetly underfoot, but left nothing as clear as a print behind them.

'Oh, good.' He nodded. 'So there you go – something to put a smile on your face, then?'

She gave that some thought. 'This is minimizing our overall contamination liability.' Her gaze shifted from their feet back up to him. 'Correct. That makes me . . . happy.'

'There you go, you miserable sod,' he replied cheerfully. 'Things are looking up. We'll be home soon enough.'

They clattered down through the wet shingle until the first warm waves of tropical water hissed up to and around their feet. Up ahead the others had decided to wade knee-deep into the sea and were splashing each other noisily. She pursed her lips in thought as she watched them, a curious gesture she must have picked up from one of the girls, Liam decided. A gesture that Bob's muscular face would have struggled to reproduce. 'If we successfully complete the mission, Liam O'Connor, and we return to the field office, do you intend to retire me?'

'Retire? What do you mean?'

'Terminate this body and replace it with a male support unit? I heard Sal Vikram refer to this organic frame as a "mistake".'

He'd not given it much thought. Becks was Sal's error – she'd not bothered to check the gender marker on the containment tube – and they'd not had time to consider growing another. But certainly neither Maddy nor Sal had mentioned terminating her and disposing of her body.

'Why would we want to go and do that, Becks?'

'The male support frame is eighty-seven per cent more effective than the female frame as a combat unit.'

'All right, maybe that's true, but why'd the agency give us female babies as well, then?'

'Female support frames can be useful for covert operations where a female cover is required.'

He scratched his head. 'Well now, I really don't see why we can't have one of each of you, you know? A Bob and a Becks. There're no agency rules, are there, you know, against us having two support units in a team?'

'Negative. I am not aware of any agency rules on that.'

'So, well, there you are . . . why not? We'll have two of you instead of one.'

They walked in silence for a while, Liam intrigued by how *human* her question had sounded.

'Have I functioned as efficiently as the Bob unit?' she asked after a while.

'Yes, of course. I don't know what we'd have done without you so far. But you know it's still so very weird. Aren't you actually Bob anyway? Or at least a copy of Bob in a different skin?'

'Negative. My AI has adapted enough since being copied to be considered a different AI ident. I have experienced data that Bob has not. Also, the organic brain that is interfaced with the AI is genetically different between the male and female support frames.'

'Right. But . . . you remember being Bob, right?'

'Of course. I recall all the incidents of our first mission, right up until the moment you removed my chip.'

Liam wished he couldn't remember that as well. 'Ugghh. Not something I'd like to do again in a hurry.'

'You successfully preserved the AI. It contained six months of adaptive learning,' she replied. 'Both Bob and I are six months closer to fully emulating human behaviour. We are both grateful.'

He shrugged modestly. 'Oh, you know, it's nothing. Just part of the job.'

'I am able to kiss you,' she said. 'This would be an appropriate gesture of gratitude. I have data.'

She began puckering her lips and Liam felt that odd conflicted sensation he'd felt after they'd first arrived in 2015: a tingling excitement offset with a sense of revulsion.

Bob, in a girl suit . . . remember.

'Uh . . . that's OK, Becks. A *thanks* is more than good enough.'

'Affirmative. As you wish.'

'Anyway, where the hell did you learn about *kissing*?'

'I have a detailed description from a book I was reading while I was installed in the mainframe.'

'Eh? What sort of books have you been reading?'

'The book is entitled *Harry Potter and the Deathly Hallows*.'

'What's that?'

'A novel. The digital file is in early twenty-first century PDF format. The file's original replication date is –'

'Hold on,' said Liam, stopping. 'Do you have that file in your database still?'

She nodded. 'My reading was interrupted. I wished to complete it. So I added it to my short-term cache.'

'And would Bob also have the exact same file on the computer system?'

'Of course.'

His mouth hung open. 'There's the code, then! Right there! That's the code you could use! Isn't it?'

Her eyelids fluttered as she processed the thought. 'You are talking of a book code?'

'That's right, a *Harry-Whatever-mijingamy* book code.'

CHAPTER 41

65 million years BC, jungle

Howard noticed the young boy walking alongside him, sloshing through the warm seawater.

'Hey,' he said.

Edward smiled. 'Hey. You always called Leonard, or do your friends call you Lenny?'

Howard shrugged; not a question he'd anticipated being asked. 'Uh . . . mostly just Leonard,' he replied. 'My mom calls me Lenny, but I hate that.'

'I heard someone say your best subject is math.'

He nodded. 'It was my –' He stopped, inwardly cursing. 'It . . . *is* . . . my favourite school subject. Always loved math. It's like, well, I dunno . . . I suppose it's like a sort of poetry that only a few people *get*. If you know what I mean? It's, like, exclusive.'

Chan nodded. 'Yeah, I know what you mean. That's why I like it. It's something I know and other people don't. It makes me feel kind of special, I guess. Maybe that's why I don't have any friends at school, cos they think I'm odd.'

Howard nodded. 'Yeah, I guess I'm the same. A loner.' He squinted up at the bright sun. 'Never ever get picked for sports, because I'm the geek.' He shrugged. 'But that's OK, cos I never liked sports anyway.'

Edward nodded. 'Me neither. It's for jocks and ditto-heads.'

'Ditto-heads?' Howard laughed. 'I like it.'

'You never heard that expression?'

Not in my time, he almost answered. But instead he just shook his head.

'Hey!' said Edward suddenly, and bent down to scoop up a curious twisted ammonite shell from the shingle.

'See? There are even bigger ones of those,' said Howard, nodding at some of the others, wading waist deep in the clear blue water, occasionally ducking down to pull shells out of the water to admire them.

They walked on in silence for a while, going a little further into the warm water. Up ahead, leading the way and deep in conversation, Howard could see the two 'agents' – Liam and his robo-girl. He shook his head at the irony of it. Despite their turning up in 2015 to 'save' Chan, they were all on the same side really, all trying to prevent the nightmare of time-travel technology from destroying the world. Same goal . . . different methods. He wondered how he'd never come across this agency in all the years of his campaigning, all the rallies and protests he'd been to . . . and no one, *no one*, had ever suggested, even as a joke, that there might be an agency out there actually using time travel itself to combat the corruptive effects of time travel. He wondered who was behind it, who'd set it up. Surely not the American government? Not any government, in fact. The internationally agreed penalties for that were severe. No politician would have the guts to risk having anything to do with time travel, because international law was brutal and strict on this matter. It was an automatic death penalty for any involved. The great Roald Waldstein had been a powerful speaker on the horrendous dangers of it. A great man, an influential man. Howard's small campaigning group had achieved far less. His group was little more than bunches of students in universities and colleges around the world.

But this secret agency, they were going about matters in the wrong way. Attempting to repair history that had been damaged by careless travellers? That was very much like trying to close the barn door after all the horses have bolted. No – worse than that . . . it was having to go out and hunt all those horses down then drag them kicking and screaming all the way back to the barn. On the other hand, his campaign group's approach had been far simpler.

Destroy the possibility of time travel at its very root. Instead of closing the barn door, they were burning the cursed thing down with all the horses still inside.

He looked at Edward Chan. The boy smiled back at him then looked down at the lustrous pink and purple sheen of the shell in his hand. He stroked the smooth surface, then held it out. 'You can have it if you want it, Leonard.'

Howard shook his head. 'No, it's er . . . no thanks.'

He has to die, you know that, Howard? Burn the barn, right? Burn it long before any horses get out.

He realized he was delaying the necessary, putting it off and putting it off. And yet he knew it had to be done. In theory the future – the future after the year 2015 – must *already* be changing, must *have changed* by now. It would be a world where this boy vanished in an explosion and never got to fulfil his destiny. It was surely a world where a man called Roald Waldstein would never become the figurehead of an international campaign, never become a billionaire from all his other inventions, never become a household name. And, yes, this world would still have its problems: dwindling supplies of resources, global warming, rising seas, migrating billions and dangerous levels of over-population. But . . . at least it would no longer have the ever-present threat of complete and utter annihilation dangling over it.

He'd once heard a speaker at a rally ask the audience what must lie beyond the dimension of space-time we all exist in. Is it Hell? And to meddle with dimensions beyond what we know was surely no different from opening a door to the devil himself and inviting him right on in. He'd spoken of a medieval artist called Hieronymus Bosch who'd claimed he'd once caught a glimpse of the devil and the underworld and painted endless nightmarish visions of what he'd seen. Perhaps, the speaker had said, perhaps what he'd glimpsed were dimensions beyond our understanding, a momentary rip in space and time. Howard shuddered at the thought.

You know the boy has to die, Howard. Burn the barn. Burn the barn. What are you waiting for?

He was so deep in thought he didn't at first register the voices from further up the beach. Voices crying out a warning, screaming a warning back at them.

Edward grabbed his arm and yanked him hard. Howard's thoughts were shaken away.

'What the h–?'

'RUN!' screamed Edward, pointing his finger at something behind him. Howard turned round to see an odd-looking dark wave approaching him fast. Water rolled down either side of an enormous grey hump, sliding up the shallows towards him like a gigantic torpedo. He spotted a large fin at the top of the large grey hump – large, very large . . . the size of a car, no, bigger – the size of a bus!

Edward was still pulling him back from the thing, trying to get Howard's leaden fight-or-flight response to do something. Howard started to react, but far too sluggishly, too clumsily. He stumbled backwards over something in the thigh-deep water and an instant later was flailing on his back, his head underwater. Surfacing a moment later, spluttering for air, his legs scrambling to find a steady footing below, all he could see now was an approaching dark cave, riding up out of the shallow water at him like a freight train, a cave lined with stalactites and stalagmites of razor-sharp teeth and dangling tatters of rotting meat swinging between them.

'*OH NO!*' was all he could scream as the gliding mass of glistening grey hide finally came to an abrupt rest and the cave, easily six foot across, snapped shut round one of his feet. He felt a vice-like grip on his ankle, the tough leather of his combat boots compressed agonizingly tight as something hard and sharp pressed from the outside. Then the beast began shaking its head vigorously from side to side and he knew bones had to be breaking and splintering in his ankle as he swirled through the water.

Howard's head was underwater. He felt pebbles, rocks and shells grind painfully up his back, and knew that meant the creature was now manoeuvring itself back from the shallows into deeper water.

He was holding his breath amid the tumbling underwater chaos . . . and, for a fleeting second, wondered why he was bothering to do so.

I'm gonna die. Surely better to breathe out now and drown than experience the agony of being ferociously dismembered by this thing?

Then, without warning the incredible pressure round his now-shattered ankle was gone. He flailed with his arms to right himself, to find solid ground on which to place his feet. He caught something with his hand, the rounded side of another ammonite shell. *So that's down.* He tried to stand up and realized the creature must have pulled him further out than he'd thought in those few seconds. Finally his head broke the surface and he realized the water was chest deep.

The air was thick with screaming voices and spray.

And the first thing he saw was Chan, a few yards away, screaming abuse at the giant shark and jabbing his spear repeatedly at the creature's nose. Its head snapped and swung from side to side, trying to get a grip on the fragile spear, trying to get past the spear to Chan, on whom it had decided to vent its frustration.

Howard waded through the water, painfully slowly, the chest-high sea in collaboration with the giant predator, wanting to slow him down. His one good foot kept slipping on the slimy rocks below, barely giving him enough purchase to make his way to shallower water. Behind him he heard Chan still hurling abuse and still stabbing and prodding, and the hiss and roar of water turned frothy white by the enraged shark thrashing in the shallows. Then he slipped again and fell under the water.

He felt a hand under his arm, then another, lifting him clear again. It was the robo-girl.

'Remain calm,' she said emotionlessly.

'What . . . about . . . Chan?' he found himself gasping.

She dragged him back to water shallow enough for him to crawl on his hands and knees. Then she let him go and headed back into the sea.

He turned and sat in the gently lapping waves, exhausted and vaguely aware of the burning agony of snapped and twisted bones down at the end of his leg. He watched Becks splashing through the water towards where Chan was still managing, incredibly, to keep the shark at spear's length.

That's a very big fish, was the last coherent thought his mind managed to put together before the world seemed to slump over on to its side.

*

Liam watched the young man as he came round. 'Leonard? How are you feeling?'

'Hurts,' he grunted thickly.

Becks leaned over him. 'There are no broken bones, but your Achilles tendon has snapped and there is a significant contusion and several abrasions to your lower leg. This will hurt, but it will also mend.'

'On the other hand,' said Liam, 'the bad news is your boot didn't make it.'

Howard half smiled, half winced. A fire crackled brightly high up on the beach, throwing dancing skeins of amber light and dark shadows across the shingle down to the softly lapping waterline.

Edward Chan joined them. 'Hi,' he said. 'You OK?'

Howard looked up at him. 'You . . . you saved my life.'

Edward shrugged. 'I just poked my stick at it for a while.'

'My God, we were lucky,' said Howard, wincing again as he adjusted his position.

'No,' said Liam sombrely, 'no, we weren't. Ranjit's missing.'

Liam vaguely recalled he'd been at the back of their party, wading slowly through the water, falling behind the others. They'd foolishly allowed themselves to become strung out all along the beach, enjoying the tropical sea like holidaymakers. They'd allowed themselves to feel a false sense of security with the peaceful flat sea to one side and a wide open beach on the other.

'Poor guy,' whispered Howard.

'That shark thing must have got him first.'

Liam wondered about that. He'd been about a hundred yards back. Surely they would have heard the rush of water as that shark slid out of the surf? Surely they would have heard Ranjit scream? He looked out into the dark and wondered whether it had been that shark, or perhaps it had been those dark shapes he thought he'd seen earlier this afternoon, scattering to the ground and disappearing like ghosts as he'd turned back to look over his shoulder.

Now, was that real? Did I really see that?

'We were lucky,' said Kelly, 'that it only got the one of us. I mean, did you see the size of that thing? Bigger than a killer whale.'

'This *is* the age of the big predators,' said Whitmore. 'Big ones. The golden age for the giant carnivores.' He looked ashen-faced, shaken still, even several hours after the incident. 'And we're prey.'

'It's not the golden age for much longer,' said Franklyn. 'If this *is* sixty-five million years ago, then we're near the end of the Cretaceous era. Something happens soon on Earth that wipes out all the big species. Fossil hunters call it the K–T boundary. Beyond that thin layer of sedimentary rock, you don't find dinosaurs any more. Certainly not the big ones.'

'Good,' said Laura.

'The big asteroid?' said Juan. 'That's what killed them all, right?'

Franklyn shrugged. 'It's still debated. Could have been an asteroid, or a super volcano. Or it could simply have been a sudden climatic shift. Whatever extinction event happened, the large species were extremely vulnerable to it.'

'It won't happen while we're still here, will it?' asked Jasmine. She looked as unsettled and shaken as Whitmore.

Franklyn snorted dismissively. 'Unlikely.'

'So,' Edward muttered softly. 'Now there's only fifteen of us. If no one comes for us, we won't make it, will we?'

The others huddled around the fire heard that and it stilled their quiet murmurings until all that could be heard was the soft draw and hiss of the waves and the crackle of burning wood.

Becks broke the silence. 'Leonard, I have constructed a pair of crutches for you.'

Howard eased himself up on to his elbows. 'We're still going on?'

Liam nodded. 'Yes, we're nearly there.' He pointed up the beach. 'Another four or five miles around this bay and we should be there. It's our only hope . . . so we're going on.'

Whitmore nodded. 'Right. We can't go back now.'

Laura shuffled closer to the fire, hugging her shoulders against the cool night air. 'This will work, won't it? Somebody will find your message and they'll come for us?'

Liam grinned. 'Sure they are. They're already looking for us. And hopefully leaving them this message will help them narrow down their search. Trust me . . . it's going to work out all right.' He looked at Becks. 'Right?'

She nodded, seeming to understand that the others needed to hear something positive and certain from them. 'Liam is correct.'

CHAPTER 42

2001, New York

Sal looked at her. 'How can you be so sure?'

Maddy shrugged. 'I can't be a hundred per cent certain. But look, if Liam and the unit survived the jump, I'm pretty sure that's exactly what they'd do. I mean, that's all they *can* do.'

Sal looked up from the mug of coffee in her hands, across the dim archway, illuminated by the fizzing ceiling strip light, towards the shutter door. It was gone eleven now. By this time on any normal Tuesday, the three of them would have been settling in for the evening: Liam on his bunk with his nose in a history book and a bowl of dry Rice Krispies on his chest and Maddy surfing the Internet. But tonight she and Maddy were both up and sitting at the kitchen table, waiting for midnight to come. Waiting for the 'reset'. She could hear the softly growing hum of power being drawn in through the mains, building up and being stored in the capacitor. Come midnight they would feel an odd momentary sensation of falling as the time field reset and took them back forty-eight hours to 12 a.m. Monday morning.

Maddy was certain, or at least working hard to give that impression, that immediately after the reset happened and they appeared in Monday one stroke after midnight, there'd be a welcome party waiting outside in the backstreet and very eager to meet them.

Who, though?

Maddy said that 'secrets have a way of drifting up'. What she meant by that was that advance knowledge of a time machine appearing in New York in 2001 would surely ultimately end up in the hands of some shady government agency, men in dark suits. Something as important, something so profoundly monumental as that could only end up in the hands of secret service spooks. If that was the case . . . then, Sal hoped, Maddy was going to find a way to cooperate with them to get Liam back.

And then what? What exactly?

Interrogation? For sure. Because they'd sure as shadd-yah want to know every little thing about this place and the machinery inside and how it all worked. They'd want to know *every little thing*. There'd be endless questions about the rest of this mysterious agency, how many others? Where are they? Who's in charge?

Sal really wasn't so sure she wanted to jump back to Monday and face that.

There was the other possibility, of course – that they jumped back and no one was there waiting for them.

Maddy's logic was quite black and white about this. Sal realized she'd thought this all through very thoroughly. If nobody was waiting for them, then that could only mean one thing. If there was nobody outside waiting for them, then Liam and the support unit had never survived the explosion. Or, if they had survived, then they'd been unable to get a message to them; they were lost in time for good, never to be seen again.

She looked at the digital clock on their kitchen table, red numbers that glowed softly and changed all too slowly.

11.16 p.m.

Oh jahulla . . . I rea-a-a-ally hate waiting.

CHAPTER 43

65 million years BC, jungle

Liam stared up at the steep slope in front of them, rising up from the turquoise sea and the narrow strip of gravelly beach. It was covered in canopy trees, dangling vines and the swaying fronds of ferns. Thick jungle once again. He'd grown used to the reassuring comfort of being out in the open, where he could see anything coming their way from afar.

'It's just beyond that?'

Becks nodded. 'Affirmative. One and a half miles north-east of this point.'

The rest of the group were wearily bringing up the rear along the broad beach, none, though, daring to splash through the water this morning. Leonard was struggling at the back on the shingle with his crutches, but there was Edward and Jasmine helping him along.

'I have the calculation now,' said Becks.

'What's that?'

'When in time we are.'

'Oh.' Liam arched a brow. 'When did you do that?'

'I set the routine running thirty-three hours ago, identifying and cataloguing each tachyon particle in our vicinity before and after the jump. Two billion, ninety-three million, three hundred and twenty-two thousand, nine hundred and six particles before. And seventy-three million, one thousand, five hundred and seventy-two identified particles after.'

Liam rolled his eyes. He didn't need a blow-by-blow account of the maths. 'That's great. So . . . what's the answer?'

'With a constant particle attrition rate, my calculation is that we are located sixty-two million, seven hundred and thirty-nine thousand, four hundred and six years into the past.' She smiled proudly. 'Accurate to five hundred years either side of that date.'

'Well done, Becks.' He watched the others slowly staggering across the shifting, clattering pebbles. 'So we have a date we can put in the message. And we can encode the message with your Harry Potter book code?'

'Affirmative.'

'And of course the date and location of the field office.' He drew in breath through his teeth. 'Jay-zus, this does really feel like we're meddling with time in a big way.'

'We are,' she replied.

'We've just got to figure out the best way to ensure our *get me out of here* note lasts . . . sixty million whatever years.'

'Sixty-two million, seven hundred and thirty–'

He raised a hand to shush her. 'To ensure it lasts a long, long time.' He picked out Whitmore and Franklyn walking side by side comparing some of the shells they'd collected. 'I just hope those two fossil geniuses know where best to leave our message.'

In the distance, four or five miles down the beach, he saw several long necks hastily emerging from a cluster of jungle and out on to the beach, a small herd of those alamosauruses hurrying out into the open.

Something just spooked them over there. Didn't it?

He watched as they thundered along the beach, kicking up a trail of dust in their wake.

His gaze rested on Edward and Jasmine supporting a limping Leonard up the shingle. They finally caught up with the rest of them gathered at the foot of the steep slope of jungle.

'We've just got to hike over that, ladies and gents,' said Liam, 'and we're there.'

Franklyn was exhausted, out of breath and dripping with sweat. He was pretty sure the climb up this steep slope of jungle was one or two degrees short of full-on vertical rock climbing. He wondered how the huge canopy trees with their mushroom-like roof of leaves were managing to keep a purchase on the craggy rock sides.

The others seemed to be faring better than him, even that poor kid, Leonard, who was hopping and clattering up awkwardly, his bad leg dangling behind him. But then Franklyn was carrying twenty more pounds in weight than them, most of it round his middle. 'Puppy fat' he preferred to call it, in a vain hope that come college it was all going to magically disappear and the trim athletic body of sports jock was going to emerge. He'd still be a geek on the inside, though. But a cool jock on the outside.

A smart sports jock.

Now there's something you don't see every day.

He was so pleased with that observation that he misplaced his step and stumbled to the ground, barking his shin on a rock. 'Ow!' he hissed.

'You OK, man?' asked Juan, six yards ahead and above.

'Yeah, I'm f–' His rucksack slid off his shoulder as he picked himself up and started sliding down the slope. 'Oh no!' he muttered, watching it bounce off a tree trunk and continue its rolling, bouncing, tumbling descent. 'Just great,' he sighed. 'Now I gotta go down, get it and climb this bit all over again.'

'I'll tell the others to hold up while you get your bag, 'kay?'

Franklyn nodded a thanks and began his descent. He could see his yellow rucksack down there, swinging from a low branch. Good, it wasn't going any further, then.

Several minutes later he was nearly there, pushing his way through the large fronds of a fern on to a small level clearing of dried cones and needles and soft soil. Across the clearing – on little more than a wide ledge – was his bag, still swinging from a shoulder strap tangled round the broken stump of a branch. If it hadn't caught there, it would have rolled over the edge and he'd be backtracking another tiresome ten minutes' worth of climbing all the way to the bottom.

He stepped across, unwound it from the stump and put the straps over both shoulders this time, determined not to lose it again. He turned round to begin his ascent once more when his eyes picked out something on the ground: the familiar shape of a human footprint in the dry soil. One of theirs, but either side of it he saw three small dents – the distinctive marks of a three-toed creature. He stooped a little lower to get a closer look.

My God. It looked just like the tracks he'd seen all around that carcass they'd discovered a while back. The dawning realization came suddenly and his mouth all of a sudden felt tacky and dry.

We've been followed.

He knelt down and traced another three-pronged footprint in the ground with his finger. And another. And another.

We've been followed . . . all the way from the camp.

It was then that he heard the soft rustle of dislodged leaves, something emerging from the foliage on to the ledge behind him.

'Oh boy,' he whispered.

CHAPTER 44

65 million years BC, jungle

Broken Claw could sense the new creature *knew* they were there; his nasal cavity picked out the faint smell of fear coming from it, a chemical cocktail of sweat and adrenaline, not so different from the large plant-eaters. The new creature had cleverly spotted their tracks. The new creature had finally realized it was being stalked.

Maybe now was the time to know a little more about these strange pale beasts. His soft bark ordered the others to remain where they were for now, out of sight. The new creature was holding one of those sticks-that-catch in one of its puffy pale hands. He'd watched one of these creatures fend off a giant sea-dweller yesterday with one of those sticks. So he eyed it warily as he stepped low under the sweeping fronds of a fern, under the branch from which the new creature had moments ago retrieved something bright and colourful and emerged over the rocky lip of ground to the small level clearing. That salty smell of fear grew suddenly much more powerful as the new creature turned slowly round to face him. Broken Claw rose from his crouching posture on all fours, up on to his hind legs, to stand fully erect.

It fears.

So close now, he could see the new creature more clearly: the eyes, curiously large, behind rounded shiny transparent discs. Its face, all loose pale flesh, unsculpted by muscle or sinew or bone carapace. It made noises with its mouth, noises that sounded so unlike all the other beasts in the river valley they called home. Noises, in fact, that didn't sound too unlike the simple language of coughs, grunts and barks Broken Claw's pack used.

Franklyn in turn studied the creature that had just emerged. It had a body shape he could best describe as halfway between one of the smaller therapod species, and . . . well, and a *human*. But incredibly thin, almost birdlike in its agility. A pair of long thin legs hinged backwards like a dog's legs, meeting at a bony, very feminine-looking pelvis thrust acutely forward. A tiny waist beneath a protruding rib cage, a curved, knobbly spine that hunched over and ended with a delicate tapering neck supporting an elongated skull. Apart from the distinctive head, seen from a distance, and if one squinted a little, it could almost pass as a hominid – human-like.

'Oh my . . . m-my God,' he whispered.

It cocked its head, a head that fleetingly reminded Franklyn of a hot-dog sausage, long and bone-smooth, at one end a lipless mouth full of rows of lethal-looking teeth. Above the mouth were two holes that suggested a nasal cavity around which flesh puckered and pulled as it silently breathed, and above that two reptilian yellow eyes that seemed to sparkle with a keen intelligence. The thing's skin was a dark olive green, that seemed to pale to an almost human pink colour around the vulnerable belly and pelvis.

The creature's jaws snapped shut and opened again, and it made a whining noise that reminded him vaguely of the contented murmuring a baby made after a feed. It sounded almost human. And those curious, intelligent, eyes, studying him as intently as he was studying it.

It made another noise, grating, slightly deeper this time. Beyond the teeth, he could see a black tongue twitching and fluttering and curling, like a restless animal in a cage, experimenting with different shapes to produce different sounds.

Did it . . . did it just mimic me?

'Hi,' said Franklyn.

The long head tilted to one side, like a dog listening for its master's voice. The mouth opened again, and the tongue rolled and curled. '*Ah-eeeee*,' was the noise that came out, lower in pitch now, lower than a baby and almost matching the timbre of Franklyn's as yet unbroken voice.

He felt some of the terror replaced with the slightest flush of excitement.

It's trying to communicate.

'Hi, my name's *Franklyn*,' he said again, louder, bolder, slower.

That long head tilted over to the other side now, the gesture almost comical. One of its long arms, muscular, lean and ending with three digits that curled into lethal-looking long curved serrated blades, flexed in front of it.

Is that a hand signal?

Franklyn attempted to duplicate the gesture, bringing his short pudgy hand up before his face and curling his fingers in the same way. The creature snorted air out of its nostrils and clacked its teeth. He wondered if that was the creature laughing at his attempt.

Suddenly, he heard the crack of twigs, and the clatter of dislodged rocks; something coming down the slope above.

Becks leaped out of the foliage on to the ground between them, landing in a fight-ready and perfectly balanced stance. She spun round to face the reptilian hominid. 'Run,' she said calmly as she crouched ready for action, one of their crude jagged metal hatchets in one hand, a spear in the other.

Franklyn was frozen in place, unsure what to do. The creature had dropped down low, on to all fours, its elongated banana-like skull tilted back and resting flush in the spinal dip between two protruding shoulder blades. It hissed and barked and a swarm of others began to emerge over the lip of ground that sloped steeply down to the bay below.

'*RUN!*' screamed Liam, tumbling out of the foliage clumsily on to the ground beside Becks. 'Run, for Jayzus sakes, RUN!!' he shouted, getting up and readying his spear.

Franklyn's moment of indecision passed as he took in the crawling carpet of dark olive bodies slowly, warily gliding on all fours across the clearing towards them like a deadly lava flow. He turned, grabbed a branch and pulled himself up the slope and into the jungle, panting with panic and effort as he and his yellow rucksack quickly disappeared through the thick green fronds.

'*What?*' hissed Liam. 'Oh, sod this! I thought it was just the one of them!'

The creatures were spreading out around the clearing, attempting to flank them, encircle them.

'Recommendation,' Becks said, turning to look at him, 'leave!'

Liam could hear the sound of footfalls from above – the others. He couldn't tell if it was the sound of them coming down to help, or scrambling up the slope to get further away.

'Uh . . . right, OK. You going to be . . . er . . . all right?'

Becks ignored his stammered question as she swivelled the hatchet in her right hand with the grace of a martial arts master. The yellow-eyed creatures had moved too quickly, encircling them so that Liam already had no choice but to stay. He backed up against her until their shoulders were touching.

'Oh . . . boy . . . oh b-boy . . . I'm really n-not . . . uh, oh God . . .'

'Stay close to me,' Becks uttered over her shoulder.

'S-sure . . . and w-what are y-you going to –?'

Becks was already in motion. He glanced round to see her leap forward, swinging the spear like a baton. The sharp end punctured the flank of one of the hominids and with it still lodged between two ribs she effortlessly flicked it off its feet. Liam backed up, keeping his spear aimed at the creatures closing the gap in front of him.

Becks stepped forward again with the grace of a ballet dancer, the jagged hatchet flickering and flashing in the blur of movement. It caught the long clawed digits of one of the creatures and they spun in the air spraying droplets of blood in messy arcs.

In front of him, one of the creatures made a sudden lunge for Liam, hoping to catch him off guard as he backed up in Becks's wake. He caught the movement in his peripheral vision and had only the time to swing the spear tip round towards it before he felt the impact rattle down the frail bamboo shaft.

He turned to see the creature's deadly sickle-shaped claws flailing inches from his face and the teeth in its long skull snapping and grating and dripping spittle-strings of saliva. It was impaled on the bamboo, but so very far from incapacitated and quite enraged.

'Oh Jay-zus! I got one skewered!'

Becks was busy.

He held on to the rattling spear as the creature thrashed and drummed and swung and slowly, eagerly pulled itself further down the shaft, thick gouts of its dark blood running on to his hands. 'Help!' he screamed.

He could see one of the other hominids lowering, coiling, ready to leap on to him, when the air was split with a child-like shriek from one of them. In an instant, the beat of a heart, the dark olive-coloured bodies snaked, scrambled and swarmed with incredible speed towards the lip of rocky ground and out of sight into the jungle slope below.

Gone. Just like that.

Except for the creature still struggling halfway down his spear. A sickle claw swiped across his upper arm, cutting through the material of his shirt and digging into his muscle with the ease of a butcher's blade through tenderized beef.

'*Gah!*' Liam bellowed. '*Help me!*'

Becks was there in the blink of an eye and with a blur of movement swiped the hatchet across the creature's elegant neck. It froze in shocked realization of its fate. The long head tilted for a moment like a cocked gesture of curiosity, then swung backwards on to its hunched spine, almost completely decapitated yet still attached to the body by a frayed strip of exposed pale pink tendon. It collapsed a second later, pulling the spear out of Liam's trembling hands.

They both stared down at the tangle of lean grey-green limbs and bony protrusions, and the rhythmic jet of almost black spurting gobbets of blood across the floor of dried pine cones and needles. One of its legs still twitched and flexed; a post-mortem response.

Liam looked up at Becks. She had a spatter pattern of blood across her pale face and chest and her normally expressionless cool grey eyes were wide and wild. But that passed in an instant as artificial intelligence regained control of her face. She regarded him calmly.

'Are you unharmed, Liam?'

Liam looked down at his bloody arm, cut deep, but nothing arterial going on there. He was vaguely aware that he was in a state of shock as he said, 'Can I be put back on the *Titanic*, please?'

CHAPTER 45

65 million years BC, jungle

Liam and Becks emerged at the top of the steep hill twenty minutes later, a bald outcrop of rock with a view down all three sides to the tropical sea far below.

Liam collapsed on to the rocky ground.

'W-where are they?' asked Franklyn, looking past Liam towards the edge of the sloping jungle. 'Are they coming?'

'They are no longer pursuing,' answered Becks.

'My God, you're wounded!' cried Laura, dropping down beside him and ripping a strip of cloth from his shirt to use as a bandage.

'What the hell happened back there?' asked Kelly, undoing his loose tie and passing it to Laura to use as a tourniquet. He looked at Franklyn, still gasping from the exertion of climbing up the last half a mile of jungle. 'He's just been jabbering to us something about a load of creatures jumping him.'

Liam nodded. 'Yeah.' He pulled a plastic bottle out of his backpack and chugged the last of his water. He pumped air in and out of his lungs for a few moments, gathering enough puff to be able to say something more. 'Yeah . . . we got attacked all right. Lots of them . . . dozens of 'em.'

'Dozens of *what*?' asked Whitmore.

'A species of pack hunter,' said Becks.

Whitmore went pale. 'Oh God, don't tell me there *are* raptors?'

'Worse,' said Franklyn. 'Much worse.' He sat down next to Liam, took off his glasses and wiped the fogged lenses of his spectacles. One of the lenses was laced with a spider's web of cracks.

'They're not like anything we've ever seen,' he began, carefully rubbing dry the fractured glass. 'No one's ever come across fossils of this . . . come across *anything* like this species.'

Whitmore squatted down opposite the boy. 'Tell me, what's back down there? What did you see?'

Franklyn shook his head. 'I . . . I really don't know. They're . . . they're human-like and raptor-like.' He looked up at the teacher. 'They're unlike anything . . . *anything*, you know?'

'Not a sub-species of therapod?'

The boy shook his head vigorously. 'No . . . no, definitely not. Maybe millions of years ago there's some kind of shared ancestry, but these things . . . they're just . . . they're . . .' He was fumbling for words, for some way to describe them.

'Unique?' said Liam. He winced as Laura pulled the dressing tight one last time and finished a knot.

'Yes.' Franklyn nodded, putting his cracked glasses back on. 'Unique. That's it. They must be some kind of evolutionary dead end. A form of super-intelligent predator.'

Kelly stepped forward. 'That doesn't make sense, Franklyn. If they're, as you say, super-intelligent, they'd have thrived. We'd have found their fossils everywhere, surely?'

'How intelligent? What level of *intelligent* are we talking about?' asked Laura.

'Oh, they're smart,' said Liam. 'Very smart.' He looked up at the others. 'I think I saw them back on the big plain at the same time Becks punched that dinosaur on the nose. I looked back behind us, just as that stampede was happening . . . and

I think I saw them. Like a whole pack of monkeys . . . in fact that's what I thought I saw –'

'That's ridiculous,' said Whitmore. 'The only mammals alive now are the size of shrews.'

'They're not mammals,' said Franklyn. 'They're reptilian, all right.'

'Like I say,' continued Liam, 'I *thought* they were monkey-like. But then I wasn't sure what I saw, because they were gone in a flash. Just went to ground when they saw me looking at them.'

'They've been following us all the way from our camp,' said Franklyn. 'Did you see their tracks?'

Liam shook his head.

'Three prominent depressions at the end of a long foot?'

Liam recalled the sickle claws, four on each hand, three on each foot. 'Yes . . . that's right.'

'Those same tracks were around that carcass . . . I'm sure of it. That was their kill.'

Liam looked down the jungle slope at the broad curve of the long bay glimmering in the daylight. And, far off, the broad expanse of the open plain. Beyond that, lost beyond the shimmering air and the fogging of twenty miles' distance, would be the low hummock of a slope and a cliff edge, and their jungle valley beyond.

'They must have been watching us,' he said, feeling his skin cool and the hairs on his arm stir. 'Watching us and following us ever since then.'

'But that was . . . like . . . over a week ago,' said Juan.

'Nine days,' Becks added.

Juan made a face. 'All that time?'

'They've been *studying* us,' said Liam. 'Learning about us, so they have. Working out how much of a threat we are to them.'

'Yes . . . I think you're right.' Franklyn pulled himself up and studied the fringe of jungle several dozen yards down the slope from them. 'They're curious. That makes them intelligent. Maybe almost as intelligent as us.'

'A species of dinosaur as intelligent as us? Come on, Franklyn, that's –'

'They've got a language! I heard them communicate.'

Liam nodded. 'He's right. When they were surrounding me and Becks, there was some sort of *talking* going on among them.'

'And one of them tried to communicate with me . . . before you and robo-girl arrived. It was trying to speak like me!'

'This is just crazy!' said Whitmore. 'There's no record of any species, or any *similar* species with the cranial capacity for a brain big enough to develop a spoken language . . . or able to make human-like vocal sounds.'

'But that's the thing, Mr Whitmore, just because no fossil of these things has survived, doesn't mean they didn't exist.'

'The lad's right,' said Kelly. 'Don't palaeontologists say we've only got an incomplete record of prehistoric times? That there are large gaps in our knowledge?'

Whitmore rubbed his beard and stared down at the fringe of jungle. 'Well, then, that's one huge goddamn gap out there, isn't it?'

They were quiet for a while, all staring at the nearby canopy trees, and the dark forbidding undergrowth beneath, imagining eyes staring out from the gloom back at them.

'What do we do now, Liam?' asked Laura.

He pulled on his bottom lip in thought. 'We carry on with the plan.' He turned away from the jungle he'd emerged from minutes ago and looked down the slope on the other side of the peak. Below he could see the pale apron of a small sheltered sandy cove nestling at the bottom of the ridge and another equally high ridge on the far side, like the protective embracing arms of a rocky giant. He could see the twinkle of a small stream meandering down through thickets of bamboo and reeds and spilling out on to the cove. It was an inviting, secret bay of turquoise-green water that lapped along the crescent of a pale cream-coloured beach. In another time, another place . . . a secluded tropical paradise. A picture-book pirates' cove.

'Is it down there?' he asked Becks. 'The place we need to be?'

'Affirmative. That is it.'

'Yes,' he said, nodding his head firmly, hoping he looked every bit the decisive leader. 'We can be down there in less than half an hour. We'll make a camp on the beach and be sure to have a huge fire going. Hopefully that'll keep those things at bay. And we'll have half of us sleeping, and half watching, and we'll do that in shifts.' He looked at Becks again. 'We'll make this message, so we will, and tomorrow we'll plant it.'

'How are we going to do that?' asked Kelly.

Liam was about to answer that he wasn't sure yet, when Jasmine replied. 'Clay.'

The others looked at her.

'Clay,' she said again. 'If we could find some we can make a tablet. You can write your message on it then we can bake it hard in the fire.'

Liam stroked his cheek thoughtfully. 'Right, yes . . . good idea. That's what we'll do. So? Any questions before we get moving?'

'What about them things back down there?' asked Juan with another pointed glance towards the jungle.

'Well, I suppose they've learned something about us, right?'

The others looked at each other, not quite sure what Liam meant by that.

'They've learned we can kill them.' He gestured at Becks. 'And they've learned our robo-girl is not to be messed around with, so they have.'

Becks frowned indignantly at that. 'My ident. is Becks.'

He shrugged. Too tired and winded to apologize. 'Right, then . . . I suggest we get going.'

CHAPTER 46

2001, New York

The alarm clock on the table between them was showing 11.45 p.m. Maddy noticed Sal's eyes nervously glancing at it. 'Fifteen minutes to go.'

'I'm a bit scared,' whispered Sal.

If Maddy was being honest, she would have admitted she was a little jittery too. Instead she smiled, reached across the table and grasped Sal's arm. 'It's going to be fine, Sal. I promise.'

'Maybe I should go get Foster's gun from the back? You know? Just in case somebody unfriendly turns up.'

'Really?' Maddy cocked an eyebrow. 'Do you think that's going to be sensible? We might be answering the door to a backstreet full of very excitable armed men in suits and dark glasses.'

'You think it'll be like that?'

Maddy shrugged. 'I really don't know what's going to happen, Sal . . .'

If anything at all . . .

'But,' she continued, 'if a whole bunch of secret service types turn up, we're not going to achieve much standing there with one gun between us, are we? I'm sure they'll come *prepared*, if you know what I mean?'

'I guess so,' muttered Sal, her head drooping down to the

table, a fold of her dark hair flopping over darker eyes. 'How come you're so calm about this?'

Calm, am I? But then she realized she actually *did* feel calm . . . No, not calm . . . *resigned* . . . resigned to whatever history was rolling up through the aeons to meet them in a few minutes when the archway's bubble reset. She'd figured this out yesterday while she was out there anxiously looking for Foster; there really was nothing much they could do other than wait and react to whatever turned up. Wait. That's it. Wait until a ripple or a time wave arrived, or, as she hoped, a message. Then, and only then, could they do anything at all useful.

'I'm calm, Sal . . . because, I dunno, because it's not in our hands now. Because we have to just wait and see. No point worrying about what's out of our hands.'

That sounded lame. But it was all she had right now.

'But, if it's *bad* guys, Maddy . . . if it's bad guys who want to get their hands on the time machine, what are we going to do? We can't just let them.'

'I've got that covered.'

'How?'

Maddy smiled. There was something she'd managed to get right. 'I've instructed Bob to lock down the computer system if he hears me say a codeword out loud.'

'Right.' Sal nodded, silent for a moment. 'But . . . but won't they have computer experts who could hack their way in and, I dunno, deactivate that command or something?'

'Maybe, eventually. That kind of hacking takes a lot of time. And they won't have enough time to do that.'

'Why?'

'Because he's under orders to trash absolutely everything if he doesn't hear from me again.'

'Huh?'

'If he doesn't get a second password from me within six hours, he's under instructions to go completely mad and wipe the hard drives clean and send a power surge through the displacement machinery's circuits and fry them. There'll be nothing left but frazzled silicon and garbage-filled drives if they try anything funny with us, Sal.'

Sal nodded, regarding Maddy with renewed respect. 'Oh jahulla, that's clever, Maddy.'

Maddy shrugged. 'I saw it in a film once. It worked in that – don't see why it shouldn't work for us.'

'You're a good planner,' said Sal. 'I know you think you're a bit rubbish, and I know you blame yourself for the explosion . . . but I don't know anyone else who could have picked up all that you have so quickly.' She glanced away from Maddy, self-conscious, flicking her fringe behind one ear. 'I'm just saying, that's all . . . you're pretty good at this.'

'Thanks, Sal.'

They watched another minute vanish on the clock.

'We'll see soon enough. If it's bad guys out there and they really want to get their grubby paws on our tech, then they're going to need us, aren't they?' Maddy took a deep breath, feeling the tickling sensation of growing anxiety claw its way up her spine as the clock flickered to 11.47 p.m. 'And they're freakin' well going to have to be real nice about it too.'

CHAPTER 47

65 million years BC, jungle

Broken Claw cradled the organ in his hands, still, cold and lifeless now; its colour had drained from a vibrant red to a dull purple as the sun slowly sank in the sky. Now the sky was dark, a half moon bathing the dark jungle with a quicksilver light.

He stood where the new creatures had been just hours ago. Evidence of their presence was everywhere in the form of footprints in the soil, droplets of dried blood on the rocks and boulders and the smell, their unique smell of fear thick on every surface. They had waited here for a while. And they had been so very frightened.

The new creatures fear us.

And yet Broken Claw had been so certain up until now that it was his pack that needed to be afraid of them. The others were looking at him, waiting for him. He looked down at the organ in his hand, all that remained of his pack-mate, the mother of many of the young males before him. She would have led them all if Broken Claw was to die before her. The wisdom of age was more than enough to make up for her smaller frame . . . and no young buck would have challenged her. Unlike the other simple-minded animals in these lands with their crude pack hierarchies that relied on the brute strength of an alpha male, Broken Claw's extended family understood the power of wisdom.

But now she was dead. Her slim neck had been almost

completely severed and she'd had a wound through the chest cavity that would almost certainly have been fatal anyway.

They had returned to the ledge to find her body still warm, but her life gone. And so they'd consumed her, torn the flesh from her bones in ragged strips – skin, muscle tissue, organs – all of her stripped down to bloodied bones. None of her to be wasted. She was loved too much to leave her flesh for smaller scavengers to gnaw at.

Her heart was his, though, and his alone.

Broken Claw had cradled it now for hours, unwilling to let go of the last thing of her. But now was the time. Now, as he stared down through the dark night to the cove far below and the flickering orange flower on the beach surrounded by those pale creatures.

His serrated teeth tore a chunk from the purple organ and he vowed as he chewed on the fibrous tissue that every last one of those new creatures would die. He would be sure to stare closely into their eyes as his claws dug deep into their chests and pulled the pumping source of their life out.

The others began to wail and mew softly, young males grieving at the loss of their mother, as Broken Claw placed the rest of the organ in his mouth and bade farewell to his lifelong partner. He turned to the others and silenced them with a soft bark.

We do not need to fear new creatures.

The others understood this too.

They are as plant-eaters, harmless without their sticks-that-catch.

And they were careless, foolish creatures that often placed these lethal tools on the ground and walked away from them, unaware that without them their clawless hands and small, even, white teeth made them as vulnerable as freshly born cubs.

Broken Claw watched their distant movements on the beach, illuminated by the yellow flower. Of course they all had to die to avenge her . . . but also to be sure his kind were the only intelligent pack hunters in these lands. To allow these pale things a chance to breed and increase their number would be foolish.

He opened his mouth and his black tongue curled and twisted as he softly tried to reproduce again the strange sound the short fat creature with ginger hair and those strange eyes had made. Broken Claw's throat gargled and whinnied, and his tongue shaped the sound into something that sounded, to his recollection, to be a very passable facsimile.

'*Aye . . . ammmm . . . Fanck . . . leeeennn . . .*'

CHAPTER 48

65 million years BC, jungle

The morning sun was already warm on his back and shoulders as Liam poked at the smouldering remains of their campfire with his spear, carefully probing the flaking ash remains of branches for what he was looking for.

'Do be careful,' said Jasmine, standing beside him. 'They're brittle when they're still hot.'

'All right,' he said, going about it more carefully. Presently, the blunt end of thick bamboo cane hit something hard: a dull thunk.

'I got one.' He carefully pushed the ash out of the way and traced a rough rectangle outline, something approximating the size of a brick. 'It looks like it survived the cooking without cracking.'

Using a fistful of waxy fern leaves as an oven glove he reached down and pulled it out, then quickly dropped it on the soft sand. 'Ouch! Still bleedin' hot!' He squatted down beside it, gingerly wiping ash away from the rust-coloured surface of fire-cooked clay. The fine lines of letters and numbers were clogged with ash. The others gathered round and stared down at the small oblong tablet lying on the beach.

'My God, look! It totally worked!' uttered Laura.

The lettering was there to see, clear, unmistakable.

'Of course it did,' replied Jasmine. 'I know what I'm talking about. Me and my mom make ceramic jewellery all the time. We sell it on eBay.'

Liam leaned over and blew at it, the ash fluttering out of the inscribed lines and curls of his handwriting in little clouds.

Take this to Archway 9, Wythe Street, Brooklyn, New York on Monday 10 September 2001.
Message: -89-1-9/54-1-5/76-1-2/23-3-5/17-8-4/7-3-7/5-8-3/12-6-9/23-8-1/3-1-1/56-9-2/12-5-8/67-8-3/92-6-7/112-8-3/234-6-1/45-7-3/30-6-2/34-8-3/41-5-6/99-7-1/2-6-9/127-8-1/128-7-3/259-1-5/2-7-1/69-1-5/14-2-66. Key is 'Magic'.

Whitmore was reading it over Liam's shoulder. 'You think that book code of yours is going to work? I mean, I don't know what book you've used but I know every book has different editions. You know that, don't you? And the page layouts and numbers change from edition to edition. Are you using some kind of internal agency manual or something?'

Becks answered. 'It will work. My duplicate AI is working from the same database.'

'Magic?' said Juan. 'Is that some kinda clue for which book it is?'

Liam nodded. He looked at Becks. 'Do you think Bob will understand that clue?'

She pursed her lips and shrugged – yet another teenage gesture she seemed to have picked up in the last fortnight from the students. 'I am unable to give you an accurate answer to that question, Liam.'

'Well, put it this way . . . would *you* get it?'

Her eyelids flickered. 'I have thirty-one thousand listings in my database against the word "magic".'

'Ah, Jay-zus,' muttered Liam, frustrated. 'Maybe we should have put more thought into the clue there. Maybe that one word on its own isn't going to be enough for Bob to –'

'Saleena Vikram will understand,' said Becks. She looked at Liam. 'As "Bob" I discussed the book with her.'

Liam snorted. 'You're kidding me? You can actually discuss literature?'

'I told her I very much enjoyed the magic in Harry Potter.'

Whitmore stood up straight and put his hands on his hips. 'This is a joke, right? You're not seriously telling me your super-secret-ultimate-time-police agency uses a *kids' book* as a code key?'

Liam and Becks both looked up at him and nodded.

'Jesus!' Whitmore shook his head. 'What kind of a Mickey Mouse outfit are you?'

'Mickey Mouse?'

Liam waved at Becks to be silent. 'It's what works, Mr Whitmore!' he replied, surprised with himself at how angry he sounded. 'It's what works . . . that's what counts!'

Whitmore was a little taken aback by Liam's uncharacteristic outburst. 'Well, it's just . . . it just seems so, I don't know, a bit . . .'

'Amateur,' chimed in Franklyn. 'We were thinking you guys had some sort of already-organized code system. You know? Like *proper* secret-agent types do?'

'Yeah . . . don't mean to be dissin' you guys an' all,' said Juan, 'but it does look like you makin' this stuff up as you go along.'

'Look,' said Liam. 'I'll not lie to you . . . I'm quite new to this time-travel thing myself. And this is certainly the first time I've gone back to dinosaur times. So, I suppose if it looks to you like me and Becks are not working from some . . . from some sort of *manual*, well . . . you'd be right.' He stood up, brushing ash from his hands. 'But I'll tell you this much for nothing: the agency has saved you many times over. And the thing is each time it does that for you, each time it's saved history and the world around you . . . well, it's happened. And you all go on with your lives happily never knowing how close it's all come to disaster.'

Liam pressed his lips together. 'Me and Becks here have saved you once before.' He half smiled. 'A certain Hitler chap who won a war instead of losing it. Now that was a fine bleedin' mess, so it was. But we managed to fix it up again. So will you not give us some credit here? We're not completely useless, all right?'

'What about your agency?' asked Kelly. 'Who are they?'

Liam was about to answer when Becks grabbed his arm to stop him.

'Lemme guess,' said Kelly sarcastically, '*classified data*.'

'I'm sorry,' said Liam, 'that's how it is. We return you to 2015, then the less you know about us, the better. But I'll tell you this, though . . . they're organized and they've got the *best* technology out there; computers and . . . and "robots" like Becks and oh . . . loads of other stuff. So, look –' he smiled – 'you're in good hands.'

They looked at him with an unreadable mixture of expressions.

Come on, Liam . . . be decisive.

'Right, then, enough prattling like old fishwives. We have a job to do, so we have. These tablets, Franklyn? Mr Whitmore? Where exactly do you suggest we go and place them?'

They both looked at each other, an exchange of absent-minded gestures – Franklyn pushing his cracked glasses up his nose, Whitmore scratching at his scruffy beard – and a muttered exchange of ideas.

Finally Franklyn turned to them. 'I suggest we embed a couple in the beach. Dig a hole, deep . . . as deep as you can. And the rest –' he turned and nodded towards a nearby thicket of bamboos and reeds – 'that freshwater stream. There's silt banks and a bunch of marsh either side of it. I'm pretty sure that's how they describe the fossil bed in Dinosaur Valley, that it was once . . . marshy.'

Liam looked at Jasmine. 'And these clay tablets will last sixty-five million years?'

She shook her head. 'Uh, well, no . . . I never said they'd last that long.'

Franklyn shook his head. 'You really don't know a great deal about fossils, Liam, do you?'

Liam hunched his shoulders. 'Nope, Franklyn, I don't. But you do. So why don't you tell me how this works, then?'

Franklyn sighed. 'They'll most likely break up long before there are even monkeys on planet Earth, let alone *Homo sapiens*. But the *impression* they leave behind – like a cast or a mould on the sand – on the silt, which eventually will become a layer of sedimentary rock, *that's* the fossil.' He offered Liam a patient if somewhat patronizing smile. 'Not those tablets. They'll be long gone dust.'

Liam nodded thoughtfully. 'All right, then. So now I know . . . strikes me that it makes no real difference – there's still *something* left behind that a person can read, right?'

Franklyn nodded.

'Good, so best we get started. The sooner we're done, the sooner we can leave.' He turned to address them all. 'I don't know about you but come sundown I'd rather be camping out on that big, very wide beach than down here.'

'With those things out there?' said Whitmore, looking up the jungle slopes surrounding them. 'Sure . . . getting out of here sounds good to me.'

CHAPTER 49

2001, New York

'Three minutes to go,' said Sal.

'Three minutes,' Maddy echoed. They could both hear the machinery below the desk beginning to hum noisily as it sucked energy greedily from their mains feed. Not for the first time, Maddy wondered who paid the electricity bill for their archway. It had to be astronomical, the amount they used.

She smiled at her dumbness. Yes, of course, *no one* paid any bills. As far as the world outside was concerned, as far as their neighbour – the car mechanic in the archway near the top of their little backstreet – were concerned, this archway normally sat vacant with a ripped and graffiti-covered sign pasted on the roller shutter outside offering three thousand square feet of commercial floor space at a reasonable rate.

Except of course, for a Monday and Tuesday in September when, to anybody who bothered to notice, it would appear three young squatters had decided to move in, only to vanish again on the Wednesday.

'Oh,' said Sal, 'I forgot . . . I saw a funny thing the other day.'

'Yeah?'

'Yeah, in a shop nearby. A junk shop. Well, not funny really. Just a coincidence.'

'What?'

'A uniform, a steward's uniform . . . from the *Titanic.* Just exactly like Liam's.' Sal shook her head. 'Isn't that weird?'

'Seriously?'

'The lady in the shop said it wasn't a real one, though. Just a costume from a play. But, still, kind of funny. I suppose I could buy it for Liam as a spare.'

'I'm sure he's in no big hurry to go back to the *Titanic*, you know? Given what he'd have to face.'

Sal's smile quickly faded. 'No,' she said. 'I suppose he wouldn't . . . none of us, really.'

The numbers on the clock flickered and changed. Two minutes left.

Maddy really could have done with Foster sitting right here beside them. Calm, relaxed, with a reassuring half-cocked smile on his old wrinkly face. Skin that looked like weathered parchment, skin that looked like it had seen way too much sun –

. . . I wouldn't mind feeling the sun on my face . . .

Foster's last words. He'd said that the morning he'd taken her out for coffee to say goodbye.

'Sun on my face,' she uttered under her breath.

Sal cocked an eyebrow. 'Uh?'

. . . I guess I wouldn't mind feeling the sun on my face whilst I enjoy a decent hot dog . . .

That's exactly what he'd said, wasn't it? One of the last things he'd said. That's what he fancied doing with whatever time he had left to live. Sun and a decent hot dog. With all these skyscrapers, she knew there was only one place you could count on un-obscured sunlight in Manhattan, sun . . . and, yes, hot dog vendors a-plenty. One place and one place only.

'I think I just figured out where Foster's gone,' she uttered.

They watched the clock's red LEDs flicker to show them 11.59 p.m.

'Where?'

Maddy stood up and pushed the chair back from the breakfast table with a scrape that echoed across the archway. 'I'll uh . . . I'll explain another time. We're about to have guests.'

Sal stood up and joined her in the middle of the floor, both facing the shutter door, and counting down the last sixty seconds as, behind them, the deep hum of machinery began to build to a final fizzing crescendo.

The strip light above them began to flicker and dim.

'Well, here goes nothing,' said Maddy, reaching out instinctively to hold Sal's hand.

CHAPTER 50

65 million years BC, jungle

'Do you think it's deep enough?' asked Liam.

Becks squatted down beside the waist-deep hole in the mud, and studied the oozing sides, slowly sliding downwards, and the bottom, already beginning to fill up around Liam's ankles with cloudy water. 'I do not know,' she said.

'*Don't know*, is it? Great.' He wiped at his sweating brow, smearing mud across his forehead. 'Well, who knows how deep is deep enough? May I have the tablet?'

She passed it down to him.

He turned the brick of clay over in his hands and studied the inscribed letters and numbers.

So, my little silent messenger, you go get us some help, all right?

He bent down and placed the brick writing-side down in the cloudy water and gently pressed it deep into the mud. 'We're counting on you, Mr Tablet, counting on you to do your very best for us. Last as long as you can, all right? And, like my Auntie Loretta used to say, *you be sure to make a good impression*.' He looked up at Becks with a grin plastered on his face amid the mud. 'Uh? Make a good impression? See what I did there?'

She stared down at him, grey eyes coolly analytical. 'A pun,' she replied. 'A single word with multiple meanings dependent on contextual framing.'

'Aye, a pun . . . you know? It's meant to be funny.'

She frowned for a moment, and then her face suddenly creased with an insincere mirth and she bellowed a mock laugh. He cringed at the sound of it.

'Jay-zus, Becks, if it's not funny . . . just don't laugh. I'm serious – it's embarrassing.'

She stopped immediately. 'Affirmative.'

Liam pulled himself out of the hole as the wet sides of it began to slop down into the bottom. He and Becks scooped up handfuls of mud and silt and helped the self-filling process until all that was left was a barely noticeable mound on the stream's bank. Liam produced a length of bamboo and plunged it into the top and tore a ragged strip of neon green material from the bottom of his shorts. He tied it to the bamboo stalk. 'And that's so we'll find it easy enough when we come back for it.'

Becks nodded. A part of the plan she'd insisted was necessary: to return to this time-stamp once everything else had been put right and retrieve every single one of the five tablets that were being put into the ground.

Liam looked downstream. The small trickling artery of fresh water twisted and curled out of sight beyond a thicket of reeds. 'I wonder how the others are doing?'

Kelly stood up straight and placed his hands on his tired back. Their two tablets were now dug deep into the fine sand of the beach at either side of the small cove, both marked with bamboo flags and strips of material ripped from the sleeve of his office shirt.

'Done!' He smiled at the others. There was a muted cheer from Juan, Laura, Jasmine and even Akira, a girl as shy as Edward, self-conscious about her thick accent and faltering English.

He looked up the beach towards the line of reed thickets and clusters of bamboo, and the small delta of fresh water and silt that spread out and trickled down a fan of flow-worn grooves in the beach, down into the warm salty sea.

'The others should be done pretty soon,' he said. 'Then we can head back.'

Laura's gaze drifted to the steep peak of jungle they were going to have to ascend. 'I wonder if those things are out there still.'

Juan looked up. 'We got our weapons, and we got robo-girl. We're going to be all right.'

'Maybe we're safer now than we were,' said Kelly. 'One of them was killed trying to attack us. So maybe they're more wary of us now.'

Laura tightened the grip on her spear. 'Yeah . . . I guess you're right.'

Franklyn finished piling a small cairn of stones around the base of the bamboo stake in the ground and looked up. Whitmore was leading the other two: Edward and his seemingly adopted big brother, Leonard, a hundred yards down towards another hump of silty bank they'd identified earlier as a good place for their second tablet.

'You coming, Franklyn?' the teacher called out.

'Just a sec!' he replied. The bamboo stake kept flopping over to one side and the rocks were very nearly, but not quite, holding it up. 'I'll join you in a second!' he called back, reaching for another large river-smoothed stone.

He heard it then. A soft, muted cry. Like the whimpering of a small child. He froze, listening for it over the stirring hiss of the reeds and the chuckle of the stream. And there it was again, a little louder, a little clearer. It sounded like someone in pain.

'Hello?' he replied. 'Who's that?'

One of the girls perhaps? Maybe slipped on a wet rock and broken something?

'Jasmine? Laura?'

The cry again, pitiful, wretched and insistent. It seemed to be coming from the reeds. 'Akira? Is that you?' He stepped towards them and fancied he saw someone shifting on the ground at the base of the reeds. He pushed his way in.

'What? Have you slipped? Hurt your –'

The form slithered back from him through the reeds and out of sight, moving in a fast – too fast for human – way. It was then his peripheral vision picked out eyes watching him intently from among the reeds to his right. It shifted forward, silently revealing itself a mere couple of yards from him: distinct yellow forward-facing eyes at the front of an elongated, tapering skull that sloped back over hunched bony shoulders and a hunched spine. The curious shape of its skull vaguely reminded him of the aerodynamic helmets worn by speed cyclists, or downhill skiers at the winter Olympics, only much longer, like the aliens in those DVDs his older brother kept watching over and over. It scrutinized him, perfectly still, perfectly poised. And then its scalpel-sharp teeth parted and he saw its black tongue coiling and unfurling like a snake.

'*Aye . . . ammm . . . Fanck . . . leeennnnn . . .*' it hissed softly.

My God. This creature – he realized now, the very *same* reptilian hominid he had faced back up the hillside in the jungle yesterday – had remembered his name, had remembered their fleeting moment of communication, the exchange of a spoken word. Something that wasn't going to happen again on this world for tens of millions of years. What's more, this thing had actually the voice-box and the oral dexterity to reproduce a human word!

'Yes!' he whispered excitedly. 'Yes . . . that's me!' He gestured to himself. 'My . . . name . . . is . . . Franklyn.'

Its long tapered head tilted to one side and silently it glided a step forward out of the reeds towards him.

In his rucksack, nestled at the bottom beneath the last couple of parcels of grilled fish meat wrapped in waxy leaves, was his phone still with some charge left on it. Enough, he hoped, just enough to take a few photographs and maybe a short recording of this thing actually *speaking*. He eased the rucksack off his shoulders.

'I'm just going to get something,' he said softly, soothingly, moving slowly. 'OK?'

The creature remained perfectly still, yellow eyes curiously watching his every move. He unzipped the bag and reached inside, the rank smell of fish spilling out. The skin flaps around the hominid's nasal cavity began to twitch.

He can smell the food. Change of plan. Franklyn grasped one of the packages, pulled it out and unwrapped it. 'Here you are . . . look! Food.' He held the small hunk of barbecued flesh out in one hand towards the creature.

Further off, he could hear the voices of Whitmore and the others echoing back over the reeds, less than a hundred yards away. He was torn between hoping they'd turn up and scare the thing away, and hoping they didn't. He could call out to them. But then what might that trigger? An attack? Or perhaps it would vanish for good, never to be encountered again.

He realized that would be a tragedy. Because this . . . thing, this species, like every other species of dinosaur, just wasn't going to make it. The world of dinosaurs hadn't much time left in geological terms. A thousand? Ten thousand years? Maybe tomorrow it was going to happen: a mass extinction event, either an asteroid or a mega-volcano was going to choke the world and kill every land-based species larger than a dog. And this intelligent species, so close in many ways to human, closer in some than man's own ape ancestor, was going to vanish along with all the other dumb dinosaurs. They were going to vanish without leaving a trace, would never be known about, never leave any fossil markings, never have a Latin name or be exhibited in a museum or discussed by palaeontologists. And that was the cruellest irony. Because here was something that, given just a few more million years . . .

. . . could have been us.

The dominant intelligence, a reptilian version of *Homo sapiens*.

'My God . . . you . . . you're incredible,' he whispered.

The creature was now just a couple of yards from him, yellow eyes on the hunk of meat, crouching low, its rib-and-spine-lined back looked so human, like the back of some size-zero catwalk supermodel or some lean gymnast.

'. . . fankk . . . leeeen . . .' it uttered again.

Franklyn realized he *had* to take a picture. The species deserved some evidence, at least one shred of visual evidence, that it had once upon a time existed. He gently placed the meat on the ground in front of him then delved back into his rucksack for his mobile phone.

The creature advanced another foot and then strained its long neck and curiously elongated head to sniff the meat. One slender arm swept forward and a hand with three lethal-looking sickle-shaped claws tapped it, rolled it over . . . then casually pushed it aside.

Its head cocked; its nostril flaps puckered. And then Franklyn realized the creature wasn't the slightest bit interested in the stale odour of the mudfish. It was smelling him, reading his odours like a witch-doctor reading bones, like a medium reading the creased palm of a hand.

'I-I mean no harm. I . . . just . . .' Franklyn stuttered nervously.

Its jaw snapped open, and the tongue inside twisted and curled. 'No harmmm . . .' it mimicked.

'Y-yes . . . friend . . . f-friend,' said Franklyn, tapping his chest. It was now so close he could have reached out and stroked the bone-hard carapace of the front of its skull. He could feel warm, fetid puffs of air coming from its nasal cavity.

Franklyn had the mobile phone in his hand now. His eyes still on this thing's reptile eyes, he fumbled with the touchscreen menu and finally got it into digicam mode and pressed the RECORD button.

'A species,' he said softly, panning the cell's camera up and down the beast, 'p-possibly a remote ancestor of the v-velociraptor . . . or more likely the smarter troodon.' He hated that his voice was shaking like some nervous girl's. If this was going to be a few seconds of footage that was going to make him famous . . . he wanted to sound like a pro, like a true hardcore adventurer, not some knee-trembling geek. 'This species . . . is q-quite incredible. Capable of copying a human v-voice . . .'

The hominid's mouth suddenly snapped shut with a loud clack of teeth and then the cluster of reeds began to rustle with movement all around him.

Franklyn looked up. 'Oh God . . . n-no . . .'

CHAPTER 51

65 million years BC, jungle

Liam heard it. A brittle scream, long and ragged and then suddenly silenced. 'Did you hear that?'

Becks nodded. 'Affirmative.' She straightened up. 'The hominid pack hunters may have returned. We should rejoin the others immediately.'

Liam grabbed his spear. 'Come on.'

They splashed across the shallow stream, kicking up fans of water, and then along the bank on the far side. No more than two hundred yards closer to the beach, that's where Whitmore and the others had been left to place their tablets. That seemed to be where the scream had come from. Liam couldn't tell if that one long cry had been a male or female voice, but it had rattled with horror and ended in a way that hadn't sounded good.

They splashed back across the water again to avoid another thicket of reeds as the stream weaved around a smooth boulder the size of an automobile. A minute later, up ahead, he could make out the others gathered in a group, standing closely together and studying something on the ground.

'What happened?' he called out.

None of them replied. They looked up at him with faces as pale as bed linen. Kelly and his group had heard the cry too and had come up from the beach. They must have arrived there only a minute or so earlier.

'What happened?' he called out again as he and Becks splashed across the stream one last time and finally joined them on the silty bank.

Then he saw it for himself.

Blood.

Blood everywhere, and a few tattered shreds of clothing that he recognized as belonging to Franklyn. But no sign of the boy himself. 'Oh no,' he uttered, blessing himself absent-mindedly. 'That isn't really . . .?'

Whitmore nodded. 'Franklyn's. He . . . was . . . we were just down there,' he uttered, pointing downstream. 'Just there . . . just b-beyond those reeds.'

'Didn't hear anything,' said Howard. 'Or see anything. Just heard him scream. We came up here and . . . he was gone. Just gone.'

It was Kelly who decided to say first what they were all thinking. 'Those things . . . it's those things, isn't it? They've damn well come after us.'

'We don't know that for sure,' said Liam. 'There are *other* predators.'

'Oh, we know,' said Laura. She passed Liam a mobile phone, dappled with droplets of congealing blood. On the small screen, a shaky low-resolution image looped over and over: nothing but the bright pale blue sky, and then the jerky image of something stepping over just the once. But that was all he needed to recognize it: lean, almost skeletal, and that long tapering skull. The image was pale sky again, occasionally shuddering as the camera was knocked, and through the small speaker the sound of growling, snapping teeth and the frenzied noise of something being torn to pieces.

Liam swallowed, his mouth and throat suddenly dry. He felt his face drain of blood and blanch, just like theirs now, pale as a ghost. 'We're leaving,' he said quietly. 'Leaving right now.'

'Uh . . . I left my bag at the beach,' said Juan.

'Forget the bloody bag!' snapped Liam. He glanced at Becks, ready to bark at her to be quiet should she decide to caution him about potential contamination. But she seemed to understand. Instead she pointed out which way they needed to go. Up the steep slope, thick jungle. 'I will lead the way,' she said. 'Recommendation: you should all remain close.'

'Oh, don't you worry about that,' uttered Liam under his breath. He pulled one of their homemade hatchets out of his bag and hefted his spear in his other hand. 'Everyone ready?'

The others nodded, all of them with a weapon of one sort or another in their hands. None of them keen to step back into the thick canopy of leaves and vines and dense clusters of fern leaves that could quite easily conceal death, but even less keen to remain here a moment longer.

'So, what about Franklyn?' asked Chan in a small voice. No one seemed to want to answer that question. The boy looked up at Howard. 'We're not looking for him, Leonard?'

Howard answered. 'He's gone, Edward. He's gone.'

Becks nodded. 'Correct. Information: approximate calculation – at least five pints of blood on the ground. Franklyn cannot be alive.'

'Come on,' said Liam, resting a hand on Edward's shoulder. He looked up at the sloping jungle ahead of them. 'We should go.'

CHAPTER 52

Clay tablets, five of them, buried deep in mud and sand, silently count the passing of years. Above, as they slumber in their own dark tombs, tides rise and fall, and individual layers of mud dotted with the decaying bones of generations of creatures accumulate like the rings of a growing tree.

Two hundred and seventy-six thousand, nine hundred and two years after a group of *Homo sapiens* placed them in the ground, the planet Earth shudders under the impact of a rock the size of Manhattan travelling at forty thousand miles an hour. A wave of incinerating energy spirals hundreds of miles out and tidal waves engulf millions of miles of lowlands across the world. The sky turns dark for the best part of a decade. A ten-year night in which almost all of life on land vanishes, except hardy small rodents from which those very same *Homo sapiens* will one day descend.

The giants of the plains die off quickly, first the plant-eaters, then the predators. A holocaust followed by a nuclear winter. Massive extinction on an unimaginable scale.

Yet through this five tablets lie still, and dark and oblivious.

In the aftermath of the asteroid impact, the Palaeogene period begins: a vast stretch of time, forty million years in which mountain ranges are born, live and die. A period in which a vast inland sea riding up a backbone of hills that will one day be called the Rockies recedes, surrendering ground that has only ever known the darkness of a seabed, ground that will one day have names like Utah, Colorado, Wyoming, New Mexico.

The dinosaurs are long gone, now nothing more than fossils waiting silently, like the tablets, for the constant attrition of erosion, the movements of ground, to finally push them near the surface and sunlight, again.

Above, in the world of daylight, a brand-new ecosystem exists, a world utterly rewritten. It is a cooler one than the tropical world of the dinosaurs, and the small hardy rodents have grown, evolved, diversified and cover the land with a million different mammal species, many of which a traveller from the present might even begin to recognize.

Near the end of this era, one of the five tablets, now no more than an impression on the surface of a stratum of sandstone, is lost forever when a minor earthquake fractures and grinds the strata to loose gravel. The subtle etchings of words and numbers imprinted from the long-gone clay tablet, erased.

Four companions, however, live on, still separated after so many millions of years by the same distance that existed between them the day they were buried, mere hundreds of yards apart.

Around twenty million years pass and the Palaeogene period becomes the Neogene. The world grows cooler, and for the first time, for a long time, ice-caps begin to form at the polar north and south. Species of grass colonize the land in a way that prehistoric ferns could only dream of, and small four-legged mammals that will one day look very different and be known as 'buffaloes' graze blissfully upon it.

Around seven million years ago, the hard-rimmed hoof of one of these small grazing creatures catches the tip of a broken slab of sandstone, and pulls it out of the ground. It lies there in the darkness of night, moonlight picking out strange and subtle patterns of raised markings on one side. But the roaring of a night predator spooks the herd. As one, they surge away from the sound, and the night is filled with the rumble of thousands of hooves on hard-baked soil.

By dawn the curious slab of sedimentary rock is no more than dust and fragments, destroyed by thousands of trampling beasts.

Three silent witnesses remain as endless aeons pass in darkness, like the soft ticking of an impatient clock. Above ground, one species of rodent that took to the trees during the early Palaeogene, has finally ventured down to the ground once more to forage for food as the Neogene era begins. It is larger, with a more muscular frame and a head larger in proportion to its tree-climbing ancestors. It's a species that will one day, in another more million years, be known as 'ape'.

In 11,000 BC, early one morning as warm sun spills across a plain, a young Indian brave carefully scouting the grazing buffalo ahead runs his hand over the coarse grass and dislodges the sharp corner of a stone. A chunk of flint emerges from the orange soil, a flint, he notices, with curious markings on it.

For a moment the markings incite his curiosity. They look deliberate. But then his mind moves on to the size of the flint itself. He can see how three separate *tamahaken* blades could be struck from it, and he thanks Great Father Sun for the find.

Now only two silent messengers remain.

In 1865, a young Confederate lieutenant on the run from Union forces, leading a ragtag band of soldiers unwilling to accept that the civil war is over, rests his aching back against a rock. With tired eyes, too old for such a young face, he watches the languid river in front of him as his fingers twist through coarse grass. And, yes, they find the sharp edge of a stone.

Before the war he was a student of history, and the faint lines of writing on the stone fascinate him. He puts the curious piece of rock in his saddle-bag and resolves to take it to a professor of natural history he once knew in Charleston when he eventually can. But later that same day the Union cavalry regiment finally catches up with the lieutenant and his men. And before the sun has set they – soldiers and officer – lie in a shared unmarked grave not far away from the Paluxy River.

And so just one last tablet remains.

CHAPTER 53

2 May 1941, Somervell County, Texas

Grady Adams watched his brother goofing about in the water below with growing irritation. 'Watch it, Saul . . . you gonna scare off all the fish!' His brother ignored him and surface dived into the sedate Paluxy River.

Grady ground his teeth. His younger brother could be a complete ass at times. No, strike that . . . *all the time*. He settled back on his haunches, his toes curled over the lip of tan-coloured rock overhanging the river. The stone was hot against the bare skin of his feet, *egg-frying* hot, that's what Pa would say. The sun had been beating down on it all morning, and the pool of water that had dripped off him from his last swim in the river half an hour ago had long since evaporated.

He looked up at a nearly cloudless sky and realized there wasn't going to be any momentary respite from the heat of the sun. To his left, several dozen yards along the ledge of rock, a small, withered cypress tree was clinging to the side of a large craggy boulder. He could see it was casting a small pool of shadow, at least big enough for a part of him to keep out of the sun.

He stood, grabbed his fishing rod and walked carefully along the narrow ledge. Carefully, because from time to time, right near the edge, bits of the sandstone rock broke away and splashed into the river a yard or so below. That had happened to Grady before, scratching up his hips and chest as he'd slid into the water.

Saul came up again, noisily splashing the surface of the river, no doubt scaring any remaining fish well away from the float bobbing nearby.

'Saul! For crying out loud!'

His brother gave him a toothy grin and paddled across to the far bank, deliberately kicking his feet on the surface and making as much of a ruckus as he could.

Grady hunkered down in the shadow, his back now against cool rock, and to his right a dried earthy wall of orange soil and gnarled roots from the small tree poking out from it. He prodded at the loose layers of soil, light and dark, like the layers of some fancy sponge cake. He'd once found a Paiute *tamahaken* blade among a bank of earth like this. Those layers folded away such fascinating things along this river. He remembered there was that team of men last summer, digging around along portions of the riverbank, looking for monster footprints in the rock. *Dinosaur tracks*, that's what they'd said they were looking for.

Grady and Saul had seen a few in their time along here, big ones like he'd imagined an elephant might leave, and small ones too, three deeper dents and a shallow one. Saul even claimed he'd once seen a human footprint in the rock, just exactly like a shoe. Silly ass was always coming up with doofus nonsense like that.

Grady knew no cavemen wore shoes back then in dinosaur times.

The people up in Glen Rose had started calling this place Dinosaur Valley on account of the men and women from the museums and stuff who came digging for fossils last year. He smiled at that as he tugged at one of the twisted roots. It sounded kind of cool . . . *Dinosaur Valley*. He could imagine some of the gigantic beasts he'd seen in picture books striding across their Paluxy River, walking up and down the riverbanks, their long necks craning down to drink from the river . . .

Grit and dry soil tumbled down on to his arm. 'Ouch!'

He let go of the root and it sprang up, releasing another small avalanche of loose clay-like earth. And then he saw it, half hanging out, and resting on a coil of tree root that looked like a pig's tail. A palm-sized slate of shale. He reached up for it and it fell heavily into his hands.

For a moment, as he stared down at the almost triangular shape, he wondered whether it might just be another one of them *tamahaken* heads. But it didn't have the telltale signs of being worked on, shaped by some skilled hand.

It was just a plain ol' slice of rock.

He held it in his throwing hand, wondering how many bounces he'd get from skimming it across the river. It was nice and flat . . . a good spin on the throw and maybe he'd count seven, perhaps eight, before it settled and sank. He stood up, saw Saul on the far bank sunning himself on a dry boulder. 'Hey! Saul!'

His brother's head bobbed up. 'What?'

'I got me a skimmer. Reckon I get an eight with it?'

'Nah,' he called back, 'cos you throw like a girl an' all.'

Grady shook his head and sighed. His brother really could be annoying. 'Well, why don'tcha just look and learn, you foo-bat!'

He cupped it in his palm, wondering which side was flatter . . . and then turned it over.

CHAPTER 54

2001, New York

On Sunday 9 September 2001, Lester Cartwright, a small narrow-shouldered man facing his last five desk years before his long-awaited retirement, went to bed with his plump wife. A man who, if you asked him to be honest, would admit to being a little bored with his unchallenging life. His job – yes, it might sound interesting if he was allowed to talk about it – was as a *projects budget assessor* for a low-profile US intelligence agency. But, in actual fact, despite the intriguing sound of working for a secret service, the work simply involved crunching numbers and balancing costs and expenditures. He might as well have been doing that for Wal-Mart, or McDonald's, or some carpet store . . . the job would have been exactly the same.

Not exactly where he'd hoped to end his career when he'd first joined them back in the 1960s, a young man ready to serve his country in the field. A young man ready to kill or be killed for Uncle Sam. Now he was an old man who rubber-stamped expense forms.

That night he went to bed after walking their dog, Charlie, climbed into his pyjamas and picked up a Tom Clancy spy novel, hoping to enjoy at least a few aimless thrills today before turning the light out on his bedside table.

Later, as he slept, change arrived in the form of a subtle ripple of reality. A wave of reality systematically rewriting itself, a wave of change that had started in 1941 . . . with a young boy's discovery of a strange rock beside a river in Texas. A boy who turned over a rock and saw something curious.

Lester's boring life in that moment of darkness was replaced in just the blink of an eye, with a far, far more interesting one.

'Sir! Sir!' Knuckles rapped gently against the car's rear passenger window. Lester Cartwright stirred, his mind had been off again, considering the incredible, the impossible.

Only, it isn't impossible, is it, Lester?

He looked out of the window at Agent Forby, dark glasses, a suit, crew-cut hair and a face that looked like it had never told a joke while on duty. Lester wound his window down an inch. 'Yes?'

'Sir, it's time,' said Forby.

Lester looked down at his watch. Three minutes to midnight. Dammit . . . he must have been napping again.

Getting too old for something like this.

'Forby, the area's completely secure?'

Forby nodded. 'We have a two-block cordon set up. Police and state guard are manning those. The Williamsburg Bridge has been closed and all civilians have been evacuated from the perimeter.'

Cartwright nodded. The cover story had been an easy no-brainer to come up with: a bomb threat. American civilians seemed to react very well to that. 'So, we're certain we have just agency personnel within?'

Forby nodded. 'A hundred per cent, sir. Just us guys.'

Cartwright looked out of the window past Forby's hunched form. The Williamsburg Bridge towered over them, the nearby intersection was deserted and there, fifty yards away, was the entrance to the small backstreet running alongside the bridge's brick support arches.

My God . . . finally. This is it. This is finally it.

He felt his chest tickled by butterfly wings and the short hairs on the back of his neck rise.

'Very well.' He opened the car door and stepped out into the warm evening. 'Then let's begin.'

Cartwright led the way across the quiet road, lit by several fizzing street lights and the intermittent sweep of a floodlight from a helicopter holding position high up in the sky. Apart from the far-off *whup-whup-whup* of its rotors, this three-block-wide area of Brooklyn was ghostly quiet.

There was a barricade across the entrance to the backstreet, manned by more of Cartwright's men. No soldiers or police this close to the *target*, on Cartwright's insistence. Only personnel he trusted within the perimeter. Only personnel he'd recruited himself into this small covert agency, an agency he and his men referred to as *the Club*.

He nodded at them as they raised their guns and let him through. He looked down the narrow cobbled street, littered with garbage, an abandoned skip halfway along.

Good grief, I feel . . . like a kid.

All of his professional life had been leading up to this one moment, ever since he'd been quietly headhunted from the FBI to come and work for the Club. Forty years of *knowing*.

Lester Cartwright began to make his way down the row of archways, past the first one, clearly being used by some one-man auto-repair business.

When he'd first joined, his superior had been prepared to reveal only some of the facts: an incredible find in a place called Glen Rose, Texas – a find that had major national security implications. That was all he got for quite a few years. But time passed, and Lester gradually climbed several ranks, finally becoming the senior serving officer in the Club. His departing boss had handed him the complete dossier on his very last day, handed it to him with eyes that looked like they'd been staring far too long into an abyss.

'*Do me a favour, Lester,*' he'd said. '*Sit yourself down and drink a finger of bourbon before you open this file, all right?*'

'*Sir?*'

'*You're about to join a very, very small group . . . those that know.*'

And it *was* a small group.

Presidents had been briefed – Roosevelt, when the news of the *artefact* had first been unearthed. Then Truman, then Eisenhower. But they'd stopped briefing presidents when that silly fool Kennedy had threatened to go public on it. That was the year after Lester had joined the Club, the year of the Dallas incident. A very messy business. But the Club had a responsibility.

They hadn't bothered to tell presidents since then.

Cartwright passed the third and fourth archways, both open-fronted and unoccupied. He could see needles and bottles back there in the darkness. His men had checked in there for vagrants and unearthed only one grubby, stinking and utterly bewildered alcoholic. He could feel his heart pounding in his chest as his feet slowly brought him up outside the metal roller-shutter door of the fifth archway.

Forty years he'd known of a thing called the *Glen Rose artefact*.

But only for the last fifteen years had he known exactly what it was.

Figuratively speaking, a message in a bottle, with a date on it. A bottle that couldn't be opened until a certain date. He looked down at his watch and saw that that certain date was a mere forty seconds away.

There hadn't been a single solitary night during the last fifteen years that he hadn't lain in bed and wondered what they'd find inside this address. He'd been down this street on a number of occasions and looked at that corrugated metal; he'd even been inside and looked around on several occasions. Empty, unused.

But now, finally, there were occupants inside. Occupants from – his heart fluttered and his breath caught as he considered the phrase – *another time*.

Cartwright instinctively reached into his suit jacket for the service-issue firearm he kept there as he looked at his watch and realized that after forty years of waiting and preparing he was finally down to counting off the last ten seconds.

'So . . . this is it,' he uttered.

The second hand of his watch ticked past midnight and all of a sudden he thought he felt the slightest puff of displaced air against his face.

He leaned forward, balled his fist and knuckled the shutter door gently.

CHAPTER 55

2001, New York

Maddy looked at Sal. 'Oh my God! You hear that? That was a knock, wasn't it?' She hadn't fully expected to be right, that come the stroke of midnight and the reset there would actually, for real, be a knock on their door.

The roller shutter rattled again, and they heard the muffled sound of a man's voice outside.

'So we're going to open it, right?' whispered Sal.

'I . . . uh . . . yes, I guess we've got no choice.' She stepped forward towards the button at the side and pressed it. With a rattling whirr of a winch motor begging for oil, the shutter slowly rose. Both girls looked down at the ground, at the gradually widening gap, and the soft glow of the street lamp outside creeping across their stained and pitted concrete floor.

Two shoes. Two dark-suited legs. Finally the person outside ducked down slightly to look in, and his wide eyes met theirs.

'Hello there,' said Maddy, raising a limp hand. 'We were . . . kind of expecting you.'

The shutter rattled to a stop and the man stared at them for a long while in silence.

'I . . .' he started, his voice croaky with nerves. 'You . . . but you're just kids.' He narrowed his eyes, looking past them at the dim interior. 'Are there any others here?'

'Just us, I'm afraid,' said Maddy.

He looked at her; his old creased face seemed to be struggling to cope with the moment. 'Are you two . . . are you f-from the future?' he asked.

Sal looked at Maddy and she finally nodded her head. 'You've got a million questions you want to ask us, I'm sure,' Maddy addressed the old man. 'And we're prepared to answer some of them. But . . . you have something, right? Something for us?'

He eyed her cautiously. 'Perhaps.'

'A message?'

He ignored the question. 'Are you time travellers?'

'I won't answer anything until you answer me. Do you have a message for us?'

He took a step forward, squinting at the machinery on the far side of the arch. He nodded towards it. 'Is that some sort of time machine?'

She bit her lip. 'I'm not saying anything until you answer me.'

'It is, isn't it?' He smiled. 'My God . . . this is incredible.'

'Please!' called out Sal. 'Something brought you to us. It's a message from our friend, isn't it?'

The old man turned away from them and barked an order down along their backstreet. A moment later Maddy could hear the slap of boots on cobblestones. She retreated from the entrance and into the arch, taking several steps towards the computer desk.

'I'm sorry,' said the old man. He reached into his suit jacket and pulled a handgun on them. 'Please remain perfectly still. Do not touch anything! Do not do anything!'

Half a dozen men emerged from the backstreet, all of them wearing bio-hazard suits, faces hidden behind tinted fascias of plastic. All of them armed with what looked like television remote controls.

Oh no. Maddy felt lightheaded. *This isn't good.*

'We're going to talk,' said the old man gently. 'But we're going to talk safely away from this place. Please,' he said, beckoning for them both to come forward, out of the archway and into the street, 'step forward, away from the equipment.'

Now! You have to do it now!

Maddy spun to face the computer desk. 'BOB! *OMELETTE!*' she screamed, desperately hoping the desk mic across the archway had managed to pick up her voice. The last thing her conscious mind registered was every muscle in her body contracting with a sudden jolt, and then keeling over on to the hard floor, her forehead smacking heavily against the concrete.

Cartwright watched in silence as the older of the two girls was wheeled away on a hospital gurney, and the other one, younger, Asian or Indian by the look of her, was escorted down the backstreet towards the containment van.

He ordered the remaining three agency men in containment suits to stand guard outside the shutter door once they'd made a sweep and reported that the archway was clear. Good men, trusted men . . . but still better they knew as little as possible.

He stood alone now in front of a giant perspex cylinder of water, metal steps up the side and what looked like a toddler's swing seat fixed at the top. Obviously something to do with time travel . . . like the bank of computer equipment, the other tall thin perspex tubes in the back room, the power generator . . . all these things clearly played some part in the process.

He wandered back to the long table – a pair of scuffed office desks pushed end to end and cluttered with monitors, a keyboard, a dozen crumpled cans of Dr Pepper and a few empty pizza boxes. He could hear the soft whirr of activity from beneath the desk and ducked down to see the muted glow of blinking green and red LEDs. It looked like there were a dozen or more PCs, the kind you could pick up from any Wal-Mart or PC World, linked together into a network.

Beside the desk was a battered old office filing cabinet. He pulled out one drawer after another, each filled with nests of tangled cables and bits and pieces of electronic circuits, like somebody had ripped off a RadioShack store for bits and not yet figured out what to do with it all.

He felt a small stab of disappointment. In his mind's eye he'd imagined this moment; he'd conjured up visions of some futuristic arrangement, technology from centuries ahead, something that looked like the bridge of the *USS Enterprise* set up in this old brick archway. Instead, everything he could see here seemed to have been obtained from the present.

He sat down in one of the office chairs and it squeaked under his weight.

The answers to this place, why they were here in New York . . . why they were also in the Cretaceous past, how all this machinery worked, and what it could do . . . all of those answers he presumed were on these quietly humming computers. He picked up the mouse and slid it across the desk. One of the screens flickered out of screen-saver mode and lit up to reveal a relaxing desktop image of an alpine valley and, right in the middle of the screen, a small square dialogue box.

> System lockdown enabled.

Cartwright cursed under his breath. The older girl, the one with the frizzy reddish hair, had barked something out just before he'd tasered her. He'd thought she was calling out to someone else in the arch, but he realized now that it must have been a voice-activated command.

He tried to remember what she'd said. Oh yeah . . .

'Omelette,' he said into the desk mic.

> Incorrect activation code.

'Dammit!'

> Incorrect activation code.

He tried a dozen other candidate words and phrases: egg, broken eggs, scrambled eggs, boiled eggs, Easter egg, fried egg. Egg hunt, egghead, egg-nog. All of them produced the response on the screen.

Absently he tapped his fingers on the desk. If he was being honest, this wasn't how he imagined the moment of discovery was going to be: two scruffy kids, a computer system that looked like some bedroom hacker's dream set-up, and that big plastic cylinder making this place look like some kind of homemade brewery. And this locked-down computer system was obviously not going to tell him anything. He decided it was time he had a little chat with the girls.

He stepped out towards the open door and punched the green button on the side. The metal shutter started to clank and rattle slowly down.

'No one goes in, or comes out. You have permission to shoot to kill anyone who tries. Understood?'

The three men guarding the entrance nodded.

CHAPTER 56

65 million years BC, jungle

The wide-open plain was alive with the echoing calls of nocturnal life. Liam had assigned half of them to remain on watch and the other half to try their best to get some sleep, although he doubted anyone was managing that.

A fire was burning in the middle, not for the meagre light it provided, but for the effect it seemed to have on the creatures roaming around out there, keeping them all well away. It was bright enough anyway. The full moon seemed to illuminate the night enough that it felt little darker than an overcast winter's afternoon in Cork.

'That moon is actually bigger, right? Or am I going mad?'

Becks looked up at it. 'Affirmative. It is approximately twenty per cent larger.'

Liam's eyebrows shot up. 'A larger moon? So what do you think happened to it? Did it sort of *wear down* over time or something?'

Whitmore looked at him oddly and tutted. And Becks . . . he wondered whether she'd just rolled her eyes at him or whether that was just a trick of the light. 'Negative, Liam. It has not changed size.'

'It's just a little closer,' said Whitmore.

'Oh.'

Becks resumed her silent vigil, slowly panning her eyes

across the plain, watching for the dark furtive shapes of the creatures moving beyond the dancing circle of their firelight.

'What do you think of those things?' asked Liam. 'Are they really a species of super-smart dinosaur? That lad, Franklyn . . .' He paused for a moment, realizing the ensuing panic-stricken retreat from the cove, over the jungle peak and down on to the beach hadn't permitted him a single moment of reflection for the poor boy. He could only imagine what those creatures had done to him, if that carcass from nearly a fortnight ago was anything to go by.

The others were waiting for him to finish what he'd started saying.

'Franklyn said *all* dinosaurs, even the smart ones, were pretty stupid.'

Whitmore sucked in a breath of warm night air. 'Those hominids could well be a dead-end evolution, a branch-off species that maybe shares a common ancestor with troodon.'

'Troodon?'

He nodded. 'Palaeontologists commonly agree that the troodon was quite possibly the most intelligent species of dinosaur. Smarter even than their evolutionary cousins, the raptors. Very similar in appearance, both therapods . . . saurischian dinosaurs.'

'What's that mean?'

'Bipedal . . . they walk on their hind legs. Like the T-rex does.'

Liam shook his head. 'Those creatures didn't look anything like any dinosaur I've seen, big or small. I mean . . . their heads?'

Whitmore nodded. 'Like I say, some dead-end evolution. Perhaps if the K–T event never happened, the asteroid, or volcano or whatever it was, many more sub-species with similar long skulls might have evolved from them. Perhaps that's why they're so smart – a greater cranial capacity, a larger brain.'

'The species exhibits high levels of intelligence,' said Becks. Her neutral voice seemed to have adopted an ominous tone. 'They appear capable of tactical planning. They appear to have a language. They do not, however, appear to have developed tool-use.'

'Why not? If they're so smart? Why don't they use spears and bows and arrows?'

Becks had no answer. Whitmore shrugged. 'Who knows? Perhaps they've never needed to *use* tools? Maybe nature already made them so lethal they've never *needed* tools? Or perhaps, because they only seem to have four digits and no thumbs, tool-using is just something they're unlikely to ever do?'

'But they're smart enough?' asked Liam. 'Is that what you're saying? If they had thumbs an' all . . . they'd be smart enough to make a spear or a bow or something?'

Whitmore scratched his beard absently. 'Who knows?'

On the far side of the campfire, Howard and Edward stood watch. The robo-girl had been standing with them for a while and then gone to rejoin her Irish friend and Whitmore. Howard decided now was quite possibly the best time he was going to have to say what he needed to say.

'Edward?'

The small boy looked up at him.

'Thank you, you know . . . for saving me from that shark thing yesterday.'

Edward shrugged like he'd done nothing more than buy him a Coke. 'OK, Leonard.'

'No . . . seriously, Edward, that was something . . . what you did. It could just as easily have gotten you. But you . . . you stayed right by me. You saved my life.'

Edward smiled. 'Sure, Lenny. You're my best friend.' He sighed. 'Well, my *only* friend. Like I said, I don't do so good back home. You know, making friends and stuff.'

Howard felt a sour twist of guilt churn away in his guts. He'd come to kill Edward – that's how he'd ended up here – and yet this boy seemed like a ten-years-younger version of himself. He'd had things the same way when he'd been at school: lonely because he dared to be different. It never changed, did it? Not even in his time, the 2050s. Kids always found a way to single somebody out.

'Edward, I've got to tell you something,' he said before he could stop himself.

'What?'

'I'm . . . I'm not who you think I am.'

Edward frowned and smiled at the same time, bemused. 'You're Lenny.'

'No,' replied Howard, 'that's just it, I'm not. I'm not Leonard Baumgardner. I'm not seventeen.' He lowered his voice and his eyes flickered across the campfire towards the other three people on guard duty. 'And I'm *not* from the year 2015.'

'What? Serious?' Edward's eyes widened. 'You're one of *them*? An agent from the future too?'

Howard shook his head. 'Not an agent. I don't work for the same people. I belong to another group, a group trying to stop time travel, but . . . but in a different way.'

Edward stared at him silently. 'Not Lenny. So what *is* your name?'

'Howard.'

He heard Edward mouth the name quietly.

'But listen, Edward . . . I . . . I managed to go back in time to find you . . .' He hesitated, toying with how best to continue, when Edward spoke the words for him.

'To get to me. That's it, isn't it?'

Howard looked away.

'To stop me going to university? Stop me doing a degree?'

Howard couldn't bear to meet his eyes.

'Not to . . . oh no . . .' Edward's voice dropped. He'd figured it out. 'No. Don't say you came to *kill* me?'

Howard nodded. 'I'm sorry, Edward . . . but yeah. To short-circuit history, to cut out a chunk of the past that should never have happened.' In the dark he couldn't see how the boy was taking it, just the outline of his round head and narrow shoulders gazing out at the dark plain.

'That means you're not really my friend, then?'

Howard felt that twist of guilt curl and flex like some restless eel making a nest in his belly.

'That mean you're still going to kill me?'

Howard shook his head. 'No, not any more.'

'Why?'

'Because I don't need to. We're stuck here now.'

Edward turned back towards him. 'But we're gonna get rescued. Those messages that we –'

'No one's going to find them,' he replied, shaking his head.

'How do you know?'

'If they'd ever been found –' he nodded towards the others – 'and Liam and robo-girl's people were able to come and rescue us, then they'd know what happens in 2015, wouldn't they? They'd know about me. And they'd make sure you were *never* on that field trip to the TERI labs. They'd make sure you were kept as far away from that assassination attempt as possible.'

Edward's face clouded with thought for a moment.

Howard offered him a smile that was probably lost in the dark anyway. 'So, I've done what had to be done. I'm truly sorry it's landed us here. I really am . . . but the world after 2015 is a much safer place without you. There's no you, there's no maths thesis, no Waldstein and no time machines. For good or bad . . . I know the world's heading for dark times ahead, certainly it is where – *when* – I came from: floods, droughts, billions starving, oil running out, wars. But the world will get through that eventually. It can survive that.'

'But it can't survive time travel?'

'No. We've been messing around with stuff we can't understand, can't control. We're like children playing catch and toss with a neutron bomb. But that's finished, Edward . . . It's not going to happen. I'm relieved, but I'm also sorry it's landed you and the others here.'

'Why be sorry?' said Edward flatly. 'Mission successful. You did it.'

'I'm sorry . . . because, I think, well, I hope, you and I have become friends. And I've put you in this situation.' Howard could understand if the boy walked away right now and told everything he'd just heard to the others. Then, of course, they'd confront him and perhaps even exact a brutal revenge on him. Howard could understand that and was ready to face the music.

Instead he felt Edward's small hand on his forearm. 'It's OK. I'm not angry with you.'

He laughed. 'You have every right to be.'

'No point,' said Edward. 'We're stuck here forever, then. So we've got to work together. Right, *Leonard*?'

Leonard . . . it sounded like Edward was going to keep this confession to himself.

Howard nodded. 'So?'

'So, I'm not telling. You're Leonard still.'

He smiled. 'OK . . . I'm Leonard.'

'Right.'

'Right.'

CHAPTER 57

2001, New York

Maddy's mouth was dry and her head was pounding. She slowly opened her eyes and winced them shut against the painful bright glare of the light overhead.

'Sorry about that,' she heard someone say. The lights in the room dimmed slightly. 'Better?'

She cracked her eyes open again, and then nodded. She felt something cool pressed into her hands.

'Water. Have a sip. It's just water, I assure you.'

Maddy lifted a plastic tumbler and gratefully slurped a mouthful. Her eyes blinked and she tried to focus on her surroundings: a small room with a low ceiling, what looked like a medicine cabinet, a strip light overhead. She was lying on what appeared to be a hospital bed and beside her she saw the old man who'd come knocking at their door sitting on a stool. He'd taken his jacket off, rolled up his shirtsleeves and loosened his tie.

'You took a knock on the head when you went down. I'm sorry I had to taser you.'

Yes . . . that was it. She'd felt like every muscle in her body had locked and an unbelievably agonizing sensation had coursed through her whole body.

'Where am I?' She realized she was lying on some sort of a

hospital gurney. But then this didn't look like a hospital ward, or a private ward.

'New York still,' he smiled. 'And somewhere perfectly safe.'

She sipped the water again. 'Who are you?'

The man pulled the stool forward. It rattled on castors across a smooth linoleum floor. 'My name's Lester Cartwright,' he answered warmly. 'And yes – if that's your next question – I work for a, shall we say, a quiet little intelligence agency on behalf of the American government.'

Maddy nodded and smiled blearily. 'I figured it would be someone like that who'd come to our door.'

'Well . . . who else would it be?' he asked. 'Something like this, knowledge of this . . . it's far too important for any old Joe to have in his possession. I'm sure you'd agree.'

Maddy shrugged, her hand reaching up to her forehead and finding a dressing there. 'I suppose.'

'So,' he said, leaning forward. 'I have just about a million goddamn questions I've been wanting to ask someone like you. Questions I've been waiting for answers to most of my adult life. And, in return, I have a curious message that I'm sure you're rather keen to see.'

She was encouraged by the old man's directness. No beating about the bush, no attempting to fool her, beguile her. Just the straightforward declaration of a *quid pro quo.*

She nodded. 'A message from a friend.'

'Yes,' he said as he got up and reached for his jacket neatly draped on a small storage cabinet in the corner of the room. He fumbled for the inside pocket and finally pulled out a folded sheet of paper. 'A friend who apparently decided to take a holiday during the, if I'm not mistaken, the late Cretaceous period?'

Maddy's jaw dropped open. 'I . . . uh . . . *when* did you say?'

'The late Cretaceous. We've tested the rock. It's definitely from that time.'

Her lungs emptied a gasp. 'You mean, like, dinosaur times?'

Cartwright nodded. 'Yes, I believe it was a popular time for dinosaurs.'

'Oh my God, I didn't think the machine –' She stopped herself before she blurted out anything else. She decided it would be far smarter to keep as much as possible to herself for now.

'Yes.' The man's eyes narrowed curiously. 'Yes, you *do* look genuinely surprised at that. What were you going to say?'

She shook her head. 'Nothing.'

He studied her silently for a few moments. 'This is someone you lost, isn't it? Someone you've been unable to retrieve? To find? Some kind of mistake? Is that it?'

'May I see the message, please?' she replied.

'You didn't think time travel that far back was possible?' he said, fishing for a reaction on her face. 'Am I right?'

'We lost someone, all right? Now, can I see the message?'

'Where are you from?' he asked, then shook his head. Comically, he gently slapped his forehead. 'Stupid, stupid me . . . it's *when* are you from I should be asking, isn't it?'

Maddy couldn't help a smile and a dry laugh. 'It does that to you, this business . . . makes you want to slap your head.'

The old man shared the smile. 'I can imagine.' The smile eased away. Business again. 'You're American, that much I've worked out. Boston?'

She nodded. No point trying to hide that. 'Yes.'

'When?' He looked at her T-shirt, the faded Intel logo on the front, her jeans, her pumps. 'Not too far into the future is my guess.'

'Maybe.'

'You want to see this?' he asked, unfolding the message.

She nodded.

'Then can we start having some *precise* answers from you?'

She shrugged. 'OK.'

'Your name is?'

'Maddy. Maddy Carter.'

'Hello, Maddy.' He nodded politely. 'And what year are you from?'

'I'm from 2010,' she replied.

The answer seemed to stun him. His eyes widened involuntarily and beneath the folds of his wrinkled skin above the crisp white collar of his shirt, his jaw worked as teeth ground. Finally he pursed his lips. '2010 you said?'

'Yup.'

'You actually *know* the future? The next nine years of it?'

'Of course.'

His face drained. 'Then you . . . you're saying you know, for example, what this government's foreign policy goals might be? Long-term strategic plans? Those kind of things?'

She smiled. 'Oh yeah, I know what's round the corner.'

That silenced him for a long while. She watched the folded paper flutter in his hand.

'Do you know just how dangerous that makes you to certain people?' he said softly. 'I can think of quite a few colleagues in my line of business who'd want to put a bullet in your head right now. Quite a few more who'd want to torture every last little fact out of that head of yours . . . oh, and *then* put a bullet in it.'

'The message?'

He nodded his head absently and then handed it over. 'It might amuse you to know,' he said, 'I can recite every word and every last number of the coded section. I've known off by heart what's written down on there for the last decade and a half.' He laughed humourlessly. 'Like an old poem drummed into your head at school and you never ever forget.'

Maddy reached for it and unfolded the paper. She saw handwriting. She presumed it was the old man's handwriting.

> Take this to Archway 9, Wythe Street, Brooklyn, New York on Monday 10 September 2001.
> Message: -89-1-9/54-1-5/76-1-2/23-3-5/17-8-4/7-3-7/5-8-3/12-6-9/23-8-1/3-1-1/56-9-2/12-5-8/67-8-3/92-6-7/112-8-3/234-6-1/45-7-3/30-6-2/34-8-3/41-5-6/99-7-1/2-6-9/127-8-1/128-7-3/259-1-5/2-7-1/69-1-5/14-2-66. Key is 'Magic'.

Oh my God, Liam . . . you're alive. You made it.

'Now, the first bit makes sense to me . . . clearly designed to make sure the message finds its way to you –'

She cut him short. '*Where* did you get the message from?'

He cocked a wiry grey eyebrow. 'A fossil, would you believe? A fossil discovered by some boys in 1941. The second of May, to be precise. Along a river near a town called Glen Rose in the state of Texas. It nearly caused a sensation, but . . . the wartime secret service worked quickly to hush up the find. And, of course, people were far more concerned about the war then than silly rumours about mysterious fossil finds.'

He smiled. 'The place was taken over by secret service goons, and guess what else they found?'

Maddy shrugged.

'A few months after the message was discovered, they found a human footprint.' He looked up at her. 'Oh yes, a genuine human footprint, from the same strata of sedimentary rock. The print of some sort of a running shoe.' He was amused by that. 'That's what they called it back then, *a running shoe*. They didn't have training shoes back then.'

'Uh?'

'A forensic expert matched the print pattern to the *Nike* brand last year.'

'And no one else knows?'

He laughed. 'Of course not. The boys who originally discovered the artefact . . . well –' he glanced at her – 'our methods were a little *uncivilized* back then.'

'Killed?'

'Hmmm . . . *vanished* . . . is the term I think we prefer. And, of course, it turned out a few years later that some other local rockhound had found fossilized human footprints the previous summer . . . so again there was need for some damage limitation.'

'*Vanished* too?'

He shook his head. 'News of the human footsteps got to the local newspapers before it could be contained. We simply discredited the story. Easily done, the same old boy swore blind his dead mother lived in the attic and came down once a year to bake his birthday cake.' He snorted. 'Complete loon by all accounts. Anyway, go look it up sometime. I'm sure it's on some conspiracy website somewhere: "Humans Walked with Dinosaurs – Dinosaur Valley, Texas".'

She looked down at the message again. 'So, you know exactly how old the fossil is?'

He shook his head. 'No, not exactly. Of course not. It's identified as coming from a seam of sedimentary rock that pre-dates the end of the Cretaceous period. What they call the K–T boundary. That's as precise as we can be, I'm afraid. Geology works in aeons and ages, not months or years.'

He gestured at the piece of paper. 'The numbers . . .

I presume the numbers contain specific information that would help you retrieve your friend?'

She could deny that, but it was quite obviously the information Liam would have put down there. 'I hope so,' she said.

'But unfortunately it's encoded,' he said. 'Now, the secret service boys who pre-dated my little club's involvement in this matter identified this pretty quickly as some sort of *book code.* See? The numbers follow the page, line, word structure. And about a decade ago, we managed to secure some very expensive time on the Defence Department's mainframe and ran every single book in the Library of Congress through it.' He splayed his hands tiredly. 'We got diddly squat for all our troubles, of course. Which leads me to think, as I sit here with you now, that that was a big waste of time as this probably is a book that hasn't even been published yet. How about that?'

Maddy shook her head. 'I . . . I don't know. I really don't.'

She glanced at the last words of the message. 'Key is "Magic".' She looked up at Cartwright. 'That's the clue, right? But I just . . . I just don't know . . . If that really is a clue to a book, I wouldn't know which one.'

'What about your colleague?'

'Sal?' She sat up and groaned with the effort. 'Is she OK? Where is she?'

'Oh, she's just fine,' he said, waving his hands dismissively. 'And she's nearby. Maybe it's time I had a chat with her.'

'You won't hurt her?'

He looked sternly at her as he reached for the piece of paper, got off the stool and picked his jacket up off the cabinet.

'Because, see, if . . . uh . . . if that's what you're planning to do,' Maddy continued, 'then don't b-bother.'

'Oh, let me guess, because the pair of you are heroes and neither one of you is going to talk, huh?'

'Because –' she shook her head and laughed nervously – 'because there's really no need. Neither of us are heroes. We'll talk, OK? Just promise me you won't hurt us.'

CHAPTER 58

65 million years BC, jungle

Kelly struggled up the steep incline, cursing under his breath as low-hanging thorned vines scratched at his face. Ahead he could hear the others pushing their way noisily uphill, the snapping of branches and vines, the clatter of dislodged rocks and soil rolling downhill.

'Leonard? Edward?' he called out.

'Here,' gasped Edward.

'Come on, you need to pick it up . . . we're lagging behind the others.'

Their sweat-drenched faces emerged through a curtain of waxy leaves. 'I'm exhausted,' gasped Howard. 'My leg . . .' He failed to finish his words between ragged puffs of air. He dropped uncomfortably to his knees on to an uneven bed of dried cones, twigs and jagged rocks.

'It's slowing him down,' said Edward. 'His ankle.'

'I know, I know, but we can't let the others get too far ahead.'

Around their campfire last night the discussion had turned to why those creatures hadn't attacked them again, instead choosing to discreetly follow them at a distance. The conclusion they'd come to was that they were playing a tactical game, waiting for the group to become spread out enough to be able to pick them off one at a time. This morning as they'd made their way across the rest of the plain towards the last stretch of the journey, down into the jungle valley, they'd been almost comically bunched up.

But now, hacking their way through dense foliage, the group was getting dangerously strung out.

'Come on, Edward, help me get him up.'

It was then that Kelly caught a glimpse through a gap in the leaves of some dark form fifty yards below them.

'Oh Jesus,' he hissed. 'I saw something back there!'

'What?'

'Just . . . just . . . .there's no one else behind us, is there?'

Edward shook his head.

Kelly saw it again, a dark form hurrying between the trunks of two trees, then dropping down out of sight. 'Oh my God! They're down there!'

Howard was on his feet again.

'Go! Go!' snapped Kelly. 'I'll watch our backs!'

Edward and Howard stumbled forward again, Kelly reversing uphill, keeping his eyes on the downhill as he fumbled his way after them. Again, he saw it. Closer now, the flicker of dark olive skin, leaping between the gaps in the leaves. More than one of them, and moving so terrifyingly quietly. More worryingly . . . they didn't seem to care that they were being seen.

Oh no.

Now they were in the jungle they were closing the gap.

I'm not going to outrun them.

He realized he stood a far better chance squaring up to them, perhaps even skewering one of them on the end of his spear. Maybe another kill would buy them another day of caution, enough time to get back over that river to the camp.

'Come on,' he hissed. 'I know you're down there!'

He heard Edward calling down. 'Mr Kelly?'

'Go!' he shouted. 'I'm just coming!'

The sound of the two boys' clumsy staggering slowly receded from him until all he could hear was the occasional snap of a branch echoing off the tall stout trunks of the canopy trees.

'Come on!' he whispered again. He was surprised that it wasn't abject terror he was feeling right now, but anger. Rage. He wanted to grab one of those scrawny things and rip its ridiculous marrow-shaped head off. His throat filled with a dry laugh.

Who do you think you are – Tarzan?

A far cry from his normal life: PR guy, meeting and greeting visitors with his cheesy tanned smile and his nice linen suit and expensive polo shirt. Right now, standing legs apart in trousers ripped off at the knees to make shorts, bare-chested, revealing a pale torso tufted with silver-grey hair and drooping man-boobs that spoke of a lapsed gym membership . . . right now he felt like that commando character in the film his sons liked, the one with the alien with a crab face and dreadlocks.

Oh yeah, he was ready for them.

'Come on . . . you want some of me? Then COME ON!'

As if in answer, in the stillness of the jungle around him, he heard a soft, high-pitched voice.

'*. . . Come . . . on . . .*'

Then ahead of him, as if it had appeared like the Cheshire Cat, only yellow eyes first instead of a big grin, there stood one of the creatures, a dozen yards downhill of him, cocking its head and studying him intently.

Kelly took several steps downhill, lunging with the tip of his spear. 'Yeah? So that's what you things look like up close.'

It recoiled at the sight of the spear, ducking back into a patch of waxy leaves, only to emerge again a moment later.

'Oh yeah! I can kill you with this spear,' muttered Kelly triumphantly. The spear seemed to be warding off the creature, its yellow eyes warily locked on the sharpened tip of bamboo.

The sound of the others moving through the jungle was all but gone now. He couldn't afford to remain like this much longer. He needed a kill pretty soon, and for the rest of those things to hopefully bolt like rabbits.

'Come on,' he said quietly, 'just you and me. Man versus ugly lizard thing.'

Its jaw snapped open and a dark tongue curled like a serpent inside. '*. . . Lizz . . . arrrrd . . . ting . . .*' A surprisingly close approximation of his own voice.

'So you do impressions, huh?'

The creature cocked its head thoughtfully, and it was then, as the creature was distracted, working out how to replicate what he'd just said, that he decided to make his move. He took a quick step and a short leap forward and thrust the spear hard. It caught something soft and the creature flapped and flailed on the end of the bamboo, howling with a voice that reminded him of the awful noise a dog can make if you step on its tail.

'YES!' he snarled.

First blood. He pulled the spear back out, leaving a large puncture wound in the creature's belly, out of which thick dark blood began to sputter as it flailed in screeching agony on the jungle floor.

He was about to stab the thing again, but he felt the spear yanked roughly out of his hands.

'Whuh?'

He turned to see a larger hominid, standing fully erect, maybe a foot taller than him. It snarled angrily, a rattling croak in the depth of its throat. He saw others behind it, then became aware of yellow eyes all around him.

The creature held his spear in both of its clawed hands, closely inspecting the long thick shaft, and then finally the sharpened tip, wet with dark blood. It looked at the tip, cocked its head and then looked down at Kelly, who now no longer felt so much like a commando. His knees buckled beneath him and he found himself in a helpless squat on the jungle floor.

Oh God, oh God . . .

'Run,' he whimpered. 'Why aren't you r-running? W-why aren't you running?' That was what was meant to happen. If this was a film, that's what would happen, right? The weedy office guy finally finds his inner hero and saves the day?

'I k-killed one . . . so why . . . w-why aren't you r-running?'

The creature holding the spear took a step forward and once more inspected the bloodied tip of the bamboo before turning it round so that it pointed towards Kelly.

'Oh . . . no . . .' he found himself whimpering. 'P-please . . .'

The normal everyday sounds of a Cretaceous jungle, the distant lowing of large ambling leviathans on the far-off plain, the chatter and squeak of small foraging creatures going about their business, were punctuated by a peculiar sound: the protracted, rattling scream of a human being. It echoed up through the jungle and out through the tops of the canopy trees, startling flocks of small anurognathus from their branches and into the air.

CHAPTER 59

2001, New York

'I'm not saying another thing to you!' snapped Sal.

Cartwright shrugged. 'Well, OK. But then I guess I'm not going to show you what I've got.'

It was silent in the small interrogation room, except for the soft hum of an air-conditioner. It was warm and stuffy. He casually loosened his tie.

Sal's narrowed eyes softened, piqued with curiosity. 'What? What have you got?'

He smiled. 'Hmm . . . now there was me thinking we weren't going to be talking to each other.'

'Oh shadd-yah! Please. Just tell me!'

He pursed his lips, giving it some thought. 'And are you going to tell me the things I want to know?'

She clamped her mouth shut, said nothing.

'You know? I suspect you probably will,' Cartwright relented. 'After all, you, me and Maddy all want the same thing: to bring your friend back home safely.'

'He's alive? Liam's alive?'

'I believe so.' He nodded and reached into his breast pocket. 'He decided to write home.' He passed her the folded sheet of paper and she quickly began to scan the handwriting.

'Your colleague Maddy and I were discussing it just a few minutes ago. She's really rather keen to bring him home too.

And you know I'm prepared to help you girls do that. Whatever you want, whatever you need. But . . .'

She looked up. 'But?'

He splayed his hands almost apologetically. 'That technology in the arch. I'm afraid that's going to be US government property now. And we're going to need your help in figuring out how it all works.'

'We can't do that,' she started. 'We can't just let you have it. It's too dangerous!'

'Too dangerous for the government? But apparently not too dangerous for a pair of kids to mess around with?'

'We were recruited. Specially recruited.'

'Recruited by?'

Sal hesitated. 'I can't really say.'

He shrugged. 'Well, that can wait until later. It's not so important. The fact is somebody needs to take charge of what's in that archway.' He cocked a questioning eyebrow. 'I mean, *somebody's* got to be in charge, right? Making sure there *aren't* loads of other time machines and people running around when and where they shouldn't be.'

'And what . . . that someone's going to be *you*, is it?'

'Me for now, perhaps. In time I'll brief the current president on what we have. But believe you me, far better you have someone like myself looking after this on behalf of the American people than some terrorist group or some mad dictator looking for a world-beating weapon, a madman like Saddam Hussein or Osama Bin Laden. Hmm?'

She shrugged a 'Whatever' at him.

'Now,' he said, nodding at the paper in her hands. 'There's a code there. Maddy seems to think you might know how to decipher it.'

She looked down at the numbers, a meaningless jumble of

digits that meant absolutely nothing to her at first glance. But then, very quickly, the pattern began to speak to her. Groups of three numbers, the first into the hundreds, the second being numbers no greater than thirty-five and the last seeming to peak at numbers no greater than fifteen, sixteen. She knew exactly what that was.

'It's some kind of a book code.'

'Clever girl. But now, here's the sixty-four thousand dollar question. Which book?'

She scanned to the bottom of the numbers and saw the last word of the message.

Magic.

Magic? What the jahulla sort of a clue was tha–?

She looked up at him, a smile slowly spreading across her face. Of course, if Bob had it in his database, so the duplicate AI in the female support unit would also.

'You know, don't you?' said Cartwright.

'Uh-huh.' She was almost tempted to tell him the book's title anyway, since it wasn't going to be published for another few years yet. Instead she attempted to suppress an irresistible urge to giggle.

The old man sighed patiently. 'Well, you could, of course, just tell me. Which would be far more pleasant for the pair of us. Or we have a medicine cabinet full of interesting drugs I can pump into you. Some of them with some quite horrific side effects. And failing that there's always the old-fashioned way.'

'You take us back to the archway,' she said, 'and I'll decode the rest of this message for you.'

He shook his head. 'Hmm, now see, my concern is that we get back into that archway of yours and one of you kids'll shout out something else, and – *pop!* – you and all that machinery vanishes in a puff of twinkly time travel sparkles and smoke.'

'She hasn't told you yet, has she?'

He frowned. 'Told me what?'

Sal's smile widened, a nervous twitchy smile. 'That's actually really funny.'

'Funny?'

She nodded. 'Funny.'

'Why? What's funny?'

'She's playing with you. How long have I been in here?'

'Why?'

'Please . . . tell me how long?'

He looked down at his watch. 'A few hours. Why?'

'Exactly. Please.'

'Five hours . . . five and a half hours.'

She giggled again. 'You don't have much time left, then.'

The last of the congenial expression was lost from his rumpled face. 'Stop messing around and tell me what the hell you're talking about!'

'Sure,' she said amicably. 'Our computer system is locked down for six hours. After that, it's got orders to totally *brick* itself if Maddy doesn't give it another codeword.'

'Brick?'

'Fry all the data. All the machinery. Everything.'

His bushy eyebrows both arced, and beneath his jowls his jaw began grinding away again.

'You ready to take us back now?' asked Sal politely. 'I'll even say "please".'

CHAPTER 60

65 million years BC, jungle

Broken Claw looked at the others in his family pack, predator eyes meeting predator eyes. In his claws he was still holding the bamboo spear, the bloodied end of it embedded in what was left of the new creature.

His mind worked hard trying to understand what he'd done. Trying to comprehend the fact that it wasn't his claws that had ended this pale creature's life, but the long device that he was holding, something *other* than him. Something he controlled. Something he had . . . *used*.

He turned to the others, clicked and growled and mewled softly.

Do you see? We killed the new creature with this.

Their minds, all younger, less developed. His children stared, yellow eyes burning with hatred, but not quite understanding, not just yet.

But he did. And his older, wiser mind stretched a little further. This long stick he held, he understood now what it was and where it came from. They grew along the river in thick clusters. But now it was no longer simply a plant – the new creatures had fashioned it into something else entirely: a deadly weapon.

Something deep in his reptilian mind *shifted*. Concepts, very simple concepts, looking for each other amid a busy crowd of instinct-driven brain signals, finally finding each other and embracing.

His pack had no communicable sound for the concept. His mind had no word for the idea. But if he'd had a wider range of words to construct his thoughts from then his mind would have been full of words like *use*, *make*, *build* . . .

His small mind suddenly produced an image, an image of a fast-flowing river and a tree trunk lying across it – a device the new creatures had *built* to cross the river.

He turned to the others, clicked his teeth and beckoned them to follow.

What he had growing in his mind is what any human being would have called . . . *a plan*.

CHAPTER 61

2001, New York

They approached the archway. Cartwright nodded at his men still standing guard outside. He gestured to Forby to join them inside as the shutter cranked noisily up. The other men he instructed to continue guarding the entrance, allowing no one else inside.

One by one they all stooped under the shutter as it clattered to a halt. As he followed the others in, Cartwright glanced up at the sky above Manhattan, beginning to lighten with the first grey stain of dawn. Another hour and it was going to be daylight, New Yorkers getting ready to go to work, and disgruntled civilians building up around the road blocks either end of the Williamsburg Bridge. Traffic police, TV film crews and journalists were surely soon going to add to that, asking his men and the National Guard soldiers where their orders had come from. What the hell was going on? He and his discreet little under-the-radar agency could do without attracting that kind of attention. The terrorist-bomb cover story those men had been given would hold for a little while longer, but not forever.

The last one inside the archway, he pressed the button and the shutter rattled down noisily again. Forby removed his bio-containment hood and then unslung his machine pistol.

'It's all right, no need to aim it at the girls,' said Cartwright. 'But just have it to hand, uh?'

Forby nodded and lowered his aim.

'So,' he continued, approaching the desk stacked with monitors, 'the computer? Before it's all fried?'

Maddy nodded. 'Yes, of course. DOMINOES.'

Cartwright shook his head. *Of course. You idiot, Lester.* He looked at the Domino's pizza boxes strewn across the desk, and would have slapped himself if he'd been alone.

The dialogue box on one of the screens flickered to life as a cursor flashed and scuttled across the screen with new text.

> Welcome back, Maddy.

'Hi, Bob,' she said. 'I'm in time, aren't I?'

> No system files have been erased yet. You had another seven minutes before I proceeded with your instructions.

'Christ,' muttered Lester, 'you weren't kidding.'

Sal shook her head. 'Nope.'

> My camera detects unauthorized personnel in the field office.

'Yes,' said Maddy, 'we have guests.'

> Are you under duress?

'No, it's fine, Bob. These guys are OK, for now.'

Cartwright tapped Maddy's arm and spoke quietly to her. 'Anything funny, I mean it . . . you say anything to that computer that sounds remotely like a warning and it'll be the very last thing you do.'

She nodded. 'Don't worry . . . I'm not stupid.' She sat down in one of the office chairs and faced the computer's webcam. 'Bob, we got a message from Liam.'

> I am very pleased to hear that.

'Yes, so are we.'

Sal joined her at the table. 'Hey, Bob.'

> Hello, Sal.

She held up the piece of paper Lester Cartwright had

produced earlier. 'This is the message. Can you see it clearly?'

> Hold it very still, please. I will scan it.

A moment later the scanned image from the webcam appeared on one of the monitors and the image flickered light and dark as Bob adjusted the contrast to get a clearer resolution of the handwriting. Then a highlight box flashed around each handwritten letter in rapid succession, until finally a text-processing application opened itself on yet another monitor with the entire message typed out clearly.

> Some of the message is in code.

'That's right,' said Sal. 'It's a book code.'

> The encryption clue is 'magic'. Is this correct?

'Yes.'

> I have more than thirty thousand data strings that include the word 'magic'.

'I think that's referring to the book you were reading the other day. Do you remember? We were discussing it.'

> *Harry Potter and the Deathly Hallows*.

'Yeah, that's the one.'

Cartwright and Forby leaned forward. 'You have got to be kidding,' mumbled the old man.

'Hey, my daughter is reading those books,' said Forby. 'Is that the *next* one?'

'It's the *last* one,' said Maddy. 'Book seven.'

'Jeez! What my girl wouldn't give to get a look at that!'

Cartwright cocked an eyebrow at his man. 'Forby . . . please be quiet.' The man obediently drew back and resumed his wary stance, the gun held loosely in his hands.

Sal sat down beside Maddy. 'Bob, you and the duplicate AI will have the same digital book file, right?'

> Affirmative. The file was in my short-term memory

cache when we downloaded the duplicate AI into the support unit.

'Then this should be pretty much straightforward,' said Maddy.

'Yeah.' Sal flicked her hair out of her eyes. 'You've just got to replace each three-number code with the letter. You understand how the code works, Bob, yeah?'

> Affirmative. Page number. Line number. Letter number.

'That's right.'

> Just a moment.

They watched in silence as clusters of numbers were momentarily highlighted on the document, while on another screen, pages of the book flashed back and forth in a blur. The task was completed in less than thirty seconds.

> The complete message is: Take this to Archway 9, Wythe Street, Brooklyn, New York on Monday 10 September 2001. Message: Sip, two, sehjk, three, npne, gour, zwro, aix. Key is 'Magic'.

They stared at it in silence for a few moments, trying to make sense of it.

'Well, that's just gibberish, isn't it?' said Cartwright.

'Are you sure you're working from the same digital book file?' asked Maddy.

> Affirmative.

'The original numbers on the fossil,' said Cartwright, 'some of them were indistinct, or incomplete. I have access to the original piece of rock.'

'No . . . it's OK,' said Sal. 'If it's just numbers it's really easy to work out. *Sip* is six. *Sehjk*, must be seven.' She worked quickly, writing the numbers down on a scrap of paper.

'There.'

6-2-7-3-9-4-0-6

'It's not in the usual time-stamp format,' said Maddy.

> Please show me, Sal.

Sal held the piece of paper up to the webcam.

> It is a number. 62,739,406. Suggestion: it is the AI duplicate's best estimation of their current time location.

'Oh my God!' gasped Maddy. 'It actually managed to work it out?' She looked at the cam and smiled. 'Well, that's *you*, actually, isn't it? A copy of you, Bob. Well done!'

'To the exact *year*?' said Cartwright. 'To the *exact* year? That's . . . that's incredible. How could anyone possibly –'

> Negative. The best resolution guess can only be to within 1,000 years of that year.

That silenced them all.

They could be up to 500 years before or after the specified time location.

'Oh *jahulla*,' whispered Sal. 'Then that's no good to us.'

'The nearest *thousand* years?' Maddy's head drooped. 'How are we supposed to find him in that?'

Cartwright looked down at both girls. 'So your machine can't bring back your colleague?'

Maddy shook her head. 'It takes time to build up enough charge to open a portal, particularly for one that long ago. I don't even know how long it would take to accumulate enough to open one then anyway, let alone do it thousands and thousands of times over.'

> Information: approximate charge time – nine hours.

'So we *can* do it,' said Sal.

Maddy laughed drily. 'Yes, we can . . . but a thousand years? If we opened one window for each year it'll take us nine thousand hours . . . what's that? Just over a year of constantly opening and closing portals.'

'So? We'll do that for Liam, right?'

Maddy sighed. 'That's opening one window per year. What are the chances of Liam standing right there in the two or three seconds of that year? Hmm? What if he was asleep at that moment? Taking a leak? Hunting for food? To stand any sort of chance we'd need to open one . . . like . . . every day!'

'This sounds like a needle-in-a-haystack problem,' said Cartwright unhelpfully.

'Oh.' Sal bit her lip. 'But we could try, couldn't we?'

'Three hundred and sixty-five thousand attempts!' replied Maddy. 'Do you want to have a guess how many years that would take us? Hmm? Lemmesee,' she muttered, as she gnawed on the nails of one hand. 'Oh, there . . . three hundred and seventy-five years or something.' She made a shrewish face, growing pink and mottled with frustration and anger. 'So, what do you say we get started, then?'

'Then I'm sorry, that's it,' stepped in Cartwright. 'I'm afraid your friend is stuck where he is. This facility will need to be packed up by the end of today and shipped down to a more secure government facility.'

'You can't do that!' snapped Sal. 'This is our . . . this is our *home*!'

'It's now a US government asset,' he replied calmly. 'And so are you, my dear.'

> Suggestion.

'You can't do that! We've got . . . like, human rights and stuff!'

Cartwright's smile was humourless and cold, the calm and empty gesture of someone who cared not one whit. 'I wonder . . . who exactly is going to miss the pair of you? Hmm? Family? Friends?'

'The agency,' snapped Sal. 'And if you mess with us, if you

hurt us, they'll come for you! They're from the future! And they're –'

'Sal!' barked Maddy. 'Shut up!' She grabbed Sal's arm. 'Don't say anything more about the agency! Do you understand?'

She clamped her mouth shut and nodded mutely.

Maddy looked at Cartwright. 'I think I can guess what you have in mind for us; you'll keep us under lock and key in some remote Area Fifty-one facility, like freaks, like lab rats. And that's where we'll remain until you're sure you know everything about this technology . . . then I guess you'll dispose of us, right? A drive out into the middle of the Nevada Desert and one shot in the back of the head for each of us. Is that how you lot work?'

Cartwright shook his head. 'Nothing so brutal, Maddy. You're worth far too much to us alive. Even when I'm sure you've told me all that you know, we're still going to need guinea pigs to test your time machine on.' He sighed. 'Mind you, it would have been good to have your colleague too . . . I'm not sure I'm entirely comfortable with the idea of him being out there roaming around history. But I suppose if he's sixty-two million years away, I can't see him doing –'

Sal cast a glance back at the monitor.

> Suggestion: rapid-sweep density probes.

She pointed at the screen. 'Maddy! Look!'

Maddy spun in her chair to look at the monitor and quickly digested the words. 'Oh my God, yes! Probes. Density probes . . . that could work!'

'What?' said Cartwright, shaking his head irritably at the distraction. 'What're you on about?'

'Tachyon signal probes to check a return location is clear of obstructions and that someone else isn't wandering through it before we open.'

Cartwright looked none the wiser.

'It's like . . . it's like knocking on a door before entering. Like asking *is anyone in there?* It's a lot quicker than actually opening a portal. A lot less energy needed.' She turned back towards the mic on the desk. 'Bob, what are you suggesting? We can't scan *every* moment over a thousand years . . . can we?'

> Negative. We scan a fixed moment of each day, 500 years either side of the calculated year. That is a total of 365,250 density probes.

'But that's going to take you what? Months? Years?' asked Cartwright.

> Negative. Small signals, no more than a few dozen particles per signal, would be enough to identify a transient mass. Movement.

'Yes,' said Maddy. 'That's it! And all the signals that came back with some movement detected could become a . . . become our candidate list: a shortlist of times we could try to open a portal on. Bob, how long would it take to do that many probes?' She turned back to Cartwright. 'It'll take a lot less time, I promise you! Maybe just a few days, tops!'

He shook his head. 'Unacceptable. I want this archway empty by the end of today. Empty and everything inside in boxes and en route to –'

'Please!' begged Maddy. 'We can't leave Liam out there!'

Cartwright silently shook his head.

'He knows the location of all the other field offices,' cut in Sal.

Maddy's jaw dropped open. 'Whuh?'

'He alone knows where they *all* are. Locations, time-stamps.' She turned to Maddy. 'I'm sorry . . . I was going to tell you, but . . . but Foster swore me to secrecy.'

Cartwright studied her silently. 'There *are* others, then? Other places like this?'

Her face hardened and her dark eyes narrowed. 'I'm not telling you any more. I don't know any more, but . . . like I say, *Liam* knows.'

'Hmm.' He thumbed his chin thoughtfully.

'Bob,' said Maddy, 'how many days would it take to do those density scans?'

> Calculating . . . just a moment . . . just a moment . . .

'Nice try, young lady,' said Cartwright eventually. 'You know, that was almost convincing. But it's the sort of nonsense that only happens in movies.' His croaky voice raised in pitch to that of some damsel in distress. '*Oh, please don't shoot, mister . . . If you let me live, I'll show you where the loot is hidden.*'

Cartwright laughed, pleased with his impression.

Sal shook her head. 'Oh, I'm not lying. Where do you think the time machine came from?' she replied. 'What? You think me and Maddy put it all together by ourselves?'

He had no answer for that.

Maddy could see where Sal was going with this. A good bluff. 'She's right, Cartwright. Where do you think we get spare parts from? When the displacement system breaks down, *who* do you think we call to come and fix it? Some spotty kid from PC World?'

Sal nodded. 'You think our people are going to let you walk away with one of their time machines?'

There were questions there that the old man needed time to consider carefully. The room remained a motionless tableau, while from somewhere overhead came the faint muted sound of a circling helicopter.

The blink of the cursor running across the dialogue box suddenly caught everyone's attention.

> Information: running at 11 scans a second, 365,250 scans will take approximately nine hours.

'Nine hours,' said Maddy. 'See that? Nine hours.' She looked at her watch. 'By three this afternoon, we'll have an idea exactly when he is and we'll be able to bring him back.' She smiled sarcastically at him. 'Then you'll have three lab rats to play around with instead of two.'

'Yes.' Cartwright nodded appreciatively. 'I suppose there is that.'

'Please,' whispered Sal, her hard-bargaining face softened to that of a begging puppy.

'All right. But if either of you tries anything silly, like dialling for help with one of these signals –' he reached into his jacket and pulled out a handgun – 'in fact, if you do *anything* that isn't explained clearly to me first, I will shoot you dead. Do you understand?'

They both nodded quickly.

'There'll be no shouted warnings, girls. I will simply pick up my gun and I will blow your brains across that messy desk of yours.' He offered them that cold lifeless smile. 'And, believe me, you'd be in very good company. It won't be the first time I've blown a person's brains right out of his head.'

Maddy swallowed and puffed out a fluttering breath, her eyes resolutely on the wavering muzzle of Cartwright's gun.

'Sure. Uh . . . O-OK. Nothing silly, then . . . I totally promise you that.'

CHAPTER 62

65 million years BC, jungle

Liam heard the roar of the water through the trees ahead of them.

'Becks? Are we close?'

'Affirmative. The river is a hundred and twenty-six yards ahead of us.'

He grinned a mixture of relief and bravado. 'Jay-zus-'n'-Mary, am I glad to be back!'

By the look on the faces of the others they couldn't agree more with that. The thick canopy of leaves above them began to thin out as they approached the jungle's edge, lances of late-afternoon sunlight stabbing down past loops of vine and dappling the ground with pools of mottled light.

With a final glance back at the forbidding darkness behind them, and an almost complete certainty that those things were still somewhere back there watching them from a distance, they hurried forward into the light.

Up ahead the river frothed and tumbled like some endlessly enraged beast. On the far side, he could see their bridge, dangling like a crane's arm above the water. He was relieved to see it was raised; the four they'd left behind had maintained a wary caution.

Liam stood on the bank and cupped his hands. 'Hello-o-o-o-o!'

The others gathered beside him. They'd lost three of their number, Ranjit, Franklyn and, earlier this morning, Kelly. All of them had heard his cry, and it had hastened their efforts down into the jungle valley, knowing those things were somewhere behind. And they'd grouped together more cautiously, realizing now the creatures were looking for stragglers.

Being bunched together seemed to have paid off. There'd been no sign of them throughout the morning, midday and now into the afternoon. Not even when they'd cleared the bare peak. Liam had looked back quickly in the hope of catching their pursuers unawares. But he saw nothing.

Now they were back. Job was done.

Liam craned his neck to look into the thin veil of jungle on the far side of the river. He could see some slivers of light through the dark tree trunks, the clearing beyond. But no sign of anyone coming their way to lower the bridge yet.

'Try again,' said Laura.

'H-E-L-L-O-O-O-O-O!'

Liam's voice echoed above the roar of the river, and startled a flock of miniature pterodactyls from a nearby tree. They waited with growing anticipation for a few minutes.

'They'd have heard that surely?' said Whitmore.

Edward stood on tiptoes to get a look through the jungle opposite. 'Unless they're all sleeping.'

'There'll be hell to pay if they are,' muttered Liam. He cupped his hands again. 'WE'RE BACK!'

Still nothing.

'Maybe they gone huntin'?' said Juan.

'I gave instructions that someone always has to keep an eye on the windmill,' replied Liam irritably.

Laura nodded at the bridge. 'Someone would have to stay behind *anyway*, to lift that for them and lower it.'

He nodded. 'True.'

'So someone must be home.'

'This is not good,' he muttered under his breath.

Becks had been examining the fast-flowing water. 'I am able to cross this,' she said.

'The current's too strong,' said Liam.

'I do not need to swim across all of it, Liam.' She pointed along the bank on which they were standing. Fifty yards down, it rose to a moss-covered hump that was well on its way to being undercut by the river. 'Information: I calculate I will be able to jump across between thirty and forty per cent of the river's width from that point.'

He looked at her. 'And you know how to swim?'

'Affirmative. I also know how to walk, run, jump . . . talk.'

He cocked a sideways glance at her. Was that actually *sarcasm*? Was that another example of Becks's emerging sense of humour? She returned a smile.

'Oh, you're so funny, Becks.'

'I am developing several files on humour traits.' She nodded towards the mossy hump, changing subject. 'I will not be long,' she said, turning to walk down the bank towards it.

'Where's she going?' asked Whitmore, unhappy to see their robot bodyguard leaving them alone.

'She's going to do her superhero thing,' said Liam.

They watched in silence as she examined the river for a moment then turned to regard the height of the hump. After a few seconds she walked away from the river's edge and came to a halt just as she was about to enter the shadowy fringe of the jungle. She turned round and without a second's hesitation broke into a sprint towards the river.

Whitmore's eyes rounded. 'She's gonna *jump* it?'

She bounded up the side of the hump and launched herself out across the river. Subconsciously everyone gasped and rose on their tiptoes as she gracefully sailed a dozen yards out over the water, her arms pinwheeling to give her extra momentum. Then she arced down into the water, disappearing beneath the stampeding white horses of the river.

For a long half a minute Liam couldn't see her anywhere, then, finally, he spotted a dark head bobbing among the churning swirls of suds, gone again, back again, then as the river rode over a bed of large boulders and became a chicane of lethal-looking rapids, it curved round and she was lost from sight.

'She gonna make it?' asked Juan.

Liam nodded. 'I'd put money on it.'

Whitmore nodded with admiration. 'What I wouldn't give to have her on my school's athletics team. We'd win every cup going.'

They waited an interminable ten minutes before they spotted her again, jogging up the riverbank on the far side. She reached their jury-rigged bridge, carefully untied the counterweight of bundled logs and then, taking on the weight of the main trunk, muscles in her arms bulging from the effort, she slowly lowered it, the vine ropes creaking and groaning under the strain.

Above the busy rumble of the river, they heard the crack of one of the vines snapping.

'It's gonna go!' shouted Liam.

It looked like Becks had heard that too. She began to pay out the rope more quickly. But another vine snapped under the increased burden, *twanging* up to the overhanging branch like a rubber band.

'Stand back!' barked Liam to the others. 'It's gonna drop!'

And it did. The other vines snapped in quick succession and the tree trunk swung down from its forty-five degree angle and clattered heavily on the boulders on their side. Everyone heard the crack, loud as a gunshot. Halfway along the trunk, jagged splinters of wood protruded from the side, and their bridge sagged down in the middle almost into the water.

'Oh, great!' shouted Laura.

'Lemmesee . . . it may be OK,' said Juan. Before anyone could stop him he'd stepped up on to the boulders and then carefully on to the end of the log. He inched his way a few yards along it. It bowed a little further, now dipping into the water itself midway along, but it seemed to be holding.

Juan dropped to his hands and knees, then straddled it, bum-shuffling his way across. At the midway point, he gingerly eased his way over the jagged fracture, water catching his dangling legs and threatening to pull him off. But he got over, and a minute later jumped off on the far side.

Liam nodded. 'All right, then. It seems like it'll hold for us. Let's go.'

Whitmore ushered Edward to cross first, then had Laura, Akira and Jasmine line up to go next. Meanwhile Liam turned round. 'Have your spears ready.' He nodded at the dark jungle behind Howard and Whitmore. 'They may still be out there.'

Waiting until it's just the one of us left? Then what?

He didn't care to think about that.

Whitmore went after Jasmine, panting with exertion and fear as he inched his way across, the fractured trunk wobbling and creaking with each movement he made. Finally, he made it to the far side and beckoned for whoever was coming next.

'Leonard, you go.'

The dark-haired boy eyed Liam. 'You sure?'

'Uh-huh,' replied Liam, his eyes remaining on the dark jungle. 'Just be quick, will you?' he added, flashing him a quick nervous smile.

Howard nodded, and then was on the trunk and shuffling. Liam waited until the student was nearly halfway across before taking one wary step on to the end of the log. He could feel the vibration of Howard's movements.

If they're gonna come for me . . . it's gonna be right now.

Then as if on cue he thought he saw movement, some dark shape leaping through the undergrowth, moving from one hiding place to the next. Getting closer, but not quite ready to commit to leaping out into the open.

'What is it?' he grunted under his breath. 'You scared of me? Is that it?'

That sounded good to him, fighting talk. For a fleeting moment there he almost *didn't* feel completely terrified. But that soon passed as his eyes assured him something else had just shifted position one tree closer to him.

He finally felt the trunk under his foot wobble as Leonard presumably jumped off at the far side. He heard Whitmore's voice over the din of tumbling water calling him over.

'Coming!' Liam shouted over his shoulder. Keeping his eyes on the jungle, he reversed on to the log, still not daring to turn his back on what he knew was in there and waiting for him to do just that.

Pull yourself together, Liam.

He dropped down to his hands and knees. Unwilling to turn his back on the jungle, he began bum-shuffling *backwards*, one hand still holding the spear half ready, in case he needed to defend himself at a moment's notice.

After a minute's slow progress, he finally felt a sharp splinter of wood scrape the inside of his thigh and realized he was now just before the fractured halfway point. Cool water rode up his dangling legs, soaking him to his thighs. As he shuffled to get past the jagged shards of the fractured trunk, he heard it crack and felt it lurch as it sagged lower into the river. Water suddenly rode up over his knees and over his lap, pummelling his gut and chest like an enraged boxer sensing the faltering resolve of an opponent.

Oh no . . . please, no.

Water. Drowning. Suddenly the fear of being snatched and torn apart by some vicious predator was matched by the idea of being snatched away by the river.

'It's going to break!' shouted someone.

Liam could feel the trunk being buffeted and kicked by the strong current. It flexed, creaked and twisted under the punishing weight of energy slamming into it. He realized it wasn't going to hold out much longer and a rising tide of panic compelled him to get off his backside and crawl. He struggled on to his hands and knees, now, finally, turning his back on the jungle he'd moments ago thought was hiding the most frightening thing in this world.

No . . . the most bloody frightening thing right now was this churning white monster roaring hungrily at him, doing its best to pull him off. He could see the others waiting for him at the far end of the bowing log, all frantically waving at him to get a move on.

'All right . . . all right, I'm coming!' he yelped. He began to crawl forward on hands and knees. One hand carefully placed after the other on the treacherously wet bark.

Come on, Liam, come on. You're nearly there. He managed to make his way a yard closer to the bank, and even managed to flash the others a cavalier *I'm gonna be just fine* grin, when his hand found a slick patch of moss.

'Uhh . . .' was all he managed to gasp before his hand slipped round the side of the trunk and the unsupported weight of his body carried him over.

CHAPTER 63

65 million years BC, jungle

Suddenly he found himself spinning amid a roaring chaotic swirl of swiftly moving water. Instinctively he'd snatched a lungful of air as he'd gone under, his body doing the thinking for him while his mind shrieked uselessly with blind panic.

Drown! I'm gonna drown!

He knew it. His lungs were only going to buy him a half minute of life. His mind was all of a sudden back in the narrow confines of a corridor groaning with the sound of stressed bulkheads, flickering wall lamps and the distant roar of ice-cold seawater finding its way up from the deck below. The certain promise of death a mile down in the cold dark embrace of the ocean.

Oh no, no, no, no, not this! Not like this!

Then his head suddenly broke the surface. He flailed in the foam, still holding on to the stale breath in his lungs. He caught sight of their log bridge thirty or forty yards behind him already and fast disappearing as the swift current carried him away.

His legs thumped heavily against a boulder and he found himself being rolled over its hard rounded surface. His head again under the water, his ears filled with the pounding roar of the river, he felt himself being sucked down deep by a spiralling current, pressure compressing his chest.

Panic. Sheer, blinding panic robbed his mind of any useful conscious thought and left him with a curdling mental scream, knowing this dark roaring depth was where it was all going to come to an end for him.

But the river's mischievous current decided to play one more game with him and shot him to the surface to say goodbye to life and air and trees and the crimson sky of later afternoon once more. Liam gasped for another lungful of air, half aware that perhaps the kindest thing he could do was simply breathe out and prepare his mouth, his throat, his lungs for an invasion of water.

But then his shoulder thudded hard against something. Something he could grasp hold of and fight the incredible pull of the river. He opened his eyes and realized it was a fallen tree. For a moment he wondered if the river had carried him right the way round their island in some logic-defying loop-the-loop and he was right back where their crudely constructed bridge was.

He desperately grappled with the rough bark and the small leafy branches that sprouted from it, merciful handholds that their smooth and straight trunk had lacked. From branch to branch he managed to pull himself out of the strong current in the middle of the river to some calmer eddies of swirling water.

Finally his foot brushed against the river bottom, scattering pebbles, and his feet desperately fumbled for firmer footing that promised to stay beneath him. His hands followed the fallen tree, pulling on thicker, more reliable branches until he found himself wading out of the river, finally collapsing on hands and knees on wet shingle that shifted and clattered noisily beneath him.

'Urgh,' he spluttered, between ragged gasps of breath.

His breath was still pounding in and out as he finally pulled himself, exhausted, to his feet. He turned to look at the fallen tree, trying to get his bearings and work out which side of the river he was now standing on. The base of the tree was on the far side; he could see a frayed and splintered stump that looked like it had been hacked at by a team of inept carpenters armed with blunt chisels . . . or beavers even.

Not beavers, obviously. Perhaps some species of termite had cannibalized the tree, or it had simply rotted and split. Either way, he thanked it for saving his life. He noticed a mess of disturbed shingle and footprints around him among the leaves and branches of the felled tree and realized that perhaps Lam and the others must have felled the tree for wood, but foolishly allowed it to fall across the river and just left it.

Idiots.

The first thing he'd do once he found them was get them to heave the tree back into the water and let it be carried away. He turned round and squinted up the riverbank. Through a hundred yards of jungle he could just about make out crimson slivers of waning sunlight, the trees thinning, the clearing beyond . . . and their camp.

He'd lost his spear in the river. No matter, he was on the safe side now. He made his way up the shingle and into the narrow apron of jungle. Up ahead through the dangling loops of vine he could see the sun casting long shadows across the leafy hummocks of their shelters and the wooden wall of their small palisade as it began to make a bed on the horizon. But, as yet, he couldn't make out Lam and the other three kids they'd left behind.

Where are they?

'Hello-o-o-o!!' he called out again, his voice ricocheting through the jungle.

A few moments later he was stepping out from beneath the dark canopy of foliage and into the clearing. On the very far side, he could see Becks and the others emerging.

He waved at them. 'Hey!'

He saw their heads turn his way and their mouths form sudden dark ovals of surprise and relief.

'I made it! I'm all right!' he called across to them. 'I'm fine! Have you seen the others?'

Becks led them across the clearing towards Liam until finally they converged around the smouldering remains of a campfire.

'The others have not been located,' said Becks.

Liam noticed their small turbine wasn't spinning. The cross-bar was split and the school bag was on the ground, its load of round pebbles spilled. 'The windmill's broken. What's happened?'

There were no answers.

'We should get that running again first,' he continued. He looked around at the others. 'Maybe they're out looking for us?'

Becks strode swiftly towards the contraption to see whether a quick repair could be made. Liam was about to pass on some instructions to the others to split up and search for the others when he noted Jasmine's gaze, wide-eyed and lost on some detail everyone else seemed to have missed.

'Jasmine? You all right?'

She pointed at the ground. 'That,' she whispered. 'What's that?'

Liam followed her gaze down to the ground. Nestled amid a cluster of pebbles, cones and the dry brown decaying leaves of long-dead ferns, he saw a pale slender object that looked to him like an impossibly large maggot. He took a step towards it and noted the ground was stained dark around it, and at one end of it, pointed yellow-white shards poked out like the antennae of a shrimp.

He felt his stomach lurch and flip in a slow, queasy somersault.

It was someone's index finger. The antennae, shards of bone.

'What is it?' asked Whitmore, stooping to get a better look. 'My God! Is that a finger?'

The conclusion hit Liam like a punch. 'They're here.' He looked up at them. 'Those pack hunters are here, on the island.'

Whitmore's mouth flapped open and shut and produced nothing helpful.

'How?' asked Howard. 'It's impossible. No way those things can swim across!'

'They don't need to.' He looked at the others. 'They went and copied us . . . *learned* from us.'

'What do you mean?'

'I think they made their own bridge.'

CHAPTER 64

2001, New York

Everything in the archway died, leaving them in pitch black.

'What's going on?' cried Cartwright.

'Please!' cried Maddy in the dark. 'Don't shoot! Don't shoot! It's nothing I did!'

'Stay right where you are!' snapped Cartwright. 'I hear you move or do anything and I'll fire!'

'O-OK . . . we're not moving, are we, Sal?'

'Nope. Sitting still. Doing nothing.'

'Just hang on, Cartwright,' said Maddy, 'just a second . . . the generator should kick in any time now.'

On cue, from the back room, came the rumbling of the generator firing up. A moment later the strip light in the middle of the archway flickered once, twice with a *dink, dink*, then stayed on.

They all stared silently at each other as the monitors flickered in unison, the computer system rebooting itself.

'What just happened?' demanded Cartwright.

'I dunno yet . . .' said Maddy.

'That was a time wave,' said Sal.

'A what?'

'Time wave,' she repeated. 'Something big changed in the past and it's just now caught up with us.'

Maddy nodded unhappily. 'Yeah . . . she's right. That's exactly what that was.'

Cartwright looked at both the girls, then at Forby, who returned nothing more useful than a calm professional stare. 'Well?' said the old man. 'What does that mean?'

'It means outside this archway, outside the perimeter of our field-office time shield, things have changed,' explained Maddy. 'Changed a *lot* . . . if we lost power.'

'So, what's out there now?' he asked.

Maddy splayed her hands. 'I don't know! Another version of New York, I guess.'

Cartwright's eyes widened to rheumy bloodshot pools. 'Forby, go take a look.'

'Yes, sir.' He stepped across the archway and hit the green button. Nothing happened. 'Won't open.'

'The doorway's not on the generator circuit,' said Maddy. 'Just crank it up with the handle. There,' she said, pointing. Forby saw the small metal handle, nodded and started turning it round.

The computer had finished rebooting and Bob's dialogue box popped up.

> We are running on auxiliary power. Resume density probing?

Maddy turned in her chair, back towards the monitors. 'How much more probing have you got to do?'

> Information: 177,931 candidate density soundings made.

She made a face – less than half the total number that Bob had calculated they needed to make.

'Are there any good suspects?'

> There are 706 soundings so far in which a density fluctuation occurred.

'Can you narrow that down any?'

> Affirmative: I can analyse the interruption signatures returned and identify those that demonstrate a repeat or an artificial rhythm.

'Uh . . . lemme think.' She bit a ragged edge around her fingernail. 'But you're only, like, halfway through doing the probes?'

> Less than halfway.

'And if you stop now we might miss them,' she thought out loud.

> Affirmative.

'But now we're on generator power, have you got enough power to do all those probes, *and* open a window too if we find them?'

> I do not have enough data to answer that question, Maddy.

'Can you guess?'

> I do not have enough data to answer that question, Maddy.

She cursed. 'All right . . . so you're saying it's possible we'll run out of juice if you carry on doing the probes, right?'

> Affirmative.

The rattling of the cranking shutter door coming from across the archway suddenly ceased.

'OK, Bob,' she sighed, burying her face in her hands with weary frustration. 'OK . . . OK. All right, then. Stop with what you're doing and analyse what we've got already. See if we've got a hit.'

> Affirmative.

'What the –!' That was Forby.

'JESUS!' That was Cartwright.

Maddy spun round in her chair and saw the pair of them

standing in the middle of the opened shutter doorway, staring out at a canvas of emerald-green jungle.

She sighed. *Oh no, not again.*

Last time a time wave had arrived like this one, large enough to sever the feed of power into their field office, it had left New York a post-apocalyptic wilderness of tumbledown ruins under a poisoned rust-red sky. She and Sal hurried over towards the open entrance.

'Jahulla!' gasped Sal as they joined the other two.

And Maddy nodded. *Jahulla indeed.*

This time New York was gone, not just shattered ruins, but gone as in *never existed*. She looked down at her feet. Their cold and pitted concrete floor simply ended in a straight line where their invisible force field's effect terminated. The ground beyond was a rich brown soil, carpeted in a mat of tall grass and lush clusters of low-growing ferns and other unidentifiable foliage.

She looked up and saw no Williamsburg Bridge, no horizon of Manhattan skyscrapers, just a broad, sedate river delta of lush rainforest.

'Uh . . . how . . . how did we end up in the middle of a jungle, sir?' asked Forby.

A slow, understanding smile spread across Cartwright's face. Finally he nodded. 'Incredible,' he whispered, his eyes wide like a child's, full of wonder. A solitary tear rolled down one of his craggy cheeks. '*This is quite . . . incredible.*'

'Sir?' Forby turned to him. His calm, professional demeanour had vanished and been replaced with barely contained panic. 'Sir, where the hell are we?'

'We haven't moved anywhere,' the old man replied. He turned to look at Maddy. 'Or any*when*? Have we? We're exactly when and where we were.'

'That's right,' she replied. 'But an alternate history has just caught up with us.'

Cartwright's ragged features seemed to look ten years younger. The face of a child catching a glimpse of the tooth fairy, or a glint of Santa's sleigh disappearing into a distant moonlit cloud bank.

'Sir? The other men? Where are they?'

'Gone, Forby,' he replied in a distracted whisper. 'Gone.'

'They're dead?'

'Nope. They were just never born,' said Sal.

'I want to see more,' uttered Cartwright, stepping off the concrete on to the soft ground beyond. He grinned. 'My God! This is real? Isn't it?'

Maddy shrugged. 'It's another reality. How New York might have ended up if . . . if . . .'

'If what?' asked Forby.

'That's just it,' she replied. 'We don't know yet. My guess is it's some change caused by our colleague in the past. I'm sure it wasn't intentional.'

Forby shook his head. 'You're telling me one person can actually change a whole . . . world?'

Cartwright sighed, clearly frustrated by the narrow-minded thinking of his subordinate. 'Of course, Forby. Think about it, man. If . . . if a certain Jewish carpenter hadn't made his mark two thousand years ago, it wouldn't be *In God We Trust* on a dollar note, but *Gods*.'

Forby frowned. A patriot. No one dissed the mighty dollar. Not on his watch.

'And our friend's much much further back in time than Jesus,' added Sal.

'Small changes in the past,' quoted Maddy, remembering the first time Foster had spoken to them, bringing them that tray of coffees and doughnuts, a simple and strangely reassuring gesture in that surreal moment of awakening. 'Small changes in the past can make enormous changes in the present.'

Cartwright glanced towards the nearby riverbank. 'We should go and explore a little –' He stopped dead in his tracks. 'Look!'

Maddy followed his wavering finger, pointing across the broad river to the low hump of island that was once Manhattan. She squinted painfully, her eyes not so great without glasses. She managed to detect the slightest sense of movement. 'What is it?'

'People?' uttered Sal. 'Yes . . . it's people!'

'A settlement of some kind,' added Cartwright.

She thought she could make out a cluster of circular dwellings down by the waterside and several pale thin plumes of smoke rising up into the sky.

'Look,' said Forby, 'there's a boat.'

Halfway across the river, calm and subdued, barely a ripple upon its glass-smooth surface, was the long dark outline of some canoe. Aboard they could see half a dozen figures paddling the vessel across the river towards them.

'They look odd,' said Sal, shading her eyes from the sun. 'They're . . . they're moving all funny.'

Cartwright seemed eager to rush down to the riverside and greet them. 'We should go and make contact.'

'No,' said Maddy. 'Really, I don't think we should.'

'Why not?' he asked. 'The things we could learn from each other! The knowledge of another –'

'Maybe the girl's right,' said Forby. 'They could be hostile, sir.'

He shook his head, his face an expression of bemusement. 'This is an *incredible* moment of history!'

'But that's just it . . . this *isn't* history. This isn't meant to happen,' said Maddy. 'Those people shouldn't exist. This is a *what if* reality . . . this is a *never shoulda happened* reality, Cartwright. Do you get it? The last thing we need to do is go and make friends with it.'

'I'm not so sure they're *people*, anyway,' said Sal, quietly watching the canoe approach the nearby riverbank. A hundred and fifty yards away, the long canoe rode up gracefully on to the silt. The figures aboard the boat put down their paddles in the bottom and began, one by one, to jump off the front and on to the mud.

Even Maddy could now make out that they weren't human.

'My God, look at their legs,' whispered Forby. 'Like . . . just like goat's legs, dog's legs.'

'Dinosaur legs,' added Cartwright. 'In fact, therapod legs. A bit like velociraptors.'

'Forget their legs,' said Sal, 'check out their heads!'

Maddy squinted, wondering whether her eyes were playing tricks on her. 'They look like bananas?'

'Elongated,' said Forby, shaking his own head. 'Weirdest damned thing I ever seen. They look sort of extra-terrestrial.' He turned to the others, his voice lowered. 'My God! Do you think that's what they are? A species of alien that's arrived and colonized our world?'

Cartwright dismissed the man. 'The legs suggest some possible ancestral link to dinosaurs. The heads? Damned if I know where that shape has come from.'

They watched the creatures spread out along the silt, holding spears in their hands and probing the mud with them.

'What are they doing, do you think?' asked Maddy.

As if in answer to her question, some unrecognizable pig-sized creature emerged from a hole in the mud and scurried across the silt towards another hole. The nearest of the banana-heads quickly raised his spear and threw it with practised efficiency. It skewered the small creature, and left it struggling and squealing on its side.

'Hunting!' said Forby a little too loudly.

One of the creatures suddenly turned to glance their way. The four of them instinctively hunkered down behind the gently waving fronds of a large fern.

'Think he saw us?' hissed Forby through gritted teeth.

Maddy looked up at the ragged outline of red brickwork around the corrugated shutter door, the portion of the bridge support that existed within the archway's field. Luckily most of it was shielded by a giant species of tree she didn't recognize; drooping waxy leaves the size of umbrellas hung low over them. A perfect camouflage.

'I think we're hidden,' she whispered.

They watched through gaps in the swaying leaves as the creature, still curious, slowly paced up the silty bank towards them, cocking its long head curiously on to one side. Closer now, they could see a lean hairless body covered with an olive skin, an expressionless face of bone and cartilage and a lipless mouth full of razor-sharp teeth.

'It's really ugly,' offered Sal in a whisper. 'I really don't want to go make friends with it.'

Maddy noticed Forby raising his gun warily, a finger slipping across the trigger. She nudged him gently and shook her head.

Don't.

He nodded.

'It's beautiful,' whispered Cartwright. 'What a magnificent creature! Look at it!'

For a moment it lingered there, scanning the rainforest in

front of it, not seeming to spot them or the squat brick shape of their archway. Then, finally, it seemed to shrug, turn away and head back towards the others, calling something out with a mewling whine and a clack of its sharp teeth.

'I've seen enough. We should go back inside,' said Maddy. 'There's work to be done.'

'Don't you want to learn more?' asked Cartwright.

She shrugged. 'Why? If we've managed to get lucky and locate Liam . . . then none of this will ever have happened.' She looked at Forby, who seemed relieved at the idea of heading back. 'Be pointless learning anything about these things really . . . if you think about it. They soon will belong to the world of *Never Were*.'

Cartwright made a face, a mixture of disappointment and frustration. 'All right,' he conceded. 'Let's get on with it.'

CHAPTER 65

65 million years BC, jungle

'Did you hear that?' said Laura, her eyes round with fear.

They'd heard it all right. Although the jungle was soon due to stir with its concert of nocturnal cries and calls, the sun had only just slipped from the sky, leaving behind thin combed cirrus clouds stained a coral pink from its waning light. The jungle was on the turn, the stillness between those that lived in the day and those that prowled the night.

But there it was again. A desperate female cry for help. It was one of the four they'd left behind, either Keisha Jackson or Sophia Yip.

'*. . . Please . . . help me . . .*'

'It's Keisha!' said Jasmine. She turned to the others. 'It *is*! It's Keisha!'

'Which direction did it come from?' asked Liam. It wasn't far off, somewhere within the apron of jungle around their clearing. Could be coming from any direction, the mischievous way voices seemed to bounce around.

'*. . . Help . . . it hurts . . .*'

'We have to go help her!' said Edward.

'Negative,' said Becks. 'The hominids could still be on the island.'

Laura's eyes darted back to the finger on the ground. The light was getting dim enough for it to be almost, mercifully, easy to overlook. '*Could be?*' she exclaimed. 'They're h-here, all right.'

'Or they've been and gone,' added Whitmore. He looked at Liam. 'We've got to go help the poor girl! She could be dying!'

'. . . *Please* . . .'

Whitmore nodded across the clearing. 'It came from over there.' He grabbed a spear and turned to the others. 'I'll need help lifting her.'

Edward grabbed a spear and joined him. Howard and Juan did likewise.

'OK,' said Liam, 'go get her.' He turned to Laura, Akira and Jasmine. 'We need this fire going again. Can you see to that? Big fire, all right? Big as you can make it.' They both nodded. 'And, Becks, we need that windmill contraption running.'

She nodded. 'Affirmative.'

'And, all of you,' he called out, particularly to Whitmore and the others already jogging in the direction they hoped to find Keisha, 'all of you, stay close together! No one goes on their own!'

He watched them go, four of them all armed with spears. In the jungle on their way back from laying down their clay tablets, they'd been infinitely more vulnerable to ambush, and yet the creatures had warily held back . . . only jumping Kelly, he presumed, because he'd been entirely on his own.

He looked anxiously around the clearing. The girls were just a dozen yards away working on the fire, and Becks merely thirty yards from him, busy trying to re-jig the windmill. Liam tried to think quickly. He wasn't exactly alone here in the middle of the clearing, but he'd have felt happier having another one or two people standing right beside him. His eyes darted to the dark entrances of a couple of the nearby lean-tos, the small gateway to their palisade, possible hiding places. Possibly containing one or two of *them*.

Liam. Stay calm, Liam. Stay calm.

Broken Claw watched the new creatures approach. Four of them armed with their killing sticks.

He turned to the others, crouched nearby, and softly hissed for them to make ready. He turned towards the younger one, crouched next to him. The youngest ones of the pack were best at this particular skill – mimicking the calls of wounded prey – their voice-boxes being smaller, allowing them a much higher pitch, the shrill pitch of fear and desperation.

He clacked his claws gently, instructing the young one to do it once again.

The young female's jaw opened, and her tongue and voice skilfully reproduced the cries the female new creature had been making earlier today as she lay dying from a fatal stomach wound.

'. . . *Help me . . . please . . .*'

They changed direction, veering directly towards Broken Claw and the others, just a few dozen yards away now, stepping out of the clearing and into the darkness of the jungle. The new creatures seemed to have absolutely no sense of how close to danger they were, their small seemingly ineffective noses unable to detect the smells that filled Broken Claw's nasal cavity: the smell of excitement from his pack, the smell of anticipation of a fine kill, the smell of their dark-skinned female brethren lying dead amid the ferns nearby – bled out hours ago.

How could they not smell any of this?

These creatures were either foolish or incapable of sensing all the warning signals in the air around them, stumbling blindly.

Certainly – he understood this now – nothing for his pack to be wary of any more. He'd learned enough about them: that they were as vulnerable as the larger plant-eaters they usually hunted, more vulnerable, in fact, since they had neither their weight or strength to throw around.

And now . . . Broken Claw and several of the stronger males in his pack now possessed *sticks-that-kill*.

The four long digits on each of his hands tightened round the thick bamboo shaft. Broken Claw was determined to use his stick-that-kills on one of them as he had that older male earlier this morning up in the hills. A fascinating way of delivering death. An intriguing tool of death.

Juan stopped and pointed at a splotch of drying blood on the back of a broad waxy leaf.

'Keisha!' he called out. 'You here?'

The four of them stood perfectly still, listening to the gentle hiss of shifting leaves above them and the fading echo of Juan's voice.

'Keisha!' he called out again.

Then, very softly, not a crying-out voice trying to be heard across acres of jungle, but a soft whimpering close-by murmur. '*. . . Please . . . help me . . .*'

'Where are you?' asked Whitmore. 'We can't see you!'

'*. . . Help me . . .*'

'Where are you, Keisha? Can you see us?'

'*. . . Please . . . please . . .*'

Juan cocked his head. 'That don't sound like her, man.'

Edward nodded. 'She sounds kind of funny.'

'*. . . Sophia . . . run . . .*'

Whitmore's eyes narrowed. 'Keisha?'

'*. . . They killed Jonah . . .*'

Juan looked silently at the others. His face spoke for him. *That really isn't her.*

Whitmore nodded and then slowly placed a finger to his lips. He waved his hands at them to back up the way they'd come. Fifteen . . . twenty yards of jungle, that's all, then they'd be out in the clearing again.

They'd just begun to carefully retrace their steps when Juan suddenly convulsed, burping a trickle of blood down the front of his varsity sweatshirt. He looked slowly down at the six inches of sharpened bamboo tip that protruded from his belly.

'Oh . . . oh, man . . .' was about all he could say before his eyes rolled and his legs buckled beneath him.

Crouching behind Juan's collapsed form was one of the bipedal creatures, its long head cocked with curiosity and its yellow eyes marvelling at the spear in its hands.

'RUN!' screamed Whitmore to the other two. 'IT'S A TRAP!'

Howard and Edward turned on their heels to head back towards the clearing, only to face another pair of those creatures, springing seemingly out of nowhere. Howard lunged quickly with his spear, catching one of them in the thigh. The creature recoiled with a scream.

'GO!' screamed Howard, pushing Edward away from the creatures. Meanwhile, Whitmore found himself trapped by a closing circle of four of them.

'You r-really . . . are . . . c-clever . . . aren't you?' he found himself babbling through trembling lips. A couple of them were holding spears just like he was holding his. 'My G-God . . . you've learned f-fast . . . haven't you?'

The creature that had speared Juan stepped over his body and approached Whitmore with an unsettling raptor-like bobbing movement. The creature barked an order to some more of its kind hiding in the undergrowth and Whitmore heard the thud of feet and the swish of branches flicked aside as several set off in pursuit of the other two boys.

Now it cocked its head, its yellow eyes drinking him in, eyes that burned with intelligence and curiosity and a thousand questions it probably wanted to ask, but hadn't yet developed a sophisticated enough language to know how to ask.

'I . . . I know . . . you can c-communicate . . .' Whitmore babbled, his man's voice broken and mewling now like a child's. 'S-s-so . . . can w-we. W-we're the s-same. Y-you,' he said slowly, pointing a shaking finger towards the creature. 'M-me . . . me,' he said, gesturing to himself. 'We're the s-same!'

Its long head protruded forward on the end of a fragile, almost feminine, neck.

'Th-the same . . . the same,' whimpered Whitmore. 'Intelli-intelligent.'

Whitmore was only vaguely aware of his bladder letting loose, a warm trickle running down his left leg and soaking his sock. A small detail. A faraway detail. Right in front of his own face, only inches away, his world was this bony carapace of another face and yellow piercing reptile eyes that seemed to grow ever larger.

Its jaw snapped open, revealing rows of needle-sharp teeth and a twisting, leathery black tongue that furled and unfurled like an angry snake in a cage.

Whitmore let go of his spear and it clattered to the ground between them. 'Do . . . d-do you s-see? No n-no harm. I m-mean y-you no h-harm!'

The tongue twisted and coiled and Whitmore heard an odd facsimile of his own voice coming right back at him. '. . . *No h-harm . . . the s-same . . .*'

He nodded. 'Y-yes! Y-y-es! W-we-we're intelli–'

Whitmore felt a punch to his chest. It winded him – like a medicine ball launched at his thorax. He gasped, spattering a fine spray of blood on to the creature's expressionless face. He would have doubled over from the blow, but claws from behind were holding him up on his feet. The yellow eyes inches in front of him looked down at something. All of a sudden, feeling oddly dizzy and lightheaded, he decided the polite thing was to do the same.

And there it was in the palm of the creature's hand, his own heart still dutifully beating away.

CHAPTER 66

65 million years BC, jungle

Howard and Edward stumbled through the jungle, skirting the clearing but unable to get to it because one of the creatures was deliberately blocking them.

'Clever,' wheezed Howard. Keeping them bottled up here amid tree trunks and dangling loops of vine, it prevented them making big sweeping strikes with their spear and hatchet; the blade or shaft was bound to get tangled or caught on something.

One beast was behind them and another to their left, preventing them from making their way to the encircling river . . . not that they'd be able to go anywhere. The pursuer behind them could easily have caught up, but he remained a steadfast dozen yards behind. He realized then that they were just wearing them out, pursuing the pair of them through the tangled undergrowth until they were certain they were spent and unable to offer much of a fight.

Howard stopped. Edward, who'd been supporting his weight on the right leg, gasped. 'Uh? We got to run!'

Howard shook his head, finding his breath. 'No . . . they're *playing* with us. Herding us.'

All three of the hominids pursuing them came to a halt a dozen yards away on each side and waited patiently for their next move, yellow eyes peering at them through thin veils of dangling, looping vines.

Howard nodded to the clearing, the edge of it fifty yards to their right. The creature blocking that way had ducked down out of sight. 'That's the way we should be heading.'

Edward swallowed nervously. 'But . . . one of th-those –'

'I know.' He sucked in breath again. 'He's in there somewhere . . . but you have to make a break for it, run for the palisade.'

'What about you?'

He shook his head. 'I won't make it . . . I can't run . . . I'll buy you time.'

'You . . . y-you'll die!'

Howard nodded, smiled even. 'Sure, I figured that.'

Edward grabbed his arm. 'We c-can *both* run!'

'Don't argue. There isn't time for this. Listen.' He grabbed the boy's shoulder. 'Run, save your life. Make it back home. But promise me something.' He glanced over Edward's shoulder; one of the creatures was shifting position, impatient for a kill and stepping closer. 'Promise me to dedicate your talent to something else . . . not time travel, Edward . . . anything but time travel!'

Edward's eyes were on the other two creatures.

'Promise me!'

He nodded. 'Yes! Y-yes . . . OK!'

'No time travel, Edward. It'll kill us all; it'll destroy the world . . . God help us, perhaps even the universe. Do you understand?' he said, shaking the boy's shoulder.

The creatures inched warily closer, long athletic legs gracefully stepping over the uneven jungle floor towards them, their lean bodies bobbing with coiled energy.

'Please . . .' he hissed. 'Please tell me you understand.'

Edward's eyes met his. He was crying. 'Yes . . . I p-promise. I promise!'

Howard ruffled his hair. 'Good.' He took the hatchet in one hand and grasped the spear in the other.

'Now, when I say,' he said softly, 'you run, Ed. You run for all it's worth. You understand?'

The boy nodded.

Howard could see the creature between them and the clearing now. Its head bobbed up and ducked behind a large fern, no longer trying to hide, but clearly still very wary of them.

Good. Then he'd take advantage of that.

'Ready?' he whispered.

Edward nodded silently. His cheeks shone with tears; his lips clamped shut, trembling.

Without any warning Howard roared 'Waaarrghhhh!' and charged forward towards the creature cowering behind the fern. The creature leaped back, an almost comical bunny hop of surprise as Howard crashed through the undergrowth towards it. He stumbled through a cluster of ferns, swinging his hatchet at the creature as it recoiled, still off balance. The jagged blade caught something and the creature screamed.

Howard spun round and reached for Edward. 'GO!' he shouted, grabbing the scruff of his collar and pulling him forward. 'GO, GO, GO!' He pushed the boy forward with a rough punch to the small of his back.

Edward scrambled past the writhing creature, across a dozen yards of stunted plants and thinning saplings, ducking loops of thorny vines that promised to snarl his throat like barbed wire.

The boy was fast and agile and small enough to make a better job of dodging the jungle obstacles. Howard turned his attention to the creature beside him, snapping and clacking teeth as it got to its feet and warily circled him, leaking dark blood from the gash on its leg.

I'm ready for this, he told himself. *I'm ready for this. I'm ready. I'm ready. I'm ready to die.*

His mantra back in the lab, back when he was approaching Edward Chan and fingering the gun in his bag. He'd been ready to die then for a cause only a few seemed to truly understand. He was just as ready to die now.

Just as long as the boy keeps his promise.

There was no knowing, but instinct, *hope* . . . told Howard that Edward had seen enough of the nightmare of time travel for himself to know that his unique talent could never be allowed to find its voice.

And that's all that matters. Right?

Howard stared down the creature in front of him. 'Mission completed,' he uttered to himself with a growing smile spread across his boyish face.

'Come on, then, ugly,' he said, advancing on the thing just as the leaves behind him shuffled and swayed with the arrival of the other two, ready to finish him off.

CHAPTER 67

2001, New York

They returned to the archway and Forby wound the shutter down again.

'So,' said the man as he shouldered his assault rifle and cranked the handle. 'What I don't get is if this is still a version of the year 2001 how come those dino-humans out there aren't a lot more advanced?'

Maddy and Sal looked at each other. 'I dunno,' said Maddy. 'I'm no anthropologist.'

'It's a good question, Forby,' said Cartwright. He turned round and crouched to get one last look out at the rainforest version of the East River delta, and the far-off cluster of rounded huts on the muddy banks of Manhattan island. 'A good question . . . and I'll hazard a guess. They're a dead-end branch of evolution.'

Forby looked at him. 'Sir?'

'Those things out there –' he flicked a finger out at the narrowing window of alternative world outside – 'if they really are the direct descendants of some species that survived the end of the Cretaceous era, a species that somehow survived as a result of something that's been changed –' he looked at the girls – 'by your friend, then they've been around for tens of millions of years.'

'Well, that's exactly my point, sir. How come they aren't

light-years more advanced than humans? How come there isn't some gigantic lizard version of *Futurama* out there?' Forby finished cranking the shutter down. The archway was dim once more, lit by the sterile fizzing glow of the ceiling tube light.

'They *plateaued*,' said Cartwright. 'Perhaps their species evolved to the best it could possibly be. And then just stopped.'

Sal made a face. 'I thought evolution never stopped. I thought it always changed, always, like, adapting.'

'Oh, but it does and can stop,' he replied. 'There are species alive today that are virtually identical to their distant prehistoric ancestors – sharks, for example. Nature had evolved them to be perfect for their environment, perfect killing machines . . . why bother adapting any further?' He shrugged. 'Perhaps in this world, those reptilian hominids out there are the dominant predator, with nothing to compete against . . . and have been that way for millions of years?

'Evolution is nature's way of problem solving. If something changes that challenges a species' ability to survive, then that stimulates an adaptive response. If there's nothing to challenge a species' existence, then why would it ever need to change?' Cartwright shrugged. 'A dead-end of evolution.'

'A dead-end world,' echoed Forby.

They made their way across the dim archway. 'On the other hand, maybe there's some practical limit to how much smarter that species outside can get? Maybe those long heads are already too heavy to develop any greater cranial capacity?'

'So their brains will never get any bigger?'

'That's right. And they'll never do any better than spears, mud huts and dugout canoes.'

'Well,' said Maddy, approaching the desk, 'whatever. We'll never know, because those creepy-looking things weren't meant to happen.' She sat down at the computer desk. 'Bob, how're you doing with those candidate signals?'

> Analysis completed. The last 1,507 density soundings before you ordered me to cease the sweep indicated the immediate location was occupied by a permanent physical obstruction. This could be a natural intrusion, for example a fallen tree or a geological event.

'So, before that?' Maddy asked impatiently.

The others joined her at the desk.

> A total of 227 transient density warnings.

Cartwright squatted down beside her and studied the dialogue box. 'That means what? So now you're down to two hundred and twenty-seven possible locations for your friend?'

Maddy nodded. 'Can we filter that any further?'

> Affirmative. 219 were single-incursion events. Of the remaining eight density signatures that demonstrated a repeated incursion, only one demonstrated a regularly timed signature.

Sal bit her lip with excitement. 'That's it! Surely? That's got to be it!'

> Affirmative, Sal. There is a high probability that this is the correct time-stamp.

'YES!' said Maddy, spinning round in her chair, her hand raised for a high-five. Sal obliged with a hearty slap and a shriek of excitement.

Cartwright smiled. 'I presume that means you've found your friend?'

'Yes . . . see?' Maddy grinned proudly. 'I told you we could do it!'

'So then . . . what happens now?'

She spun back to face the monitors in front of her. 'Bob? We're good to begin charging up to open a portal?'

> Information: we have a 24-hour time period identified in which to open a window.

'Hmm.' Maddy pulled absently on her top lip. 'Twenty-four hours. But when *exactly* do we open it?'

Cartwright looked vexed and impatient.

'We have to be sure they're *there*, right?' said Sal on Maddy's behalf. 'You know? Before we commit to opening a portal. If we spend the stored charge and they're not there, we've gone and wasted it.'

Maddy nodded. 'We'll only have enough stored energy to open one, maybe two windows. How do we make sure they're actually right there and ready and waiting to come through, though?'

'Hang on!' cut in Cartwright. 'You just said "they". Are you telling me there's *more* than just your friend stuck back there?'

Sal nodded. 'Yes, Liam . . . and some others . . . children that were caught up in an accident.'

'Good God,' the old man whispered. 'Accident? This was an *accident*? What the heck have you people been up to?'

'It was a training incident,' cut in Sal, 'that's all. It went wrong. These things happen from time to time.'

> Information: it will be possible to open a series of pinhole windows and obtain a small-resolution image of the target location.

'Right.' Maddy nodded. 'Right . . . then we could *see* exactly when – during the day – there's somebody standing around. Yes . . . yes, good idea, Bob. Let's proceed with that.'

> Affirmative.

Cartwright sighed. 'So what's happening *now*?' Clearly impatient to see the displacement machine actually finally running.

Maddy turned to look over her shoulder. 'We're taking

some images of the portal location to make sure that when we open the window they're ready and waiting to come through.'

'Why don't you just open your portal and see for yourself?'

'Sal just explained that. We could be wasting a full power-up, and we can't risk doing that.' Maddy shrugged. 'Anyway, wouldn't you want to check first? This is the Cretaceous era, right? That means dinosaurs. I'd want to know the coast is clear of T-rexes first. Don't you?'

The old man glanced at Forby and the man shook his head quickly. 'Taking a few photos first sounds like a pretty good move to me, sir.'

Cartwright laughed nervously. 'Uh, I guess you're right. OK . . . we'll do it your way. Just get a move on before those hunters down the beach find a railway arch in the middle of their jungle.'

CHAPTER 68

65 million years BC, jungle

The three girls had revived the smouldering fire; the dried brittle moss that seemed to carpet every boulder and rock made perfect kindling and already a thick column of smoke was drifting up into the evening sky.

Liam felt a little happier now. Fire had seemed to keep those creatures at bay during the last few nights that they'd been out on their errand. They seemed to have a healthy respect for it – actually, to be more precise, a morbid fear of it.

He looked up across the twilit clearing. It had got dark very quickly. He wondered how the others were doing with Keisha. Surely they must have found her by now? If those pack hunters really had felled that tree and made their way across, then he was surprised they'd allowed her to live.

He was considering that point when he heard two sounds at the same time: one a far-off scream, shrill and terrifying that rattled around the clearing like a gunshot, and the other the sound of approaching trainers slapping the hard ground. He exchanged a hurried glance with the girls, and with Becks as she stopped fiddling with their damaged windmill and snapped erect like a spooked meerkat.

'Help!' He heard Edward's voice through the gathering gloom, and then a moment later picked out of that gloom the dancing outline of his pale T-shirt.

'Edward! What's up?'

The boy joined him, gasping and looking anxiously back over his shoulder. 'They're h-here! THEY'RE HERE!'

Liam followed his gaze and saw nothing across the clearing, just the dark outline of the apron of jungle. 'Where are the others?'

The boy ignored his question, his eyes wide with terror. 'Th-they're h-here, they're h-here!'

Liam grasped his arm firmly. 'EDWARD! What about the others?'

The boy looked at him. 'Dead,' he replied. 'All dead.'

'Oh God, look!' gasped Laura.

She was pointing across the clearing. Where a mere second ago he'd seen only jungle, now he saw a line of the creatures approaching them cautiously, spreading out like beaters for a hunting party. He quickly estimated thirty, maybe forty, of them; all sizes.

The whole pack . . . Jay-zus!

In the middle of the line, he thought he recognized one of them in particular. The one he'd seen in the jungle, barking orders to the others, their leader.

'Liam,' said Becks, stepping back from the windmill to join him and the others near the smoking fire, now beginning to take hold and crackle and spark. 'Do you see the middle one?'

He knew what she was referring to. The one in the middle, the pack leader, was holding one of their spears in its claws. He nodded.

'Like my adaptive AI,' she continued, 'the species has observed our behaviour and learned from it.'

He swallowed nervously. 'Back to the palisade . . . we need to go now!'

'Negative, I must stay.'

'What?' He looked at her.

'This location has been probed in the last twenty-four hours.' She nodded towards their broken windmill. 'There are decaying particles in the vicinity of the interference device. They may scan again at any moment.'

She was right, of course. Utterly barking mad, but quite right.

'All right, all right,' he uttered, watching the approaching hominids closing the gap slowly. 'You four,' he said to the others, 'get inside the wall and wait there!'

'What are you going to do?' asked Edward.

He really had no idea just then . . . some notion of holding out beside the campfire, back to back with Becks until . . . until . . . what?

Until they've finally worn her down, and jump her. Then turn on me.

But, there was a slight chance, wasn't there? A slight chance Maddy and Sal were going to sweep this place again at any moment. And, if they did, this might be their last chance to flag the signal, to tell them they were right here. The alternative, hiding inside their flimsy palisade until these creatures finally managed to gnaw their way through the twine, pull aside a couple of the logs from the wall and get in . . . He shuddered.

'There's a return window coming,' he said. 'It's coming soon! Becks and me need to be out here waiting for it. You four will be safer inside. I'll call for you when it opens. Now just go!'

'I want to stay,' said Edward, picking up one of their hatchets from a pile of cut wood beside the fire. The other three nodded. 'We'll f-fight them t-together,' whispered Laura, her teeth chattering noisily.

Jasmine looked across at the palisade, twenty yards away beyond the flickering pool of light from the fire. 'They'll find a way in anyway.'

Liam looked at the creatures, now almost entirely encircling them, maintaining their cautious distance. 'All right. Perhaps you're right,' he uttered. 'Becks, how're we gonna do this?'

'Recommendation: I need to be in the vicinity of the interference device in order to detect any precursor particles arriving.'

Liam nodded. 'Yes . . . yes. R-right. We should hold the ground over there.' He reached down towards the fire and pulled out a branch. The end of it flickered with flames. 'Everyone grab a torch. They don't like fire!'

The others followed suit. Then moved together in a tight huddle, away from the reassuring glow of the campfire towards their contraption, a dozen yards beyond the growing pall of amber firelight.

The creatures followed them, silently padding across the soft ground, watching them, and ever so subtly closing the distance around them.

'YOU BACK OFF!' screamed Laura at them, waving her flaming stick.

The creatures hissed, warbled and mewed at that, one of the smaller ones attempting a copy of her shaking voice.

'. . . *Yoo . . . . bak . . . offfff . . .*'

Becks turned to Liam. 'This location has just been scanned again. There are several hundred new particles.'

Liam felt a surge of hope. 'Oh, c'mon! Why don't they just get on with it and open a bleedin' window?'

Becks cocked her head. She had no answer.

All of a sudden, the creature holding the spear barked in a

croaky voice and, as one, the creatures surged forward towards them.

'Oh my God! Oh my God! screamed Laura.

'Recommendation: use your spears to –'

CHAPTER 69

2001, New York

The best part of an hour passed in silence with Maddy, Sal and Cartwright gathered around the monitors watching a progress bar slowly inch across one of the screens, and an empty directory slowly fill with low-resolution JPG files.

Forby meanwhile stood beside the doorway, cranked up a couple of feet, gazing at the jungle world outside. 'They're still hunting those beach pigs or whatever those things are,' he called out softly.

'Good,' replied Cartwright absently. 'How much longer?'

Maddy shrugged. 'You can see the progress bar yourself, can't you? It's nearly there.'

The old man made a face. 'If it's anything like the Windows I got at home, *nearly there* can mean another five minutes or another five hours.'

'This is an operating system from sometime in the 2050s,' said Maddy. 'It sure ain't gonna be Windows.'

The progress bar suddenly lurched forward to a hundred per cent and Bob's dialogue box appeared.

> Process complete.

'Bob, can you do some sort of slideshow?'

> Affirmative. Images are taken one every five minutes.

A monitor to the left of them flickered to life, revealing a small pixelated image of green and blue.

Maddy squinted at the image. 'What is that?'

'Jungle,' said Sal. 'That's what it is. Jungle and some sky.'

Forby joined them around the desk. 'Yeah . . . that's a jungle, I think.'

A second image appeared, almost identical to the first, a couple of pixel blocks had changed tone slightly. 'Is this as clear as the images get?' asked Cartwright.

> Affirmative. The pinhole and image data size has been kept to a minimum to conserve on energy consumption.

'All we need is to see enough pixels change to indicate something moving around the area, right?' said Sal.

> Correct, Sal.

'Can you play through these slides a little faster, please, Bob?'

> Affirmative, Maddy. Increasing display rate times ten.

The next slide came up, just the same as the last, and another, an undecipherable flicker show of green and blue pixels. They watched in silence until approximately midway through the complexion of the image suddenly changed with a mass of dark pixels.

'Whoa! Stop!' said Maddy. She studied the shape on-screen. 'What's that?'

'That looks like a person,' said Forby. 'See? That's a shoulder and an arm.'

Sal cocked her head and frowned. 'It doesn't look right.'

'What time in their day is this image, Bob?'

> 14:35.

'Half past two in the afternoon,' said Sal.

'Give us the next image, Bob.'

Another dark image appeared on-screen, the blue pixels of sky and green of jungle almost entirely gone.

'Somebody standing right in the middle of the portal

location . . . for about five minutes,' mumbled Maddy to herself. She looked at Sal. 'That's got to be the support unit? She's sensed a tachyon particle and she's hanging around for another?'

Sal shook her head. 'Maybe . . . but the shape of the body looks all kind of funny to me.'

'Oh, come on, it's a one hundred by one hundred pixel image – everything's going to look all funny.'

She shook her head again. 'I'm not sure. It could be anything . . . it could be some animal.'

'Bob, next image.'

Another image flickered up and this time the dark mass of pixels was gone, leaving the image the same even mix of blue and green squares.

Maddy grabbed a pen from the desk and scribbled the time of 14:35 on a scrap of paper. 'Well, OK, we know someone was hanging around then. We've got one possible window. Let's get on with the slideshow and see what else we get.'

Once more the images began to flicker on-screen one after another, a second apart, the blue pixels of the sky slowly changing hue from bright blue to a rose colour.

'It's evening,' said Cartwright helpfully.

The sequence continued, with the sky pixels slowly reddening in colour, and the jungle's light green becoming a deeper darker green, until all of a sudden, in the middle of the image, they saw a single dot of bright orange.

'Stop!'

All four of them craned forward to get a better look.

'That's fire, isn't it?' said Forby. 'A flame?'

Sal nodded. 'Yeah.'

'Someone starting a campfire maybe?'

'Fire . . . right,' uttered Cartwright, 'and the only thing that can make a fire back then is going to be human.'

Maddy tapped her chin thoughtfully. 'Yup . . . so maybe this is a more reliable candidate than the other. What time is this image, Bob?'

> **18:15.**

'Give me the next image.'

The orange pixel became a dozen pixels, and half the screen was filled by a vertical block of black pixels. In the top left corner, they could just make out the sky, the pink evening becoming a deep purple with the onset of dusk.

'Someone's standing right there again!'

'And that thing doesn't look as weird as the earlier one,' said Sal.

Maddy looked at her. 'How can you tell?'

'Screw up your eyes a bit, Maddy . . . it sort of blurs the pixels slightly. You can make out shapes more easily.'

'A campfire and someone standing right there,' said Cartwright. 'Looks like the best time so far.'

'Yes,' she replied absently. 'What do you think, Bob?'

> **This image looks most probable.**

'Quickly run through the rest.'

The slideshow flickered through the last sixty-eight images, one image per second. A juddering animation of time . . . the fire slowly dwindling, dying and vanishing, the sky darkening until the final few dozen images were simply a sequence of black pixels.

> **Sequence complete.**

'Looks like we have a winner,' said Cartwright. 'Can we now proceed?' He looked up at Forby. 'You know? Before those hunters come knocking on our door?'

'OK . . . let's begin powering up, Bob.'

> **Affirmative.**

Cartwright stood up straight, his arms caressing a stiff back.

‘So . . . what happens next?’ He glanced at the large perspex tube. ‘They’re going to appear inside that?’

She shook her head and pointed to a circle of chalk scrawled across the concrete floor. ‘There. You and Forby need to stand well clear of that.’

Cartwright’s man stepped away from the table and faced the circle, unslinging his assualt rifle in readiness.

Maddy turned to regard both men. ‘I’d be happier if Mr Forby could take his finger off the trigger.’

Cartwright smiled. ‘Of course.’ He nodded at his man. ‘You can stand down, Forby. But . . . just stay alert, all right?’

Forby nodded, slackening his grip and lowering the barrel of his gun.

CHAPTER 70

65 million years BC, jungle

Liam lashed out with his hatchet, swinging the serrated metal blade in one hand and probing and prodding with his bamboo spear in the other. But the creatures dodged back with graceful agility, keeping their eyes on the weapons.

The fire nearby had taken a firm hold of the branches that had been thrown on top of it. Occasional tongues of flame lashed up into the almost dark sky, and upward cascades of sparks danced like fireflies. The flickering light, the warmth from the campfire and the dancing flames on the ends of their torches were causing the hominids' probing attack to falter.

'GO AWAY!' screamed Laura, prodding the flaming end of her branch towards the nearest of them.

Becks, meanwhile, had managed to kill one of them and severely wound another. She could move forward with the same sudden speed as these things, catching them off balance. The wounded creature, now thrashing around on the ground, had lost a limb to one vicious roundhouse sweep of her hatchet. The creature she'd managed to grasp hold of moments ago had had its fragile spine snapped over her knee.

For her efforts she'd received a deep gash down one thigh. Her left leg was red with her own blood, soaking the sock rolled over the edge of her combat boot almost black. The wound was already clotting, but Liam couldn't help notice how much blood she'd lost in that one sudden crimson gush and worried whether her engineered body was capable of replacing that blood with the same efficiency as it could staunch a wound.

The creatures probed and circled, clacking teeth and claws and mewling like foxes, occasionally testing them with a lunge and snap of jaws . . . so far the six of them were doing better than Liam could have hoped holding them back. But then he realized there was patient thinking going on behind what these creatures were up to.

Wearing us down. That's all they're doing. Wearing us down.

His eyes picked through the lean olive-coloured hides, the flickering chitinous teeth, until he found the pack leader, holding that spear and looking strangely human because of that.

If we got him . . .

Yes, if Becks could somehow be fast enough to reach out past the others and grab him, and snap his neck in her hands, then the others would surely panic and run. He had a spear in his hand; he realized he could at least have a go. The pack leader was only fourteen or fifteen feet away and, unlike the others, circling in that strange bobbing way, he stood perfectly still, watching them with keen studious eyes.

Liam dropped his hatchet at his feet.

'What are you doing?' yelled Jasmine.

'Gonna get that one there,' he said, nodding towards Broken Claw.

He steadied his balance on his back leg, lined up the creature staring at him with cocked-head curiosity down the length of the bamboo shaft and then hurled it like a javelin. A straight point-to-point throw instead of an arced trajectory. He surprised even himself with his accuracy and would probably have caught the thing square in its narrow chest, had not another smaller one bobbed in the way unintentionally. The sharp tip of the bamboo punched into its long bony skull and the creature crumpled to the ground with a short brittle scream that sounded almost like the wail of a human child.

Liam winced and cursed that he'd not got the leader. And now they were down to one spear.

Out of the black one of the smaller hominids suddenly ducked down low and swiped with a claw, knocking Akira off balance. Her leg buckled and, with a thin yelp, she dropped heavily into the dirt. Winded and worn out, she struggled to get up. Yet more spindle-thin arms emerged from the gloom and clawed digits wrapped tightly round her ankles and wrists.

'No!' she screamed, her pale face just two wide eyes and her mouth an 'O' of horror. Within a second, two beats of a pounding heart, they'd dragged her struggling form out of the pall of flickering light, her screaming voice smothered, muffled and then brutally silenced.

Becks took advantage of a careless incursion and lunged forward again, sweeping her blade and missing as the creatures leaped once more back out of her range.

'We . . . can't keep this . . . up,' said Laura. 'Not all . . . not all n-night.'

'I know,' replied Liam.

Just then something whistled past his cheek. '*Whuh?*'

He looked down and saw the shaft of a bamboo spear rattling and flexing on the ground. He looked up at the empty-handed pack leader and understood.

'Oh no!' he gasped. 'You see that? It . . . threw . . . It threw it back.'

Good going, Liam. You just taught them how to toss a javelin.

'Ah Jay-zus . . . if they start throwin' missiles at us, we'll be in trouble.'

'L-like we're not already?' muttered Laura, lashing out at one of the smaller creatures bobbing too close.

Liam watched the leader, moving around the rear of his pack, those yellow eyes no longer on him but flitting across the ground, looking for something.

Looking for another spear to throw?

'Information.' Becks's voice suddenly cut across the clacking and mewling. 'I am detecting a burst of precursor particles.'

'Is . . . is that good?' asked Jasmine.

Liam nodded. 'Yes! Oh Jay-zus, yes!' He turned to Becks. 'That's a window, right? Tell me it's a window and not another probe?'

'Affirmative. The configuration suggests an imminent window.'

'YES! Oh yes!' He grinned breathlessly.

'We must move out of this space,' said Becks. 'They will not open the window until it is completely clear.'

'Right. Together,' said Liam. 'Keep together, back to back . . . move towards the fire!'

The five of them backed up towards each other, until they were almost bumping together. Then Becks stepped a little ahead, swiping and spinning a hatchet in each hand with ballet-like precision at the creatures. They wisely backed away from her, creating a path for them to shuffle along in her wake.

'Enough!' barked Becks after they'd moved half a dozen yards across the clearing towards the increasing heat and flickering light of the campfire. She turned round to face them. 'The extraction area is now unobstruct–'

It was then a sharpened tip of bamboo erupted through her abdomen, ripping through her flesh and the tattered material of her black crop top. Becks glanced casually down at the bloody tip.

'Becks!' gasped Liam.

With a blur of movement, she reached round and grabbed the creature that had skewered her from behind. She flipped it over her shoulder on to the ground in front of her. Its claws viciously flailed at her, shredding the skin on her forearm into tatty red ribbons. With a savage jerk she twisted its long head. The creature's yellow eyes and leathery black tongue bulged under the sudden tension in its slender neck. They heard a crackling sound and then the thing stopped squirming.

'Becks! You OK?' cried Liam.

'Negative. The damage is significant,' she replied, looking down at the point of the spear, still protruding from her waist. One of her legs wobbled beneath her and she dropped to her knees.

'BECKS! Hang in there!' yelled Liam.

Then they all felt it, the solid push of displaced air. Liam looked behind him and saw a shimmering sphere: the faint, dancing pattern of a reassuringly familiar place – the archway. 'LOOK! That's it! THAT'S THE WINDOW!'

Right now, in this instant, there were no creatures between them and their way home. 'GO!' Liam yelled.

For a moment the two remaining girls and Edward stared at him, unsure what he meant by that.

'NOW!' he screamed, his voice breaking. 'THERE! . . . RUN FOR IT! GO, GO, GO!'

Laura nodded, more than happy to obey. She turned on her heels and sprinted for the window. Jasmine followed suit. Edward lingered. 'What about –?'

'NOW!' screamed Liam.

Edward turned and sprinted after the girls. Liam turned to Becks. 'Come on!'

She struggled to her feet unsteadily. 'Information: I have lost significant levels of blood –'

'Just shuddup!' he snapped, sliding his hands under her armpits and hefting her up. She staggered to her feet. 'Leave, Liam!' she ordered him. 'Protect Edward Chan!'

Liam shot a glance over his shoulder. He could see Laura hovering just outside the spherical boundary of the window, hesitating to step in. Between her and them, Edward and Jasmine sprinting.

'GODDAMMIT GO THROUGH!' he shouted. 'GO THR– . . . AGHHhhhh!'

He suddenly felt a searing pain through his leg and saw that one of the smaller creatures had grasped his shin; the razor-sharp edge of its claws sliced through his shorts, through his skin and now grated against his shin bone.

Becks swiped with the hatchet still in her left hand, and cut through the creature's thin wrist. Its claws and its hand were still attached to Liam's lower leg like the jaws of some tenacious decapitated soldier ant. Despite the grating agony in his leg, he dragged Becks with him, she barely able to drunkenly stagger, and yet still swinging her blade in powerfully vicious yet groggy ill-aimed arcs that thwacked and cracked against the hungrily grasping reach of those creatures determined enough to reach out for them.

Around him, Liam could hear a mixture of frustrated snarls and startled whimpers . . . and a sudden high-pitched scream that sounded unmistakably human. His mind solely on dragging Becks, heavy despite her slight frame, he could only fleetingly hope that it wasn't Edward Chan's voice he'd just heard.

'Mission priority –' Becks began to chastise him.

'JUST KEEP HITTING THE BLOODY THINGS!' he

bellowed back at her. She shut up and obliged, swinging a booted foot out at a long bony jaw getting ready to snap down on her blood-caked thigh. Her boot made heavy contact, and the skull spun on its turtle neck like a skittle, a handful of toothpick-sized teeth whizzing out into the dark.

Ten seconds later – ten seconds that to Liam could easily have been a minute or an hour, ten seconds of dragging, hacking, swinging, kicking and screaming – and all of a sudden he felt the hair on his head lift in response to the warm soup of energy and excited particles around him. Over his shoulder, he could see Sal, actually see her shape, dancing and undulating as if seen through a thin veil of oil, and other shapes, Edward, Laura standing beside her. He could see the flickering blue fizzing archway light that normally irritated him so much as he read on his bunk.

'WE DID IT!' he found himself yelling as his foot seemed to lose touch with solid ground and he felt that all too familiar nauseating sensation of falling.

CHAPTER 71

2001, New York

He felt his face smack against a hard concrete floor, the dead weight of Becks landing heavily on the top of his back, knocking the air out of his lungs.

'Good God!' he heard from somewhere nearby – a male voice he didn't recognize.

While his eyes were still seeing stars, he could feel Becks struggling to lift herself off his back. He heard the pounding rasp of laboured breath nearby, presumably, hopefully, Edward and the other two. He could hear the faint muted chug of the generator in the back room. And through the still-open portal hovering a couple of feet above the tangled pile of himself and Becks, the far-off sounds of a jungle night stirring to life . . . and the click-clacking and mewling of those things getting louder, closer.

'Ummpph . . . closhhhh the 'ortal!' he mumbled into the floor, his bloodied lips still mushed against the hard concrete as Becks struggled to lift her dead weight off him.

'Liam? Is that you under there?' Maddy's voice.

'Umpph. U'mm . . . yeshhh,' he mumbled. 'Closhhh the 'leedin' 'ortal!'

Then all of a sudden he felt another heavy load land on his back, and the excruciating pain of three sharp blades digging deep into his left shoulder-blade.

'What on earth is THAT?' Another unfamiliar voice, another man's voice.

The weight was gone as quickly as it had arrived and he heard the skittering of claws across the concrete floor and the startled bark of one or two of those creatures echoing off the arched brick ceiling.

'My God, Forby! Shoot it! SHOOT IT!'

The piercing scream of a girl, he couldn't be sure who. Then, with a rattling sigh, Becks finally flopped off the side of his back, her pale face spattered with dark dots of drying blood, thudding to the floor beside his. Her grey eyes stared lifelessly back at him, as if looking at something far, far away. He managed to lift himself up on to his elbows, grimacing at the sharp pain in his shoulder and his head still spinning from the impact of the heavy landing. He attempted to get his first glance at what was going on around him.

Two of the creatures had managed to follow them through and were now darting in confusion and panic one way and then the other across the archway floor. He spotted two men he didn't recognize: one old, in a rumpled suit with a loosened tie dangling round his throat like a hangman's noose. The other man was younger with buzz-cut sandy hair and an army-fit physique beneath what looked like a baggy light-green boiler suit. He raised a gun.

'Where did they go?' snapped Maddy.

They heard something fall off a shelf in a dark corner of the archway and roll noisily across the floor.

'Over there!'

With trained, quick precision, Forby squinted down the weapon's barrel and flipped the night-sight of his scope on. A soft green glow poured across his face as he slowly panned the weapon around the archway, then up towards the curved brick ceiling.

'Ahh . . . I see one.'

Liam followed the direction of his gaze and thought he could just about make out some dark shape moving among a criss-cross of old rusting pipes and loops of electrical flex. Age-old dust and the grit from crumbling bricks and mortar trickled down past the softly fizzing glow of the ceiling light, giving the hapless creature's position away.

The man fired two aimed shots in quick succession. The creature screamed, then plummeted to the floor, bringing down a small flurry of dust and grit with it. It squirmed and screamed and drummed arms and legs against the floor, until the young man put a third shot into its long skull.

As the echo of the last shot rattled around the brick walls, Liam looked around him. He could see Edward and Laura huddled together by the displacement machine's perspex tube, and Sal and Maddy beside the computer desk. All of them looking from one dark recess to another, listening intently for the sounds of movement.

'Where's the other one?' whispered Sal.

The man with the gun placed a finger to his lips to hush her. 'Hiding,' he whispered.

'Well, for Christ's sake find him, Forby!' hissed the older man.

Liam watched as Forby stepped across the floor into the middle of the archway, continuing to slowly pan his gun, studying every nook and cranny around until finally he came to a halt, aiming at the arched recess where their bunk beds were.

'Uh-huh . . . I think he's skulking under there.'

He squatted down low and pumped his finger. A single shot danced and ricocheted under Liam's cot, sparking against the metal frame.

It was then that something dropped down from above, past the ceiling light on to Forby's back – a blur of movement and flashing of claws and teeth, a bright arc of crimson.

'HEELLP M–!' His voice was cut off as the creature's claws flailed at his neck. He dropped the gun as he staggered and struggled to wrestle the thing off his back.

Liam picked himself up and scrambled across the floor, reaching out for the heavy assault rifle as Forby's legs buckled and he dropped to his knees, blood spraying from the multiple ragged wounds across his face and head. The creature leaped off his shoulders and darted towards the shutter door as Forby flopped the rest of the way to the ground. Quite dead.

Liam raised the gun and pulled the trigger. The gun kicked his shoulder as he emptied the clip with a protracted and unaimed volley that produced a dozen showers of sparks and brick-red plumes of dust.

With the gun angrily clicking in his hands, he finally eased his finger off the trigger and peered through the gunsmoke at the inert body of the other creature. Now a shredded mess.

'Jesus,' whispered the old man, his croaky voice shaking.

CHAPTER 72

2001, New York

They stared at the naked body floating amid the pink-red soup of liquid in the plastic cylinder.

'Will the support unit survive?' asked Sal.

'Becks,' said Liam quietly. His voice little more than a gentle croak. 'Her name is *Becks*.'

The soft glow of red light coming from the base of the birthing tube was the only illumination in the back room. It was enough for Maddy to see the lost expression of post-traumatic stress on Liam's face. 'She'll live,' said Maddy with the hesitant smile of someone not really sure. 'Bob said their combat frames can sustain roughly a seventy-five per cent blood loss and still be able to recover from that, given enough time.' She glanced at the shredded remnants of the female unit's left lower arm. Almost all the soft tissue had been clawed away leaving a skeletal forearm surrounded by tatters of skin and tendon that floated and swayed in the gloop like so many ends of frayed rope.

'Unlike Forby,' said Cartwright sombrely.

'I'm sorry,' said Maddy. 'He seemed, like, you know . . . like a good guy.'

The old man nodded thoughtfully. 'The best. The very best.' He sighed. 'Family man too.'

The only sound in the back room was the gentle purring

of the tube's filtration system. Maddy had shut down the generator to conserve the half a tank of fuel they had left. There was no need for the generator to be chugging away right now; a row of steady green LEDs showed the displacement machinery was fully charged and ready to use again. She'd shut everything else down, the computer systems, the lights, the other birthing tubes and the fridge containing the other embryos . . . they'd keep in their cryo-tubes for a few more hours without refrigeration.

'So how long?' asked Laura, wiping her nose on the back of her hand. 'You know? Until she's all better again?'

Maddy looked up at the girl. She could imagine her in another time, confident and popular in her high school, a baton-twiddling cheerleader, everyone's favourite, always invited to parties, always surrounded by friends and acolytes. That Texan accent – the confident bray of someone who'd never need to question her place in the world . . . Well, she didn't look quite so much like a future Homecoming Queen now. Even in this muted light Maddy could see how badly affected she was by the portal's corrosion effect. Her face looked ghostly pale, the flesh around her eyes dark and it seemed her nose was still leaking a steady trickle of blood: a ruptured blood vessel somewhere inside that quite possibly might never heal.

The boy, Edward Chan, seemed to have fared only slightly better.

Apparently, according to Chan, there'd been another girl with them, but she'd been jumped by one of those things just before she could reach the portal. If she'd suffered the same fate as Forby, then Maddy could only hope her death had been as mercifully quick. Although, after what she'd witnessed only half an hour ago, *merciful* felt entirely like the wrong word to use. She watched Chan's large round eyes staring at the mush of organic soup, at the foggy figure of the support unit inside. Both these two, Chan and the girl, seemed to be in a deep state of shock, well beyond grieving for a lost classmate. Liam said there'd been others, sixteen of them had survived the blast back in time. Only these two plus Liam and Becks had made it.

God knows what they've been through.

'How long?' asked Chan again.

'About four and a half hours,' Maddy replied. 'Four and a half hours and her condition should be stable. She'll have replenished enough blood to function again.'

'What about her arm?'

Maddy shrugged. 'I don't know whether this healing thing actually regrows limbs and stuff. Bob, our computer system, just told me she'd be able to repopulate blood cells. We'll see, I guess.'

Liam's eyes came back from far away and met hers. 'You said . . . *function again*?'

She nodded. 'She has to go back, Liam. You know that. There are loose ends that need fixing.'

The others looked at her. It was clear to her that she was the only one doing any strategic thinking here, thinking beyond the moment.

That's your job, Maddy. Team strategist . . . remember?

'She has to go back and correct what happened . . . what it is that's made the present the way it is.'

'It's those creatures, isn't it?' said Cartwright. 'The ones that came through your portal . . . they're the thing that's different?'

Maddy turned to Liam. 'Liam, is that –?'

Oh my God.

She hadn't noticed it before. In fact, she had, but she'd thought it was a streak of dust, or perhaps a dusting of some exotic jungle pollen. Looking at Liam right now, even in the dim crimson glow of the birthing tube, she could see a shock of white hair on his left temple. And his left eye . . . the white of it mottled with the web-like blur of a burst blood vessel.

'Yes . . .' he said after a few moments, not registering the look on her face. 'Yes . . . those things, they learned a few tricks from us.'

'There's more?' asked Sal.

He nodded. 'Yeah . . . thirty or forty, I suppose. A pack of them.' His eyes remained on the outline of Becks's form, curled up like a foetus. In her sleep, vulnerable-looking – just a teenage girl. 'She managed to kill some of them, but the rest are back there.'

Maddy looked at Sal and Cartwright. 'Then those hunters across the river, they must be distant ancestors. They're somehow linked, right? The long heads?'

Cartwright nodded. 'It's an unusual configuration.' He stroked his chin. 'No . . . it's a *unique* configuration.'

Maddy had lifted the shutter door briefly after they'd seen to Becks and shown Liam and the other two the jungle that now replaced New York. The hunters were no longer probing the riverbank for mud creatures and had returned to the settlement on the far side of the broad river.

'They're descendants, Liam,' she said. 'Distant . . . very distant descendants.'

'And their ancestors,' cut in Cartwright, 'must have learned something from you . . . something that enabled them to survive and prosper. Something, some sort of skill, that helped them survive the K–T event, whatever wiped out the dinosaurs.'

Liam nodded slowly. She could see he'd worked that much out already. 'So . . . someone has to go back and kill the whole pack.'

'Yes,' said Maddy, reaching a hand out and holding his arm

gently. 'They can't be allowed to live and develop any sort of intelligence that could save them. They should have died out with all the other dinosaurs.'

'OK.' He took a deep breath. 'OK . . . I'll go –'

'No,' she said, a little too quickly. She tried not to let her stare at his bloodshot eye linger. 'Not you, Liam. You need rest.'

'If not me, then who? No one else –'

'The support unit.'

'Becks?' He shook his head. 'No. She'll take days to recover, surely. And she'll not be able to face them all on her own. They'll kill her, to be sure.'

Her? She?

She held his arm. 'Listen to me, Liam.' She nodded at the birthing tube. 'I know you've been through a lot together, but remember . . . it's just a support unit in there. A meat robot. A tool for the job. That's all it is. It's *expendable.*'

'I'll go with her,' he said.

'No.' Maddy shook her head firmly. 'No. You can't go back there again.'

'Why?'

He doesn't know, does he? He hasn't looked into a mirror. He hasn't realized how much damage going so far back in time has already done to him. She wondered why he hadn't yet noted the condition of the girl and Chan. Both looked like people suffering from advanced radiation sickness. But then . . . from his time, Liam wouldn't know anything about radiation sickness. Perhaps he attributed the bleeding noses, the pallid complexion to shock. Perhaps he was too much in shock himself to have noticed.

'Because you're too valuable to lose, Liam. We need you here.'

'We need you,' added Sal, 'and . . .' Her face dipped out of range of the soft peach glow and in the darkness they heard movement, a scrape, the heavy thud of something metallic and the rattle and tinkle of a buckle. Her face returned and she held up something that glinted in the dull light. 'And she'd have this gun, Liam. Not just a bamboo stick.'

Maddy nodded. 'You saw how good it was earlier.'

'High-calibre MP15 assault rifle,' said Cartwright. 'It'll mince those monsters up no problem.'

'We'll give her a few hours to rebuild herself. OK?'

'I'll uhh . . . I'll go and see how many clips of ammo Forby has . . . *had*,' said Cartwright.

Maddy pressed out a smile, and nodded. 'You do that.'

She turned back to Liam, watching the floating body of Becks. She could see he felt something for the support unit, that they'd bonded in the past . . . that this time, unlike last time, if the support unit fell, there'd be no one to retrieve its AI, no one to dig the computer out of its cranium and bring it back.

Be the leader, Maddy. There's no discussion here. It's decided.

'Sorry, Liam, she has to go,' she said forcefully. 'That's how it is. She has to do this. We need New York back; we need our power feed back before we run out of fuel. Anyway . . .' She glanced at the silhouette of Cartwright shuffling cautiously out through the doorway by the light of a wind-up torch. She lowered her voice. 'Anyway, there's going to be one more job for you to do before we've dug ourselves out of this whole freakin' hole.'

CHAPTER 73

2001, New York

Liam watched the sun setting across the river, picking out thin skeins of smoke from the settlement perched on the muddy banks on the far side. He saw several pinpricks of light in the middle of the round huts.

Fire. One of the earliest markers of intelligence. He wondered how many aeons ago this descendant species had learned they could control it, use it. A far cry from the primitive animal fear for it demonstrated by their ancestors.

He heard the shutter rattle as Maddy stooped under it and joined him outside. 'Hi,' she said. 'How are you feeling?'

'Tired.' Squatting against the outside brick wall of their archway, watching the jungle turn dark and the sky's rich palette change from crimson to violet, he realized how utterly spent he felt. Finally, after two weeks of nervous tension, two weeks of fearing something primal, savage and hungry could snatch him away at any time . . . here he was, somewhere safe at last. Somewhere he could close his eyes for a moment and actually, properly, rest.

'She's nearly ready,' said Maddy. 'We're prepping the portal to take her back to one minute after we closed the last one. Those creatures should still all be gathered there, scratching their heads and wondering where you went.'

'How is she?'

'The arm looks like it's begun repairing itself. I noticed there's some new muscle tissue. No skin yet. I presume that regrows at some point. Anyway, Sal's bound her arm and hand in bandages to protect it.'

'How is she?' he asked again. 'Can she do it?'

'She says she can operate to forty-seven per cent functional capacity.' Maddy smirked. 'And she's really rather pleased about the weapon.'

Liam laughed softly. 'Just like Bob.'

'They could be brother and sister.'

'Well, they are . . . I suppose.'

'True.'

Liam nodded towards the village. 'It feels wrong, in a way.'

'What?'

'What we're doing . . . killing the rest of that pack. I mean, look what they became.' He shook his head and laughed.

'What's so funny?'

'I'm almost proud of them, so I am. They're like, I suppose . . . I feel like they're sort of *my* creation. We showed them how to build a bridge, how to use a spear. And, after Lord knows how many thousands of years . . .'

'Millions actually.'

'. . . millions of years, they've become this. A brand-new intelligent race and here we are, going to wipe them all out. What's that word for it?'

'Genocide?'

'Aye, that's it . . . like that Hitler tried to do to the Jews. And we're going to do it to those things. They're not just dumb animals, Maddy. They were clever back in the jungle, you could see that. Very clever, and now here they are just as smart as us humans.'

'No, Liam, they're not. Something that old man, Cartwright, said . . .'

'What?'

'Ask yourself this: just how long have they been at this stage of development? Hmm? They could have got this far – canoes, spear, huts an' all – millions of years ago and yet . . . and yet this is as far as they ever got.' She gazed at the distant village. 'Otherwise, why aren't they walking around in smart suits and talking on cell phones?'

He shrugged. 'Maybe they did once. Maybe millions of years ago they were that smart, and this place was a big city like New York.'

'And what? They chose to become savages again?'

'Who knows? Maybe they had some sort of war? Maybe they once had an incredible civilization that eventually collapsed into ruins. Or some doomsday weapon wiped them out but for a few poor bloody survivors.'

Maddy nodded. 'It's possible, I guess. A lot can happen in sixty-five million years.'

'Aye, and who's to say it doesn't one day happen to us too, eh? And soon.'

She looked at him. 'Kramer's time?'

'Foster's time, perhaps. You remember the things he told us about the future? The dark times ahead. All that global warming, the flooding, pollution and the poisoned seas . . . the starving billions?'

She did. It was a future she'd thought she was beginning to see in her lifetime. That big meeting in Copenhagen that was supposed to be the last best chance for the world to agree on how to stop global warming – it had failed miserably. She wondered whether historians from midway through the twenty-first century would point to that day as the very beginning of the end.

'Well . . . that's the future whether we like it or not, Liam. And it's our job to fight to keep it that way.'

He nodded. 'Hmm . . . but do you ever wonder, Maddy?'

'Wonder what?'

He looked at her, with his bloodshot eye and thin shock of snow-white hair, and for a moment he looked both old and young at the same time. 'Do you wonder whether that future, the one Foster told us all about, whether that's the *right* future to fight for?'

'I dunno. I suppose we just have to trust him that it is.'

The sun dipped behind the far horizon of trees, behind the thin lines of campfire smoke. From inside the arch they could hear the voices of the others: Sal helping the support unit . . . Becks . . . get ready.

'She's been given orders to kill them all, then destroy your camp. Burn everything so there's nothing left behind to leave fossil traces. We'll know if she's successful –' Maddy nodded out at the jungle – 'when this all goes and we get New York back, and . . .' She lowered her voice a little. 'And the tricky situation we were stuck right in the middle of just before jungle-land arrived . . .'

'Cartwright?'

She nodded.

'So . . .' He cocked a brow. 'I'm presuming he, and the poor fella with the gun, are the chaps who found our message?'

'Not exactly. It was found a lot, lot earlier. In the 1940s, apparently. But Cartwright runs this little government agency,' she snorted, 'an agency a bit like ours, I guess – small and secret. Its job for the last sixty years has been to be a custodian of your message. And to finally make contact with us in 2001.'

'And he came knocking?'

'Oh, he came knocking all right. Just before the last time wave, we had men with guns standing guard outside in the backstreet. In fact, they had several areas of the neighbourhood sealed up with roadblocks and soldiers and stuff. Helicopters overhead and everything. Quite a big deal. You'd have loved it.'

'My fault.' Liam looked guilty. 'Sorry about that.'

She shook her head. 'Don't be. You had to send the message. There was no other way we would have found you.'

Sal was calling out for her. It was time.

'Thing is, Liam,' she said hurriedly, 'we have to be ready to move, and move quickly. If Becks is successful . . . we'll get all of that situation right back in our faces. We'll be right where we were. So, I'm going to need to send you back to make sure they don't get your message.'

'Dinosaur times?'

'Oh no. Not that far.' She managed to stop herself saying *because that would probably finish you off.* 'No . . . it'll be the second of May 1941. You need to prevent some kids from finding a particular chunk of rock.'

He smiled. 'And Cartwright and his agency will never have existed?'

She was ducking down under the shutter when she paused. 'Well . . . his agency might not exist, or maybe it will, but it will be busy with some other secret it's trying to keep from the American people.'

'Right.'

'When that time wave comes, Liam . . . we'll need Cartwright standing *outside* when I turn on our time field. His life will be rewritten along with the rest of the corrected reality. He'll have no memory of all of this.'

Liam bent down and looked under the shutter and into the archway. He could see Forby's dark boots poking out of the end of the blanket they'd wrapped his body in.

'And what about him?'

'Forby? Not sure. If his body is outside the field I suppose he gets to live again, doing whatever job he was doing before Cartwright and his agency suddenly winked into existence. The point is . . . whatever that means for him and the old man, we *won't* have a backstreet full of spooks with guns. We'll be back to normal.' She grinned up at him. 'Which would really be quite nice.'

'True . . . but do we not still have to get Edward Chan back home?'

'One thing at a time,' she sighed. 'Come on, let's send Becks on her way.'

Liam followed her under the shutter and then cranked it down after him.

He rejoined Maddy and the others gathered around the computer desk. He saw Becks standing in the middle of them, the assault rifle cradled in her arms, one of them swathed in bandages up to her elbow.

'How are you feeling?' he asked over the hubbub of other voices: questions from Cartwright and the kids that Maddy was busy trying to field as she configured the return time-stamp.

'I am fine, Liam.'

'What about that spear wound? That looked pretty bad, so it did. Are you sure you're fit enough to go?'

'My organic diagnostic systems indicate my kidney was ruptured and is no longer functioning. The organ can be repaired later,' she added. 'It will not affect my performance.'

'Your arm?'

'My arm is operable.'

'OK,' said Maddy. 'I've set it to one minute *after* the other window. There'll still be background tachyon particles around from the previous window, but I've moved the location thirty feet away so there shouldn't be any disruptive effect on your arrival portal. OK?'

'Affirmative.'

'You understand the mission parameters?'

'Kill all the reptile hominids. Destroy all evidence of our camp. Return window set for two hours after arrival.'

Maddy nodded. 'You got it. And, of course, remember to bring the gun back with you.'

One of Becks's dark eyebrows arched slowly. 'Well . . . duh,' she said flatly.

Sal giggled. 'That's cool!'

Maddy grinned at Liam. 'Looks like she's been doing some learning of her own.'

He nodded.

'All right, we haven't got time to fill the tube. She's going back dry. Stand clear of that circle on the ground.' She pointed to the circle of chalk, and within it, a patch of concrete floor darker than the rest. She sighed. 'We're gonna need to fill in the floor once again after all this is finished.'

The others pulled warily back and Becks wandered over and planted her feet inside the circle, her knees bent, ready to react at a moment's notice, the gun loaded, cocked and raised, the assault rifle's butt pressed firmly against her shoulder and ready to fire.

'Be careful, Becks,' said Liam. 'We want you back safely.'

She nodded hesitantly. 'Affirmative, Liam O'Connor. I will be careful.'

'Are we all set?' asked Maddy.

'Affirmative.'

'All right, Bob.' Maddy turned back to the desk mic. 'On my countdown. Ten . . . nine . . . eight . . .'

The archway filled with the sound of power surging into the

displacement machine, the green LEDs winking off one after another as they indicated the drain of stored energy. A three-yard-diameter sphere of shimmering air suddenly enveloped Becks. The ceiling fluorescent light dimmed and flickered.

'Seven . . . six . . . five . . .'

Her cool grey eyes turned to rest on Liam and she smiled uncertainly.

'Four . . . three . . . two . . .'

'Good luck,' he mouthed, unsure whether she could read that in the flickering fizzing light.

'. . . one . . .'

And then she was gone. Air whistled past them all to fill the sudden vacuum created.

'Wow,' whispered Edward.

'Now we wait,' said Maddy. She shot a glance at Liam. 'And we make sure we're ready.'

CHAPTER 74

65 million years BC, jungle

Becks emerged from the surrounding sphere of undulating air, and dropped the last few inches with a soft thud of boots on hard mud.

Crouched, ready for action, her eyes panned across the fire-lit clearing: a dancing, flickering impression of hell. The creatures had converged in the centre of the area, picking through the shelters, the palisade, watching the campfire hungrily consuming the last of the branches that had been stacked on it.

A knot of them were gathered around the space where, only a minute ago, the return window had opened. They were examining the ground, a cluster of low ferns nearby, their heads cocked with confusion and bewilderment like curious crows studying road kill.

None of them had yet noticed her standing there.

She had a thirty-round ammo clip, and in the blink of an eye had organized the order in which she was going to drop the targets: larger male creatures first.

The first rapidly fired half-dozen shots echoed across the clearing like so many dried and brittle branches snapping, and five out of six of her targets dropped like leather sacks of bone and meat. The one she'd missed had bobbed unpredictably, the shot skimming across the top of his head.

The other creatures froze where they were, uncertain as to what the rapid cracks of gunfire actually meant.

Becks took advantage of the moment of stillness and confusion and selected another six targets, all the larger males again. But this time the muzzle flash of her gun had attracted their attention and they began to bound towards her. She killed four and wounded another, before their short-lived charge faltered. They drew up a dozen yards away and fanned out, snapping and snarling.

Beyond them she could see the others, females and cubs being herded away from harm by a large male. She recognized it as the pack's leader, a claw from one of its four digits missing on its left arm. It was holding one of their spears, waving it around and using it to prod and cajole the pack away into the darkness.

[Assessment: primary target]

The pack leader, the alpha male . . . logic and observation dictated that that particular creature was the one who'd been learning from them; the shrewd one, the clever one whose genes and unique acquired knowledge were going to pass onwards to its offspring. In only a few nanoseconds of silicon-based analysis, she realized that the one creature she had to be absolutely certain of killing was the one with the missing claw. She was striding forward like an automaton as she fired another rapid succession of single shots, killing half of the creatures bobbing and snarling in front of her; those still standing turned and fled. The noise and the muzzle flash were as startling to them as the sudden inexplicable death it seemed to deal out. The entire pack was in motion now, scattering like birds startled by a handclap. But her eyes remained on the back of the alpha male. She swung the assault rifle towards it, aimed and fired.

The shot spun the creature off its feet.

CHAPTER 75

2001, New York

Maddy looked over at Cartwright. He was with the two children and Sal, standing beside the half-raised shutter entrance, staring out at the jungle and eagerly waiting to see the spectacular sight of a new reality arriving from a distant past. Sal was doing a great job keeping them all over there, telling them all about time ripples and waves and her job as an *observer*.

'You understand what you've got to do?' she asked Liam quietly.

He nodded. 'But are you sure it's the right date?'

'Well, I hope so. He said your fossilized message was discovered on that day. I presume he's not lying. I've got the Glen Rose National Park entered in as the location. I'm sure he mentioned a river called the Paluxy River . . . so that's what I've put in. And you're looking for the two boys that found it.'

'Boys? How old?'

'I don't know . . . You know, boys.' She shrugged. '*Boy* age, I guess.'

Liam glanced furtively over her shoulder at the others. 'Well, then, what do they look like?'

She ran her hand tiredly through her frizzy hair. 'Jeez . . . How the hell am I supposed to know!' she muttered irritably, then immediately felt guilty and angry with herself. She looked at Liam . . . his bloodshot eye, the streak of white hair . . . and felt like a snappy cow. 'I'm sorry,' she sighed. 'I guess they'll look all excited and very pleased with themselves. OK?'

She turned towards the desk. 'Bob, are we ready for a portal?'

> Affirmative. There is sufficient charge for this displacement.

'OK.' She nodded. 'All right.' She looked at Liam's face again, pale like the other two, but not as bad. No nosebleeds, no apparent nausea or any other apparent haemorrhaging. 'You sure you're OK to go, Liam?'

He nodded. 'I'm fine, so I am. Tired, I could sleep for a year, but I'm all right.'

Why not go in his place, Maddy? Look at him . . . look at the damage that last portal did to him. And now you're sending him through again! She stilled that guilty voice in her head quickly; she needed to be right here, coordinating Becks's and Liam's bring-backs. It was all going to be rather tricky.

She wanted to tell him what she knew, what Foster had told her. She wanted to tell him so that at least he could decide for himself if it was worth it, killing himself slowly, one corruption at a time.

'Shall we?' he said.

She pressed a digital watch into his hand. 'Six hours,' she said softly, then glanced at the chalk circle and the concrete already gouged out of the floor in the middle. Liam understood. He had six hours back in 1941 and then she'd open the return window. He casually ambled across the floor towards the circle as Maddy silently initiated the countdown sequence. The machinery began to hum – there was no way to avoid that – and the ceiling light flickered and dimmed.

She was hoping Cartwright would be too engrossed in

listening to Sal and watching for the time wave to immediately notice something was going on, but the wily old man spun round and looked back into the arch. 'What's going on?'

Liam stepped smartly into the chalk circle just as a sphere of air began to twitch and fidget around him.

'What's happ– Hang on, what's . . .?' His eyes widened. 'Where the HELL IS *HE* GOING?'

Maddy ignored him. Cartwright reached into his jacket pocket.

'No! Don't shoot!' shouted Maddy, realizing what he was going to do. 'Please!'

Cartwright pulled out his pistol, straightened his arm and aimed. 'STOP IT, NOW!'

'I can't! Please . . . I can't stop it. Don't sh–'

He fired a single shot at Liam just as the sphere wobbled and collapsed in on itself with a puff.

1941, Somervell County, Texas

At the very same moment that Liam landed on a riverbank of pebbles something whistled past his ear and off into the sky.

'Jay-zusss!' He ducked and then looked around, wondering what the hell that was. He saw nothing, just a narrow river, rolling sedately along a shallow creek of sandy-coloured rock, small and mean-looking yew trees and arid tufts of sun-bleached grass that hissed softly alongside the soothing gurgle of water.

Perhaps a bird? A bee? A fly?

It could have been. A fast one, though.

His mind turned to more pressing matters – which way to go? He had no idea, no idea at all, other than to look out for a pair of boys. He looked at the digital watch, Maddy's. She'd set a countdown on it: five hours and fifty-nine minutes.

'Right,' he muttered to himself, 'where do I start?'

A midday sun beat down on his head as he stood there, unsure which way to turn. He decided, before walking anywhere, that he was going to mark the window location with a small cairn of rocks: a dozen fist-sized worn and rounded rocks stacked in a small pyramid. Big enough so that he wasn't going to walk right on past and miss it.

Then, caught on a lazy midday breeze that had the nearby yew trees stirring and hissing, he heard the faint call of a voice and what sounded like a splash of water.

That way . . . downstream. He set off, walking along the riverbank, shingle and pebbles clattering underfoot. For a moment he recalled an image of that huge sweeping bay and the calm prehistoric green sea spreading out to an infinite horizon on his right.

It was here. Right here, an incredible tropical sea.

Quite a breathtaking notion, that . . . in the vast dimensions of geological time, even seas and oceans, just like any other living creature, had lifespans that came and went.

He heard voices again, echoing up the creek. The sound of children playing, larking about.

CHAPTER 76

65 million years BC, jungle

Becks followed the spatters of dark blood into the jungle. By moonlight the streaks of blood were black and glistened wetly. The trail didn't lead too far into the jungle, fortunately. If it had, she suspected she'd have been unable to follow it; the moonlight was beginning to fail her, blocked by the drooping leaves from the canopy trees above.

She heard them before she saw them: the rattling breath of one snorting like a winded buffalo and a chorus of mewling voices that sounded like a pitiful choir of simpering children. Her eyes picked them out. The creature she'd managed to hit was curled up on the jungle floor. Around it an array of the smaller creatures, females and cubs, all pawed and stroked the wounded one, as if somehow that would magically heal their pack leader.

She stepped forward until she was looking directly down at the creature with the broken claw. The pack, perhaps twenty of them here, became quiet; a forest of yellow eyes that glowed with soft fluorescence and narrowed with fear looked up at her.

'. . . *Help* . . . *me* . . .' The facsimile of a human voice came from one of the females. Becks recognized it as an attempt to duplicate the cries of the human called Keisha.

A part of her computer mind calmly informed her that a mission parameter remained outstanding, and could not be successfully flagged as completed until, at the very least, the wounded creature was confirmed dead.

But another part of her mind, a very much smaller part, a part that contributed thoughts as foggy sensations rather than runtime commands, spoke to her.

Just like me.

She remembered being born, released from growth amid a cascading soup of warm liquid, lying like this creature, curled like a foetus on a hard floor; feeling bewildered, frightened, confused. An animal mind of sensations, feelings . . . but no words.

She squatted down to get a closer look at the creature. The wound was in the middle of the creature's narrow chest, and from the pulsing of ink-black blood down its olive skin, was almost certainly going to prove to be fatal.

'You will die,' she announced coldly. And then realized talking to them was illogical and pointless – these wild things were no more intelligent than monkeys. But, on the other hand, it felt like another way of processing, filtering her own thoughts . . . giving words to that part of her mind that wasn't high-density silicon wafer.

'I am here to kill you,' she said. 'This is a mission requirement.'

The yellow eyes studied her silently. Perhaps those eyes were trying to communicate something, pleading for mercy.

She stood up again and changed the clip in the assault rifle for a fresh one. The mission voice had no time for such an irrational sentiment and gently cajoled her to proceed with the task.

Complete Mission

1. Terminate alpha male of species

2. Terminate remaining hominids (optional)

3. Retrieve all evidence of human habitation

'I am . . . sorry,' she said. She cocked her head, curious. There'd been a strange effect on her voice. It had *fluttered* ever so slightly. It had actually made her sound more convincingly human; she'd sounded almost indistinguishable from the school students she and Liam had spent the last fourteen days in the jungle with. Those three words really had sounded so very human. For a moment she was almost tempted to say them once again. Instead, she raised the rifle swiftly to her shoulder, her bandaged finger slipped on to the trigger and beneath the dressing the recently vat-grown muscle tissue tightened and pulled. A shot rang out. Her finger muscles released and pulled again . . . and again . . . and again.

By the time the last of the creatures flopped lifelessly across the body of Broken Claw, the clip was empty and the barrel warm.

The jungle was still, every nocturnal species stunned into silence by the rapid crack of gunfire. For a few moments she listened to the shifting breeze, the muted rumble of the nearby river.

'I am . . . sorry,' she said again, and realized this time her voice sounded flat and emotionless, as it always did.

She turned on her heels and headed back towards the remains of their abandoned camp.

2001, New York

'Where did you send him?' barked Cartwright, swinging the aim of his gun on to Maddy.

'I . . . I j-just sent him back . . . to help Becks kill the –'

'You're lying!' he snapped.

'Honestly I –'

He fired a shot past her head. Behind her one of the computer monitors exploded amid a shower of sparks and granules of glass.

'Really,' he said, 'I wouldn't advise lying, young lady. I can put a bullet through your stomach right now . . . and believe me when I say that's one of the most painful ways to go. Slow and very, very painful.' He took a dozen steps towards her. 'Now, I'll try again . . . *where* did you send him?'

Maddy swallowed nervously, her eyes on the gun. 'I . . . just . . . I . . .'

'Maddy!' yelped Sal. 'Something's coming!'

Cartwright stopped where he was. 'What's that?' he shouted back over his shoulder, keeping his eyes firmly on the older girl.

'Did you feel it? A tremor?'

'No,' he replied, his eyes and aim still on Maddy. 'I didn't feel anything.'

'I felt something,' said Edward.

'Oh my God . . . the jungle's changed,' said Laura. 'Something different. I don't know what. Something –'

Sal nodded. 'The settlement's gone. It's an early ripple . . . the big change will follow.'

Cartwright cursed. He desperately wanted to see this. 'You!' he snapped at Maddy, waving his gun, 'over there by the entrance. NOW!'

Maddy nodded meekly and hurried across the archway to join the others standing in the entrance and looking out at the jungle. Cartwright joined them, keeping a cautious few yards' distance and holding his gun on them as he watched the evening jungle. 'What happens next?'

'The *big* wave,' said Sal. 'You'll feel dizzy just as it . . .' She looked at him, her eyes round. 'Do you feel it *now*?'

His eyes widened. 'My God, yes! Like an earth tremor!'

On the horizon the orange stain of dusk was blotted out by what appeared to be a rolling bank of raincloud, a storm front rushing in from the Atlantic at an impossible speed.

'What is that?' he gasped.

'The wave?' whispered Edward.

Maddy nodded. 'Another reality.'

It crossed over the island beyond the broad river and amid a churning soup of thick, shimmering air, realities mixed and became fleeting impossibilities. Amid the churning reality soup they saw the winking flickering outline of tall buildings warping and twisting and Maddy thought she saw for a fleeting moment a swarm of creatures in the sky like gargoyles, dragons – a possible reality, a possible species that in this correcting reality had no place, existing for a mere heartbeat, then erased.

Then the wave was over the river and upon them.

The archway flexed and warped around them, the ground beneath their feet momentarily dropping away, becoming void.

Then, just like that, they were staring at a brick wall, ten feet opposite, across a cobbled stone backstreet. The rolled-up tarpaulin with Forby's corpse inside, that they'd placed just outside the entrance, was gone. Instead he was standing to one side of the entrance, talking in hushed tones with two other armed men. A spotlight flickered across the backstreet as overhead they heard the *whup-whup-whup* of a circling helicopter.

Cartwright's jaw hung slack and open, his gun arm lowered down to his side. 'This . . . is . . . *incredible*.'

'Isn't it?' said Maddy.

Forby looked up from his conversation. 'Whuh? Oh, sir?' He looked perplexed, as did the other two men. 'I uh . . . didn't hear the door opening. You OK, sir?'

Cartwright's face was still immobile, still frozen with incredulity.

'Sir? Everything OK?'

He looked at his man. 'Uh? Yes . . . yes, just fine.' Alive

once more. A faint smile of relief stretched across his thin lips. 'Good to er . . . it's good to see you again, Forby.'

Forby frowned and nodded. 'Sir?' Then he noticed Edward and Laura. 'Who are these?'

Cartwright shook his head, gathering his confused wits. 'I'll . . . I'll explain later.' He turned to Maddy and the others. 'Inside, you lot. Let's close this door.'

Forby stepped forward but Cartwright waved him back. 'You best stay outside for now, Forby, all right?'

He flicked his gun at Laura. 'Close the shutter.'

She began to crank the handle, but Sal stepped in and pressed the green button. 'It's OK, we've got power now.' The shutters clattered down as a small motor beside the door whined.

The old man took a moment to compose himself, to try to make sense of what he'd seen, and what he may yet see before the night was through. The shutters clattered down and the whining motor was silent.

'All right,' he said presently. 'All right, so this means your friend and the cloned girl . . . they've been successful. They've killed those freaks in the past. So that means no reptile hominids.' He nodded as he talked. 'All right . . . I get that. I understand that.'

'Cartwright,' interrupted Maddy.

'And . . . and Forby's alive now, because . . . because . . .' His eyes narrowed as he tried to make sense of things. 'Because what happened . . . didn't happen. No reptile monsters means he couldn't have been attacked. But then that's just crazy . . . that doesn't make any . . . I mean . . . I actually saw that thing rip his . . .'

He was rambling.

'Cartwright,' said Maddy again. 'Listen to me, you need to hear something.'

'. . . and he was dead.' He turned to look at the floor. Halfway across, a pool of blood had congealed. Forby's blood. 'I mean . . . there! Look! It's his blood! He was –'

'Cartwright!'

The old man's confused eyes darted from the blood back to Maddy.

'This new reality is still *wrong*,' she said. 'This reality with you and Forby and men outside and a helicopter buzzing overhead and your secret agency. It's all wrong too. This is something else that should never have happened.'

'What?' His face creased with confusion.

'Your life,' said Sal. 'Should be a very different one.'

'In *our* timeline . . . in the *correct* timeline, you've lived a different life to this.' Maddy tried appealing to him with a friendly smile. 'Perhaps even a much better life . . . I dunno, with children, grandchildren?'

'I'm not married!' he snapped. 'I don't have children!'

'But, see, that's what I'm saying –'

'This *agency* is my wife! This secret! *This secret! Time travel!* It's my secret. I know things that even our president doesn't. I know time travel's already happening! *That's* what I'm married to! This . . . this knowledge! That's my life!' He raised his gun again and aimed at the frown between Maddy's eyes. 'And you're not going to take that away! Do you hear? NO ONE IS GOING TO TAKE THAT FROM ME!'

CHAPTER 77

1941, Somervell County, Texas

Liam spotted them further up the river, two boys. One splashing around in the water, the other perched on a shelf of rock, sheltering from the scorching hot sun in a cool nook of shade.

Neither had seen him yet. His first instinct had been to call out to them, to find out what they'd been doing so far today . . . to ask them if they'd found anything interesting. But then if they hadn't yet, his intrusion on their day might alter what they did; change the sequence of events for today, and they might not make their discovery.

So he decided to lie low and watch. He hunkered down in the shade of a yew tree and waited.

An hour passed, another, and another. The sun was well past midday, the shadows slowly shifting and lengthening. He checked his watch again. The countdown was telling him he had less than two hours to go. He was beginning to wonder whether he was watching the wrong two boys, and perhaps another several hundred yards up the river two different lads were right now cooing and marvelling over some incredible fossil writing they'd just discovered. Then the boy on the rock ledge called out something.

'Saul!'

'What?'

He couldn't quite make out what the lad on the ledge said next, but from where he was he could see the boy was turning something over and over in his hand. The boy in the water, Saul, didn't seem particularly interested, content to continue paddling around in aimless circles. The other, frustrated at his companion's lack of interest, suddenly leaped off the ledge and into the river, swimming across to join him in the shallows. He showed Saul what he had in his hands, and among a garble of exchanged words Liam made out two distinct ones: *look* and *message.*

That's it, then!

He pulled himself up, grimacing at the stab of pins and needles in his feet, and made his way towards them. 'Hey there, lads!' he called out.

Both of them turned to look at him. 'Hey there!' he said again, trying to sound as friendly as possible and not frighten them off. But as he drew closer he could see both of them regarded him warily.

'Hey . . . it's all right, now. I'm not going to eat you. Just saying hello is all I'm doing.'

'Ma says we cain't talk to no strangers, mister,' said the boy holding the rock.

Liam drew up a few yards short of them. He hunkered down on his haunches and offered them a friendly smile. 'Well now, my name's Liam, Liam O'Connor. So I suppose I'm no longer a stranger.'

Both boys nodded at the unfailing logic of that.

'I'm Saul. This here's m' brother Grady.'

Saul looked at him. 'You sound funny,' he said. 'An' you got strange clothes. Where you from?'

'Ireland,' said Liam.

The boy looked at his face curiously. 'What's wrong with you, mister?'

Liam shrugged, bemused by the odd question. 'Nothing's wrong with me.'

'You sick or something?'

He really didn't have the time for this. 'No, I'm perfectly fine.' He gestured at the rock Grady was trying to keep from his prying eyes. 'What's that you got there, lad?'

Grady hid the rock behind his back defensively. 'Ain't nothin'.'

'Oh, come on.' He inched a little closer. 'Is it money? Did you find some money up there?'

'No.' Grady shook his head warily. 'Didn't find no money.'

'It's just some words on a stupid stone,' said Saul. 'Somebody made a message on a stone.'

Liam offered them a look of mild interest. 'Really? How interesting. Can I see?'

Grady shook his head. 'It's mine.'

If he'd been a bit smarter about this, if he'd thought ahead, he'd have brought something to trade – a cool toy, a pack of baseball cards, a bag of sweets or something, even some . . .

Of course. He suddenly remembered he had on him something way better than any of those. Something either boy couldn't fail to be entranced by. 'Hang on,' he said, digging into the thigh pocket of his tattered shorts. It was in there somewhere still. He'd . . . ah, his fingers found the sharp edge. A moment later he pulled out a four-inch-long fishhook-shaped object. He held it out in front of him and their eyes widened. 'It's a claw,' said Liam. 'A *real* dinosaur claw.'

Saul's and Grady's jaws dropped open synchronously as four young eyes admired the vicious-looking nicks along the curved edge of the claw.

'See, I just found it this morning, up the river, so I did. I heard you can find all sorts of fascinating old things along this river. Want to hold it?'

Both their heads nodded vigorously.

'We could swap,' said Liam. 'You can take a look at my claw . . . and I'll look at that message stone of yours.'

'Sure,' said Grady quickly, the passing fascination with his curious find more than trumped by the four-inch glistening claw dangling from Liam's fingers. He passed his rock over without another look at it. 'Message don't make no sense to me anyways.'

He reached out for the claw.

'Careful, it's quite sharp,' said Liam.

Grady took it off Liam and then hunched over, turning his back on his brother.

'Hey! Grady, lemmesee too.'

Grady shook his head. 'My stone, my first look-see.'

'Aw, come on, lemmesee! Lemmesee!'

Liam found a boulder nearby and let himself stiffly down on to it, ignoring their squabbling. As he turned the flat nugget of dark slate over in the palm of his hand, his heart silently skipped a beat.

Jay-zus . . . there you are again. After all this time. My silent messenger.

There it was, his own handwriting, reversed and faintly embossed with web-thin ridges and grooves of rock compressed and preserved by time.

'You're right,' he said, looking up from the rock, 'the words make no sense at all, do they?' But Grady wasn't listening. He was entranced by the vicious-looking claw and too busy fending off Saul's grabbing hands.

'It's just a load of gibberish,' he said, a knowing half-smile spread across his face.

'Wanna swap, mister?' asked Grady. 'My stone for your claw?'

Liam shrugged as casually as he dared. 'I dunno . . . my claw's a pretty good find an' all –'

'Please . . .!' The boy dug deep into the pockets of his own trousers and produced a wooden yo-yo. 'I'll throw this in for extra!'

Liam made a show of interest in the toy. He'd had one just like it back in Cork: large, cumbersome and one he'd never managed to get on with.

'Well . . . all right, then, I suppose. Yo-yo as well, you've got yourself a deal.'

They exchanged a solemn nod in silence – a deal officially sealed – and then Liam picked himself wearily up, for some reason feeling as old as the hills, and politely bade farewell. But both boys were already stuck back in a heated debate about the rights of access to the claw, and who was going to hold it all the way home.

He picked his way back along the shingle of the riverbank, through sliding, clacking wet pebbles, running his fingers across those faint embossed lines and his eyes looking for that small cairn of stones.

CHAPTER 78

2001, New York

Sal felt it again, the early ripples, the faintest sensation of dizziness. But it looked like no one else had felt it. Cartwright still had his gun on Maddy.

'This . . . *this* is my life. This world. This reality!'

'Y-you have to step outside now . . . rejoin your men,' replied Maddy firmly.

Sal was impressed with her calm, her cool in the face of his wavering gun.

The old man shook his head and laughed. 'What? You're expecting me to just walk away from this? The greatest discovery in the history of mankind . . . and what? I just walk out into that backstreet and try to forget about it?'

Sal glanced at the other two kids. They met her gaze; eyes exchanging a shared imperative.

We've got to do something.

'Listen!' cut in Maddy. 'If the wave comes and goes while you're in here . . . y-you'll be left behind. It'll rewrite the present *without* you –'

He smiled. 'Oh . . . I think I could live with that, Maddy. In fact, I've been waiting a long, long time for something like –'

Her eyes narrowed. 'This isn't about state security any more, is it?'

He shrugged. 'All right, yes! And why not? This thing . . .

this time machine . . . it's a *boy's* dream! It's a *man's* dream! *Mankind's* dream, goddammit! To travel anywhere, to any time, to see it all. To see things no other human will ever see!'

'It's not a toy, Cartwright. You know you . . . you just can't think of it that w-way.'

'Oh, right! You . . . some snot-nosed teenager and her buddies . . . you're to be entrusted instead, are you? You're the guardians of time, huh?'

Sal glanced at the others again, then took a hesitant step towards the old man. She looked to see if the other two were going to do likewise. Laura remained where she was, trembling, face ashen. She shook her head. Too frightened. Edward, however, took a silent step forward along with Sal.

She had no idea what she intended to do – make a grab for the gun?

Oh God, the thought made her knees wobble.

'I was selected!' replied Maddy. 'I didn't freakin' *want* this, Cartwright! Jesus! In fact, I didn't have much of a freakin' choice at all!'

The old man shrugged. 'Guess what? I don't really care.' He stepped towards her, across snaking cables. 'This is what *I* want. And I've spent my life waiting for it. Preparing for it.'

Sal noticed something blinking on one of the monitors.

'I'm an old man,' he continued, stepping on to concrete floor in the middle of the archway, clear of any cables that could trip him up. All the while the aim of his gun remained resolutely on Maddy. 'My whole life, my whole adult life, has been leading towards this moment. And I've known for so many years that a time machine was going to arrive under this bridge, in this archway, on September tenth, 2001.' He sighed. 'Can you imagine what knowing about something like that does to you? Knowing that near the end of your natural life

. . . something truly *wonderful* is going to happen.' He shook his head. 'And what?' He laughed drily. 'You're telling me to just forget about it? Just walk away and forget about it?'

Over Maddy's shoulder Sal could see the blinking cursor in Bob's dialogue box. He was trying to tell Maddy something. A warning of the impending time wave?

'The things I've wanted to see, Maddy Carter . . . the things I've dreamed of seeing over the last fifteen years, the destruction of Pompeii, the fall of Atlantis, the crucifixion of Christ . . . the battle of Bunker Hill, George Washington crossing the Delaware, Lincoln giving his Gettysburg address! The arrival of Columbus . . .' His rheumy old eyes were alive with naive wonder. 'My God! The impact of the K–T asteroid that ended the time of the dinosaurs! Can you imagine actually seeing that impact for yourself?' He shook his head. 'How far back can I go? Do you know?'

Maddy spread her hands. 'I . . . I don't know. I –'

'The beginning of life on earth? The first division of cells?' Cartwright seemed lost in his reverie, of the things he could see, the places he could go. All his now for the taking.

Sal suddenly felt the hairs on her forearms stand on end, and knew it was here – the time wave. A moment later the ceiling light dimmed and flickered and they all felt it, a moment of imbalance, the floor dropping away beneath their feet. The monitors over Maddy's shoulder all flickered and went dead. Laura cried in alarm and Edward gasped as the ceiling light flickered off, leaving them, for a moment, in complete darkness.

Then the monitors flickered back on and the ceiling light fizzed, blinked and bathed the archway in its cold blue glare once more.

Cartwright giggled joyously. 'Good God! That was it? Wasn't it?'

Maddy nodded slowly. 'Yeah . . . I think it was.' She looked at him accusingly. 'You should've been outside our field. You should have been out there with your people. This messes things up. This –'

'But I wasn't outside,' he said calmly. 'So why don't you just get over it?'

'You don't understand . . . you've been written out of the present. I've got no idea what that means to you or –'

'That suits me fine,' he smiled.

Sal noticed the blinking cursor was back on-screen and all of a sudden it occurred to her what Bob was desperately trying to tell Maddy.

'Maddy!' she cried, pointing at the monitors. 'You need to look!'

Maddy turned to glance over her shoulder. 'Oh no!' She turned back to Cartwright. 'GET OUT OF THERE!'

His wiry brow furrowed. 'Uh? What's up?'

'*MOVE!*' she screamed.

The displacement machine's hum changed in tone as stored-up energy prepared to be released.

'LOOK!' shouted Maddy, pointing to the ground at Cartwright's feet. He looked down, wondering what was so special about a chalk circle and, within, a small irregular section of the grubby concrete floor scooped out and . . .

'OH GOD, CARTWRIGHT, GET OUT!'

It happened in nanoseconds, the instant appearance of a sphere of energy around the old man. Most of him was inside, all but his left hand.

Sal thought she saw in that fleeting moment dark shapes swirling around him like demons or ghosts, a window on to some world that an uneducated person, a superstitious person, someone from the Dark Ages, might have called *Hell*.

Then he was swept away. Gone.

The sphere pulsed and shimmered, and now she could see what appeared to be an undulating Texas-blue sky, and an arid and drab landscape . . . and the wavering outline of a shape stepping through. Liam staggered into view with a distinct look of nausea on his face, and a moment later the sphere of supercharged tachyon particles vanished with a soft pop of rushing air.

'Jeez, that was an odd one,' he said queasily, bending over, nauseous and heaving.

'Liam!' yelped Maddy. 'Oh my God . . . I thought you were going to get all mushed up with Cartwright! I . . .'

He raised a hand to hush her. 'Just a second, just a second . . . I'm gonna –'

He threw up on the floor and on to the still-twitching hand Cartwright had left behind.

Sal rushed over to him. 'Liam? You OK?'

He wiped his mouth and looked up at her with his bloodshot eye. 'I . . . I just . . . I'm all right now.' He straightened up and looked down in disgust at the hand and the acrid-smelling puddle at his feet. 'That wasn't like I'm used to. That one felt really odd, so it did.'

Maddy shook her head. 'I'm not sure what happened. Cartwright was standing in the circle. I forgot the countdown was due.' There were tears in her eyes, running down her cheeks. 'Oh God, Liam, I thought you were going to end up a twisted mess with him and . . .'

'Well . . .' Liam rubbed his mouth dry and grinned. 'I'm all right now, aren't I?' He spread his hands and looked down at himself. 'Or have I got an extra arm or something stuck on the back of me head?'

She nodded, wiped her eyes and laughed. 'No . . . no, you're just fine as you are.'

'Did it work?' asked Liam. 'Has anyone looked outside?'

'I think a time wave came,' said Laura, looking at Sal for confirmation.

'That's right.' Sal nodded. 'I'll go see.'

She turned back to the entrance, hit the button and the shutter slowly began to crank up. They gathered around the rising corrugated shutter and as it lurched to a halt they stepped outside into the dark night.

Manhattan glistened brightly across the river, a towering wedding cake of lights. A commuter train rumbled overhead along the Williamsburg Bridge, and the evening was filled with the soothing white noise of far-off traffic and the echoing wail of a police siren.

'Normal New York,' said Liam. He puffed out a weary sigh. 'That was a bleedin' mess and a half we got out of, so it was.'

Sal reached out and hugged him tightly, embarrassed by the tears rolling down her cheeks. She squeezed him in a self-conscious way, just like anyone might a big brother, and then let him go.

'But here we are again,' she whispered.

They watched New York in silence, each of them lost in their own thoughts for a long while.

Maddy stirred. 'I better go and sort out the return window for the support –' she corrected herself – 'for *Becks*.' She turned and headed back inside.

The rest of them savoured the evening panorama, watching beads of car headlights edging forward along FDR Drive across the river, and a ferry cutting the mirrored reflection of Manhattan with its wake. Finally, it was Edward who stated the obvious as-yet-unfinished business.

'Me and Laura, we got to go back, don't we? To get things back to the way they were?'

'Yes,' Liam nodded. 'But I don't suppose it has to be tonight.'

'Good,' whispered Laura, 'I'm not feeling so good.'

'We've got some beds back inside,' said Sal. She looked at the girl and the Chinese boy. Both looked pale and ill, their faces smudged with a fortnight's worth of grime. And Liam . . . She realized he looked disconcertingly old and young at the same time with that streak of white hair at his temple.

'I'll go make some coffee,' she said.

CHAPTER 79

65 million years BC, jungle

Becks watched the pyre of logs and branches burn. Amid curling tongues of flame she could just about make out the outline of the several dozen bodies she'd stacked on top. The log bridge was gone now, its counterweight device dismantled like their windmill and tossed on the fire as kindling. The palisade, the lean-tos, all gone as well. The assorted rucksacks, baseball caps, jackets, mobile phones that had flown back into the past, all of them tossed on the fire.

By morning those things would be nothing more than soot or contorted puddles of plastic that would eventually break down over tens of thousands of years into minute untraceable contaminants.

Her computer mind took a moment to make a detailed audit of all the other items of forensic evidence that marked their two-week stay here. The human bodies she'd been unable to retrieve: Franklyn, Ranjit and Kelly. Of those, only Franklyn had died in a location that would one day yield fossils, and even then it was statistically unlikely that his body was going to be preserved in a way that would produce anything. A corpse needed to be almost immediately covered by a layer of sediment to stand a chance of that. Those three bodies, wherever they lay, were exposed to the elements, to scavengers.

Bullets and casings littered the clearing. But they too would soon become unidentifiable nuggets of rust in this humid jungle. Perhaps, a hundred years from now, no more than stains of oxidized soil on the jungle floor.

She was satisfied that the sheer weight of time and natural processes would wipe their presence clean. There was always the remote possibility that a footprint or the unnatural scar of an axe blade on a tree trunk might just, somehow, become an immortalized impression on a fragment of rock. But the probability factors she crunched yielded an acceptable contamination risk.

Her partially healed stomach wound had ripped open as she'd laboured on the funeral pyre, but a dark plug of congealing scab prevented any further valuable blood leaking out of her. The dressing on her arm had also unwound earlier, revealing red-raw muscle tissue and bone. A layer of skin over the top of that would have offered her damaged limb some protection – instead the fragile workings of her arm were now clogged with dirt and twigs and leaves and all manner of bugs.

An infection advisory flashed quietly in the background of her mind, along with several others that warned her that her biological combat chassis had suffered enough damage to warrant immediate medical attention. As she watched tongues of orange lash up into the Cretaceous night sky towards a moon a hat size too big, she detected the first precursor particles of the scheduled window and stepped towards the open ground where it was due to open.

She looked back one last time at the fire and picked out the dark twisted limbs of the hominid species amid the flames. For a moment she felt something she couldn't identify: sadness, was it? Guilt? All she knew was that it came from a part of her mind that didn't organize thoughts into mission priorities and strategic options.

A sphere of churning air suddenly winked into existence in front of her and calmly, impassively, she stepped forward through sixty-five million years into a dimly lit brick archway.

The first face her eyes registered through the shimmering was Liam O'Connor's. He smiled tiredly and she momentarily wondered if his mind was flashing the human equivalent set of damage advisory warnings.

'Welcome home, Becks,' he said softly and then, without any warning, he clasped his arms around her. 'We did it!' he muttered into her ear.

She processed the curious gesture and her silicon swiftly came back with the recommendation that returning the demonstration of affection would be an acceptably appropriate response. Her good arm closed around his narrow shoulders.

'Affirmative, Liam . . . we did it.'

CHAPTER 80

2001, New York

Monday (time cycle 50)

They stayed for a few days, Edward and Laura. Maddy said they were probably suffering some sort of radiation sickness from the lab explosion and needed some rest and recuperation. It was nice to have some new faces around here for a while, anyway. But Maddy said they had to go. She was right, of course. They had things to do, lives to go and lead.

But not long lives . . . not Edward, anyway.

I read his file on our computer. This is so sad. He will write his great maths paper in 2029 that will change the world, and he'll be just twenty-two when he does that. But then he'll be dead from cancer before his twenty-seventh birthday.

Cancer at twenty-seven?

That seems so unfair. Twenty-seven years isn't a life. It's just a taster of life, isn't it? I know I couldn't have told him that and, even if I could, would it have been fair to tell him? Would anyone want to know the exact day they were going to die? I know I wouldn't.

We were going to send them back to 2015; that was the original plan. But Maddy figured that wasn't going to work: they've both seen too much; they both know too much. Maybe that's not so important for the girl Laura. Maybe her life isn't ever going to affect the world that much. But Chan . . . he's everything the future's going to be. It all kind of starts with what he's going to one day write in a paper.

So what did we do? We left them outside when the field reset. We watched with the shutter open. We watched time come and take them away. Reality just erased them, like someone deleting files off a computer. Maddy says she's pretty sure that's going to make things all right again. Reality will bring them back. They'll be born once more, like all the other kids who died; they'll be born . . . be babies, toddlers, kids, teenagers a second time. Only this time they'll visit some energy lab in 2015 and then get to go home and tell their mums and dads what a totally boring day trip they had.

Well, at least that's what we're hoping.

And what about the person, whoever that was, who tried to kill Edward? I suppose we'll know whether history's been changed enough that he or she makes some different choices. If we get the same message again from the future . . . then, well, we'll have to deal with this all over again, won't we? Hopefully not.

We just have to wait and see if this fixes everything. Nothing's certain. Nothing's final.

'Everything's fluid'. . . that's Maddy's phrase. What does that really mean?

So, the female support unit, Becks (still trying to get used to that name), is still healing. Those creatures really messed her arm up by the look of it. Bob says the regrown skin will probably show a lot of scarring, and the muscles and tendons may never be fully functional again. Which led to an argument between Maddy and Liam.

Maddy suggested flushing the body and growing a new support unit, one of the big tough male ones. But Liam got angry. He said 'she deserves better'.

I don't know what I think. After all, they're just organic robots, aren't they? And whatever knowledge her AI picked up would be saved, right?

But Liam says there's more to them than just the computer . . . there's something else in there, something human-like in their heads. So maybe he's right. It does seem unfair to do that to her. After all, it seems she did really well.

Anyway, she's got a name . . . I mean, how can you just flush something away that's got, like, a name? It's wrong, isn't it?

Seems like the argument's all settled now, though. Looks like we're keeping her but also growing another Bob. Maddy said there seemed to be nothing in the 'how to' manual that says we can't have two support units.

So why not?

CHAPTER 81

2001, New York

The old man was sitting on the park bench and throwing nuggets of dough from the crusty end of a hot-dog bun to a strutting pack of impatient pigeons.

'I knew I'd find you here,' said Maddy.

He looked up at her and smiled a greeting. She closed her eyes and turned her face up towards the clear blue September sky and for a moment savoured the warmth of the sun on her pallid cheeks.

'Unobscured sun and a good hot dog . . . that's what you said,' she added, 'and where else in Manhattan's forest of skyscrapers are you going to get that?'

Foster laughed drily. 'Clever girl.'

She flopped down on the park bench next to him. 'We've really missed you. *I've* missed you.'

'It's only been a few hours,' he said, tossing another doughy nugget out among the birds.

'What? It's been months –'

'Yes, but for me,' he said, 'just a few hours.' He looked at her. 'Remember, I'm out of the loop now. I'm out of the time bubble. I said goodbye to you on a Monday morning.' He looked down at his watch. 'And now it's nearly one o'clock on the very same Monday.'

She shook her head. 'Yes, of course. Stupid of me. I knew that.'

They sat in silence for a while and watched a toddler on reins attempt to scare away the pigeons by stamping her little feet. The birds merely gave her a wide berth as she ambled through and then returned, to hungrily resume pecking at the crumbs of bread on the ground in her wake.

'You hinted you'd be here, didn't you? When we parted?'

Foster nodded. 'I suppose I felt a little guilty leaving you so soon.' He puffed out his sallow cheeks. 'But I'm dying, Maddy. I won't last very much longer.'

'The tachyon corruption?'

'Yes. It plays merry havoc at a genetic level. It's like a computer virus, rewriting lines of code with gibberish. Out here,' he sighed, 'outside the time bubble, I might get a little longer to live. I might get a week or two more. Maybe a month if I'm lucky. That would be nice.'

She thought about that for a moment. 'But . . . you'll always be . . .?'

'That's right, Madelaine. From *your* point of view, I'll *always* be found here in Central Park, at twelve fifty-two a.m. on Monday the tenth of September. Like all these other people,' he said, gesturing at the busy park, the queue of people standing beside the hot-dog vendor across the grass, 'like them, I've become part of the furniture of here and now . . . part of the wallpaper. That's the other reason why I left.'

She frowned, not getting that.

'If I'd stayed with you and the others . . . I'd be long gone by now. This way, I can still help you. Someone to talk to.'

'Ah.' She nodded.

'But each time you come and find me, Madelaine, remember, each time you come and find me . . . it'll be the first time *for me*. Do you see what I mean?'

Of course it would. She realized, for the old man, Monday

had been a coffee and a bagel and a goodbye. And now, three hours later, a momentary reunion in Central Park. Each time the field office reset itself, any conversation he had with her . . . never happened. For Foster there'd be no memory of it.

He laughed. 'It'll be like visiting some senile old fogey in a madhouse. You'll have to get used to repeating yourself.'

She shared his chuckle. 'I had a boyfriend like that once. He never listened to me.'

He sniffed. 'You came here, I presume, because you need help?'

'Well, we did have a problem, but it's all fixed now, I think.'

He patted her arm. 'See? I knew you lot were ready.'

'Hardly. We scraped through this one, Foster. It was a close-run thing.'

She gave him the bare bones of their story. Foster shook his head. 'Dinosaur times?' he whispered. 'I . . . I never thought the machine could take us so far back.'

'You never did that?'

'No. Never that far. How's Liam?'

'Well, that's just it. I don't know how much damage that did to him. It's definitely done something to him, aged him in some ways. He has . . .' She looked at Foster, and for the first time, she noticed the rheumy whites of his eyes were faintly laced with the scars of old burst blood vessels. 'Like you, haemorrhaging. And a streak of white hair. Who knows what's been damaged *inside* him. I mean, that's just what I can see. Foster, how long can he take this kind of punishment? How long do you think he will live?'

He sucked in air through his teeth. 'Well, he's a tough old soul. I can tell you that. But, you see . . . it all depends on where and when he goes, Madelaine. Who knows how long he's got?'

That didn't help much.

'Do I tell him or not, Foster? You know, he's not blind. He's seen his bad eye, he's seen his hair. He jokes about it, but he's not stupid. He must know this isn't good for him.'

He shook his head. 'I know he'll cope. But whether you tell him has to be your call. You're the one in charge now. I can give you what advice I can, but command decisions are yours. That's how it is.' He tossed the last of his bun in among the birds. 'I can't run the field office from out here on a park bench. You're the boss now.'

'But what about the agency? Is there someone else I can talk to? Someone in charge?'

'I . . . I'm sorry, Madelaine. That's . . . that's off limits. You have to treat this like you're entirely on your own. Do you understand? You're on your own.'

She cursed. 'What sort of useless freakin' agency is this?'

He pursed his lips sympathetically. 'I'm afraid that's just how it is.'

She ground her teeth in silent frustration for a while, knowing there was nothing more Foster could offer her on the subject of Liam. In any case, there was a new pair of glasses she was due to pick up from the opticians. They'd promised her they'd be ready in a couple of hours and another day of squinting at monitors and getting a migraine for her troubles was something she could live without.

She stood up. 'I'd better go. Things to do.'

He stood up, slowly, achingly. Polite, like a true gentleman.

'You'll be here again?' asked Maddy. 'For sure? Every Monday at this time?'

'Of course,' he grinned. 'I do charge by the hour, though.'

She laughed then hugged him, awkward and faltering. 'Enjoy your day, Foster.'

'Oh, I have a fun-packed afternoon planned.'

She squeezed his arm. 'Take care. I'll drop by and see you again soon.' She turned to walk down the path leading to the south-west gate. But a thought suddenly occurred to her. She stopped, turned and saw him standing there among his pigeons, watching her go, almost as if he'd been expecting her to stop and turn.

'Foster? How can you be so sure Liam will cope? What if he works out he's dying? What's he gonna do? He might choose to leave us.'

'He'll do the right thing,' he replied. 'You'll always be able to rely on that . . . the right thing. He's a good lad.' He turned away and began to wade through a parting sea of ruffling grey feathers and curious beady eyes.

'Foster! How can you be so sure?'

He stopped in his tracks and looked back over his shoulder. 'How can I be so sure?'

She nodded. 'I mean, come on! Who the hell would be stupid enough to keep doing something they know's killing them? What makes you think you know him so well?'

'Oh, I know –' he cocked an eyebrow – 'because he's me.'

HISTORY AS WE KNOW IT

65 million BC
Late Cretaceous era – dinosaurs roam the earth

2001
New York: as we know it – busy, noisy and colourful

HISTORY ALTERED

65 million BC
Liam, Becks and a class of students end up stuck in the late Cretaceous era

1941
A mysterious fossil is found in Texas. A fossil with Liam's handwriting on it . . .

the first time wave

2001
New York: unchanged – but a secret government agency tracks down the TimeRiders field office

But a previously undiscovered species of predator study Liam and the others. They learn to use tools and weapons

The predators learn and evolve. 65 million years of new history ensue and the predators' ancestors inherit the earth . . .

the second time wave

2001
New York: jungle! Primitive reptilian bipeds have replaced man

THE
ADVENTURE
DOESN'T
STOP
THERE

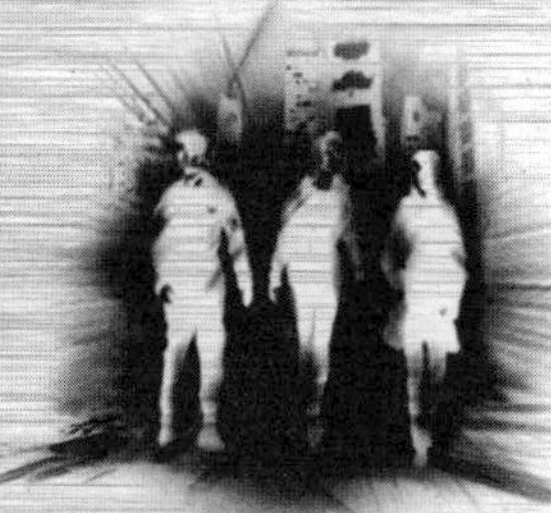

NEXT STOP:
ROBIN HOOD . . .

FEBRUARY 2011

WANT MORE ACTION? MORE ADVENTURE? MORE ADRENALIN?

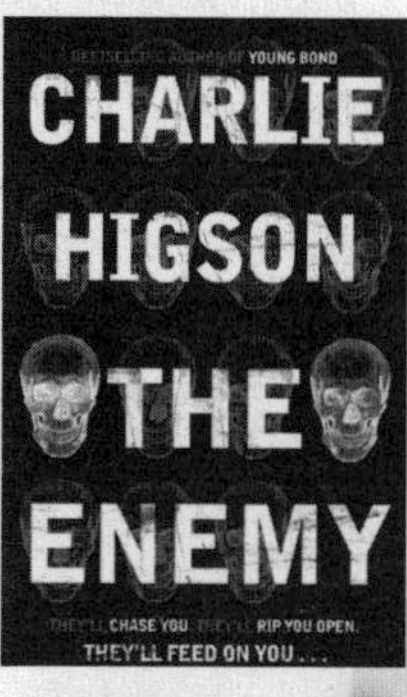

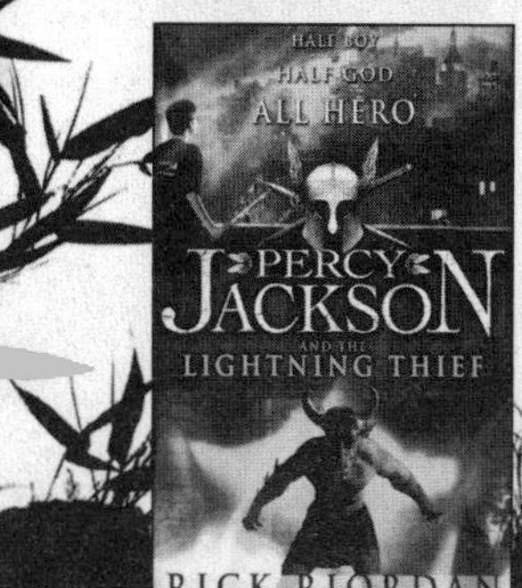

GET INTO PUFFIN'S ADVENTURE BOOKS FOR BOYS

It all started with a Scarecrow.

Puffin is seventy years old.

Sounds ancient, doesn't it? But Puffin has never been so lively. We're always on the lookout for the next big idea, which is how it began all those years ago.

Penguin Books was a big idea from the mind of a man called Allen Lane, who in 1935 invented the quality paperback and changed the world. **And from great Penguins, great Puffins grew, changing the face of children's books forever.**

The first four Puffin Picture Books were hatched in 1940 and the first Puffin story book featured a man with broomstick arms called Worzel Gummidge. In 1967 Kaye Webb, Puffin Editor, started the Puffin Club, promising to **'make children into readers'**. She kept that promise and over 200,000 children became devoted Puffineers through their quarterly instalments of *Puffin Post*, which is now back for a new generation.

Many years from now, we hope you'll look back and remember Puffin with a smile. **No matter what your age or what you're into, there's a Puffin for everyone.** The possibilities are endless, but one thing is for sure: whether it's a picture book or a paperback, a sticker book or a hardback, **if it's got that little Puffin on it – it's bound to be good.**